MOTHER TRUCKER

Book One

Mother Trucker
Copyright @2016 by CRLE Publishing
Mitchell, Robyn

This is a work of fiction. All names, characters, places, and incidents are the products of the author's imagination or are used fictitiously. Any resemblance to current or local events or to living persons is entirely coincidental.

Library of Congress Cataloging-in –Publication Data

                                                p.   cm
ISBN: 978-0-9972129-0-7   PCN: 2016930851

I. Truckers—Fiction II. Trucking Industry—Fiction III. Adventure Fiction
Fic Mit   PS 3606.A775M46

Editor-in-Chief: Mindy Reed, The Authors' Assistant
Interior Designed by Danielle H. Acee, The Authors' Assistant
Cover Design by Douglas Brown, Album Arist

Printed in the United States

MOTHER TRUCKER

a novel by

ROBYN MITCHELL

PUBLISHING
Odessa, TX

For my husband, C.L.
Thank you for your patience and unquestioning support throughout the process
of bringing this story to fruition. Without you, there would be no book.

Chapter One

The gunshots came down from the top of the hill into the pit, making it sound like a war zone. Shelby tried to look up to see what was happening, but the dust was thick from the spray of bullets that were hitting everything in sight. "STOP THE DAMN SHOOTING!" she yelled as she covered her head with her hands and put her face in the ground. *Just how did I get here?* she wondered.

◊◊◊

"Ouch, dammit that hurt!" Shelby put the injured finger into her mouth and then quickly removed it. She looked at the nicely-painted, half-broken artificial nail. "I just had these nails done last week." As she reached down toward her stuck high-heel, which had caused the incident in the first place, her purse slid from her shoulder, hitting her leg. "Stupid shoe." She pulled at the lodged heel stuck in a crack of cement, near the rubber mat that lead into the grocery store.

Shelby hobbled into the store and used the handle of a shopping cart to balance as she replaced her shoe. Then she placed her handbag in the child seat. "What else can go wrong today?" she mumbled.

Just as she was about to push the cart forward toward the produce section, a hand gently tapped her shoulder. "Shelby? Shelby Mathews? I knew that was you."

Shelby turned, catching her blonde hair in her old college friend's ring. She pulled her hair away and the two women embraced each other. "Jayne Edwards, wow, it's been like forever since we've seen each other. How are you?"

Jayne let Shelby go and smiled at her old friend. "Oh, it's been too long. Funny, I've been thinking about you lately, which must be why we crossed paths today. I'm doing well. How about yourself?"

Shelby lifted up her finger for her old friend to inspect. "Just hanging in there really, and this little mishap is the icing on the cake for me, I think. My father always told me I was a magnet for mishaps and mischief." The two women laughed. Shelby was glad to see her friend, but with everything that had happened over the last few weeks, all she really wanted to do was burst into tears. "Trying to keep my chin up and move forward."

Jayne could tell that her college chum needed to talk. "Hey, why don't we find a seat over at the coffee bar and chat?"

"That sounds wonderful, I would love to catch up. Steven, my son is home with Jack, so I'm sure he won't need me for anything for a while."

The two women ordered their coffee and took their cups to an empty table. When they were settled, Jayne began, "Last thing I remember was you marrying Jack Mathews, and I think you sent me a couple of email announcements, about the birth of some children."

"Yes, I married Jack, and we have three boys—all grown up. She paused, "Jack just came home from the hospital a few weeks ago—heart attack."

"Oh, no. How is he? How are you?"

"We're coping…trying to keep things running smooth. I'm a teacher, and Jack—well, Jack used to be an executive in his company. He's been with them since we got married, but right now he's on long-term disability. Believe me, that isn't easy financially either. I had to take a job at a local convenience store to help supplement, so we can at least pay most of our bills."

"That's terrible. It's a shame that teaching just doesn't pay like it should. I remember when I got divorced it was nearly impossible to keep up on just one check. That's why I changed careers."

Jayne and Shelby sipped at their coffee.

"Tell me about those boys," Jayne said.

Well, we have three now. Jack Jr. the oldest looks and acts just like Jack. He has two children. Can you believe it? Me, a grandma."

"Congratulations!"

"Mark, the middle boy is a Marine. He's more like me. He got leave when he learned of Jack's heart attack; we just sent him back to North Carolina." Shelby sipped her coffee again, holding back the tears she wanted to shed. "We're very proud of him. It's amazing how much being a soldier has changed him. He's so grown up, yet so young."

"Wow, has he seen combat?"

"Yes, he was in Iraq and Afghanistan."

"At least he's safe on American soil now, right?" Jayne took another sip of her coffee. "So, what's the youngest boy like?"

"Steven. He's in college, and he still lives at home. He's my quiet man."

"Sounds like you've been busy," said Jayne. "I'm sorry to hear about Jack—"

"We're taking it one day at a time."

Jayne put her hand on Shelby's. "He'll be okay. One day at a time is all you need to be doing right now. Have faith, Shelby."

"Thanks…so what have you been up to all this time? I feel really bad I haven't kept in touch."

"Well, I got married…but it wasn't a good marriage. Like I said, I got a divorce, but I have a great son out of it, and I'm glad I'm on my own. I drive a truck for a living now, so I get to see a lot of the states and make a good living at the same time. Life's been good to me health-wise, and I enjoy every day that I'm given."

"You're a truck driver?" Shelby said, shocked. "Are you telling me that you drive one of those great big things all over the country?" She gaped at the smart, pretty woman who sat in front of her.

Jayne grinned. "Yep, I'm a big eighteen wheel truck driver. I drive all over the country, and I love it. Besides getting to see a lot of great things, I meet nice people and get paid really well for just delivering stuff from one side of the country to the other."

"Wow!"

"Don't be so shocked," Jayne said. "A lot of us women are driving rigs now, especially single women who have to take care of their families. Truck driving is a good way to make a living, even for those of us with college educations."

Shelby sat back and studied her old friend. Before her was a happy, healthy, educated, put together woman. "I hope I haven't offended you. I guess I'm just a little confused. Hell, I know women work in almost every industry these days; you just don't seem the type."

Jayne laughed. "Well, I am. After my divorce, I had to find something that paid well if I was going to raise my boy and send him to college. My job as a college professor just wasn't cutting it financially."

"You make more driving a truck than you did teaching at that community college?"

"You bet. At least twice as much."

Shelby wanted to know more. She looked at her watch. *Time to get back to Jack.* "Jayne, I would love to continue this conversation with you. May I have your number so we can talk? Or maybe you can come by my house sometime and we can have coffee again?"

Jayne reached in her purse and pulled out a business card. "Here. I own my own trucking company, and although I'm gone a lot, I'd love to talk with you again. Call me any time. I've always had a special place in my heart for you."

Shelby took the card and got up from the table. Jayne got up too and gave Shelby a hug. "I'll be in touch soon, I promise."

Shelby grabbed her shopping cart and disappeared into the store.

CHAPTER TWO

Shelby was glad when summer break arrived. Although she was still working at a local convenience store in the evenings, she hoped she'd have time to work in her yard and plant some new flowers. Jack was regaining his strength, but he still needed a lot of rest. Steven took on a job at the mall for extra money, hoping to help take some of the pressure off his parents' current financial woes.

It bothered Jack that his wife had to work a minimum wage job to bring in extra money. Her teacher's salary had been the supplemental income for the extras they wanted, but now it just wasn't enough, especially with the mounting medical bills. It humiliated him that friends and neighbors saw her in the corner store. *They probably assume I'm not able to take care of my family anymore,* he fretted.

When the part-time work became full-time, he confronted her. "Look Shelby, you were supposed to work part-time and now you're gone at least fifty hours a week. Look at what they pay you for all those hours." Jack held up the pay stub. "I love you, but that job has got to go. Look at you. You're worn out, and I hate the fact you have to scrub those floors and bathrooms. Not to mention the danger of being robbed!"

"What do you want from me, Jack? I'm trying to keep our heads above water." As she left for the store, she thought, *I know he's right, I just don't know what to do about it.*

◊◊◊

Shelby was finishing the last hour on her shift when a huge eighteen wheel truck pulled up. This was unusual since the parking lot was not large enough for a big truck. Shelby watched through the window as the man got out of the truck and came into the store. He smiled at Shelby, went straight for the cooler, grabbed a water bottle, and then headed to the register.

"Sorry about blocking the drive," he said, resting the bottle on the checkout counter. "I was so thirsty I couldn't wait to get to the next truck stop for a drink. I'll be gone in a minute, promise." He handed her correct change and left just as quickly as he had entered.

The big rig left with a puff of smoke and the sound of the unique gear changes.

Shelby stared into the empty parking lot, long after the truck disappeared. She remembered running into Jayne. She went back to sweeping the floor but couldn't put Jayne's words out of her mind: *"I make at least twice as much driving a truck, and I love it."*

She tried to dismiss the thought forming in her brain, *You idiot, you could never drive one of those big things. Besides, Jack would never allow it,* she scolded herself.

As she drove home, she was consumed with the crazy idea that had preoccupied her since seeing the big truck: *Could I really drive a big truck? How hard would it be to learn? Who would teach me? Could I really make the kind of money Jayne does?*

By the time she got home, Jack was already in bed. She turned on the television, got a glass of wine, kicked off her shoes, and sat down in her chair. She hoped that the wine and some ridiculous late night show would bring her back to reality. Try as she might, she could not shake the idea of being a truck driver.

◊◊◊

"Are you out of your mind? No wife of mine is going to drive a truck, and that is final!"

"Look, Jack, I know this is something neither of us ever thought I'd do, but let's just stop and think about it." She hoped she could bring him around. Her mind was made up and she was going to do this with or without his consent. "I talked with Jayne yesterday, and she gave me the complete lowdown. She's been doing this for fifteen years. Hell, Jack, this tiny woman gave up being a professor. She owns her own trucking company, takes care of herself, and has put her son through college. She gets to see new places, meets new people, and loves what she does. She says the work isn't that hard—even easier than what I'm doing in the corner store."

Jack listened, but remained quiet. He turned and looked at his beautiful wife, the woman who he had married years ago because he loved her so deeply he couldn't stand the thought of not having her by his side forever. *This woman's given me three great sons, made our home a castle, has worked as a teacher for decades, all while loving me. God only knows why. Now she is asking me to let her go out into a world mostly dominated by men, a world of stinky, dirty, smelly diesel and oil motors.*

The closest Shelby had ever come to an engine was taking her car in for an oil change. *This truck driving idea is insane. How can I possibly let the woman I've protected all these years into a world like that?*

But he also knew she would not be denied. Her mind was made up, and the best thing he could do was support her. "Shelby, baby, this is crazy," he said slowly. "You can't even back the car into the garage without help, and now you want to back a big truck and trailer into docks? I must be completely out of my mind letting you do this… but I guess if you want to try—"

"Oh, thank you, Jack!" Shelby ran and kissed him passionately. She broke herself away from his lips and jumped around the room like a child at Christmas. "I knew you would understand! I have so much to do."

That's my Shelby—completely reckless, unconcerned with consequences, ready to take on the whole world. He slumped back into his chair. *What have I just done?*

◊◊◊

By the middle of June, Shelby had taken the required DOT physical and drug test, worked out the finances with Jack to pay for the course, and registered with the truck driving school that Jayne had recommended. To her surprise, the school was totally dominated by women. The director of operations, Jerri and Evelyn, the lead classroom instructor, as well as one of the driving instructors, were both retired female truck drivers. The only men in the school were John and Troy, two driving instructors from other schools who came in to help out from time to time.

Jack was feeling better lately and was spending time in his shop, working on his favorite pastime—motorcycles. He loved fixing them, cleaning them, and especially riding them. He was in a good mood. However, he became reticent when Shelby approached him about using the last four thousand dollars of their savings for the school. "What if you can't learn to drive or pass those tests you'll have to take to get your CDL? That'll leave us down four thousand dollars and nothing to show for it. Besides, even if you do get your CDL through this school, what if you can't find anyone who will give you a job because you don't have any experience?"

"You don't think I can do it, do you? You don't believe in me," She challenged him. "You gave me the okay to do this, but you're hoping I fail. I can't believe you. I'm busting my ass to keep us afloat, even willing to make a big change in my life so that we can continue to have everything we own, and you sit there playing with your stupid toys, hoping I'll fall on my ass." She stormed out of the shop and back to the house. Jack knew he was in trouble.

He followed her into the house where he found her in the kitchen. "I'm sorry. I love you, and you're right, I was wrong. Take the four thousand bucks, learn to drive one of those big old trucks, and make us lots of money."

His concern was relieved when she explained that the school had a money back guarantee. "Furthermore, when I do get my CDL, Jayne will line me up with several local companies, and if I pass their driving tests, they'll give me a job. A good friend of hers owns one company that likes hiring drivers from the school I'm attending. I guess because he can train them to drive his equipment the way he wants it driven and not have to deal with the, 'I already know everything' types.

"I figured you would go to work for Jayne at her company," Jack said.

"Well, at first that was what I had in mind, but Jayne runs what they call long haul only, and since I really want to stay closer to home right now, to be closer to you, that really isn't a good option."

Jack was pleased that Shelby wasn't jumping into this truck driving adventure feet first, but had also considered all the outcomes to be successful.

He still cringed as he thought about what his friends were going to say when they found out that his wife was a truck driver. *I'll never live those joke down.* He was actually relieved he was stuck at home and didn't see many folks.

◊◊◊

Trucking school was nothing like the traditional classrooms that Shelby was accustomed to in her previous profession. It was more like training. Her class was small—just her and one male classmate, Omar. After decades as a student and then a teacher, the classwork and testing came easily for Shelby.

Their test dealt with driving rules, laws of the road, what to do to avoid an accident, and how to handle a big truck in different types of weather conditions—what Shelby called "common sense." Other parts of the testing, however, were a little more complicated, such as knowing different parts of the truck—including air brakes, and how to test them before driving. She also had to learn about hazardous materials, which was more involved than the placards displayed on the trucks she saw on the highway. Although she had little to no clue about most of what she had just been tested on, she did quite well on the tests. Within a week's time, she proudly announced, "Look, Jack, I did it, I got my learning permit."

Jack kissed her and then asked, "That's great sweetheart. When are you going to learn to drive a truck? I want to be sure and stay off the road," he laughed.

"Asshole," she quipped.

◊◊◊

Shelby was both nervous and excited when the day came for her to get inside her first big truck. Her instructor had introduced her and Omar to the rig a few days earlier. They were shown how to perform an air brake test and how to record their pre- and post trip exams on the training truck each and every day. Now they were actually going to be behind the wheel, driving a great big piece of metal.

The previous eight weeks had been a blur. Shelby tried to cover the bags forming under her eyes with makeup. She had not given up her job at the convenience store, nor given the school district her notice for a long term leave of absence. She went to driving school from seven a.m. to five p.m., went home for dinner with Jack, then worked at the convenience store from eight p.m. to one a.m.

The eight weeks of hell ended on graduation day. Shelby knew there were times during the past few weeks when she felt like she wasn't going to make it. Especially when it came to backing up that big rig and putting it smack between those two yellow lines at the practice course. Her instructor had been tough, and wouldn't let Shelby quit until she could back the "son of a bitching" truck up, and put it where the instructor had wanted it. She hoped everything she learned would stick with her.

◊◊◊

The week after graduation, thanks to Jayne, she had job interviews lined up, which meant more driving tests. She had already been to the DOT office where she had to perform her driving and air brake skills for the nice but very intimidating DOT officer.

She remembered the moment the DOT officer told her she'd passed the driving part of her tests and could go into the office and get her Class A, CDL drivers' license. She jumped off that big truck and ran, screaming, "I PASSED," to Omar and her instructor.

The one job Shelby had set her heart on was the job Jayne had recommended as, "the best fit"—sand hauling. Jack, had been in the oil industry for years and also felt it was a good fit. The job was not difficult and the equipment, which Jack had checked out for himself, seemed to be in good condition.

A few days after her interview she received a call. "This is Eddy at ESCC, and I was wondering if you could come in and visit with me tomorrow." Although he sounded formal, Shelby got the impression that the sand hauling company's manager was a friendly person, who was willing to give her a chance.

◊◊◊

ESCC was small, dusty, and untidy, with manly smells: a combination of oil, dirt, grease, and sweat, which she knew well having a husband and three sons.

There was no reception area or secretary in sight, so Shelby had to maneuver through an unorganized maze of rooms. A young woman who Shelby assumed was a secretary, although her clothing did not resemble that of an office professional, came around the corner. Shelby was about to introduce herself and ask the woman if she could speak with Eddy, but before she could get the words out of her mouth the woman had moved quickly past her and out the front door.

Wow, people move quickly around here, she thought. She looked closer at the room that appeared to be the hub of this operation. *Man, this place needs a secretary bad if they don't have one. Or if they have one, she needs to be better at her job*, Shelby thought.

Her thoughts were interrupted by a nice looking man who entered the room and approached her. He stuck out his hand and looked at Shelby, "Hi, I'm Eddy. You must be Shelby. Wow, not exactly what I was expecting, if you don't mind me saying."

Shelby wasn't offended by the comment, but hoped it wasn't something that was going to keep her from getting the job, "Nice to meet you," Shelby muttered.

Eddy moved toward another office and motioned for her to follow him. "Come in and have a seat, Mrs. Mathews." He pointed toward a dusty leather chair that faced what obviously was his desk. Shelby sat down in the dusty chair in her less than appropriate business suit.

Eddy got straight to the point but humor seemed to be a dominant part of his personality. "Well, I've gone over your application, and although I don't have any trucks available right now, I do have a position available for a secretary."

Shelby was taken aback and a little let down by the offer. *I could have gotten a secretary position weeks ago and without spending four thousand dollars*, she thought.

He saw the confused look on her face and let out a big laugh. "Not really, Shelby. I was just joking."

Shelby sat back in the chair, relieved. She tried to get a handle on this man, who she hoped was soon to be her boss.

"I really think you'll be a good asset to this company, and I really don't, at this moment, have a truck for you. I'd like for you to begin training with us as soon as you can. You'll have to take a driving test with one of my lead drivers and of course, the usual drug and DOT physical will have to be done."

He searched through a stack of papers on the top of his desk and produced a packet of paperwork and handed it to Shelby. "Here. Fill these out and bring the packet with you tomorrow if you don't mind. Seven a.m. Does that work for you?"

Shelby nodded.

Eddy picked up the phone and called a local doctor's office to set up an appointment for her. He wrote the time and location on a sticky note and handed it to her. He stood up and extended his hand toward Shelby, "Welcome aboard."

Shelby couldn't believe it as she stood to shake Eddy's hand. *I did it. I landed a job driving a truck! Wow, is that all there is to this? Surely there's more.* "Thank you, Eddy," she said, trying not to let her giddiness show. "I'll be back tomorrow with this paperwork and get those tests at the doctor's office done right away."

Eddy shook her hand and said, "You really look nice in those fancy clothes, but you'll ruin them here. You might want to dress in jeans from now on, and you'll need a pair of steel-toed boots." Then he quickly turned around, grabbed a hard hat off one of his messy shelves along with a pair of glasses and handed them to Shelby. "You'll need to wear these whenever you're in the yard or on location making a delivery. Most of the places that you'll be picking up sand from will also require these, so be sure and keep them with you when you're working."

Shelby took the items from her new boss. These were not strange items to her. Jack worked in steel-toed boots every day. She had also seen him wear a hard hat and safety glasses many times at his job. Now she had her own hard hat, safety glasses, and a totally blue-collared, hard-working man's job.

◊◊◊

Jack was fixing the vacuum cleaner when Shelby got home. She kissed his forehead and teasingly mentioned, "Got the job," as she walked toward their bedroom to change.

Jack got up and followed her to the bedroom. "You got what?" he asked as he entered their room and was literally attacked by his overly enthusiastic wife. She jumped into his arms and wrapped her legs around his waist. She kissed him deeply as he moved them both toward their bed, hoping to get there before he dropped her, not because Shelby was all that heavy but because he still wasn't that strong yet.

He put her on the bed and placed himself over her with their lips still locked in a passionate kiss. Shelby finally let his mouth go as she explained once again, "I got the job at ESCC today. Your wife is a truck driver, a sand hauling truck driver."

Jack rolled over off of Shelby and laid flat on his back on the bed, still a little exhausted from carrying them both to the bed. He wasn't really sure how he felt about Shelby's news yet. *Happy, sure—now she'll be making more money—at least she won't be working at the stupid convenience store anymore.* But he was also a little afraid. Shelby, his beautiful, non-mechanically inclined, and totally naïve wife was entering his world, the man's world. Something deep inside him didn't feel right about it.

He didn't verbalize all the thoughts running though his head about what possibly could happen to her out there, and probably would happen to her. He hoped she wouldn't get hurt, but before he could continue his thoughts, Shelby was on top of him, wanting to know what he thought about her new job.

"Well silly, aren't you going to congratulate me on getting the job?" She brushed his arm with her hand as if to hit him, then rolled off and stepped toward the closet to get something comfortable to wear.

Jack knew he had better snap out of his less-than-positive attitude, and show some happiness toward the news if he wanted to avoid a battle. So, he sat up reluctantly and called out toward the closet. "That's great, baby. I'm really proud of you. When do you start?"

Shelby came out of the closet half naked with a shirt in her hand and a pair of short shorts on her ass. Her golden brown skin shimmered a little from the sunlight coming in the window, giving Jack additional concern. *Shelby is beautiful, trim, and sexy. Those three things alone are going to make my wife a total magnet for almost every man out there. She's never been placed directly in the face of temptation before.*

He quickly snapped out of his nightmarish thoughts and was brought back into reality as Shelby answered, "I start tomorrow."

Great, he thought to himself, *my wife is doing this tomorrow.* Jack did not show his real feelings. He simply pulled Shelby to him on the bed and kissed her, hoping she would believe from the kiss that he was happy about everything so he wouldn't have to lie to her.

CHAPTER THREE

Shelby's first day at ESCC was great. Eddy introduced her to the young woman who had rushed by her without talking. "Tiff, this is Shelby. She's going to be one of our new drivers. Shelby, this is Tiff, my right-hand girl."

Shelby could tell from Eddy's voice that he had feelings for this young woman, but it was more fatherly than romantic. Either way, she could tell they had a close bond. Tiff shook Shelby's hand and welcomed her. Eddy heard the phone ring. "Tiff, go and take Shelby around the yard and introduce her to whoever is here," he said, reaching for the phone. "Show her the trucks and how we do things."

Tiff began explaining the floor plan of the office areas. "This is where our new dispatcher will be when she comes back from training," said Tiff. "She's at the home office being orientated for her new job. She'll be your direct supervisor under Eddy. She'll control all of the loads you pick up and deliver. Be nice to her—she's like blood to your heart when it comes to making you money."

Shelby was glad Tiff had explained all that because she didn't know what a dispatcher was, and she also thought she better listen to this lady's advice since she obviously knew this business well. "Thanks, I'll remember that," Shelby said, smiling.

Tiff led her out the front door and to the yard area. "Sandy should be back on Friday; so right now, Eddy and I are dispatching. You won't need to worry about that for now, though, because I think Eddy is going to put you with one of our lady drivers for training. We have three lady drivers, and with you coming on board, we'll have four. We have sixteen male drivers and five yard hands."

Tiff led Shelby toward some buildings and then pointed toward the east. "Over there, beside those rail cars, are what we call silos. You'll eventually learn to load your truck out of those and also out of those rail cars behind the silos."

Shelby looked at the monstrously tall white cylinder-shaped silos, wondering how she was going to load a truck out of them. She looked behind the silos, and wondered, with even more confusion, how someone would load a big truck with sand from a rail car. *I can't imagine we'd be using a shovel...*

Tiff interrupted her thoughts by leading her into a building. Inside, the building was dark and dusty, but Shelby could see well enough from the light coming in through the door that it was stacked full of large, white bags full of something.

"This is our sand bag warehouse," Tiff explained. She opened a bag and let Shelby see its contents. "We store several different types of sand in here that come to us from different parts of the country and different parts of the world."

"I had no idea there were different types of sand," Shelby muttered. "I thought all sand was the same, you know, like the kind you find in a sand box?"

Tiff laughed, but turned toward a conversation from the corner that was becoming a little louder. Tiff responded half-heartedly, "Yeah, lots of different sands. Okay, who's in the corner over there?" After Tiff confronted the two people having the conversation, they both came forward into the light of the doorway.

In the light, Shelby could see that one was a man and the other was a woman. They were still conversing as they walked toward Tiff, who shook her head in disbelief.

"What the hell are you two doing in here?" she asked with unmistakable sarcasm in her voice. "Don't you have some loads to deliver?"

The woman replied sarcastically, "Yes, but it's a little difficult to deliver a load of sand when the yard hands are too busy taking their break instead of loading our trucks." The woman looked at Shelby with a little smirk, which Shelby didn't notice because of her fascination with the sand. "Who's the blonde?" the woman asked, nodding toward Shelby and elbowing the man standing next to her.

Tiff dropped the sand she had in her hands and brushed them off on her pants.

Shelby dropped her sand and brushed the sand dust off her hands by rubbing her hands together, realizing that she was soon going to be introduced to what she assumed were two of her coworkers.

Tiff pointed toward Shelby. "Betty, Ted, this is Shelby. Eddy just put her on as a new driver. She's probably going to be training with Marie."

Shelby put her hand out to shake the other drivers' hands, but Ted was the only one that shook her hand and he quickly took it back after Betty gave him a less-than-happy glance. Shelby realized right away that Betty was one of those territorial types, and Ted apparently was part of that territory as was this job. She pulled her hand back and put it into her pocket simply replying, "It's nice to meet you both."

Betty turned abruptly away from Shelby and toward Tiff. "So, are your yard hands going to load us today or not?" Tiff motioned for Shelby to follow her out the door, turning her back on the arm-crossed snob who just stood there, waiting for a response.

Tiff replied while walking out the door, "They'll load you soon, they aren't on a break, Betty. They're loading other trucks on the other side of the rail cars. You two need to get out of here and check out your trucks. People might start believing the rumors if they keep finding you two hiding out." Tiff laughed as she left the building with Shelby.

"Very funny, Tiff!" Betty called out as Tiff and Shelby walked away. "Just get your damn yard hands on our trucks. We need to get to location before dark."

Tiff did not respond, and that seemed to make Betty even more upset. She turned toward Ted, who was standing there like a lost puppy waiting for a scolding from his master. "So what do you think about little Miss Barbie? She didn't wait for his response before walking toward the open door that Tiff and Shelby had just exited. Then she paused, glaring at the two women as they walked to the other building. "I don't think she'll last," she told Ted. "She looks too much like a Barbie doll. Did you see those nails? I give her a couple weeks at the most."

Ted laughed, glad that his master had not given him a tongue lashing for being polite to the new kid on the block.

◊◊◊

That afternoon Shelby met the mechanic, Ed, who would be taking care of all her truck's needs. He was a sweet man, and after Shelby was given a tour of the shop area, she realized that Ed was going to be her best friend, especially since she was not mechanically inclined.

Shelby was also introduced to the yard hands: Maquel, Omar (a different Omar), Jesse, Manly, and Trey. They were all more than happy to show Shelby how sand was loaded not only onto ESCC trucks, but also onto trucks from other companies. Maquel pointed to a machine that looked like a duck. "This is what we call a loader," he explained. "We place that flat belt under the belly of the rail car, we open up the belly with that metal pole, and let sand flow onto the belt and up into the holes on top of the trucks."

Shelby followed Maquel's hand motions all through his explanation and finally found her answer as to how they got sand out of the rail cars and into the trucks.

After a short time watching that process, Tiff pulled Shelby away from the loading dock and led her to the line of pretty red and white trucks that were lined up in what seemed to Shelby a perfect formation. Tiff pulled a key out of her pocket and walked with Shelby over to the fleet line and directly to one of the trucks near the end. She opened the door. "This is one of our lead driver's trucks. Here, hop in and have a look around. You won't be able to take her out until after your driving test, but you can at least see what you'll be driving."

Shelby hopped into the truck. It was a lot taller than the one she had driven in school. "Wow, this is so nice! It's nothing like the trucks we drove in school. The knobs and buttons on the dash actually work in here." Shelby touched the steering wheel and looked around the inside of the truck in awe. "Do you know when I'll be testing and training exactly? I really want to start driving one of these."

Tiff moved back so that Shelby could back down out of the truck. She locked the truck back up. "I'm not sure what Eddy has in mind, but I think you'll test with Marie this afternoon and maybe even go out with her on a little job if she is scheduled for a load. I'll check on that with Eddy when we get back to the office, but I'm sure it will be today."

Shelby felt a twitch in her stomach, but whether it was nerves or excitement, she couldn't decide. "I hope it's today," she told Tiff. "I can't wait. I know I'm going to enjoy this work."

They walked across the dusty yard toward the main office. Shelby was used to the wind and dust in West Texas, because that was the way it usually was in the desert, however the yard was dustier than the normal terrain. She was going to have to get used to the dirt or get a mask to cover her mouth and nose.

They returned to the office, and Shelby was surprised to see that the break room was filled with people. Tiff introduced Shelby to several of her new coworkers. "Everyone, this is Shelby, our newest driver." Several of the drivers came forward and shook Shelby's hand, giving her their names.

A cute Mexican man came forward and introduced himself. "Hi, I'm Speedy."

Shelby shook his hand and smiled. She could sense that she was going to like working with this driver.

"I'm Slick Stick," said another young man—this one smaller than the others. But from his handshake alone, Shelby could tell he could handle just about anything that came his way, much like her son, Mark.

A tall man stepped up to her next and said, "They call me Fast Man. I like to get the job done quickly."

Shelby shook the man's hand.

"I'm Phantom 309," said another. This one was thin with long hair. "Got the name from my daddy years ago."

Another female driver came forward and introduced herself to Shelby. "I'm White Eyes, she said, smiling and shaking Shelby's hand. "That's right, I'm Indian." The woman was a little older than Shelby and wore a dress and heels. She didn't look like the stereotypical female truck driver. Shelby knew she was going to have fun getting to know this driver.

Seated at the table were the two people whom Shelby had met earlier in the warehouse. Neither stood to introduce themselves; they just sat there.

White Eyes, seeing how her coworkers were behaving, was kind enough to introduce them to Shelby, not realizing they had already met.

"The smart ass is Cheeks and the dumb ass is Sport Bottle, she said, gesturing at the pair. Everyone in the room cracked up, making Betty get up from the table with her puppy right behind her as they headed toward the door. They pushed through everyone without even a polite "excuse me." Betty—or Cheeks, as Shelby reminded herself—yelled, "Shut the hell up, White Eyes!"

White Eyes looked at Shelby. "Don't worry, kiddo. They act like that all the time, especially the little bitch. Sport Bottle only acts that way because he's afraid he might get cut off."

That comment made everyone in the room break out in another round of laughter. Shelby wasn't too sure what to think about her new coworkers, but she knew one thing—they all had funny names.

Shelby innocently asked, "I thought their names were Betty and Ted?"

Tiff tried to compose herself, then spoke through a few more chuckles in order to explain the names. "Those are their handles, Shelby. They use those names on the CB radio in the trucks."

"Oh, I understand," Shelby said, quickly, feeling a little stupid. She knew what a CB was—they had explained that during school and she had talked on one at her uncle's house when she was a little girl—but she really had no idea they used aliases on those things.

Fast Man came forward and sat at the break table, looking at Shelby who had found a comfortable corner to stand in. She felt a little overwhelmed. "So what's your handle, Shelby?" he asked.

Shelby thought for a moment and, not being able to come up with one fast enough, simply replied. "I don't have one."

Fast Man sat back in his chair. "That just won't do. Everyone has a handle. Let's see…." He sat there as the whole room of people started throwing different names into the air. "Blondie, Blue eyes, Stacks, Newbie, Tweedy, Rosebud …." The names kept filling the air as three other drivers entered the room.

Tiff pointed toward Shelby as the drivers entered the room, found themselves chairs, and loudly placed their briefcases or folders on the table in front of them. "This is Shelby, our new driver."

"That's Jumpstart," she said, pointing toward a smiling black man, "…and that's Diego." She pointed at an older gentleman who appeared less than happy to be there.

The third gentleman didn't stay seated or wait for Tiff to introduce him. Instead, he quickly rose to his feet and presented his hand to Shelby. "I'm Luscious. Really, I am."

Shelby took his hand and shook it as the whole room once again broke out in soul-filled laughter. "It's nice to meet you."

Luscious took his seat again and placed his hands on his hips. "What? I am. Just ask my wife."

The laughter continued for a few more minutes until Eddy and a really tall lady walked into the room. "What's so funny around here? Oh, let me guess—Cheeks and Sport Bottle must have just left." Again the room filled with laughter and Shelby finally realized that Betty and Ted were definitely the brunt of everyone's fun around this place.

Eddy tried to calm the room down. "Okay, okay save it for the road." He looked directly at Shelby. "Shelby this is Marie, a.k.a. Long Legs, and she will be your trainer. She is also going to give you your driving test today. She'll be filling out this form while you're driving for her." Eddy handed the form to Marie as Shelby moved out of her corner and extended her hand toward Marie. "Hi, it's nice to meet you," Shelby said.

"Same here," Marie responded.

Eddy moved back toward his office, but before he was completely out of the room, he used a few words to motivate his employees. "Alright, all of you that are in here screwing off. Hit the door and move some sand. The rest of you, get your paperwork done and go home. Marie, bring me that form back when you're finished with her driving test, and then load for that job south of town. Shelby, once you've done the driving test, I want you to ride with Marie for today. I want you to observe what we do out in the field. Marie, until I have a chance to go over her driving exam, no driving, alright?"

Marie nodded her head, letting Eddy know that she understood his instructions. "Tiff, hit the yard and move those yard hands! We're running behind, and I want those trucks loaded yesterday."

Shelby moved in behind Marie toward the front door that led to the yard. She was amazed at how quickly everyone moved. "Wow, everyone really listens when Eddy tells them what to do, don't they?"

Marie laughed. "Eddy's a pussy cat. But, everyone knows that cats have claws, and that cat can scratch if he wants to."

Shelby understood what Marie was talking about, but she didn't have Eddy pegged as a cat—more like a tiger, maybe.

It didn't take long for the girls to get across the yard and to Marie's truck. Marie held out the keys to her truck in Shelby's direction. "Okay, starting now, I want you to show me exactly what you'll do each and every time you're called out on a job. I want you to pretend that my truck is now your truck and you're leaving for a job."

Shelby was a little nervous, but she took the keys from Marie and opened up the cab.

Within moments, Shelby had activated all the lights and started walking around the truck, checking for leaks, air pressure in the tires, making sure the lights were all functioning, and that there was nothing broken or missing from the tractor or the trailer within her line of vision. She then disengaged the lights and opened up the hood of the truck where she checked fluid levels, joint movements, and belt tightness. After she found that nothing seemed to be in need of attention, she returned the hood to its proper position and secured the latches. Shelby then got into the truck, pulled the seat forward, made slight adjustments to the mirrors, and quickly ran through an air brake check before firing up the truck's engine.

Marie seemed impressed that Shelby didn't need to be reminded of anything on the pre-trip inspection. She made a quick note on the form Eddy had given her. "I see you had a good instructor at that driving school you attended. Most new drivers need to be reminded of several items during the pre-trip inspection, but you did really well."

"Thank you." Shelby sighed, relieved. Although she knew the hardest part was yet to come.

Marie went around to the other side of the truck and got into the passenger side seat. Once inside, she and Shelby secured themselves with seat belts and Marie instructed Shelby on how she wanted her to exit out of the truck parking area and in which direction they would be traveling for the test. "Okay, now I want you to pull out and move the truck to the left, following all the way around the rail cars and out past the front offices. Once you're at the front entrance to the yard, I want you to exit left and follow the service road for three miles or a little further, to the county road exit."

Shelby knew exactly where this exit was, and after checking her mirror and honking her horn, she pushed in on her clutch and brake pedals, placed the shifter into low gear, and pushed in on her air brake button. She once again checked her mirrors, slowly eased off the clutch and then the brake, moving the truck forward slowly without killing the engine. Shelby liked the feel of the wheel in her hands. The truck bounced some as she took on another gear, but eased back on the accelerator so that she wouldn't exceed the five mile an hour speed limit in the parking lot.

Shelby didn't understand it exactly since before she went to school she had never even been in a big truck, but she really liked the way these big trucks sounded and moved. It was like sitting above the rest of the world in a big chair, as though being carried down the street like a queen or princess, while the whole world looked up at her.

Shelby stopped at the stop sign at the front entrance to the yard. Marie pointed toward the direction of travel she wanted Shelby to take along the service road. "Take this road to the county road exit and follow it around the turn through to the interstate."

Shelby maneuvered the truck with the huge steering wheel and shifted the whining engine diesel down the road with soft precision, praying with each move that she wouldn't grind a gear or miss a command from her trainer.

It took about an hour to get done with the driving exercise. When they pulled back into ESCC's parking lot, Marie pointed toward the fleet line. "Now, I want you to back this truck in between those other two trucks and park it."

Shelby could feel the sweat on her forehead. Backing up was still difficult for her. "Okay, but backing isn't my strongest point. It takes me some time to get it in, so I hope you're patient."

Marie didn't seem concerned. "Take all the time you need. Just don't hit the other trucks, and get it in there straight."

Shelby nodded as Marie opened the passenger side door and got out of the truck to watch Shelby from outside. Shelby moved the truck around in front of the space she was supposed to place it. There was enough room to move forward until she was straight with her trailer. She was glad for the space because she knew her abilities well now, and trying to put the trailer in from a forty-five or ninety-degree angle would have been a chore.

Shelby moved the truck back slowly, but being Shelby, she over corrected several times and turned her wheels the wrong way a couple more times. But within a few minutes, she had placed the truck, mostly straight, between the other two trucks and she hadn't hit them. She wasn't too happy with the performance, but she felt she had done the best she could. The rest of her driving test seemed to have went well, and she hoped that would offset the backing up.

Marie walked to the driver's side of the truck. "Shut it down, post trip it, and come to the office."

Shelby nodded and turned off the truck, trying not to read too much into the flat, even tone of Marie's voice.

Eddy's office was bustling with business activities—something that Shelby was now beginning to understand as a normal routine for this small but vibrantly growing company. As she approached Eddy's office, she was almost run over by several drivers who were leaving the building. She liked the constant movement, but still wondered about organization. *Things must be under control or this place wouldn't be functioning so well*, she concluded.

Shelby looked around the corner and saw Eddy in his office, talking on the phone. Several drivers hung around, waiting to talk to him, but he noticed her and motioned for her to come in as he hung up the phone. "Come in Shelby, have a seat. Out, you guys," he said, waving his hands. "I'll get with you in a few minutes on those loads, your trucks aren't even loaded yet. Get." Eddy pointed toward a dusty chair, indicating she should sit. "Sorry about that. It's busy around and everyone wants my attention."

Shelby sat down and placed her hands between her knees, hoping that would help her feel less nervous, or at least make her appear that way. Eddy looked over her driving exam. He laid it down on his desk and looked at her with an unreadable expression. "Marie gave you really good marks on almost everything but your backing. That is something that will come in time with practice. Now, I don't normally do this. Marie is a good judge of skills, and she thinks you have acquired a lot of skills in the short time you've been driving. I tend to agree.

"I don't know if you would be interested, but this just came up and I need someone to bobtail one of our older trucks to one of our larger terminals in South Texas and bring back a new truck for our yard. Would you be interested in doing that before I put you in a truck with Marie for training? You would be gone overnight and return with the new truck the next day."

Shelby took a moment to think about Eddy's request. "So, I have the job?"

Eddy laughed and then responded. "Yes, Shelby."

Shelby smiled and blushed, lowering her head to hide her excitement. "Yes, I'd be glad to go and get the new truck." She didn't have to think about it for long.

Eddy reached in one of his drawers and pulled out a truck key and what appeared to be a credit card. He handed them to Shelby. "Good. I want you to leave first thing in the morning. This is the key and gas card for truck 821; you'll bobtail. It should take you about twenty-four hours, including your ten hour break to bring back truck 1107. Then I'll have another good running truck, and I'll be able to get you in your own truck as soon as you finish training. Come in early; your paperwork will be in your box. Just give it to Casper when you get to the other yard. Directions to the yard and everything you'll need will be ready for you."

Shelby stood up and shook Eddy's hand. "Thank you, sir."

Eddy nodded and then added, "Do you always turn that red when you get embarrassed about something?"

Shelby placed her hand on her cheek and smiled. "Yes."

Eddy laughed and sat back in his chair. "We'll call you Roma. You know, like the tomato?"

Shelby blushed even more as she turned toward the door, but she liked it. "Thanks for the nickname, makes me feel like I already belong." They both laughed as Shelby left his office. "See ya tomorrow, boss."

Eddy was busy again with drivers who were filtering back into his office. "Be careful," he called as she left.

Shelby waved and went to look for Marie.

Marie wasn't anywhere in the building, and Shelby didn't see her outside the building as she left to go home. Shelby figured she had already gone out on the job Eddy had mentioned earlier for training and that she would catch up with her later. In the parking lot, however, she was confronted by the two people she had come to realize, in her short existence with this company, were not very friendly.

Betty and Ted both approached her as she opened her car door. "So how did you do on your driving test? It was Shelby, right?" Betty leered.

Her sarcasm made Shelby wish she could jump in her car and leave without responding, but she knew that if she did, it would be rude and she didn't need to make anyone feel that way about her right now. "I did okay," she answered. "I'm going to take a truck to South Texas tomorrow and bring back a new one before I start training with Marie."

Betty leaned over Shelby's car door, making Shelby feel even more uncomfortable. "Well, that's good. Be careful going down south, it's real dangerous down there. Those people like little blonde girls."

Shelby didn't really know how to take what Betty just said, but noticed she was laughing. She turned toward Ted and expected him to laugh with her. Shelby knew full well there wasn't any more danger for her in South Texas than anywhere else in the nation, but as soon as Betty moved her arm off of her door she slid into her driver's seat and shut the door. She started her car and rolled down the window just far enough to respond to Betty, before putting her car in reverse. "Thanks, I'll keep that in mind. I don't mean to be rude, but got to get home and make supper. See ya tomorrow."

She backed up the car, pulled out of the parking lot, looked in her mirror, and saw Ted and Betty. They just stood there—stunned that the little blonde bimbo had just left them in the dust.

"Man, what is wrong with that woman? I'm not sure I'm going to be able to handle that crazy bitch. Guess I'll just have to stay away from her," Shelby said.

CHAPTER FOUR

Shelby couldn't believe how wonderful she felt when she got into truck 821 and started it up. As Shelby pulled the truck onto the highway and headed toward her destination, she thought, *Eddy must have a lot of confidence in me, letting me take one of his trucks over four hundred miles and then driving a new truck back.* She was glad she'd have a chance to drive alone for a while so she could practice without someone watching her every move.

A few miles down the road, Shelby pulled into a truck stop to fuel up. She felt a little out of place fueling the big truck, especially when it seemed like every trucker in the place was checking her out from head to toe.

The gal behind the counter inside the store was so sweet and cute that Shelby took a liking to her right away. "Hey, how can I help you?" the young girl asked.

"Just a receipt for pump twenty-five please."

"Truck 821, right?"

Shelby took the receipt, made sure it was hers, and signed it.

"Thanks, Josie. See ya next time."

The clerk seemed a little surprised that Shelby had taken the time to notice her name tag. She looked at the fuel ticket and got Shelby's name. "Sure thing, Shelby. See ya soon."

Both women laughed and Shelby knew that they had just become friends.

A few miles down the highway, as Shelby began to feel more comfortable with driving the truck, she checked out the radio. It only seemed to halfway work so she tried the CB. She wasn't sure it worked either, but she left it on to see what might be happening on the road. She really had no idea how to adjust anything on the CB, so if it wasn't functioning properly she wouldn't know it. The radio showed channel nineteen and that is where she left it.

The trip to South Texas was long, but she found the conversations over the CB, which was working, interesting for the most part and even funny at times. Shelby was beginning to realize that truckers were really good storytellers, and most of them seemed like normal everyday people—at least from the conversations. Some truckers seemed really lonely; some talked nonstop; others talked about politics, some about their families, and some about breaking up with girlfriends. Across the board, there was a lot of talk about loads and where they were headed. There was also a whole lot of talk about sex, and although Shelby wasn't naïve, she knew that this was probably something she would have to get used to. This was a man's field of work, after all, and men talked a lot about sex. She lived with four of them—she should know.

Her thoughts were interrupted when someone spoke over the radio directly to her. "Hey, Blondie. What's a pretty little thing like you bobtailing a big ol' truck like that down the road for? Shouldn't you be home making cookies or loving on your old man instead of hanging out here with us dirty old men?"

Shelby didn't know exactly what to do. She grabbed the mic and pushed the button. "Are you talking to me, sir?"

The man laughed. "Yeah, you, driving that red Pete southbound. You're probably the only pretty blonde I've seen in a long time driving down this road."

Shelby didn't know what to say, so she didn't say anything at all.

It wasn't long before the man came back on the radio. "Haven't been driving long, have ya baby doll? Well don't be scared of that big ol' black mic, just pick it up and talk like you would on a phone. I'm GTO and I've been out here for a long while. What's your handle?"

Shelby was still shy about talking on the CB, although the man seemed sweet enough. Slowly she picked up the mic and pushed the button again. "Hi, GTO. I don't have a handle, and yes, I'm new at driving a truck."

GTO responded back quickly. "Well, not having a handle is just criminal out here. We'll have to come up with something for you. Where you headed?"

Shelby wasn't sure how much information to give this stranger but decided a general area would be okay. "I'm headed south to pick up a new truck for our yard. Not to be odd or anything, but just how did you know I was blonde?"

GTO laughed. "Little lady, I went around you a little bit ago, and I'm the truck in front of you now."

Shelby felt a little stupid as she vaguely remembered the truck passing her earlier. GTO continued. "So, no handle? Tell me a little about yourself, and I'll come up with a good one."

Shelby spent the next few hours talking with GTO from time to time over the radio. Before she knew it, they were coming to a splitting point in their drive. "Well, Shelby, it's been a pleasure traveling with you and talking with you, but I have to make a left here and you have to continue on about fifty more miles before you get to your destination. Be careful out there, little lady, and maybe we'll meet each other again on the road. Sorry I didn't come up with a good handle for you, but I'm sure you'll figure one out soon."

Shelby was grateful for the company. It had made the drive go so much faster, and GTO seemed really nice. "Thanks, GTO. It's been fun, and you be careful too."

"See ya soon, little lady driver. Be careful."

"You too, GTO."

◊◊◊

It took about another hour before Shelby reached the South Texas yard. It was late, so she decided to find a place to park in the yard and wait until morning before contacting Casper about taking the new truck back to West Texas. She found the dispatch office, let the dispatcher know that she was there, and to be sure to wake her up when Casper got in. Then she headed back to the truck in the parking area.

Before going to sleep, Shelby decided to call Jack and let him know that she had made her first trip safely and that she would be home tomorrow. "Hey, baby. I made it down south," she said when Jack picked up the phone.

"I'm glad, sweetheart," he sighed. I've been worried all day about you. How was the trip?"

"It was great," she said, deciding not to mention GTO. "I really needed to take this trip alone. I've had a chance to really learn to drive and shift without someone watching my every mistake."

"That's great, honey." Jack's voice sounded faint and faraway. "I can't wait for you to come home."

After they hung up, Shelby changed into a t-shirt and shorts and got into her sleeping bag in the sleeper. This would be her first time sleeping in a big truck, and although it wasn't her bed at home, it wasn't too bad. Before she knew it, she had fallen asleep.

◊◊◊

It wasn't even light out when someone knocked on the door of the truck and startled Shelby awake. "Mrs. Mathews." Shelby looked out the window of the driver's side door and saw the young man she'd talked with in the dispatcher's office last night.

"Yes?" Shelby asked.

The young man looked at Shelby through the window. Shelby quickly rolled it down.

"Mrs. Mathews, Casper will be in the office in about an hour, and I'm going home. So I thought I'd wake you up before I left. There's a restroom and shower area in that building over there, and a little store across the street if you need something to eat."

"Thank you," she said, gratefully.

"You're welcome. Have a safe trip back home."

Shelby waved goodbye and rolled the window back up.

In an hour, Shelby found herself outside Casper's office. The area was filled with men, who Shelby figured had to be waiting to talk with their boss too. Everything in that office was chaotic, she felt very much out of place and in the way. Shelby decided to wait outside until things cleared out a little bit before talking with Casper.

As she walked out the door, a nice gentleman held it for her.

"Thank you!" Shelby exclaimed as she made her way to the table and sat down.

"No problem," the man said as he exited the door and sat at the picnic table across from her. "That place gets really wild in the mornings. Oh, by the way, they call me Buck around here." Buck stood up and shook Shelby's hand.

"I'm Shelby. I just started working out of the west yard. Eddy sent me down here to get a new truck. You guys are really busy around here, aren't you?"

Buck grinned. "Sure are. So, how long have you been driving a truck?"

Shelby looked down at her lap, embarrassed. "Not that long," she said. "Actually, this is my first job driving a truck. I just got out of school."

Buck laughed. "Yeah, Eddy likes to train his drivers, and you meet two of his favorite criteria."

Shelby wasn't sure what he meant, but the conversation was interrupted by some drivers leaving the office. An older but sweet man called out, "Who's the blonde, Buck? Does your wife know you're having breakfast with a hottie this morning?"

Everyone busted out in laughter. Buck laughed too, but gave lip right back to the older man. "Papa, at least I'm young enough to have lunch with a pretty blonde. You might get too excited over tacos to enjoy the company." Again the laughter exploded.

Shelby wasn't sure whether to laugh or just smile so she did a little of both. She knew that the joking was over her, and she liked the attention, but felt a little embarrassed.

Buck saw her face turn red and decided to put her at ease. "Now look, Papa, you've embarrassed our newest driver."

Papa was a little shocked to know that Shelby was a driver. "Driver, what the hell you doing out here with all these nasty ass men? You look like you need to be in the mall with a stack of credit cards."

Before Shelby could respond, another ESCC employee joined the party. "Are you Shelby Mathews?"

Shelby straightened her shoulders. "Yes, I'm Shelby."

The young man pointed toward the door to the office. "The boss wants to see you."

Shelby moved away from the picnic table and to the door. "Okay, thanks. It was nice to meet you, Buck and Papa. I hope I have time before I go back west to get to know the rest of you." Shelby didn't understand why everyone laughed at that comment as she walked into the office area again.

The young man who had delivered her the message and another driver who had been out there laughed. "I hope you do, too."

Shelby found that the office had cleared out somewhat. She found an empty chair in front of a big, handsome man's desk. Shelby felt not only inferior but really short when this man stood to shake her hand. Her feelings changed quickly once the man introduced himself.

"Hi, you must be Shelby. I'm Casper."

Shelby stood up, shook Casper's hand, handed him the paperwork Eddy had sent with her, and then sat back down.

"Yes." Casper took the paperwork and put it in a stack on his desk. "Eddy phoned me yesterday and let me know you were coming to get the new truck. I'll have the dispatcher get you the keys and the DOT man in shop will run a check out on the truck for you. Bear Hunter will want to go over a few safety features."

Shelby nodded her head.

Casper reached for the phone when he heard his name over the intercom. "This is Casper. Can you hold on for just a minute? Okay, thanks." Casper directed his attention back to Shelby. "It will take me a little while to get things together, so you can use the company pickup and go to the store if you like. We also have a shower here if you need one. Don't take it until all these bozos clear out of here though." Suddenly he turned to the hallway and yelled, "Bolt! Come here, please."

A tall thin man came through the door in a hurry. "Yes, sir?"

"Bolt, this is Shelby from the west yard. Give her keys to the company pickup, directions to the store, and show her the shower."

"Okay." The young man motioned for Shelby to follow him.

Shelby left Casper's office with Bolt and went into the outer office. Bolt reached into a key box, took out a key, handed it to Shelby, and then pointed toward the drivers' lounge. "The shower is that door right there." Then he pointed to a map on the wall. "Just across this street about two blocks is a little store, or you can take this road and go down town where there are some restaurants."

Shelby looked at the door Bolt had pointed to and asked, "Can I take a look at the shower?"

Bolt snickered. "Sure, but don't faint. Remember a bunch of guys use that thing."

Shelby fought the urge to roll her eyes. She'd raised four men, including Jack, and knew how disgusting men could be when it came to keeping showers and restrooms clean. She could handle nearly anything.

"Bolt, do you guys have some bleach?"

Bolt laughed. "Yeah, somewhere. I'll get a hold of Dego and see if he can get you some. Not sure even bleach will work."

Shelby laughed. "Well, it can't hurt."

◊◊◊

After cleaning the shower and taking a trip to the store, Shelby went back to her truck and decided to take a nap. She had only been resting for a little while when Bear Hunter knocked on the truck door. "Hi, I'm Bear Hunter, the safety man. I'm here to show you around, introduce you to some of the higher ups, and give you a quick safety lesson."

Shelby climbed out of the truck, shook Bear Hunter's hand, and followed him toward the office building.

Inside, Shelby was introduced to Mr. and Mrs. B, along with several secretaries. Then Bear Hunter went over several company safety procedures. About the time he was finished, another gentleman entered his office, looking for Shelby. "Excuse me, Bear Hunter. Are you Shelby?"

Shelby stood and shook the man's hand. "Yes, I'm Shelby."

"Sorry, Bear Hunter, but I have to take Mrs. Mathews with me so I can go over things with her on the new truck."

"No problem DOT man, we've covered most everything anyway." He shook Shelby's hand. "It's been a pleasure, Shelby."

Shelby shook his hand and followed DOT back out to the parking area. DOT pointed at a beautiful, bright red truck with a shiny tank on it. "This is the truck you'll be taking back west. Eddy told me you were a new driver, so taking this rig back will be a little different than bobtailing."

Shelby listened intently to the instructions, and liked that this truck was at least a little cleaner than the one she had brought down here.

Before long, Shelby was once again on her way back to West Texas. DOT had been right about the difference in bobtailing and rolling in a truck with a tank on it. Shelby could feel the grooves in the road a lot more, and she even felt nervous about the directions through San Antonio that Casper had given to her before she left. Coming to the south yard was pretty easy because she followed a route around the big city. This time she would be taking a big rig right through downtown.

Once Shelby reached San Antonio, it dawned on her that Casper had played an awful trick on her. "That little stinker gave me directions straight through the middle of town," she said aloud. "I guess he wants to test my driving skills. Well, I won't disappoint you, Casper."

Outside the city limits, Shelby relaxed and was rather proud of herself for making it safely through the city. As she was basking in her accomplishment, she caught the sound of voices over the CB. Turning the radio up, she realized they were attempting to speak with her. "Hey, beautiful. Where you headed?" Shelby still couldn't get over the fact that people could see what she looked like in the truck. She nervously clicked the mic hoping she wouldn't sound stupid.

"Are you talking to me?"

The voices covered each other and then someone else let them know, "Hey, you're walking on each other, drivers."

One driver broke in and talked to Shelby. "Where you headed, little lady?"

"Heading back west," Shelby replied. "How about you?"

The driver answered, "Oh, I'm heading west too, going out to Cali."

Shelby spoke up again. "I'm just going over to West Texas."

The other driver spoke this time. "Well, that's cool, but you don't look like any lady driver I've ever seen. How long you been driving?"

Shelby rolled her eyes. *Are men ever going to get tired of asking me that?* Still, she forced herself to answer the question that was beginning to grow old. "A couple of days now. Or at least that is how long I've been hired on with this company."

"Wow, a greenhorn. And, a pretty one to boot. What do you want to drive a truck for?"

"I needed a change in my life, and I decided driving a truck would be a good one." She didn't owe anyone any more of an explanation than that.

The first driver spoke out this time. "Well, there isn't much glory in driving a truck. Fact is, a lot of people don't really like truck drivers. They like getting their stuff; they just don't care to know who brings it to them or how it gets there. You'll learn that fact when you enter certain states in this country. You'll see it by the way they regulate trucks to the max. Hell, some states won't even let us idle our trucks so we can stay warm in the winter or cool in the summer. They say it's environmentally wrong, but really, they just don't like the noise. By the way, my name's Loco. What's your handle?"

"I don't have a handle yet," said Shelby. "I didn't know until I started driving that I needed one. I haven't come up with a good one yet. Lots of suggestions, but haven't decided. My name is Shelby."

The second driver spoke up. "My handle's Shit Stirrer and my partner in the other seat is Big Bird."

Shelby laughed. "Shit Stirrer. Now how did you get that handle? Big Bird how did you get yours? Loco, I can only imagine how you got yours."

Shit Stirrer responded first. "Well, as you might have guessed, I cause a lot of trouble. Its fun—especially out here on the road—driving the other drivers crazy by being a smart ass. Big Bird got his name because he's tall and thin and kind of reminds you of Big Bird. Even acts that way sometimes."

"Ouch!" The other driver yelled. "He hit me, Shelby. You better come on up here and save me."

Loco interrupted, "You're right, Shit Stirrer. You are trouble. Shelby, don't fall for that line. He just wants to get another look at you. Hell, I want another look at you."

Shelby laughed. "Don't get attached boys. This lady driver has a husband."

"Oh, man. I knew it," Loco said. "I knew you were too good looking to be single. I promise not to tell if you don't."

Shit Stirrer spoke up, "Pick me, beautiful, pick me! I won't tell either." Shelby laughed, hoping that these boys were only joking, because she didn't want or need any trouble.

"Oh, boys. I'm the faithful type. Besides, I'm old enough to be your mom."

Loco beat Shit Stirrer over the radio. "I like older women, and I doubt you're old enough to be my mom. I'm 26."

"Yep, I have a son that old. Told you. You guys better pay more attention to your driving. Did you just see that cop that went by in the eastbound lane?"

That worked. The drivers were more interested in the cop than in her.

"Where?" asked Loco. "God, I'd better slow it down. I don't need another ticket; I got kids to feed."

"Yeah, me too," Shit Stirrer concurred. "We have to get off here in a couple of exits, Shelby. We deliver shoes to the stores out here from Dallas. It sure has been fun running with you. Maybe we'll meet up again, sweet lady."

Shelby had enjoyed the conversation, but was glad they were moving on. "It's been fun, guys. I'm sure we'll meet again, one day. Be careful and drive safe, okay?"

Shit Stirrer responded, "Sure thing, pretty lady."

Shelby watched as his truck took the ramp off the interstate.

CHAPTER FIVE

Shelby arrived early at the yard and was put into a truck with Marie Long Legs for training. She'd spend the next two weeks finally learning how to do her job.

"Hey, Shelby. I see you made it back from South Texas." Marie said, shaking Shelby's hand as the two women walked toward Marie's truck.

"Yeah, it gave me a chance to practice shifting gears." She climbed into the driver's seat as Marie climbed into the passenger side.

Marie handed Shelby a trip log and a filled out pre-trip inspection report. "Already did the pre-trip for us, and this is a trip log book. Didn't know if they showed you this while you were down south or not."

"Yeah, Casper showed me how to fill it out." Shelby said, filling out the date, state, roadway, and mileage.

"Good," said Marie. "Sometimes they get so busy down there that they forget important things."

Shelby nodded and Marie informed her they would be scaling up, loading up with 50,000 pounds of sand, and delivering it to a local site. Today they'd be doing this with several other drivers from the yard. Some of the drivers Shelby had never met before: Rude Dog Rider, Southwest Grizzly, Cowboy, and Hot Stuff. And unfortunately, Ted and Betty.

"Once we get to location, we'll be blowing our sand off into this compartment, into this unit." Marie showed Shelby the worksheet that the company gave each driver when they went out on a job. "This is probably your most important piece of equipment; make sure you read it completely and follow it exactly. If you ever have questions about the information on this piece of paper, call dispatch right away. Never, ever mix sands, which can happen if you unload into the wrong compartment or if someone else doesn't do their job right. It happens occasionally, but it's very costly to the company and you could lose your job over it. I always double check and recheck before I blow off."

Shelby could tell from Marie's tone that the information she was relaying was extremely important. She would keep that information close at hand so she could retrieve it quickly when she was unloading on her own.

"Pull onto the scale now and make sure you have the whole truck on, watch your tandems. Sandy will let you know when she has your weight and then we'll go around and get in line to load." Marie pointed her to the scale and watched as Shelby did exactly as she was told.

After they finished scaling up, they pulled in behind three other trucks. Marie removed her seatbelt and opened her door. "Now we have to get out and open our hatch on top of the tank." Shelby got out of the truck and followed Marie. Marie pointed to a red valve at the rear of the tank before climbing up the ladder. "Make sure this valve is always in the down position before you ascend to open the hatch. This red valve controls your tank pressure, and trust me, you do not want pressure in your tank when you open that hatch. Unless, you like flying without wings."

She followed Marie up the ladder and got on top of the tank. "Oh, wow this is scary. I didn't realize I don't like high places, especially when there isn't a guard rail." Shelby felt a little wobbly on top of the tank.

"Until you get used to the height, it's okay to crawl across the tank and open your hatch. Go ahead and sit down right there by the ladder, and I'll show you what you'll be doing from here on out. Trust me, I crawled for a long time when I first started. It's normal to be a little nervous about this part of the job, until you get used to it."

Shelby appreciated Marie's understanding and advice. "Thanks, Marie. I believe I'll crawl for a while. This does make me nervous."

Marie continued toward the middle hatch, stepped over it, and kneeled down to show Shelby how the hatch was unlocked. "This latch here needs to be disengaged last, even if you have already confirmed that the tank valve is in the right position. Seal this latch first when closing it up, and unlatch it last when opening it for safety purposes. Okay?"

"I got it. That one gets latched first when closing, and last when opening." Shelby pointed to the appropriate handle.

"Yep, that's right."

After Marie finished opening the hatch, she and Shelby climbed off the tank and returned to the cab of the truck. "Go ahead and move forward. It will take us a little while before it is our turn. Here, I have made a checklist of what you need to do every time you get ready to unload." She handed Shelby a small yellow notepad with a list of procedures. "I find it helpful for trainees to follow a pattern at first, and then when you learn how things work, you can adjust things to suit yourself. Every driver has a different way of unloading and every tank has its own little quirks you'll need to learn. Starting out, you just really need to understand the functions of high-pressure bulk tanks."

Shelby liked Marie. She was straightforward and professional. It was obvious why Eddy had chosen Marie to be a trainer. Shelby slowly moved Marie's truck behind the last truck in the line. She set the brake and looked over the checklist that Marie had composed for her.

"Oh great, Dominatrix and her boy toy have arrived," muttered Marie. "Sorry, but soon enough you'll learn about those two, and I suggest you stay as far away from them as you can. Betty is a vindictive bitch, and Ted will do whatever she tells him to do. Don't try to get close to either of them."

Shelby looked in her mirrors and saw Betty pull her truck in real close to Marie's truck with Ted right behind. "Are they a couple?"

Marie laughed. "Who knows? Ted is married and has five kids. Betty is single, never been married."

"So, do they always work together? Seems like they're always together."

"Yeah. The office has pretty much decided that keeping them together makes things easier. Betty has a tendency to make it hell for people that don't give her what she wants, and running with Ted is what she wants. They're both good drivers, though, so I guess that's why Eddy hasn't gotten rid of them yet. Plus, Eddy's a softy. Doesn't like letting people go. Since Sandy has gotten here, however, I personally think their time is short. Sandy doesn't seem to take kindly to having to cater to drivers. She has been a godsend to this company. She just got back from training. Have you met her yet?"

"Yeah, just briefly this morning, she seems real nice." Through her driver's side mirror, Shelby watched Betty get out of her truck and walk toward them. "Uh oh, Betty alert," she said

Marie rolled her eyes. "Great, that's all we need this morning. Just let me do the talking."

Shelby slowly rolled the window down as Betty climbed onto the driver's side of the truck.

"Hey, Long Legs. I see you got yourself a rookie. You guys going out on that job out in Hell's Kitchen today?"

Marie knew that Betty knew they were going out on the same job, that she was just playing her intimidation games as usual. "Yeah, I hope it's not one of those hard to find locations, but being in The Kitchen it most likely will be."

Betty looked straight at Shelby. "Yeah, and if your rookie is driving, you'll most likely get lost, right? Guess we will see what little Barbie here can do today, huh?"

Marie narrowed her eyes at Betty. "I'm quite sure we'll find it just fine, Cheeks. Probably long before you and Ted, since he's been at home all weekend. I'm sure you guys have some catching up to do, right? Now get off my truck. We need to get loaded."

Betty jumped off the truck as Shelby moved to release the brakes and move the truck forward. "Didn't mean anything by that, Long Legs." Betty smiled as Shelby moved the truck away from her.

"Don't pay any mind to what that bitch has to say," muttered Marie. "She acts the way she does because she wants to feel important, which is impossible because she'll never be." Marie laughed as she and Shelby exited the truck to confirm with the loaders the product they would be hauling.

Once the yard hands let them know that they were loaded Shelby moved the truck around to the scale. Sandy came across the CB and let them know that they had the right amount. "Okay ladies, come inside and get your paperwork. You're loaded."

Marie spoke out before they exited the truck. "Go ahead and get on top of the truck and close the hatch. I'll go in and get the paperwork."

Shelby was a little scared but she knew she had to get over her fear of heights she was going to do her job.

It took about two hours to get to what everyone referred to as Hell's Kitchen. "Man, this is a mess out here," Shelby said, as they drove around, making one turn after another. "How do you guys ever find where you're supposed to be?"

Marie laughed. "There are over six hundred location sights on these two ranches and getting to any one of them is a maze. Just remember, never, ever listen to Betty or Ted when you come out here. They always get lost."

"Maybe I'll get lucky and not have to run with them much."

Marie and Shelby made it to location without any problems. "You did a good job, Shelby. I believe you're going to make a fine sand hauler. At least you listen to directions. Now, move up onto location and let me find out where we'll be unloading this big girl."

Shelby moved the truck onto the location and put on the air brakes while Marie exited the truck to find out where they would be unloading.

Shelby put on her hard hat, safety glasses, and gloves while Marie was getting the specifics from the location supervisor. Marie came back and pointed, "We'll be unloading into that unit over there. Hot Stuff, Cowboy, Rude Dog Rider, and Southwest Grizzly are unloading in the other unit so we won't be in their way when they get here. You'll need to back in."

Shelby nodded.

"I'm going to get out and guide you in. You watch me, and I'll put you right into where you need to be, okay?"

"Okay."

Marie got out of the truck and positioned herself in front and walked Shelby through where she wanted her to park. Within a few minutes, the truck was backed into position and ready to be unloaded. Marie got onto the steps of the driver side of the truck. "Now, park it and bring your checklist. I'll show you how to unload this baby."

Before Shelby could reach the back of the truck, several other drivers drove up and put their trucks into position for unloading. Everyone seemed to work together as a team.

"Hey, guys," Marie told the crew. "Shelby needs to hook up so she knows what to do. There will be plenty of other jobs for you to help out the new blonde."

Hot Stuff and Cowboy both let go of the hose and went back to their trucks, but then quickly moved over to the trucks that had just arrived so they could help them hook up.

Marie and Shelby loaded up their equipment and headed back to the yard for their second load. About that time, Betty and Ted arrived. Shelby was glad they had finished before those two got there. Betty came across the radio as they passed each other on the road. "Did you leave me any room, Marie?"

Marie decided to ignore Betty and busied herself with paperwork as Shelby tried to follow the same roads she had taken to get to the location. "Am I going in the right direction?" she asked. "All these roads look the same."

"Yeah, you're doing fine."

"Aren't you afraid that Betty will do something mean to you? You did say she was vindictive."

"That bitch knows better than to mess with me. Not only would I pound her body into the ground with my fist, but I have a big family. Betty knows my brothers, and she is well aware of the trouble she'll have from them if she tries to do anything to me."

"So, she's not that dangerous? Mostly just talk?"

"No. Betty can be dangerous and she has done things to other drivers, she just hasn't and won't to me. Keeping your distance from her is best for you unless you have some good back up at home. Trust me. She tried with me when she first started at ESCC, but I let her know real quick what was what and she backed down. She can be dangerous, just don't let her have an in and you'll be fine."

Shelby nodded, a shiver running down her spine.

◊◊◊

The next two weeks were full of local deliveries. Shelby learned how to rig up, rig down, blow off sand, and load trucks out of silos. She filled out paperwork and found her way to locations in places she never even knew existed in West Texas. She met company supervisors, location supervisors, and frack crew workers. She was even fortunate enough to be on a working location where Marie talked the crew supervisor into letting Shelby up on the mixer so she could see exactly how a frack crew worked.

On Friday of the second week, Marie told her, "Well, girl, today is the last ride along. Starting Monday you'll be in your own truck. I told Eddy yesterday you were ready go out on your own. He has a truck for you, and you'll get the keys when we get back today. It's an older truck, so you might want to clean on it a bit over the weekend. Some of the drivers don't take care of their trucks."

"Wow. I'm ready!"

"Well, you'll still be assigned to a driver, but only as a follow along until you're completely comfortable running on your own. Once you let Eddy know you're ready to be on your own, he'll assign you jobs without a follower. Then you'll be answering to the team leaders and location supervisors," Marie added. "I know you can handle it, you're a fast learner."

"Thanks, Marie. I really appreciate the boost of confidence. I'm glad you trained me. I've learned a lot from you."

"No problem. You were easy to teach." Marie pointed to a road and Shelby made a fast break to bring the speed of the truck down quickly. "Turn in that cattle guard right there. We'll be going down one of the roughest roads you have yet to experience."

Marie was right. The ruts in the asphalt were deep, and it looked like the road had not been maintained in years. Shelby worked the steering wheel and shifted the gears to keep the truck as smooth as possible, but both women bounced around in the cab like rubber balls.

"Man, this road is horrible," Shelby complained.

"Yep, told ya." Marie smiled. She looked over the worksheet on her lap. "Oh boy. We're going out to a Mudd location. These boys are nice, but they're a bunch of flirts."

Shelby had heard of the company from Jack, but she had never met any of them and until recently, she didn't even know what a frack crew did.

Marie pointed toward a crane sticking up in the air a few hundred yards away. "See the tall pole in the air, and the black smoke coming from the pumpers?"

"Yeah."

"That's where we're headed."

As Shelby maneuvered the truck down the bumpy road, Marie said, "Frack boys are some of the hardest working men I've ever met, but they spend a lot of time alone on these locations, and they love women drivers. They're pretty harmless unless you give them the idea you might be interested. You'd probably be lucky to make it off location with your clothes if you gave any of them a second look."

Shelby raised an eyebrow. After all, she had a husband and son who worked in the oil patch. She decided that she would stick close to her truck, do her job, and avoid any potential unwanted situations.

After pulling up onto location, Marie got out of the truck to talk with the supervisor. When she returned, the man she was talking with moved in front of the truck and started giving Shelby hand signals for where he wanted her to put the sand truck. Shelby followed his instructions and had no trouble putting the truck into position.

Both women put on their safety equipment and exited the truck. Shelby made herself busy with rigging up while Marie talked with some of the guys who had found their way to her truck. "Hey, guys. What's up? Have ya missed me? Haven't been on one of your locations in a little while. You guys behave while I was away?"

A short Mexican man shook Marie's hand, then gave her a small hug. "Of course we've missed you, Long Legs. It's hard out here without the company of a beautiful woman like you." Others joined Marie, laughing and chatting while Shelby unloaded the sand.

Before long, however, Shelby found herself in the middle of the group. Marie had brought them over to the truck because they were curious about the new blonde driver and wanted to meet her. "Shelby, I want to introduce you to a few of the Mudd boys. My friends Jim, Sal, Myles, Alex, Troy, and Sam."

Shelby shook each of the men's hands. "Nice to meet all of you."

Myles was a tall blonde man with muscles that seemed like they were going to burst out of his shirt. He shook Shelby's hand, and for whatever reason, held onto it for a little longer than normal, which made Shelby feel uncomfortable. Marie noticed Myles and shot him a warning look. "Down, boy, she's married."

Myles left with Marie, but kept his eyes on Shelby as he walked away. As he left, she heard him say, "Oh, come on, Long Legs, you can't bring a beautiful blonde to location and not expect us to be a little horny. Come on, let's go back. I promise, I'll be a good boy."

Marie batted Myles in the back of the head. "Not a chance, Myles. Go back to work, you horn dog." Both laughed as they moved toward Myles' mixer. Most of the other men departed as well, leaving Shelby to watch her gauges. She was flattered that these men found her attractive, but she couldn't help but feel nervous that it might cause her some trouble as well.

Within several minutes, Shelby watched nine more company trucks roll down the road. *There's only room for about four more to unload right away*, she thought as she concentrated on unloading.

"Hey, Shelby. How ya doing?" Shelby about jumped out of her skin when the hand touched her shoulder.

"Oh sorry, Shelby, I didn't mean to scare you." He let go of her shoulder and smiled.

Shelby patted her heart a little and pulled out one of her ear plugs. She smiled when she saw who it was. "Shotgun Rider, what are you doing over here? Aren't you supposed to be unloading?"

Shotgun Rider folded his arms and motioned toward the road. "I'm at the back of the line. Thought I'd come up here and see if I could help you guys unload. Beats having to wait in the truck."

Shelby looked at her gauge and then used her rubber hammer to check how far the sand had dropped on the tank. "I'm getting close to finishing my second compartment. The third doesn't have much in it, so I'll be done soon."

Shotgun Rider took his hand and slapped the middle compartment. "Yeah, you should be finished soon, but I'm at the end of the line so I have to wait for those others to finish, too."

Shelby smiled but went back to watching her gauges. "Well, with me out of the way it should go faster."

Shotgun Rider shrugged. "So, how do you like hauling sand?"

"I like it a lot," Shelby answered. "It's very different from teaching, but I like the change."

"Yeah, I bet it's different." Realizing there wasn't anything he could do Shotgun decided to move on. "Well, guess I'll check on the others to see if they need any help."

"Okay, see you later." Shelby continued to unload, and wondered what had happened to Marie when she reached the last of the sand in the final pod. She went to the cab of the truck, disengaged her PTO, and began to break down her equipment.

"Need some help there, beautiful?" Myles was at the rear of the truck, unhooking the hose from the sand chief. Shelby was a little nervous that he was there with no one else in sight. She cautiously stayed away from the man who was trying to be helpful, but decided that letting him unhook the hose would keep him at the back of the truck while she worked toward the front. "Sure, that would be nice of you."

Shelby moved under the truck, unhooked the hose from the truck line, and then fiddled with the cover, trying to get it on right.

While she obsessed over the difficult cover, Myles got under the truck on the other side. "Having some trouble?"

Shelby began to forcibly hammer at the cover with her fist. "Damn it; it just won't go on right. It happens all the time. I think I got it." She hoped Myles would get out from under the truck and let her deal with the stubborn piece of equipment alone.

Myles did not get the hint. He moved in closer and worked on the cover with Shelby. She was annoyed by his assertiveness. Fortunately, just as Myles placed his hands over hers, the cover went on and she quickly moved her hands out and quickly scrambled out from under the truck. She walked to the PTO and unhooked the hose. She quickly climbed onto the deck and placed the hose in its holder. She turned around, and like she had done many times before, took the steps backwards off the deck. However, she missed the last step, and fell right into Myles' arms.

Slightly startled from the fall, Shelby quickly realized she hadn't hit the ground and was in the arms of a very strong, muscular man. She tried to wrench herself from his hold. "Uh, thank you, Myles, but you can put me down now."

Myles reluctantly put Shelby's feet to the ground. "No problem. Glad I could be of assistance. You can fall into my arms any time."

Shelby felt her cheeks turn hot—probably beet red, like they always got when she was embarrassed. She moved to the back of the truck to replace the last of her equipment so she could leave the location. Myles followed Shelby to the back and started to help her with the final bits of work. "I got this, Myles," Shelby said, dismissively. "Thanks for the help. Have you seen Marie? I need to find her, she has my paperwork."

Myles pointed toward the supervisor's van. "She's over there with Alex turning in your paperwork right now."

"Okay, well thanks for all your help." Shelby decided to put some distance between Myles and herself, and headed towards the van.

Myles laughed as she bolted. "You don't need to run off, beautiful. I'll keep you company until she gets back."

"Hey, girl. Did you finish blowing off our sand?" Marie asked.

"Yes, and I'm ready to go now."

"What's wrong, girl?"

"Nothing."

"What's wrong? You're beet red."

Shelby got to the truck, quickly jerked the door open, and mounted the steps. "Nothing. Can we just get out of here?"

Marie frowned as she climbed into the passenger seat. Shelby released the air brakes and almost moved the truck before Marie fastened her seat belt.

"Whoa, lady trucker, what happened?" Marie asked. "We're alone. You can tell me now."

Suddenly, Shelby slammed on the brakes, almost sending her and Marie through the windshield. She'd stopped inches from Myles who stood in front of the big red Peterbilt.

"Damn it, Myles. What the hell is wrong with you?" Marie yelled as she rolled down her window. "Are you out of your freaking mind, walking out in front of a truck?"

Myles looked straight at Shelby. "No, I'm completely sane, just wanted one more look at the beautiful woman who fell into my arms today."

"What?"

Before Myles could respond, Shelby rolled up Marie's window from her side of the truck and was waving goodbye. "See ya, Myles. Get off the truck, please."

Smiling, Myles jumped off as Shelby pressed the accelerator.

Marie smiled. "Oh, now I understand what's wrong. Myles got to you didn't he? That little whore. I told him to stay away from you. What did he do? What was he talking about. . .you falling into his arms? Oh god, let me guess." Marie burst out laughing. She wasn't the least bit shocked. She had known Myles for years.

"Don't worry about Myles," Marie finally said. "He's harmless. You made one mistake. You'll have to correct or he'll never leave you alone. Myles loves women who are timid…or at least thrown off guard by him. You let Myles think you were helpless." Marie started laughing again. "Poor girl, he loves you."

Shelby laughed at the notion. "He did catch me off guard. Don't worry. I'll have no trouble next time, putting that boy in his place. I have a son around his age."

"Shelby has an admirer," Marie laughed as she told Sandy and Tiff about Myles.

The women laughed so loudly that Eddy poked his head into Sandy's office, "What in the world is going on in here?"

"The rookie got a full dose of the Mudd boys today." Marie explained.

Eddy looked at the crimson-faced Shelby. "Roma, I thought you were married? Shame on you, playing around with young boys on the job."

His comment made Shelby laugh. "I slipped on the deck!" she said, wiping away the tears of laughter. "That's all, I swear."

"Sure, and he just happened to be there to catch you when you fell. Am I right?"

"He's my son's age."

Eddy looked at Sandy and then pointed at Shelby. "Told you she liked them young."

Sandy laughed. "Yep, you got to be careful about the people you hire these days. There are cradle robbers out there, you know."

Eddy smiled, and then became all business. "Roma, I need to see you in my office."

Sandy looked at Shelby. "You heard the man, you've done it now."

"Yep, you messed up big time, having a meeting with the big man already." Tiff said. Shelby quickly went to the restroom, and washed her face, hoping to clean up some before meeting with Eddy.

Shelby waited as Eddy opened a drawer in his desk and muddled through what sounded like a bunch of keys. "There, I think these are the right ones. These are the keys to truck 818, your truck. I can't promise that it's clean, but you can take it down to the car wash. The company will pay to have it cleaned up if it's too bad. Here is a gas card for that truck too."

"Thank you Eddy, I'll take really good care of the truck. I promise."

Eddy nodded seriously before breaking out into a smile again. "Remember, we don't allow hanky-panky in the sleeper, especially with young guys."

Shelby laughed as she got up to leave. "Got it boss, no playing around with little boys." She paused for effect then asked, "How about older men?"

Eddy was caught off guard. He recovered with a laugh and waved Shelby out of his office. "Get out of here."

Shelby left for the break room. "What did the boss want?" Marie asked.

"Oh, nothing." She held up her new truck keys. "He gave me my own truck keys. I'm so excited."

Marie reached for the keys and playfully tried to take them.

Shelby was quicker and held them close to her body. "No way, these are mine."

CHAPTER SIX

Shelby told Jack about getting her own truck. "See if you can bring it home so we can clean it up together," he suggested.

She asked Eddy the next morning, and he agreed.

As soon as Shelby opened the door, it was evident the previous driver had been a smoker. She got in, started it up, and headed to the yard's exit. She turned the CB on and heard Marie's voice, "How bout ya, little Blondie, ready to roll?"

"You bet, Long Legs."

"Alright, let's go see Myles."

Shelby cringed. "Don't remind me." She wondered if Sandy sending her back out to the Mudd boys so soon was out of necessity or a joke.

"What?" Marie ribbed her, "I figured you must have dreamed about being saved by those muscular arms all night."

"Very funny. I'll be lucky to live that event down, won't I?"

"Yep, going to be a hard one to forget Blondie." Shelby fell in behind Marie at the gate and the two of them rolled down the road toward the location they had left yesterday.

Shelby changed her focus. She knew her new profession meant that her truck would be like a second home, so she decided she'd make it as personal to her as her classrooms had been.

Marie and Shelby were the first to arrive on location and Marie went to find out where the supervisor wanted them to unload. When she came back, Marie pointed toward the sand chief and said, "We'll be going into compartments one and two. They don't want us to unload yet, but we can go ahead and get set up. I'm going to guide you in first, and then I'll get in. We'll need to leave as much room as possible for the trucks that will be unloading in the other chief over there." Marie pointed again to a chief that was angled to the rear of the location.

Shelby looked over the location, picturing how she was going to maneuver the truck into the small space.

Marie said, "I want you to turn around right here, and get straight on with compartment number two. I'll move my truck back and then back you into position. I know we'll catch hell from some of the other drivers for leaving them very little room to maneuver, but that is what Alex told me to do."

"Okay." Shelby nodded.

Within a few minutes, the two women had their trucks in position and busied themselves with rigging up. "Where is everyone?" Shelby asked.

Marie pointed to the cabs of the frack trucks. "Alex said they had trouble with the well last night, almost screened out, but they got it back. After being at it all night, they're resting for a while."

After the women finished rigging up, Marie told Shelby to go ahead and take a nap if she wanted. The crew would knock on their doors when they were ready for them.

Shelby nodded, but instead of her nap, she got in her truck and grabbed a can of window cleaner. By the time the can was empty, Marie was knocking on her door. "They're ready for us to start blowing off our sand. They want us to blow it off slow because they will be fracturing the well at the same time that we unload."

Shelby put on her hard hat, safety glass, and gloves; she reached down and engaged her PTO and ran up her RPM's. Then she got out of her truck, moved to open her line valve, and stabilize her tank pressure.

Within a few moments, Shelby and Marie were busy blowing off their sand. Shelby was focused on her pressure gauge box and was not aware Myles had come up from behind. Stepping back, she accidentally ran into his arms almost repeating the exact same incident that had occurred the previous day. Shocked, Shelby quickly wrenched herself away from him and moved back toward her truck. "You scared me."

Myles smiled. "Well, I'm sorry about that, but I see you found your way into my arms again. I sure like that." He inched closer.

"Back up, tiger. I have work to do." Shelby put her hand against Myles chest to keep him from getting any closer. Myles was sweaty, smelly, and from the pressure on her hand Shelby could tell, very well built.

He moved in closer. "Oh baby, I love it when you resist."

Shelby decided enough was enough. "Myles, I like you, but I'm married and old enough to be your mama. Now back up, and let me do my job."

Myles smiled, showing his big mouth full of less than white teeth. "You like me, I like older women, and what your husband doesn't know…."

She pushed him as hard as she could. "Not a chance, baby boy. You don't have anything I want. Now go on back to whatever it is you do before I call in the big dogs."

"Oh, don't do that, Ms. Shelby. I'm sorry. I didn't mean to upset you."

"It's okay, Myles. We can be friends, but nothing else. Now, go back to your work, let me do mine, and we'll get along just fine."

Before Myles could escape, Marie rounded the corner. She pointed toward the supervisor van. "Myles, I told you yesterday to leave Shelby alone and I meant it. Now go, before I get Alex over here and you get your butt run off."

"I didn't mean anything. I was just having some fun." He begrudgingly walked away from the sand trucks.

"He is really persistent, isn't he?" Shelby said.

Marie shrugged. "You think? He's a man, isn't he? They're all persistent when it comes to beautiful women."

Shelby now understood why Jack had reservations about her working out here. Her thoughts were abruptly interrupted by another welcome voice. Betty was coming straight for her. "Hey, rookie. Do you think you could have put your truck in that spot any more crooked?"

Shelby didn't quite know how to respond. Fortunately, she didn't have to. Before she could respond, Marie said, "Shut up, Betty. Shelby put her truck exactly where I told her to. If you have a problem with that, take it up with Alex."

Betty stomped off. She got in her truck and turned it around, backing it in near the other chief. It took her several shots, and because of her arrogance, she never once asked anyone to help shot her into position. After about the tenth time of trying to maneuver around Shelby's truck, and almost hitting it nine of those times, Marie came out from behind her truck and guided Betty back into her spot. "See, if you hadn't been such a bitch about things when you rolled up, you'd already been blowing off."

Betty reluctantly agreed. "Thanks, Marie. But that rookie needs some help with getting her truck straight."

"Don't worry about her, Betty. She's going to get it. Remember how long it took you to do get it right the first few times? Hey, where's Ted?"

"He's at home with that fat cow wife of his," Betty scoffed. "One of his kids had to go to the doctor this morning. I think he should have made her handle it on her own. After all, he works his job and she needs to do hers. I think if you're dumb enough to have that many kids, you should be able to take care of them all by yourself."

Marie rolled her eyes. "She didn't create those children by herself, Betty. Those are their children, and they both need to look after them. I'm sure taking care of the house and those children is a lot more work than driving a truck."

"If he doesn't work, how is he going to pay the bills? She can take that kid to the doctor alone. She just wants to dominate his life and keep him away from work."

Shelby waited by her truck while Marie went to help Betty. All of a sudden, seemingly from out of nowhere, Myles was standing next to her. "I thought Marie told you to go back to work?"

"I did," Myles responded coyly. "But I just couldn't let you leave location thinking I'm some kind of jerk. I'm sorry for coming on so strong earlier. I just can't help myself sometimes when it comes to beautiful women. I tried to hook up with Marie, but she's got something with Alex, I think. Anyway, I'm sorry. I really do want to be friends, okay?"

"I accept your apology. I'd like to be friends, as long as you don't cross the line again."

Myles smiled his big smile. "Can I help you with anything, Ms. Shelby?"

"No, I think I got it. And Marie is coming back now, so you better get out of here before she has your head on platter."

"Got it. See you later, Ms. Shelby."

Marie saw Myles leaving Shelby's truck. "Was that little bastard here again? I thought I told him to leave you alone?"

Shelby smiled as she lifted the handle on her second pod. "It's alright. He just wanted to apologize to me. I think he understands the boundaries now."

Marie moved the valves on her truck. "That's good. It's too bad that some other people we know don't understand boundaries. I swear, every time I think I have heard it all, Betty says something, and I know that crazy still exists in this world."

◊◊◊

The two women finished unloading and headed back to the yard. Before they could get off the lease road they were met by three sand haulers from one of ESCC's competitors. Marie came over the radio. "Look what the cat drug in! Three little Rowdy Boys. Hey, boys!"

The driver stopped near Marie's truck and spoke over the radio, "Yeah, how ya doing Marie? Pull over for a minute, guys, its Marie from ESCC."

The other drivers pulled over and got out of their trucks to talk. Marie came back over the radio before exiting her truck. "Pull over, Shelby. I want to introduce you to the Rowdy Boys. We work a lot with these guys."

Shelby pulled in behind Marie and got out of her truck. She was the last to join the group that had gathered around Marie's truck. "Wow, who's the babe, Marie?" A tall man with dark sunglasses said as he removed the glasses to get a better look at Shelby.

"Calm down, Little Blue Boy. She's married."

"So am I."

Marie snickered as Shelby joined the group and shook the hand of each man as Marie introduced then to her. "This is Praise Warrior, Scooter, and Little Blue Boy. These boys work for Rowdy and they take up the slack for us when we need the help."

"Nice to meet you."

"Shelby, our newest driver," Marie said.

"The truth of the matter is that ESCC can't handle their jobs, and we have to clean up after them," Praise Warrior said.

Marie giggled. "Yeah right, that's why they call us first and you guys second, right?"

Everyone laughed and argued over which company was best before Little Blue Boy changed the conversation. "So what is a pretty little thing like you doing hauling sand?"

"Money," she quipped.

"Yeah, I know what you mean, but why sand hauling?" Little Blue Boy wondered.

"It's fun," she said with a shrug.

Marie broke the group up with a quick point. "We got to go boys. We got a vehicle coming at us, and I'm sure they won't like being detained by a group of gabby sand haulers. You guys be careful, and we'll see ya around." They all headed for their trucks.

Little Blue Boy yelled after Shelby. "Nice to meet you, Shelby! Hope we see you again out here."

Shelby waved. "Nice to meet you guys, too. I'm sure we'll be working together a lot."

"I hope so, beautiful."

◊◊◊

About halfway back to the yard, Marie got on the radio. "Well lady, I had fun rolling with you today. Let's do this again real soon. I'll be gone for a few days. They're sending me to the northwest yard in Wyoming to help out, so I won't be here to run interference for you. Just remember to keep your distance from Betty."

"I think they're sending you to New Mexico on Monday with some of the lead drivers. Phantom 309 is a good guy, so stick with him or Speedy; they'll help you out if you need anything."

"Thanks, Marie. You be safe going up north. Thanks for the advice."

When Shelby arrived at the yard, she parked her truck, went to the office to do paperwork, and then checked her box. The assignment sheet confirmed what Marie had told her. She went to the break room and sat at the table, looking over the list of drivers who'd be going with her. Thankfully, Betty and Ted were not included. At that moment, Betty entered and slammed the door behind her. She was obviously in a bad mood.

"Hey, Shelby. Need any help with that paperwork?" Betty sneered.

"No thanks, I think I got it."

"Better than backing up right?" When Shelby didn't reply, she kept pressing, "I noticed you talking with Myles today. Does your husband know you have a boyfriend?"

"Look, Betty, I'm not sure what your problem is with me. I don't like people who put their noses in my business or make up stories. You can play your little mind games with everyone else if you like, but don't do it with me. In fact, let's keep our communications strictly on a business level." Shelby gathered up her paperwork and headed toward the door.

Betty snickered. "Sorry, I didn't mean to hit a nerve. I guess he isn't aware of the boyfriend. I won't tell anyone I promise."

Shelby was pissed off but left without saying another word.

◊◊◊

Shelby liked her new job, but she loved coming home even more. As she walked through the door, familiar smells hit her nose, filling her with happiness. Jack greeted her at the door. Shelby hugged and kissed Jack like she hadn't seen him in weeks.

"What's this all about, baby?" Jack inquired.

Shelby left her hands wrapped around Jack's neck and looked deep into his eyes. "Have I told you lately how much I love you?"

"Of course. You tell me every day. What is wrong with you, sweetheart? Did something happen at work today?"

Shelby let go of her hold on Jack and walked toward their bedroom. Once inside, she threw herself backwards on the bed. Jack joined her and asked her about her day again.

"Nothing really happened. Well maybe, I don't know. It's so confusing. I never realized just how much crap you have to put up with when you have to work with overly zealous people. Why do people have to be so competitive and mean and needing to control everything?"

"That's just the dog-eat-dog world, baby." Jack let Shelby curl up in his arms on the bed and continued, "It's tough out there, Shelby. People are like us—trying to survive—and sometimes they forget that stepping on others to get to what they need isn't the right way to do things."

"You remember me telling you about that woman, Betty, who seemed to rub me the wrong way the first time I met her?"

Jack nodded.

"Well, I wanted to deck her today. Not only did she try to tell me what to do on location, but she accused me of having a boyfriend on location."

Jack's eyebrows arched. "A boyfriend, huh? When were you going to let me know I was being replaced?" He tried to make light of the accusation, but he was curious. "What made her think you had a boyfriend?"

Shelby could tell from Jack's tone that he was only half joking. "Seriously Jack, you can't possibly think I have a boyfriend."

Jack shrugged. "No, but she had to have some reason for believing it, didn't she?"

Shelby shook her head and smacked Jack on the leg. "Jack, this is serious. This woman is making me nuts already. How am I going to deal with her?"

Jack tickled his wife. "You still haven't told me when I was going to be replaced by the young buck," he laughed.

Shelby giggled, trying only slightly to free herself from her husband. "Stop talking about some stupid other guy and help me figure out what to do about Betty."

Jack held her down, looked her in the eye, and gave her the answer she needed. "You're smart, beautiful, and a fighter, my sweet Shelby. I can't believe that some crazy ass bitch is able to push your buttons like this. You know what to do, sweetheart. Do your job the best you can. Ignore everything she does and says. Believe in yourself. That's really all that matters isn't it—you and me and our family?"

"You always know exactly what to say, don't you?" She kissed him deeply and before long they were entwined in passion.

CHAPTER SEVEN

Three months had gone by when one morning, Shelby found herself rolling down I-10, heading home from South Texas. She was daydreaming about all that had happened since she switched careers when all of a sudden, her cell phone rang, interrupting her thoughts. "Hello?"

"Hey, girl. This is Sandy. Can you come into the office tomorrow? Eddy needs to see you."

"Sure…" Shelby said. "Did he say what it's about?"

"No. Can you come in around nine?"

"Sure." Shelby was now concerned with what her boss wanted. She ticked off in her mind what might cause him to be upset. She couldn't think of anything that bad, except the time she hit the guardrail. *But surely he would have terminated me long before now if that were the case.* She decided she needed to stop thinking about it and get home to Jack, who would put things into perspective for her.

"Shelby, let it go," he advised her. "There isn't anything worrying will do for you tonight except make you lose sleep. It's probably nothing important or you would have been made aware of it long before now."

"You're right. I'll find out tomorrow."

◊◊◊

Sandy pointed toward Eddy's office when Shelby arrived the next morning. "He's waiting for you." Shelby went in.

"Hi, Shelby. How are you today?"

"I'm good."

"It's time for your job review. I've already filled this out, but I need you to read over it and sign it if you agree with it."

Shelby breathed a sigh of relief. She'd been through many of these in her career as a teacher. "Sure," she said, feeling lighter than she had all morning.

"After you've read and signed your evaluation, I need to inspect your truck."

"Okay."

The evaluation was positive. "Thanks for the nice evaluation, Eddy. It means a lot to me."

Eddy grinned. "Don't thank me yet. I haven't inspected your truck."

Then they went out to inspect her truck. Eddy took many trips around the outside of it. He checked the engine and oil level, as well as lights and hose condition. He entered the cab of the truck and wrote down a few items while Shelby stood by the truck and waited for him to finish. He finished, exited the cab, and locked it. "Well, the truck is in good condition, but I'm going to have to keep the keys."

"Did I do something wrong, Eddy?"

Eddy started to walk off in the direction of some of the newer trucks. "No, but you won't need the keys to that truck if you're driving one of the newer ones."

Shelby covered her mouth in astonishment. "What? You're giving me a new truck?"

"No, Shelby," Eddy taunted playfully. "I just thought I'd pretend to give you a new one, silly. Of course, I'm giving you a new one. This one in fact." Eddy pointed to a bright red truck and dangled the keys on his fingers.

"Oh, thank you, Eddy! It's beautiful!" Shelby grabbed the keys, then went and opened the truck's door, and jumped into the driver's seat. She checked out every detail of the control panel. She started to thank Eddy again, but he was already on his way back to the office. She quickly picked up her cell phone and called Jack.

◊◊◊

"Time really flies," Shelby told Sandy as she thought about how quickly the last few months had gone by in her new truck.

"I hope I'm keeping you busy enough?"

"Oh yeah, you're keeping me plenty busy, and I really appreciate it. I wasn't sure at first how I was going to like or handle this longer haul stuff, but I actually enjoy it."

Shelby liked Sandy, and although Sandy was technically her boss, she hoped they would continue to be friends. "If you get a chance one of these weekends when I'm home, maybe we can go shopping or out for a drink?"

Sandy nodded. "That would be great! I haven't had much time to go out lately. Maybe this weekend, if you're back from Arkansas in time; we should also invite Tiff."

Shelby looked up from her paperwork, a little surprised. "Arkansas? You've never sent me any further than South Texas and Northeastern New Mexico. I didn't know we even went that far. You trust me to go all the way to Arkansas? Do you think I'm ready?"

"Of course I think you're ready, otherwise you wouldn't be going. Oh, one more thing. Before you leave the yard, I need you to find one of the yard hands and have a small load of CLT put on your truck for a drop off before you head to Arkansas tomorrow.

"Check the warehouse first, or they might be out behind the rail cars. They left the radio here in the office, so I can't relay that information myself. Be sure one of them checks in with me after they finish."

Shelby nodded, placed her paperwork in the receiving box, and went out toward the warehouse. She didn't like going into the warehouse. It was so dark, even with the doors open. She reluctantly shuffled her steel-toed boots through the sand that had accumulated on the ground near the building. She figured the West Texas winds were probably to blame for most of the sand around this building since they didn't load many trucks near the old warehouse.

Inside the warehouse it was just as Shelby had remembered—dark and dusty with a little spooky added in for good measure. She walked around the stacks of sand bags that were close to the front of the building and looked to see if any of the yard hands were in sight. She did not see anyone in the building and with a sense of relief, believing she didn't need to go any further into the building, Shelby turned around and headed back toward the entrance.

Before she could make her exit through the door and back into the light of the yard, she suddenly heard some noise coming from the southeast corner of the building. She turned to see what it was, but all she saw was a sunbeam of light full of dust particles, streaming across the warehouse from a small window. Near the window in a darker corner of the building was a door that Shelby never remembered seeing before.

"Damn it," Shelby spoke aloud, realizing that she was going to have to go back into the dungeon-like atmosphere she had almost escaped from. She decided the faster the better and moved toward the door in the corner.

Shelby opened the door and shut it as quickly as she had opened it, moving at almost a run toward the exit of the warehouse. She wanted no part in the confrontation she knew would ensue with those she had just caught in a rather compromising situation in that room. Shelby wasn't naïve about these kinds of activities going on in the workplace, nor was she shocked at the act that was being performed behind that door since she herself had given birth to three boys and was married to a man who loved sex. What troubled her was whom she had caught, and what they might do if they knew she had just been the one who had opened the door to their dirty little secret.

She felt some sense of relief after reaching the yard, but kept running until she reached the other side of the rail cars. Shelby hoped being with the yard hands near the rail cars would conceal her identity from Ted and Betty if they should decide to slither their way out of the warehouse to find their intruder. "Damn it, damn it, damn it," she muttered as she hurried toward the yard hands and moved into position by them, hoping to appear as having been there for a while.

Omar smiled at Shelby with humorous curiosity as she almost ran into him. "Hey, Shelby. What's the hurry?"

Shelby grabbed Omar's sleeve and then bent over to catch her breath before hurriedly explaining what she needed. She wanted to get away from the yard before the two lovers left their love nest. "Sandy needs you to load my truck with that small load of sand for J&B tomorrow before I leave for Arkansas." Shelby took another deep breath. "Sandy said you need to confirm it with her after you're finished since you left the radio in her office earlier."

"Okay.… But why did you almost run us down?"

Shelby waved goodbye with her hand over her head without turning around again to respond.

Shelby decided not to stop in the office and let Sandy know that she had relayed the message to the yard hands. She just wanted to get into her car and drive off as quickly as possible. The last four months had proven to be difficult during the times when she had to work with Ted and Betty, and she wasn't about to make things worse simply because she had opened the wrong door.

◊◊◊

"Ted, get the fuck off me and give me my pants. That stupid little bitch, Shelby, just opened the door, and I know she saw us."

Ted moved quickly as Betty sat up, retrieved her bra, placed it into position over her breasts, and quickly hooked it in the back. "Damn it! I knew that nosy little snob was going to be trouble for us. GIVE ME MY FUCKING PANTS, YOU DUMB ASS!"

Ted hobbled around the floor like a calf that had just been roped at a rodeo, trying to get away. Finally, he spotted his lover's desired article of clothing. He reached for the pants that were just slightly out of reach, and fell forward on his face. Betty had found her shirt and was on her feet placing buttons in the holes of the shirt when she saw Ted fall. "You moron!"

Betty leaned down and snatched the pants she wanted out from under Ted's arm, leaving him in his less than dignified position. "Shit, Ted. Sometimes I wonder about you."

Betty quickly pulled on her pants while Ted muddled his way around on the floor, trying to get untangled from his own clothes. Ted was still on his back on the floor, trying to button his pants, when Betty had finished and headed toward the warehouse doors. "Would you please get the hell off that floor and come on?"

With Ted practically jumping to his feet and still adjusting his clothing, the two reached the warehouse doors as Shelby was leaving the parking lot in her car.

Betty crossed her arms and leaned her back up against the building as she watched Shelby drive off. Disappointed with the fact that her little victim had just gotten away, she quickly began to contemplate what she would do to get even with Shelby. "You can run, sweetie pie, but you can't hide."

Betty looked at Ted who had been fiddling with the zipper on his pants the whole time and hadn't noticed Shelby driving out of the yard. "Damn it, Ted. Quit messing around and walk me to my car. I have to go home and figure out how we are going to get rid of that little bitch before she tells everyone about us."

Ted immediately stopped working with his zipper. "What? Do you really think she will tell everyone about us, Betty? What will we do if she tells my wife? Oh hell, Betty, my wife will kill me. Or worse, she might divorce me, and I'll have to pay child support on all my kids. Oh god, Betty, that would be horrible. What are we going to do? This is bad. Really, really bad."

Betty backhanded her fist into Ted's stomach as she walked toward her car. Ted doubled over, the wind knocked out of him.

"Come on, you idiot. Walk me to my car so I can think. Don't worry about Barbie. She won't say anything if she's smart, but we do have to get rid of her just in case she gets a hair up her ass to use what she knows against us. She might want to blackmail us for something."

Ted was still holding his belly as the two of them reached the parking lot. "Why would she want to blackmail us, Betty? We don't have any money, and we aren't famous or anything. What could she possibly want from the two of us? We're just sand haulers."

"Oh shut up, Ted," Betty practically growled. "People do crazy things for crazy reasons, and I'm going to make sure that little Miss Shelby doesn't get any crazy ideas."

◊◊◊

Shelby sat parked in her driveway with both hands on top of the steering wheel. She lowered her forehead on top of them. She was home, safe and well away from the sand yard. *How is it possible that this one woman can intimidate me so much? I'm a sophisticated, well-educated, socially-skilled individual, yet here I am, running away like a child. I need to get a grip or these people are going to take advantage the first opportunity they get. At least I'm home.*

When she entered her house, Jack was sitting in his easy chair watching television. "Hey, sweetheart. How was your day?" When she didn't answer immediately, he frowned and turned off the TV. "Did you have a bad day, baby?"

Shelby walked toward Jack and practically fell into his lap. "No, it wasn't a bad day at work. I just happened to see something tonight I really wish I hadn't."

"What did you see that has you this upset, baby?" Jack reached over and patted Shelby's hand.

"I caught a couple of people at work not exactly working."

"Not working? So? A lot of people don't work when they go to work. Why are you upset about that?"

"I caught them having sex in the warehouse."

Jack laughed. "Oh yeah, I guess that wouldn't exactly be working, unless they were making a movie."

Shelby stood up. "Jack, you're an ass. It wasn't about catching them having sex, it was *who* I caught."

Jack, still laughing, followed Shelby into their bedroom. He watched her undress. "Who was it? Was the woman as sexy without her clothes on as you?" Jack grabbed Shelby around her waist.

Shelby turned around and placed her arms around Jack's neck. "I caught Betty and Ted, the only two people I haven't been able to make friends with. I know this sounds like high school, but Betty is such a nasty, domineering person. Catching them could really be bad for me. He would do anything for her, and I'm afraid of what they might do to me at work. Maybe I'm just paranoid, but I've always felt so vulnerable around them, and it's even worse now."

Jack held Shelby in his arms. "Don't worry, baby. Everything is going to be alright. Try not worry so much about things. I'm sure they have no idea who saw them, and even if they did, they won't do anything."

Shelby buried her face in her husband's chest. "I hope you're right, Jack."

Jack went back to his chair to watch TV while Shelby showered and put on clean clothes. As she placed her hair in a scrunchy, she remembered she'd be leaving for Arkansas tomorrow. She went into the living room, "Hey, Jack. Through all the confusion I forgot to tell you that Sandy is sending me to Arkansas tomorrow. I'll be gone for a few days."

"You're driving all the way to Arkansas to deliver sand? Don't they have sand in Arkansas?" he asked, perturbed.

"I'm not delivering sand. I'll be picking it up and bringing it back here. I'll also be doing some load deliveries there for a few days before I bring the load for this area back. Will you be okay without me, or should I have someone come over and stay with you?"

"I'm not a child, Shelby," Jack sniped. "I think I can handle being here without you. I just thought this job was going to be more local stuff. You seem to be delivering or picking up loads out of town a lot more."

"I didn't mean to treat you like a child, Jack; I was simply concerned with how you would be health-wise without me. I do like to think I'm still needed around here. As for why they're sending me out of town so much lately, it's because that is where the work is right now. I'm doing a good job, and they trust me to haul loads longer distances. Maybe your wife is just one hell of a trucker; you know, your little mother trucker.

Shelby chuckled and went to the kitchen to start dinner. But Jack was in no mood to laugh.

CHAPTER EIGHT

The next morning, Shelby saw Betty sitting in the driver's seat of her truck, doing what appeared to be paperwork. She was glad that Betty didn't even look up when she started the pre-trip inspection on her truck. *Maybe Betty and Ted didn't see me and have no idea I was in the warehouse yesterday.* Shelby decided not to say anything to her coworkers. Instead, she would concentrate on doing her job.

After finishing her pre-trip and starting her log for the day, Shelby was about to leave the yard when Betty knocked on the door of her truck. "Hey, I noticed your paperwork was still in your box. You might want to stop and get it before you leave."

Shelby was a little confused. "What do you mean?" she asked. "Sandy gave me my paperwork yesterday."

Betty smirked. "Maybe there were some changes or something. You can check it out if you want. Or don't—it doesn't matter to me. Just thought you might want to know."

Shelby didn't want to strain her working relationship any further with Betty, so she gave a tight-lipped smile. "Thanks, Betty. I'll go and see about that paperwork right now. Are you going to Arkansas, too?"

But Betty was already walking away from Shelby's truck, so she didn't answer.

Shelby let it go and drove her truck to the front of the yard near the of-fice building. As she retrieved the new paperwork, Shelby looked it over and headed back to her truck. Once in her seat she compared the new paperwork with the paperwork that Sandy had given to her yesterday. There were differ-ent directions for the load she was delivering today and the type of sand she was picking up to bring back to West Texas. Feeling that the new paperwork was probably a revision of the prior, she put the old paperwork away and followed the new directions to the location.

Shelby headed toward the store where everyone went to fuel their trucks. The girls who worked in this store were always so friendly, and the coffee was just what she needed to start her day. After fueling, Shelby went into the store to get her receipt and coffee. "Thanks Rosie; have a good day," Shelby told the little lady behind the counter and turned to leave, almost running over Ted. "Oh sorry, Ted. I didn't see you there," Shelby explained, catching her balance with Ted's arm.

Ted smiled and helped Shelby catch her balance. Suddenly, Betty shoved her fist into his back, and he let go of Shelby in such way that she almost lost her balance again. Shelby knew from his expression that he was going to be in trouble for being nice to her, so she steadied herself and left the store. She wanted to get away from Betty and Ted as quickly as possible.

Shelby felt sorry for Ted in some ways, but he was a grown man, after all. *If he allows someone like Betty to control him like a dog, then maybe he deserves everything he's getting,* she thought. Still, she couldn't help feeling relieved that neither Ted nor Betty had mentioned her opening the door on them. *It's a good thing they didn't know it was me, and I want to keep it that way.*

◊◊◊

Betty glared at Ted after Shelby had left the store, and then pushed him out of the way to get her receipt. "Enjoy your close encounter with little Miss Barbie, asshole?"

"I just tried to keep her from running into me, Betty, that's all," Ted muttered.

"Yeah right." Betty signed her receipt and rudely threw the clerk's half of the receipt back at her without a thank you. "Did you get my email this morning?"

Ted smiled at the clerk, apologetically. He signed his receipt and gently gave it to Rosie. "Thank you."

Betty grabbed Ted's arm and pulled him away from the counter. "Stop being nice to that girl and let's go. I want to see Shelby screw up. I made the directions close to where we'll be unloading so we'll have front row seats to her stupidity. Maybe it will be bad enough mistake that Eddy will get rid of her. Did you get the email?"

Ted was moving as quickly as possible to keep up with Betty. "Yes, but what makes you think she will follow the new directions?"

"She will, dumb ass. Trust me, she will."

"I guess if you say so, Betty, but I don't think she's going to say anything. She didn't say anything today."

"SHUT UP, TED!" Betty yelled over the truck engines. The two co-workers got in their trucks and headed in the same direction as Shelby.

◊◊◊

It took Shelby about two hours to get to the location with the directions that she had been given on the new paperwork. Once she reached the location, however, there wasn't a crew or a sand box in sight. She looked over the directions again. *Maybe I made a mistake on my turns, but I don't think so. This has never happened to me before.* She decided to contact Sandy. "Sandy this is Shelby. I'm out here on location and there isn't anyone, or for that matter, anything but a wellhead out here. Do you know where the crew is or did the directions change again?"

"The crew should be there since that is already a working job, and no, the directions haven't changed," Sandy was clearly annoyed. "Are you sure you went to the right place? You should have been there at least an hour ago."

Now Shelby was frustrated. "Yes, I'm sure I followed the new directions just as you put them on this work sheet, and these directions are really out here. I even left earlier since it was so far out. I can't help that the location changed."

"What are you talking about? The directions didn't change."

"What? I picked up the new worksheet this morning out of my box."

"What new paperwork? I didn't give you any new paperwork. Read me the purchase order number off the top."

"C14578450."

"Oh god, that is an order for next week." Sandy cursed under her breath. "How did you get that paperwork? It was on my desk."

"I found it in my box this morning," Shelby explained. "I thought it was new directions for this load."

"Calm down, Shelby. We can fix this. I'm not sure why that paperwork was in your box, but I'll have Buck from the south yard meet you halfway near the interstate. Buck and some of the other drivers from the south are up here doing some work. We'll transfer your load to him and have him deliver it to the right location so you can get to Arkansas."

Shelby wasn't sure why she felt like such an idiot since she had only done what was on the paperwork. "I'm so sorry, Sandy. I really thought the paperwork was a change in my load and it was in my box."

"It's alright, Shelby. Just turn around and head toward the interstate I'll call Buck and have him meet you. I'll also get in touch with the fracture team and explain the situation. Maybe they're far enough behind that it will be alright. Don't worry about this anymore, just get to the interstate so that you can meet Buck and make your pick up time in Arkansas."

"Okay," Shelby answered quietly. "Sorry." Shelby wanted to cry but she knew that crying would only show weakness, and right now, she was determined to make sure no one could see her vulnerability.

"Damn it, how could this have happened?" she said aloud to the empty truck. She quickly turned around and headed back toward the interstate.

◊◊◊

Shelby had no idea that Betty and Ted were watching her just behind a little hill that covered them from detection. "That's what you get, Miss Shelby, nosy little witch. I'll teach you to spy on me." Betty laughed.

"Betty, I didn't know Shelby was spying on you. Why didn't you tell me?" Betty rolled her eyes. "Oh, shut up, Ted."

"But—"

"Shit!" Betty yelped, causing Ted to jump. "Hurry up and finish getting unloaded. I guess that bitch Sandy figured out something to get Shelby out of her mess. She's leaving the location. Move it, and I'll keep a watch on her so we can tail her to Arkansas. If this doesn't get her fired, I have plenty of ideas up my sleeve to make it happen."

◊◊◊

It took Shelby about an hour to reach the place that Sandy had arranged for her to meet Buck. She remembered Buck, Inspector General, from when she was at the south yard a few weeks ago. Buck was funny and she liked working with him. But she wasn't excited about working with him this time. She figured he would probably think she had created today's work out of stupidity. As she approached the meeting spot Buck was already there waiting on her.

Buck was a nice looking Mexican man who had been with the company for a long time. As Shelby approached, Buck was already near the back of his truck ready to guide her into position so they could unload her truck into his. Shelby placed the rear of her trailer to the rear of Buck's trailer, got out, and walked toward Buck. "Hey, Buck. How are you? Done any inspecting lately?"

Buck laughed, a little surprised Shelby remembered what he had done to her. "I'm good, Shelby. How about you? Any surprise inspections lately?"

Shelby and Buck laughed as they shook hands. Then they put on their gloves and walked toward the trailers. "I'm good except for this mess. I keep wondering when the next surprise inspection will come from the general though."

She reached for her hose in the tube and pulled it out so they could make the connection between the trucks and transfer the sand. "I really was doing much better until this happened. Now I just feel like an idiot."

Buck helped her make the connection, and then they walked to the front of their own trucks for the transfer. "Don't be too hard on Sandy. She has a lot to do, and sometimes paperwork gets mixed up."

Shelby reached out and grabbed Buck's arm. "What? Did Sandy tell you what happened?"

"Oh, she just said she put the wrong paperwork in your box and needed me to take this load to the right location so you could get on your way to Arkansas."

Shelby was surprised that Sandy had taken responsibility instead of blaming her, and respected her even more, if that were possible.

It took about an hour to finish the transfer of sand, and Shelby was feeling better. Buck and Shelby broke down the equipment they used in the unloading of the sand, but before they could finish, they were joined by several south drivers who had decided to show up for the party.

"Make sure you get that cap on nice and tight, Shelby. We wouldn't want any sand to fall out of the truck," Stray Dog kidded.

Shelby knew that tightening the cap wasn't going to stop sand from falling out of a trailer that didn't have any sand. She smart mouthed Stray Dog. "Very funny, Stray Dog, the trailer is empty, but maybe we should have inspector general Buck here, check it out for slippage or confided space violations." Everyone had a good laugh over that one since it had become common practice now to tease the blonde driver. Shelby didn't mind the way the other drivers messed with her. In fact, it made her feel like one of the guys.

"Oh, that's right. We are here because you didn't make it to the right location." White Lightning laughed, knowing it wasn't really Shelby's fault, but wanted to rub it in a little.

Shelby gently socked him in the arm. "Very funny, I already feel bad about all this."

White Lightning held his harm, pretending she had actually hurt him. "Damn, for a little girl you pack a good punch."

Shelby laughed.

"Well, thanks for the help, guys," she said. "I really appreciate you. I do have to get going since I have a long haul to Arkansas. A ten-hour drive in eight hours. It's going to be interesting to see how I get that done without a ticket."

White Lightning spoke up. "Shelby, just stay on the interstate and catch a couple fast runners. They will probably take you right through the Big D."

"Thanks, guys, I'll do that, and thanks again for all the help." Shelby waved goodbye and steered her big truck up onto the road toward Arkansas.

Soon after getting on the interstate, Shelby called Jack. "Hey, sweetheart. How are you?"

He heard the glum tone in her voice. "What's wrong, baby?"

"Oh, paperwork got messed up, and I got sent to the wrong location. Now I have eight hours to get to Arkansas."

"That's nothing for my little mother trucker." Jack said, clearly trying to make her feel better.

Shelby smiled. "Very funny. I know I can do it; I just hate being in such a rush. You know how I like to take in all the scenery when I travel. Now I have to hurry and that takes all the fun out of it."

"Don't worry, baby. You can check it all out on your return trip."

"Yeah, you're right, sweetheart. You always make me feel better. Well, better go. I need to find me some fast runners so I can make it on time."

"What are fast runners?"

"Fast runners are truck drivers that ride in packs and run over the speed limits to make time. They have a front door, or leader, and a back door, or the last driver that watches for DOT for the rest of the drivers in the pack."

"You mean like a convoy from the nineteen sixties, right?"

"Yeah, I guess so."

"Not a good idea, baby. That's a good way to get a ticket."

Shelby sighed. "I know, but I have to make my load time. It's part of my job. I promise I'll be careful."

Jack sounded unsure. "Alright…Just come home to me safe. I love you."

"Me too, baby. I'll see you soon. I'll call you tonight."

Jack had the last word. "Bye, baby."

CHAPTER NINE

Betty and Ted had finished unloading and had followed Shelby as close as they could off the lease and toward the interstate. They found a little turn off away from where Shelby had made connections with the south drivers and held up there until they spotted Shelby leave. They gave the south drivers time to get on their way so no one would become curious as to why they were in the same area at the same time as the mess up. Betty figured they would be able to keep up with Shelby if she used her radio. And if she didn't, it still wouldn't be too hard to catch up.

Outside their trucks, Ted was making his hands busy with Betty's boobs while they waited. Betty watched the road, waiting for Shelby to leave, allowing Ted to move his hands over her body. As soon as she saw Shelby leave, she pushed Ted off of her. "There she goes. Get back in your truck as soon as those south drivers leave. We need to catch up to Blondie."

Ted wasn't happy about being denied his toys, and he moved his hands back to her boobs. "Come on Betty, we can play until they leave."

Betty removed his hands forcefully. "Get in your truck, moron. You can play with them later."

Ted looked like a little boy who just had his bike taken away by his mommy as he walked back to his truck.

Betty yelled at him on her way to her own truck. "Make sure you're on our channel! We don't want to be on nineteen in case she's still in radio range."

Ted indicated with a wave over his head that he got the message as he walked to his truck.

◊◊◊

It didn't take Shelby long to find a pack of runners. As soon as she spotted them, she quickly got on the radio to see if she could invite herself along for the ride. "How about you? Eastbound front door?"

Within seconds, a voice came over the radio, "You got eastbound front door."

"Eastbound," Shelby replied. "I'm in a bit of a jam. Got to be in Arkansas for a pickup in eight hours. Mind if I catch a lift with you guys?"

A man's voice came back along with several others, "Be glad to have you along, little lady. Most of us are getting off at the Big D, but you can catch a ride as far as that if you like."

"Thank you, front door. Believe I'll slip right in here between these two pretty Petes, if that's alright?" Both drivers, knowing what was going on because they had been monitoring the conversation, made room for Shelby to slide into position between them. The front driver had not seen Shelby, but the driver that had backed down to let her into position had gotten a glimpse of her as she passed him. "You can slide in front of me any time. We got us a hot little lady driver with us, blonde and beautiful. What in the world are you doing driving a truck, little lady?"

Shelby was used to this question by now. "Oh, just figured I'd learn to drive a truck so I could come out here and drive all you handsome men crazy." Shelby knew that was going to start a firestorm of chatter.

The same driver that backed down for Shelby came back over the radio with a little laugh. "Well, the way you look darling there ain't no doubt you're doing a fine job of that."

Shelby tried to respond, but she wasn't able to get a word in through all the chatter between the drivers in the pack. "Choctaw, she's a looker, huh?"

"Yeah, she's a pretty little thing."

Poacher jumped into the conversation. "Damn, come on up here, little lady, and let me have a look."

King Fisher chimed in, "How good looking?"

Magnum from Kentucky who was back door gave his opinion. "She looked pretty good when she came by me. What's your handle, lady driver?"

Shelby knew she was clear to respond to all the chatter. "Well, I really don't have one yet. I've had lots of suggestions but haven't taken one on yet."

Red Rider, a little one-ton truck hauling cars, said, "How about Blonde Bomb or…."

Red Rider was cut short by King Fisher who was front door. "Bring it on up here, little lady, and let me have a look."

Shelby was blushing now from the attention and tried hard to get the men's focus back onto the task of getting to the big D, but it was impossible. The guys were having fun rolling down the highway, messing around with a lady driver.

"Come on, guys, I'm just a driver like you."

Breeze spoke up. "No way, baby, you got—"

Breeze was interrupted by Roaster. "How long you been on the road, little lady? 'Cause you don't look like a normal lady driver."

Bootlegger replied with a laugh. "You can bet she hasn't been out here long, or she would know better than to hook up with the likes of us."

◊◊◊

Shelby was having a great time running with these guys, and had no idea that her every word was being monitored by Betty, whose hatred toward Shelby was growing by the minute as she listened to their banter.

"Ted, are you listening to the crap those morons are feeding little Miss Blondie?"

Ted hadn't been listening because Betty had ordered him to go to their private channel. "No, I've been on our channel."

"Doesn't matter anyway, she's just being a whore," Betty said. "I think we are getting close to them, and we can ride the back door until the Big D. They're going to separate there, and then Shelby will have to roll north all alone. We'll hang back, and I'll make plans for our next move on Shelby."

All Ted said was, "Okay."

◊◊◊

Several hours later Gizmo, a westbound driver, interrupted the playful conversation that was still going on between the eastbound drivers. "Eastbound drivers, you got yourself a full grown about the 389 your side with a customer. Better back it down fast runners."

Shelby knew exactly what that meant in trucker language. There was a weights and measures DOT man with a vehicle on the eastbound side located around mile marker 389. King Fisher, being the front door, responded, "We appreciate that, westbound. Haven't seen anything since the I-10 and I-20 split. You have a safe ride, driver. Back it down drivers. We are almost to the Parker County line anyway, and you know what those boys are like in that county."

"Thank you for the information, eastbound," responded the westbound driver. "You all be careful now. We'll see you on the turnaround maybe."

Shelby knew that they were getting close to the Big D. She found it hard to believe that they had made such good time, and she had made up at least an hour and a half in time. "Well, thanks, you guys, for letting me roll with you. I'm going to get off at the 409 for coffee and restroom break before I head north. I truly appreciate you letting me tag along. It sure has been fun."

Choctaw and Poacher responded, "Anytime, little lady."

"Yeah, you be careful, and maybe we'll meet up out here again."

Shelby headed into the truck stop once they reached her exit.

◊◊◊

Betty was still monitoring Shelby's channel. She went back to her and Ted's channel. "Ted, we're getting off at the 409. I have an idea to make sure Shelby doesn't make her pick up time."

Ted had been listening to the stereo and didn't get all the information. "What?"

"GET OFF AT THE 409!"

Ted knew he had made her mad again. "Oh, okay."

Meanwhile, Shelby found a parking spot and went into the truck stop to get some coffee and use the restroom. She liked most of the truck stops that she had been in, but she always made sure she left most of her money in her truck. She was always so tempted to buy knickknacks for her collection.

She looked a lot, but knew she couldn't spend too much—at least not until Jack went back to work. She spent a little time looking around and stretching her legs before returning to her truck in the parking lot.

Shelby almost dropped her coffee cup when she noticed that the two rear passenger side tandems on her truck were flat. Running to the truck she briefly examined the tires. "Shit."

She could also hear an air leak. She put her cup down and crawled under her truck to inspect the area with the air leak. "Damn it, how could this have happened? Can anything else go wrong?" Shelby took hold of the broken airline, and then threw the hose line down in anger.

Shelby crawled out from under her truck, grabbed her coffee, and sipped at it while she sat on the ground, trying to figure out what she was going to do.

A couple of truckers walked up to her while she sat next to the destruction. "I'm Ramjet and this is Kat Doctor. Can we help?" Ramjet looked at one of the tires. "Looks like you have a problem here, little lady."

Ramjet offered a helping hand to Shelby as she got up off the ground. After dusting off her butt, she shook hands with the men. "Hi, nice to meet you. I'm Shelby." Shelby pointed out the tires and the hose hanging beneath her truck. "Yeah, I went in for coffee and came out to two flat tires and an air leak. Guess I was pushing it too hard, trying to make my load pickup time."

Kat Doctor examined the airline. "This line's been cut, sugar."

Ramjet looked at the tires. "Yeah, and these tires are flat because someone put a knife in them. This wasn't an accident, Shelby; this was intentional."

Shelby looked closer at the tires. She couldn't believe it. "Why would someone do this to me?"

Ramjet shook his head as he ran his hand over the slice in the tire. "Hard to tell, little lady; crazy people do crazy things for no reason these days." Ramjet pointed toward a mechanic shop about 500 yards away. "You can get these things fixed right over there at that shop, but it will take some time. We were on our way to dinner, why don't you join us after you get your truck over there to be fixed?"

"Thanks, guys, I'll need to see how long it's going to take to fix. I also need to call my boss and let her know what's happened. She's not going to be happy. If I have time, I'll come over to the restaurant and join you. Thanks again for helping me out."

"Sure, no problem," Ramjet said as he and Kat Doctor headed toward the café. Shelby walked toward the garage to talk to the mechanic about her truck. With trepidation, she pulled her cell phone out of her pocket and dialed Sandy's number.

Sandy answered on the second ring. "ESCC, this is Sandy. Can I help you?"

Shelby took a deep breath and explained to Sandy what had happened.

◊◊◊

Betty was beside herself. "See Ted? Little Shelby has to get her tires and airline fixed. Now, I wonder how that could have happened." She laughed with an evil glee, grabbing Ted around the neck and kissing him with a rough, almost painful kiss. "Now, take me to your truck and give me a quick fuck before we leave. I think she'll be here a while."

Betty grabbed Ted's hand and led him to the door of his truck. "Sandy is really going to be irritated with Miss Perfect now. I still have some things in mind for Shelby that will definitely get her fired if this doesn't work." She opened his cab and climbed in. "Did you see her face when she realized she wasn't going anywhere?" Betty laughed again, but Ted only muttered a "yeah" as Betty continued to recount the event. "I just don't understand why people keep helping her out though. Did you see those two guys almost fall over themselves? They probably thought they were going to get lucky with the blonde. I guess they left after they found out she wasn't the type to put out."

Still talking, Betty moved into the sleeper area of Ted's truck. Ted had learned never to say much when Betty was talking, because he usually said the wrong things. He hated upsetting her, especially when she was in the mood. "I'm good. You better know not to mess with Betty, right?" she warned as she stripped her clothes off and waited on the bed in the sleeper for Ted to do the same. "Hurry up and shut the curtain before everyone sees your bare ass. Give me some of that before I don't want it anymore." She forcibly pulled Ted on top of her, although he hadn't quite finished undressing or getting the curtain completely shut.

◊◊◊

Shelby was still talking to Sandy when the mechanic from the shop came back from inspecting Shelby's truck in the parking lot. "Hey, Sandy. The mechanic is here, I'll call you back in a few minutes." Shelby put the phone in her pocket and gave her full attention to the young man with greasy hands and coveralls that looked like they hadn't ever been washed.

"Well Miss, I sent Charley over there to change the tires, and it will take me about an hour to fix that line. They sure did a number on your truck. Who did you piss off?"

"Wish I knew. This has been a really bad day altogether."

"Well, Charley and I'll have you up and running in no time. Have a seat in the waiting room, and I'll let you know when we're finished."

Shelby walked to the sitting area while the mechanic wiped his hands off with a dirty rag and grabbed his tools. He took a roll of line off the wall and walked out of the shop toward Shelby's truck.

Shelby took her phone out of her pocket and called Sandy back. "Well, I should be rolling again in about an hour. I have no idea how this happened."

"Calm down, killer. It isn't your fault. Stuff happens in those truck stops like that all the time. I called the yard where you'll be loading and gave you Ted's load time and moved him up. He and Betty should be ahead of you now, so switching times shouldn't be a problem for him. I tried to call him but he isn't answering right now. He's with Betty, so I'm sure they're playing patty cake somewhere." Sandy laughed.

Shelby suddenly realized everyone at the yard obviously knew what was going on between Ted and Betty. *I can't believe all this time I've been trying not to acknowledge the Ted and Betty situation because I'm not the gossiping type. But it really doesn't matter—everyone knows.*

Sandy's voice interrupted Shelby's thoughts. "I'll keep trying to get a hold of him, but you can relax. Instead of your time, I have you set up for four hours later. You'll be taking that load you're picking up to a location in Arkansas sometime tomorrow after your break, instead of coming straight back here. Then I set you up for a couple more loads out of the east yard for the following two days, until I can get you a load back on Friday for West Texas. Be careful, and call me if anything else goes wrong, girl."

Shelby hung up the phone and felt a sense of relief, knowing that she wasn't going to have to kill herself now getting to Arkansas. She went to the coffee machine, got a cup of coffee, then waited for her truck to be finished.

"Hey, little lady. How's the truck?" Ramjet asked as he and Kat Doctor walked into the waiting room of the mechanic shop.

Shelby was glad to see her new friends. "Oh, everything is going to be fine. I should be out of here within the hour. I talked with my boss, and she has worked things out for me so I don't have to hurry."

Kat Doctor replied, "That's good, no use in trying to make a deadline you know you can't make. We just stopped in to make sure you were okay."

"Thanks guys, I really appreciate it."

Ramjet and Kat Doctor grabbed a cup of coffee and sat in the waiting room with Shelby, talking about trucks and truck driving until the mechanic came in and told her that her truck was ready. "She's all fixed, ma'am."

Shelby was ecstatic. "Alright, thank you, gentlemen. I sure appreciate you working so quickly on my truck." The mechanic rang up the charges and gave Shelby her receipt. Shelby and her two new friends walked out of the building. "Thanks so much for keeping me company, guys. I sure appreciate it."

They responded in unison, "You're welcome, sweet little lady."

Soon Shelby was pulling out of the parking lot and headed once again toward Arkansas.

◊◊◊

Betty was sitting in the passenger seat smoking a cigarette as she watched Shelby come out of the mechanic's shop with her two friends. Ted was dressing himself and checking on the beep coming from his cell phone.

"Look, Ted. I told you those guys were working the little blonde Barbie. They're both walking with her to her truck. Wonder if she's going to take both of them on, or one at a time." Betty let out her usual evil laugh.

Ted sat in the driver's seat, looking at his cell phone instead of watching at Shelby.

"Put the cell phone down, Ted! Watch little Barbie get friendly with those drivers."

Ted glanced up at the show, and then looked down at his phone again. "I missed a call from Sandy. I really need to call her back, Betty."

Betty rolled her eyes and continued to spy on Shelby. "Fine."

Ted punched the redial button. "Hey, Sandy. This is Ted. Sorry I missed your call. What's up?" He became upset. "What? I can't make that load time either! I stopped to get something to eat and a nap, thinking I had plenty of time to get there."

Betty motioned for knowledge about what was happening without speaking.

"Oh, I see. She did? Wow, that's terrible. No, I can't make that load time either. Betty? No, I'm not sure. She was ahead of me somewhere. Yeah, okay. Bye."

Ted closed his cell phone. "Well, what did the bitch want?" Betty asked impatiently.

"She wanted me to take Shelby's load time tonight. I told her I couldn't, and she wanted to know why. Well, you heard what I told her. Now she's looking for you to take that load time. We need to be more careful Betty, or we are going to get caught."

"That's bullshit, everyone having to change everything for poor little Shelby. Well I'm not changing my load time for that little bitch." Betty angrily pulled on her boots. "I'm not answering my phone, and I'm not changing my load time."

Betty jumped out of the truck and slammed the door. "I can't believe this. How is it that everyone has to change their whole life for that blonde bimbo? Not me; no fucking way, not me. She is going down, that little bitch!"

◊◊◊

Shelby was glad to be back on the road although she was beginning to get a little tired. She hadn't driven that many miles today, but with all the troubles she had, it seemed like she had been driving and working for hours. Fact was, she was close to houring out for the day, and she didn't even realize it until she checked the time. She didn't want to go over her hours, but she knew she needed to get as far as she could before shutting down for the night. Shelby figured she could drive another five hours and at least be close to her pickup point.

After a couple hours, Shelby was getting sleepy and decided she'd turn up her CB and see what was happening out there. She had gotten into the habit of tuning it down just to avoid the noise, but when she got bored or tired she would use it to stay awake. Sometimes there were good conversations that she would either get involved in or just listen to. However, there didn't seem to be anything on the radio tonight. She was ready to turn the radio down again when a voice came over the radio. "How about you, northbound sand hauler? You got your ears on?" Shelby knew they were talking directly to her. "You got northbound sand hauler."

The voice came back. "What did y'all leave behind in the Big D, little lady?"

"Didn't see a thing except for a black and white on the southbound side around Anna."

"We thank ya for that info, little lady. You're clear all the way to I-40. Were the scales closed at the line?"

"Yes, sir," answered Shelby. "The scales are closed."

"She sounds like she might be a pretty little thing, Bulldog."

"You could be right, Wilde Coyote. But being our usual luck, she's headed in the wrong direction."

"Ain't that about right? We find ourselves a sweet little lady driver and she's going in the wrong direction."

"Sorry guys, wish you were going in my direction too. I need someone to talk to so I can stay awake."

The two drivers tried hard to continue the conversation but before long, they were out of radio range and Shelby was once again listening to static.

To Shelby's surprise another voice came over the radio. "Lady driver, you still looking for someone to talk to?" Shelby keyed up the mic and hoped that the driver wasn't going to be some kind of weirdo. "Yeah, I sure could use some conversation to keep me awake. Where you headed driver?" The driver came back over the radio with a nice friendly voice. "I'm headed over to my little home in central Oklahoma. How about you?"

Shelby believed this guy was okay, but she was always cautious about giving out too much information when she was rolling by herself. "I'm heading over into Arkansas to one of our yards. I'm hoping to make it there before my log time runs out."

"I hear that. Seems like DOT dictates everything to us these days. By the way, they call me Triple L. What's your handle?"

"I don't have one yet. I haven't really figured out a good one."

"Well, that's just not right. You sound really sweet over the radio. Maybe we should call you Sweetheart."

Shelby giggled. "Sweetheart. I'm not sure that would really be a good handle out here. Some guys might get the wrong idea. You know what I mean?"

Triple L laughed. "Yeah, you could be right there, little lady. Well I'm sure you'll come up with just the right one in time."

Another voice joined in on the CB. "I got a good one. How about Blondie?"

Shelby was shocked. "How did you know I was blonde?"

The driver laughed. "I just passed you a little while ago, lady driver."

"I have to ask, because you're not the first one that has been able to see what I look like without me seeing them. Is there a trick to seeing into trucks when they pass you on the road? I haven't been able to see too many drivers like that unless I'm right up next to them, usually at a light or something."

"Well, lady driver, I'm not sure about that. I've been out here a while and I see pretty much what I like and I sure like looking at you."

"Thanks for the compliment, driver." Shelby decided this one was a little too aggressive for her taste.

"They call me Odd Ball. Guess I live up to my handle, right? Didn't mean to come on too strong there, beautiful. I just don't see too many lookers like you out here."

Triple L interrupted this time. "Maybe you shouldn't have stuck your nose into our conversation, driver."

"Maybe you shouldn't be telling me what to do there, driver. This is an open channel, and I'll say whatever I like."

Before things could get any more hostile, Shelby decided that she should put an end to the conversation. "Hey, guys. I have to go, I have a phone call. I'll catch ya later." She quickly reached up and turned her radio down, deciding no conversation was best. Besides, she needed to get to where she was going.

It took Shelby a couple more hours to reach the town where their northern yard was located. Once she arrived on the outskirts, she had no idea where the yard was located. She reached for the radio mic. "I was wondering if someone out there could give me some information please."

A driver came over the radio, "What information were you needing, driver?"

Shelby was glad she was able to get some help and quickly asked where the yard might be located.

"I believe it's just off I-40, exit 306 or 308 but I'm not sure exactly. That yard is probably locked up for the night. You might want to find a place to shut her down for the night. There's a truck stop at the 311 that is real nice, and they have plenty of parking. The ladies that run that stop are real nice."

Shelby was tired and liked the idea of shutting down for the night, especially in a place that seemed convenient.

CHAPTER TEN

Shelby found the truck stop with ease, and parking was plentiful. She entered the building to quickly take care of personal needs, then found her way back to her truck for some well-needed rest.

Jack had made it a habit to call Shelby every morning when he woke up whenever she wasn't home in their bed. "Good morning, beautiful. Are you awake and ready to go?"

"No, silly. I'm still sleeping. Can't you tell?"

Jack laughed. "Yeah, baby. I know, but you told me last night to call you when I got up. What time do you need to pick up your load?"

Shelby jerked awake and looked at her watch. "Oh shit, I'm supposed to be there in thirty minutes."

"Calm down, didn't you tell me last night during our phone call that you were just a couple of exits away?"

Shelby held the cell phone up to her ear with her chin while pulling on her pants. "I know, but what if I get lost? I'll be late again, and Sandy will kill me if I miss this pickup. I'll call you back once I'm loaded. Love ya." Shelby hung the phone up and threw it on the passenger's seat without hearing Jack's goodbye. She quickly got out to check the outside parameters of her truck and then went into the shop for coffee.

When she left the store, she couldn't believe how many company trucks were in the parking lot. *That driver last night was right—this is a hangout for ESCC trucks.*

She reached the cab of her truck and was about to get in when Ted approached. "I see you made it, Shelby. Sandy told me you had some trouble last night. Are you headed to the yard?"

Shelby was a little taken aback that Ted was talking to her, and Betty wasn't anywhere to be found. "Yeah, and I need to hurry."

"Do you know where the yard is?" Ted asked.

"Yes, a driver last night gave me some idea as to where it is."

Ted, on orders from Betty, spouted out some other directions trying to get Shelby lost. "But that driver last night said it was just a couple exits away."

Ted retracted quickly once he knew Shelby had the right directions, deciding that if he insisted on the wrong directions Shelby might get wise to Betty's little scheme. "Oh yeah, that's right. I'm sorry. I always get confused too. They moved the yard to that new location. Sorry. Yeah just follow I-40 to exit 308 it's just right off the exit there."

"Thanks, Ted. I think," Shelby said, waving goodbye from beside her truck.

That was a close call, Ted thought. Telling Betty her little trick hadn't worked made him even more nervous. He went to Betty's truck, wishing he could just skip the confrontation.

"So, did you send her to the old yard?" Betty asked, a cruel smile twisting her face.

"No, she already had gotten the directions to the right yard from another driver last night. I figured if I sent her to the old yard she would figure out what we were trying to do to her."

"Damn it, Ted!" Betty fumed. "You should have done it anyway. The whole idea is to get her fired. If she's late picking up another load, I'm sure Sandy would have lost it with her."

Ted shook his head. "Maybe, but she would have known it was me that sent her to the wrong yard on purpose, and I might have gotten in trouble."

"So? The little bitch would have been gone and that's all that matters to me," Betty pushed at Ted to get off her truck. "Never mind. Get off. I have some other ideas in mind to make little Miss Barbie's life complete hell."

Ted jumped off the steps of the truck and backed away from Betty's truck, avoiding the trailer running him down by just inches. Betty sped out of the truck stop like hell on wheels. Ted watched as she left and began to wonder why he did whatever that woman told him, but then he remembered. The only thing he had ever really liked about her was what she did for him in the sack.

◊◊◊

Shelby reached the east ESCC yard, but was a little worried when she didn't see any silos or rail cars. *How am I going to get a load out of this yard?* There wasn't even a warehouse full of sand bags. She parked her truck among the several other trucks parked on the lot and went into what looked like the main office. Inside, a man seated at a desk behind a glass window greeted Shelby. "Can I help you?"

Shelby told him who she was and why she was there.

"Oh yeah, we've been waiting for you," he said. "You need to go over to our load yard with this paperwork and get your load. You'll be going into northern Arkansas."

"But I was told to come to this yard in Arkansas."

The man at the desk smirked. "You were told to come to this yard in Oklahoma; you'll be loading in Arkansas. It's only about 30 miles further down the road on Highway 64."

Shelby was a little miffed that no one had bothered mentioning to her the difference in yards. She felt a little foolish not realizing that she was still in Oklahoma. She had been tired getting into town, and she didn't remember ever crossing a state line. Knowing that, however, didn't make her feel any less stupid. "Oh, I'm sorry."

"Don't worry about it, darling. Are you lost? You look like you're lost. They call me Woodchuck around here. What's your name?"

"I'm Shelby Mathews, from the west yard."

"Nice to meet you, Shelby Mathews. So what's the problem, are you lost?"

"No, not lost, I guess just frustrated." She began to explain what had happened and the frustration she was feeling from all the mishaps she had experienced in last few hours.

"Don't worry, darling, I'm headed to that yard myself as soon as I get my paperwork, so why don't you just fall in behind me and I'll take you there with me?"

"Oh, Woodchuck. That would be wonderful, thank you so much. You're a lifesaver."

"Wouldn't call myself a lifesaver, not sure I'm that sweet. Get in your truck and meet me around front. We'll be meeting up with several other drivers going out on jobs at the sand yard."

Shelby nearly ran to her truck. She was so glad she had someone to run with in this area of the country. "No problem, Woodchuck. I'll be right behind you."

Woodchuck and Shelby rolled together to the loading yard in Arkansas. The yard was full of ESCC trucks and several other trucking companies. "Hey, Woodchuck. Who's the pretty little thing in that truck behind ya?"

Woodchuck gracefully responded, "Better be minding your manners there, driver."

The driver persisted. "Oh, come on, Woodchuck. Who's the babe?"

Woodchuck didn't respond this time. He had pulled up onto the scale and gotten out of his truck.

"Guess Woodchuck is serious about keeping that little darling to himself."

Shelby heard the entire conversation but decided not to encourage the curious man. Although, it would have been tempting to tease him a bit. She pulled in behind Woodchuck, got out of her truck, and went into the scale house with several other drivers from ESCC who she soon got to know. Shelby was not aware that Betty and Ted had also been waiting to load at the same yard.

Betty had been in her truck listening to the radio while Ted was standing on the driver's steps talking to her.

"Did you hear all those sons-a-bitches trying to flirt with the new rookie?" Betty asked. "I just don't get it, Ted. What is it about that bitch that everyone likes? I'm way better looking than her, don't you think? I know I'm a much better driver."

Suddenly, Betty opened her driver door, almost knocking Ted to the ground. "Move. Keep a watch out for me. I'll be back in a minute." Betty disappeared for a few minutes and then came back with a big smile on her face. "That should fix the little bitch, or at least make things difficult if nothing else."

Ted wanted to know what she did, but decided maybe he really didn't want to know.

◊◊◊

Once Shelby and the other drivers were loaded, they headed to the location in northeastern Arkansas. The driver who had been so inquisitive, once again asked about her. "Come on, Woodchuck, who's the lady driver you guys got working for you now?"

"She's ours. Eat your heart out, HjH."

HjH responded, "Man, you guys are heartless, and your mama obviously never taught you to share."

"Share? Who said I was available to be shared?" Shelby asked.

"The lady has a voice, and she's spunky, too. I like spunky."

Shelby started to smart mouth this driver when Woodchuck's voice came across the CB, interrupting the fraternization. "Shelby, I don't want to scare you or interrupt, but have you ever driven in the Arkansas Mountains before?"

"No, Woodchuck, I haven't."

"Okay, this is what I want you to do, Shelby. Move in between Equalizer and Fat Man, and I want you to maintain the speeds that they maintain. You need to keep your truck a good truck length from the rear of Equalizer. Run with your jakes on, and stay off the brakes. Save them for when you really need them. The best way to slow down is tapping and let the jakes slow you down mostly. Do you know how to climb mountains with a full load?"

"Does Highway 10 count?"

Woodchuck chuckled. "Well, it's better than never having climbed anything. Just make sure you remember to down shift soon enough and up shift quickly going down so you can catch some speed for the next climb. Try and stay with those two drivers I'm putting you between. They will keep you straight."

"Okay, Woodchuck, I think I got it."

HjH came on the radio again. "How about you come back here with me, Shelby baby. I'll make sure you make it to location just fine. We might need to cool down the brakes for a while, but we'll get to location. I promise."

"Oh, that's okay, little yellow truck driver. I think I'll stay up here with the big strong red trucks."

Fat Man came across this time. "Ouch, that hurt, I bet."

Equalizer reiterated the feeling. "He said he liked them spunky."

HjH came back. "Man, and I thought we had feelings for each other, Blondie."

Shelby responded, "It's the yellow, I think."

Woodchuck wasn't kidding when he told Shelby about the mountains they would be climbing. He did, however, fail to mention the small treacherous roads with low-hanging tree lines that they would be traveling on once they got on the lease. The rain that they had received recently also made the roads even more difficult to travel. But Shelby did exactly what Woodchuck had suggested, and before long, the trucks were on location, being put into position for unloading.

Woodchuck met Shelby outside her truck after she had been backed into position. "You did good, rookie."

"Thanks, Woodchuck. I'm glad I ran into you this morning. It sure made this job a lot easier."

Woodchuck and several other drivers helped Shelby after everyone else was hooked up. Then they began to unload.

Suddenly, Shelby realized something was terribly wrong. Her truck wouldn't pressure up in the line, and she could hear air leaking from somewhere near the rear of her truck. She went ahead and opened up one of her pods to see if the pressure would increase. When the pressure didn't change, she walked toward the rear of the truck to see if she could find the leak. Immediately, she was stopped by Bee Be and Dave who came running around the front of her truck. "SHUT IT DOWN NOW, SHELBY! SHUT IT DOWN!"

Shelby quickly closed her sand pod and ran to the front of her truck. She swung the truck door open and quickly disengaged the PTO to stop the pressure. Dave ran to the tank pressure valve and released what was left. Woodchuck came around from the rear of the truck just as the Shelby and the other two drivers reached it. Woodchuck had already taken Shelby's hose off the chief and was inspecting the damage. "Looks like someone cut your hose, Shelby. Who did you piss off?"

Shelby couldn't believe it as she inspected the hose for herself. There at the connection point was a three to four inch cut that had torn even wider with the pressure Shelby was using to blow off her sand. "Man! I don't understand what is happening. First my air lines and tires, now my hose. This really could have hurt someone if you guys hadn't caught it in time. I just can't believe it. Who is doing this to me? I don't think anyone is mad at me."

Woodchuck had one of the other drivers get a hose so Shelby could get unloaded. "Don't worry about it now, little lady. Let's get you unloaded and we'll figure it out later. You can get a new hose at the Oklahoma yard when you get back. I suggest you inspect everything until you find out who has it in for you."

Shelby agreed. She rolled the cut hose up and placed it in her hose compartment. She was still upset over the incident when she finished unloading and followed the other drivers back to Red's. She didn't say anything during the entire trip back because she didn't want to cry in front of her coworkers.

Once they got to the exit of Red's Truck Stop, Shelby let the other drivers know she was getting off. "Well, guys, I'm getting off here. I'll be in the office in the morning to pick up paperwork for another load. I guess I'm going back to about the same place we went today."

Woodchuck keyed up. "Okay, Shelby. Get some rest and don't worry about the hose. It could have happened to any of us. And don't forget to pick up another hose when you come in to the office tomorrow. In fact, I'll let the shop guys know you need one when I go in there tonight so it will be ready for you."

"Thanks, Woodchuck. I sure appreciate the help." Shelby felt the tears coming as she tried hard to hold them back. "I'm sorry about the hose, guys. I could have really hurt someone today." It was too late, as Shelby turned off the highway towards Red's, she couldn't hold the tears back any longer. She cried. Apparently the other drivers knew from her voice what was about to happen because none of them responded and had the common decency to just let her be. Shelby parked her truck and went straight to her sleeper. She cried until she fell asleep.

◊◊◊

The sound of her cell phone woke her up.

"Hey, hadn't heard from you in a while, so I thought I'd see how my sweetheart's day went," she heard Jack's voice say.

Shelby had cried herself dry and after a couple hours of sound sleep, this situation did not seem so bleak. She tried to explain the event to Jack. "It wasn't just the hose being cut that made things so awful. It was the fact that someone could have really gotten hurt, and it would have been my fault."

"How would it have been your fault? You didn't cut that hose, did you?"

"No, I didn't cut the hose, but I didn't check it either. I didn't inspect my hoses like I was trained."

"That's ridiculous, you need to figure out who might have done this and stop blaming yourself. Did you see anything suspicious at that truck stop where the tires and air line were cut? I think they must have cut your hose there too, but you just didn't see it because you hadn't needed your hose until this job."

"That is probably when it happened. I just can't figure out who would want to damage my things like this. Maybe it was just some crazy, random vandal, but it sure has made me look like an idiot. I don't want to talk about it any longer, please. I'm getting a new hose in the morning, and I just want to forget the last two days."

"I wish I could say I'm glad you have something you like to do, but I really don't like you out there, Shelby. I'm trying to be supportive, but it's getting more difficult with all the shit going wrong." He sighed and asked, "Where you headed tomorrow?"

"Close to the same place as today, I think. Then we're picking up loads and heading back home." Shelby wanted to get Jack back on her side again. "I love you and I miss you. I'll be home soon."

"I hope so," Jack grumbled. "It's about time. I love and miss you, too."

◊◊◊

Shelby arrived early at the Oklahoma yard the next morning so she could get her hose and assignment before the other drivers arrived. She liked rolling with the other drivers, but after yesterday, she really just wanted to roll by herself. She had timed her arrival at the yard perfectly according to the dispatcher.

None of the other drivers had come in yet and probably wouldn't for at least another hour or so. Shelby went to the Arkansas yard and was loaded quickly, because there wasn't anyone else waiting to load.

She was well on her way to the location, enjoying the quietness of the morning drive, when her thoughts were interrupted by a familiar voice over the radio. She reached to turn up the volume and listened closer to the voice. Shelby tried to remember who owned the voice. Finally it came to her. "What are you doing out this way, GTO?"

"Who the hell is this?" GTO asked.

"Well who do you think it is?"

"I have no idea. Give me a hint?"

"Blonde, rookie, bobtail, South Texas, do you need any more hints?"

"Oh my, Blondie. Well, I see you have managed to make it out here in the trucking world for a few months. How are you?"

"I'm doing pretty well out here in the trucker world. How've you been?"

"I've been living good and taking it hard."

Shelby spoke with GTO for several more minutes. He was headed in the opposite direction so their communication was cut short. "Well, GTO, it looks like I'm losing you. Take care and we'll see ya out here again I'm sure."

GTO faded away. "You too, little blondie."

It started raining, so Shelby kept her concentration on the road. She looked through the movement of the wipers and wet windshield, trying to locate the county road just off the main highway. The county road would lead her to a dirt road, that road would lead her to the oil lease road. The oil lease road would then lead her to the well site. Shelby was a well-educated woman and directions or map reading were never a real task for her, but when it came to lease roads, there was always some glitch in the directions. *I do not like looking for roads I don't know in areas I haven't been, and definitely not in the rain. This is going to be a long morning.*

"Break one nine for some local information," Shelby said into her mic, hoping for a response. But nearly a minute passed without one. She was about ready to repeat her request when a hyperactive voice came over the radio. "What ya need there, little lady?"

"Well, I was wondering if you could tell me where County Road 33 might be off this highway," Shelby said.

"You still got a ways to go. We're headed in that direction if you want to fall in behind Shaggy and me. We'll get ya there. Won't we, Shag?"

"That we will, Dog Nuts. Anything for the ladies."

"Let the good times roll, my friend," said Dog Nuts, laughing.

Shelby didn't know what to think about her new road friends. They seemed harmless enough, and she really needed to find that county road in the rain. "Great, thanks."

"Perfect, little lady, just follow us. Let the good times roll."

Shelby didn't talk with the drivers over the radio much. She was having too much fun listening to their ramblings. These two drivers were a couple of strange fellows, but Shelby liked their silliness. The rain was finally beginning to slow when Dog Nuts informed Shelby that the next turn would be hers. "Right up here is County Road 33. You take care now, little lady."

"Thanks guys," Shelby said. "I really appreciate it. Be careful in this weather."

"No problem," answered Shaggy.

Shelby took the turn and headed toward the location. This first county road wasn't bad, except for being less than wide enough for a big rig and trees that hung down to the pipes. Shelby maneuvered her way down the winding path of the road until she reached the next turn. "Oh no." Shelby couldn't believe the road she was about to take. It was narrow and lined with low hanging trees. There was no blacktop, only mud. "Great! I've always wanted to go mudding in an eighteen wheeler."

She turned her truck down the road. "Oh well, this week has been a bitch anyway. Might as well keep the momentum going." It wasn't long before she was rolling slow and smooth down the mud-packed road. It wasn't as bad as she had first predicted, but she wanted to keep the speed down just in case her trailer decided it would have a better view from the front of the truck instead of the back. Catching a couple of tries from the trailer, she was soon making her final turn onto the location road.

Shelby moved the truck in close to the location, placed it in park, and put on her hard hat, safety glasses, and gloves as she dismounted her truck.

She had time before the others arrived to look over the location and plan how they would need to unload. The location was extremely muddy, causing her steel-toed boots to become caked with the slick, dark, wet stuff. She slipped and slid in the mud while confirming what was on location. There were two sand chiefs, several pieces of wire line equipment, and lots of water tanks—the usual items found on most locations. The space in front and behind the chiefs appeared to be plentiful enough for several trucks to unload at once, but she would wait for the others before unloading.

Before getting back to her truck, she was joined by a couple of the east yard hands, Stray Cat and Diehard, who slipped their way toward her. "Hey, Shelby. Glad you made it out here okay. Boy, it sure is muddy."

Shelby shook hands with her coworkers. "Yeah, I looked over things a bit and besides sliding around in this muck, we should be able to get several of us in here at the same time."

The drivers spent a few more moments discussing how to position the trucks before getting into their trucks and moving them onto the location.

Shelby was the first on the location, so she was the first to finish and head back toward the truck stop in Oklahoma. Muddy, wet, and tired, Shelby reached for her phone and called Sandy to confirm her new load time. "Hey, this is Shelby and I'm finished with what the yard up here had for me. I just called to confirm that the new load time you gave me for the West Texas load is still a go."

"Yeah, everything is a go," Sandy confirmed. "Pick up at two o'clock and haul ass home."

Shelby liked the sound of that. She missed Jack. "Great. I'm going to the truck stop for fuel, a shower, and lunch. I'll go to the sand yard from there."

"Sounds good, girl. Be careful," Sandy responded. "Call me when you're loaded so I know you're on your way."

"You got it."

CHAPTER ELEVEN

Betty slipped as she threw the muddy hose toward Ted. "Damn it, Ted. Do you think you could pull this hose to the front of my truck before I fall completely down into this shit?"

Ted was busy with his own truck, but quickly dropped everything to comply with his lover's request. "Sure, Betty."

Betty dragged her steel-toed boots through the thick mud, slipped again, and this time landed flat on her butt. "Shit. Ted, help me out of this shit hole, now!"

Ted dropped the hose he had been ordered to move and went to help Betty up. He tried lifting her up by the hands but they both ended up in the mud.

"Damn it, can't you do anything right?"

Betty grabbed hold of the truck and pulled herself up out of the mud, leaving her hose on the ground for Ted to pick up and put away. "This is just great. I'm covered in mud from one end to the other. There should be something in the policy book against having to work in mud. I want to get to the truck stop and take a shower."

Betty grabbed a towel and wiped herself off while watching Ted complete her work. Ted had to slip and slide toward his truck to finish putting away his own equipment. "Yeah, I just need to put my stuff away then we can go," he told her, fumbling with her hose.

Betty wiped at her butt with the towel and then climbed into the cab. "Hurry up. I'm nasty and need a bath." Ted moved as quickly as he could, not even taking time to clean up so that Betty wouldn't be upset with him.

Betty came over the radio. "Finally! I thought we would never get out of that mess. The rest of those bastards better have had as much trouble as we did. We should have been given a better location. Being senior drivers we should always get the best jobs."

Ted confirmed what Betty was saying, although he didn't understand how dispatch was supposed to determine which locations would be better, especially with weather conditions.

"I bet little Ms. Barbie didn't have to play in the mud."

◊◊◊

After filling up with fuel, Shelby moved her truck into a parking space and gathered her things for a shower. It was still sprinkling and the parking lot was full of little puddles of water as she walked toward the truck stop. Inside the building, Shelby went to the desk for the key to a shower.

"How are you today? Need a shower?" the sweet girl behind the counter asked.

"Yes, please."

The girl had long brown hair and the biggest smile Shelby had ever seen. "Number four," she said, pointing toward the row of showers.

"Thanks." Shelby took the key and went to the shower area.

◊◊◊

Out in the parking lot, Betty seemed to roll her truck through every puddle of water, almost as though on purpose. "Damn you! You'd think these people could fill in the pot holes around here." She found a parking space and parked her truck. Ted followed Betty through the lot, putting his truck behind hers in the parking space. "I'll see you after I get my shower. We'll get something to eat in the café." Betty didn't wait for Ted to respond, she just got out of her truck and headed into the truck stop.

◊◊◊

Shelby had finished her shower and had just shut the door to the shower room when she almost ran into Betty in the hall. "Oh sorry, Betty."

"You should probably be more careful." Betty said, cutting directly in front of Shelby and slipping into the shower room that she had been assigned.

Shelby stood there for a moment and shook her head in disbelief. "Unbelievable," she muttered.

The salad bar at the café was small, but had a few things that Shelby enjoyed. Soup and a sandwich was just the comfort food she needed after spending the morning in the rain. As she was getting up to leave, several drivers from the east yard—Woodchuck, Equalizer, Beep Beep, Fat Man, Red Rider and several others—came into the café. "Hey, Shelby. Where you going? Aren't you buying lunch?"

Shelby shook hands with most of them as they found a large table. "Well, I'd love to buy lunch for all of you, but I work for ESCC. So you know that isn't happening."

The other drivers laughed as the waitress brought them menus. "Yeah, you got that right, Shelby," Woodchuck said as he looked over the menu. "So where you headed?"

Shelby spent a few minutes talking with the drivers.

"Look at that, Ted," muttered Betty, as she watched Shelby talking with the drivers. "Little Miss Perfect is flirting with her coworkers. I wonder what her husband would think of her behavior. When the cat's away, the kitty will play. Just like at the truck stop, messing with those two guys who helped her out."

As usual, Ted didn't see anything wrong with what Shelby was doing. To him she was enjoying a good laugh with some coworkers, but he wasn't about to tell Betty what he was thinking. "Yeah, bet he wouldn't like it much."

"We need to finish and get going. I want to watch little Miss Perfect get the wrong load. That for sure will get her fired."

"How's she going to get the wrong load?"

Betty rolled her eyes as she took another bite of her sandwich. With her mouth half full, she spit out some words Ted barely understood. "The paperwork remember?"

"What?"

Betty swallowed her mouthful of food. "The paperwork, you idiot. I changed the paperwork. Remember, before we left our yard?"

Ted thought for a few moments and then shook his head. "Oh yeah, the paperwork."

Betty stuffed her face again and washed the food down with soda. She got up from the table and wiped her mouth off with the back of her hand. "Get this, Ted. I need to use the restroom and then hurry up so we can get to the yard to watch the action."

Ted tried to stuff and drink what he could into his mouth. He nodded his head to let Betty know he understood her demands. "Got it," he said with food still in his mouth.

"Don't talk with food in your mouth; it's nasty."

Ted just nodded his head as Betty walked away.

Shelby had finished her conversation and was headed out of the truck stop when Betty and Ted were leaving the café. Shelby saw them and waved as she passed by them. Betty, of course, ignored the gesture of friendliness, but Ted instinctively waved back.

"What are you doing?" Betty knocked his hand down. "Don't even pretend to be friendly with that back stabber. You know she could use the things she knows about us any time she wants?"

◊◊◊

Shelby went into the office at the sand yard and let the man in the office know she was there to pick up a load. She handed him the paperwork that she had retrieved from her box a few days earlier. The young man handed Shelby a piece of paper for her to sign. Shelby signed it and handed it back. "Okay, if you'll put your truck on the first scale we'll get you loaded."

"Thank you," Shelby said as she adjusted her hard hat and turned to leave.

"I haven't seen you around here before. You must be a new driver for ESCC."

"Yeah, I just started with them a little while ago."

The young man smiled. "Glad to see ESCC has decided to employ some good looking women."

"Thanks. First scale, right?"

"Right, I'll bring your paperwork out when you're loaded."

"Okay." Shelby left the building to go and retrieve her truck.

It took a little while to load Shelby, so as she sat on the scale she called Jack. "Hey, baby. How are you?"

"I'm good, missing you. Wish you were here instead of on that truck."

"I should be home tomorrow. I'm on the scale right now, and besides having to stop for my break, I'm going to haul ass to get home."

"Good. I really am not enjoying all this time away from you. I thought this trucking stuff was going to be local?"

Shelby tried to change the subject. "It's been raining up here. What is it doing at home?"

"Nothing really, just sunshine."

"Did you clean the pool and chemical the hot tub?"

"Yes ,baby, I've been doing a good job of keeping things up around here. Nothing seems to be falling apart, but you should be here enjoying the pool and hot tub with me. Not halfway across the country in a truck."

"I'll be home soon. We'll take a long swim together. That sounds so wonderful right now. I haven't had many things going right these last few days." After she made that last comment, Shelby knew she probably shouldn't have said it.

"Sounds to me like there are plenty of guys out there helping you out."

"Come on, Jack, that's not fair, I didn't ask for the help. They offered."

"I'm sure..."

The conversation was suddenly interrupted by someone else phoning Shelby. "Hey, I have to take this call; it's the office. I'll call you back in a few minutes."

"I'll bet."

"Hey, Sandy. What's up?"

"I was wondering how things were going?"

"Well, I'm on the scale. Wait, hold on a minute, the load guy is coming to my truck with my paperwork." Shelby put the phone on the dash of the truck and rolled down her window as the young man from the sand office climbed on the truck.

"Here you go, Shelby. 50,000 pounds of CLS 30/30." Shelby took the paperwork. "Just pull forward a little, I'll close your hatch."

"Okay, thanks."

Shelby put the paperwork on her passenger seat, grabbed her phone and put it to her ear as she put her truck in gear to move forward. "Hold on Sandy, just need to move forward a little…"

Sandy interrupted Shelby, "What kind of sand did that guy say he put on your truck?" Shelby quickly grabbed her paperwork, applying the brakes to the truck. The young man climbed on her truck to close her hatch while she read what was on the paperwork to Sandy. "I've got 50,000 pounds of CLS 30/30."

"Oh, damn Shelby, they put the wrong stuff on you. Did you give them the paperwork I gave to you?"

"Yes, I gave him the paperwork you put in my box," said Shelby, her heart beginning to race. Had she somehow messed up again?

"Tell me what the well location is on the paperwork you gave the loader," Sandy instructed.

Shelby read off the well location and could tell from Sandy's response that it was definitely a mess up.

"Shit, I'm not sure what is going on but you have the wrong paperwork again. You're loaded with stuff that needs to go to South Texas for later on in the week. Give me a few minutes and I'm going to makes some calls. Go ahead and take the load for now, I'll figure something out. If I can't get the load diverted, you may have to be unloaded and reloaded."

"God, Sandy. Not again! I'm so sorry."

"Don't worry about it. Just hang tight until I can figure out something."

The loader motioned for Shelby to move off the scale. She motioned for him to come to her cab. "Is there somewhere I can park for a few minutes? There seems to be something wrong with the load. My dispatcher is trying to figure out what to do."

"Sure. Just pull over there by the last scale. If you need something to drink or eat we have a break room in the office area."

"Oh, thanks. I just finished lunch. If we need to take this sand off, I'll let you know."

"Take the sand off? You'll be here for a while if that happens. You'll do that at the upper plant. I'm sure I'll know before you do anyway, especially if I screwed it up."

"No, I'm sure it wasn't on your part. I think it was a paperwork issue."

"Okay. Well, if you need anything, let me know." The young man dismounted the truck and went back to loading the other trucks that had been waiting.

◊◊◊

Betty and Ted had arrived at the yard shortly after Shelby, but had not checked in at the office. There were several trucks in line before them, and Betty had decided she wanted to wait and watch for a little while. Betty called Ted on his phone. "We'll check in at the office in a few minutes. I want to watch Shelby drive out of here with that load."

"Okay, the loader is closing her hatch now."

"Good, we're almost rid of that little snitch."

"Wait, Betty. She's leaving the scale, but she's stopped to talk with the loader. Now, she's moving over by the third scale. She isn't leaving Betty."

"I can see that, moron. Come on, let's check in and see what's going on."

Betty and Ted got out of their trucks and went into the yard office. "Hey, James. We're here to load. How ya doing?"

"Doing alright. How are you, Betty? Ted?"

"We're good, here's our paperwork." Betty grabbed Ted's out of his hand, handing both orders to the loader. Betty wasn't the least bit interested in how the loader was doing. She just wanted to know what was up with Shelby. Betty leaned over the counter, exposing what she felt were nice look- ing boobs. "So what's up with the truck that just got off the scale? Why are they blocking the drive?"

James wasn't stupid and had dealt with Betty a lot. By giving her the wanted gossip he hoped he would get her out of his office faster. "Well, not really sure. Seems like maybe she got some wrong paperwork. She's loaded with some stuff that was meant for South Texas. Her dispatcher is working on what they'll do with it. She sure is a nice lady."

"What? They know it's not the right load? How do they know that?"

James was surprised at the intensity in Betty's voice. *Why would she even care about someone else's load?* "Yeah, they know it's the wrong load, but no, I don't know how they found out. Why are you so bent out of shape about it? Did you have something to do with it?"

Betty turned with a jerk and pulled at Ted's arm, moving quickly toward the office door. "Damn it, Ted, how does this bitch manage to get out of everything? I can't believe they found out she was getting the wrong load. This is just fucking great. Well, I don't care. I have more ideas. I'll get her, I promise you. I will get her."

Ted didn't say a word as he and Betty left the office.

◊◊◊

Shelby paced back and forth talking with Jack on her cell phone as she waited for the situation to sort itself out. "I don't know how this is happening, Jack; it just seems like every time I turn around, something is going wrong. I'm just glad I found out I had the wrong load before I got all the way back to West Texas."

"So, what are they going to do?"

"I really don't know. I'm waiting for Sandy to call me back. I hope I don't get fired over this."

"Why would you get fired? You didn't do anything wrong. It's Sandy's responsibility to make sure you have the right paperwork, and she obviously didn't. I knew this trucking thing wasn't going to work."

"No, Jack, I don't think it's Sandy's fault, and it has nothing to do with the trucking. Somehow I'm not getting the right paperwork; Sandy is as shocked about the mess ups as I am." Shelby's phone beeped. "Got to go, it's Sandy. I'll call you back.... Hello?"

"Hey, Shelby. I think I have it figured out. You're going to leave that sand load on and go to South Texas. That sand wasn't supposed to go there until next week, but they're going to have you bring it down now. You'll blow off into a truck of one of the drivers who is on vacation. Then you'll run a couple loads for Casper before picking up a load out of George West and coming back here to West Texas. You won't be home for about a week, but you'll at least be running loaded and making money."

"Sounds good. I'm headed to the south yard. Casper knows what's going on, right?"

"Yes."

"Okay, I'm almost out of hours for today. I probably won't make it until sometime tomorrow. Casper doesn't have a problem with that, right?"

"That will be fine. Just check in with him when you get there."

"Guess I'll see you in a few days. Is anyone else going down there? Were there any other paperwork mix-ups?"

"I have a few drivers heading down there but not for a couple days. Your paperwork was the only mistake."

"Alright, I better get out of here if I'm going to make any miles tonight."

"Be careful."

"You got it." Shelby hung up and called Jack. "Hey, baby."

"What are they going to do about the sand?"

"I'm going to the south yard with this load. Then I'm going to run a couple loads for Casper before bringing a load home from George West. Sorry baby, but I'm not going to be home for at least a week."

Jack was quiet for a long time.

"Hello?" Shelby said, wondering if the call had dropped.

Finally, Jack spoke, "You're gone more than you're home anymore. I don't like this Shelby."

"I'm sorry. I know it was supposed to be local not long haul stuff, but I'm making money and that was the whole idea, right?"

"Yeah, I guess so, but I miss you. I don't like you out there on those roads all alone."

"I miss you too. I'll be home soon, I promise."

Shelby left the yard and headed to the interstate. Her thoughts were not on her driving as she moved up the ramp onto the interstate to merge into traffic. She did not realize that the truck in her lane was having trouble moving over because of a four wheeler next to his truck. "Hey, ESCC. You might want to back down, I can't make room for you with this four wheeler on my side."

Shelby quickly backed her truck down. "Sorry, driver. It's been one of those days."

"It's alright, just didn't want to have to do a bunch of paperwork."

"Yeah, I know. My mind wasn't where it should have been. I'm sorry."

"No problem. Catch you later, little lady."

She turned off on Highway 69 and headed south. It was quiet as darkness emerged. Shelby loved driving, but with all the mix-ups, and Jack unhappy with her absence, she wondered how long she'd be able to continue driving. A flatbed truck raced past her as she mused. Once the truck was clear of her front bumper, Shelby let the driver know over the CB. "You're clear, driver."

"Thank you, ma'am. What's a pretty thing like you doing out here?"

"Driving a truck," she quipped. "Pretty good at it too."

"Sorry, I meant no offense."

"It's alright. Just been a bad day."

"I understand bad days. I'm Snowmobile Flyer. What's your handle?"

"Don't have one. Call me Shelby. How'd you get a handle like Snowmobile Flyer?"

"Well, I live in the Midwest—it snows a lot, so we ride around on snowmobiles. I tend to ride mine really fast. One day we were out partying and…."

"Sorry to interrupt, but I have to stop over here at the Love's and use the little girl's room. Can I buy you a cup of coffee? I'd really like to hear the rest of your story."

"Okay, but I'm buying."

They took the turnoff for the truck stop near the lake on Highway 69 and pulled into the fuel pumps. The other driver pulled up next to her. When they got out of their trucks they shook hands and headed for the store. "My real name is Brian," he said as they walked. "You're even prettier in person."

"Well, thank you Brian, but we need to hurry. I need to get my load down south."

"Okay, you use the restroom, and I'll get the coffee."

"Great. Be back in a minute."

Betty heard the last part of Shelby's conversation with Snowmobile Flyer on the CB. "See, Ted, I told you that perfect little thing wasn't so perfect. She's stopping to meet up with that man. I'm going to pull in there and see for myself."

"I dunno…" said Ted. "I think she's just getting coffee, Betty."

"Right."

Betty went around Ted and led them to the truck stop. She pulled right in behind Shelby at the fuel pump and got out of her truck. She walked between the two trucks and looked at the emblem on the flatbed's door. Then she headed toward the store. Before Betty could reach the door, she saw Shelby and Brian walking towards their trucks with coffee in their hands, talking. She decided to spy on them further and hot-footed it back to Ted's truck. "I bet they go right over to that parking lot and find a nice cozy spot." They watched as Shelby and Brian shook hands and then got into their own trucks.

◊◊◊

Shelby glanced back at the trucks parked behind her in the fuel line. They were ESCC company trucks. She wondered who the drivers were. She keyed the mic on her CB. "Hey, ESCC trucks."

Betty ducked down behind the mirror and told Ted to answer. "Tell her I'm in the restroom."

Ted answered, "Hey, Shelby. What's up?"

"Hi, Ted. You guys sure got loaded fast. Where's Betty?"

"She's inside. You know…uh, girl things."

"Okay. See you later. Got to get going."

The flatbed and Shelby headed back onto the highway.

"Who was that?" Snowmobile Flyer asked.

"A couple of drivers from my yard in West Texas."

"Do you want to wait for them?"

"No. They run together and the female driver doesn't like me much, so I stick to myself most of the time."

"Oh, I can't imagine anyone not getting along with you."

"Well, thanks for that, Brian, but she's one-of-a-kind—trust me."

CHAPTER TWELVE

The sun was warm when Shelby opened her truck door and got out to freshen up. She went into the truck stop, used the restroom, and then went to find something to eat. She figured she'd be able to make the south yard in about eight hours. As she walked back to her truck, her cellphone rang—it was Jack. "Hey, sweetheart."

"How are you? Did you get some rest last night? I was worried about you."

"I'm fine, Jack. I slept good last night. I'm ready to roll and should be in South Texas in about eight hours or less depending on traffic."

"Well, be careful. I can't tell you how much I wish you would give up this foolish idea and come home."

"I know, but we need the money, Jack."

"I'm getting stronger every day. I think the doctor is going to let me go back to work soon. We have enough money in the bank to get by for now. Just come home, Shelby. I want you at home, not out there on those roads."

"I can't, Jack. I like driving this truck. I like being out here. You should come with me sometime. Then you'll understand why I like it."

"I don't like you out there where I can't protect you from some crazy person who might hurt you."

"Jack, you couldn't stop a crazy person from hurting me if I was going to the grocery store. If someone wants to hurt me bad enough, they'll get to me no matter where I am. You're being unreasonable and possessive. This isn't like you. What is your problem?"

"My problem is my wife isn't at home."

"Sorry, baby, but I'll be there when I get there."

Jack hung up the phone without saying goodbye. Shelby looked at the phone for a second, then put it in her pocket. *Why is Jack having such a hard time with my job? This is going to be a long trip.*

Shelby listened to an audio book as she drove to San Antonio. As she reached the outskirts of the city, she heard a little girl's voice over the radio. A weirdo was talking inappropriately to her. Disgusted, she interrupted. "Look, bozo, I'm not sure what you think you're going to get from that little girl, but you need to take your filthy mouth and go away. Little girl, are your folks around?"

The weirdo voice interrupted her question. "Look, bitch, you need to butt out of this conversation."

"I won't butt out. If you don't get off this radio and leave this little girl alone, I'm going to make a phone call to the local police and let them know there's a pervert accosting a child over the radio in their district. I'm sure they won't hesitate hunting your ass down."

The man did not say another word, but Shelby was still worried about the child. "Little girl, my name is Shelby. Are you still there?"

"Yes, I'm still here."

"What is your handle, little one?"

"They call me Coco; my daddy's a trucker and owns a truck wash."

"That's cool, Coco. Are your folks around?"

"Yeah, Daddy's in the office."

"Well, Coco, you need to be careful about talking to strangers over the CB. Some of the people in this world aren't very nice."

"I know, but I like talking on the CB. Do you drive a big truck like my daddy?"

"Yes, I drive a big truck."

"Why don't you bring it in to the truck wash? It's at the 193."

"Oh, I'd love to bring my big truck in and get it washed, but I've already passed that exit Coco. I promise, the next time I'm down this highway I'll stop in and see you. Okay?"

"Okay, Shelby."

"Now, I want you to be more careful about talking with strangers over the CB, okay, Coco?"

"Okay, Shelby. I'll be more careful, I promise."

"Okay, Coco. I'm losing you, but I promise to come see you soon."

"Bye, Shelby."

"Bye, Coco."

Talking with Coco reminded Shelby she was a teacher. She missed teaching, but liked what she was doing now, even with all the problems, sabotages, and Jack's attitude.

◊◊◊

The south yard was busy, as usual, when Shelby pulled onto the scale. Trucks were coming in, loading, scaling, and leaving. The scale houseman told Shelby where she was going to be blowing off her sand and she decided to tackle that hour-long task first before walking into the office chaos.

"Hey, Casper. I'm back."

"Oh god, look what the cat drug in! A blonde."

"Funny, Casper. You know I'm your favorite blonde, right?"

"Could be, but I'll deny it if anyone asks."

"Sandy says you got some work for me until I take that load back."

"Yeah, in fact I was just working on those loads. I need you to get some rest because I'm sending you out tonight with some of the guys to Aguilera. When you get back, you'll go for a load out of Fresno. That should keep you busy until you can pick up out of George."

"Who am I rolling with tonight, and when are they going to load my truck?"

"You can go ahead and load right now. I'm not sure about who I'm sending on this job yet, but the supervisor will be Tracker."

"You may be bad about teasing me over my blonde hair, but he's relentless."

"I can be relentless if you want."

"That's alright. One is enough. I'll go get loaded. Do the loaders know what to put on my truck?"

"Yeah, but here is your worksheet, just in case."

◊◊◊

Shelby was in the middle of a truck convoy going out to a location. A deep darkness surrounded the trucks as they bounced and smoked down the oil lease road.

"So, Blondie, are you scared of the dark?"

"Why should I be scared, when I have all you strong men around me to keep me safe?"

"That's right. You got strong, smart, and good looking men to protect you, Ms. Shelby."

Mario started to reply, "Don't forget our awesome driving skills. Oops, I think that tree just hit my truck."

Shelby could not stop laughing. "Oh my, you guys must really have a hard time fitting those heads of yours into those trucks."

"She won't be making fun of us once we get out to the location; this is a perfect night for the Chupacabra to come out of hiding."

"What the hell is a Chupacabra?" Shelby asked.

"You really don't want to know. Just discussing it could bring it out in the open," Rattlesnake added.

"That blonde hair is going to be a problem, it's too bright. You might want to put it up under your hard hat," Tracker warned.

"You guys are full of it. You haven't even told me what I'm supposed to be afraid of."

"We'll tell you when we get to location. Make sure you stay close to your truck, and in the light, until you're next to one of us so we can keep you safe," Mario added.

"No, really Shelby, the Chupacabra is real and it loves blood. Just be careful when you get out in the dark on location," Scratchy said somberly.

"Are you telling me the truth?"

"Honest. It's an old Mexican legend, but with all the sightings and victims it's left in its path, you'd be stupid not to believe it is real," Scratchy said.

"Okay, I'll bite, but if you guys are pulling my leg, I'm going to beat the hell out of all of ya'll."

◊◊◊

When they arrived at location, Shelby quickly hooked up her truck to the compartment she had been assigned to and helped the others get hooked up as well. After everyone was blowing sand, Mario and Scratchy snuck their way to Shelby's truck. Mario came around the front and Scratchy came slowly around the back.

Shelby saw Mario coming but was not expecting Scratchy to come from the back. Scratchy reached out and grabbed Shelby by the shoulder. "Hey, Shelby. Want to hear about the Chupacabra now?"

Shelby turned with a start toward Scratchy and smacked him hard on the arm. Both men were laughing and backing away as Shelby continued to swing at them. "Assholes."

"What? Are you scared?"

"Very funny. Okay, what is a Chupacabra?"

"Chupacabra is a bat-like creature that sucks the blood out of its isolated victims," Scratchy said.

Shelby laughed. "How convenient that this bat only attacks people who are alone."

While she was engaged with Mario and Scratchy, Tracker and Rattlesnake threw a plastic bag of sand over Shelby's truck. "OH GOD!" she screamed as it landed beside her.

The other drivers fell over themselves laughing.

"OH, YA'LL ARE DEAD!" Shelby chased Mario and Scratchy away from her truck.

Shelby saw Tracker and Rattlesnake holding their bellies laughing. "I"II GET EVEN WITH YOU. I PROMISE!"

All the way back to the yard the guys were teasing her:

"Oh, the Chupacabra almost got Shelby."

"Don't worry, Shelby. We'll protect you from the mean old Chupacabra."

"You guys are assholes. You better watch your backs because I'll get you. I promise," she laughed.

"Woo, the little blonde girl is going to get us. I guess we're the ones who should be scared," Scratchy said.

Everyone was having a good time teasing back and forth when they arrived at the yard.

Shelby found a vacant parking spot while the other drivers parked in their assigned spots. She wasn't happy when she had to park across the road from the usual truck parking lot. Several trucks from ESCC in West Texas had arrived while they had been out and took all the good parking spaces.

Shelby gathered her things together and went into the building to take a shower. She dropped off her paperwork and picked up the next set of papers she needed for the load she would be picking up in Fresno tomorrow. She looked at the list of drivers going on the job and was glad it was just her and Phantom 309, along with several south yard hands.

Meanwhile, Ted had found his way into Betty's truck and was resting against her pillows when Betty jumped up. "You need to get dressed and sneak out of here as soon as those drivers go into the office." She had been spying through the curtain. "Looks like Shelby made it down here. I wonder where they're going to send her tomorrow?" Betty put her clothes back on while Ted fiddled with his. "I'm going to go to the office. You get out of my truck while I'm gone."

"Okay," agreed Ted.

Betty put on her boots and made her way out of the truck. She hurried across the parking lot into the office. The weather was getting cold and even down south she was chilled without a jacket. Inside the office, she went to the coffee maker and grabbed a cup. She looked around and noticed that the shower room was busy, but no one else was in the office yet. She went to the dispatcher's desk and looked over the paperwork that was prepared for the next day's loads. She quickly looked for Shelby's before the drivers from the last job came into the office.

She discovered that Shelby was going to Fresno. She moved over to the computer and accessed the file she needed in order to doctor Shelby's load assignment. "There. We'll just change this and see if Shelby can explain her way out of this one. There is no way anyone can help you out of this mess." She printed a copy of the new paperwork and put it in place of the one she had found for Shelby.

Just as she was replacing the paperwork, Mondo, Rattlesnake, and Scratchy came into the office. Betty placed the old assignment sheet into her back pocket and pretended to be looking for her own assignment. "What you need, Betty?" Mondo asked as he sat down at the dispatcher's desk, making Betty move away.

"Just looking for my paperwork for tomorrow."

Mondo looked through the paperwork. "Doesn't look like Casper has your assignment yet. I think he was waiting to see if you guys would make it tonight."

Betty decided that she had pushed her luck far enough and backed out of the room. "Well, I'll check with him in the morning. When you see him be sure and tell him we did make it in."

Mondo was still looking over papers. "Okay, sure Betty, I'll let him know. Get some rest."

Betty turned to go and almost ran into Shelby. "Watch it," she growled.

"Sorry," muttered Shelby as she walked to the dispatch room to get her paperwork. "Man, I have no idea what I have done to that woman, but she is just the rudest thing."

Mondo spoke up. "No, Shelby she's just a mean bitch."

Shelby smirked, "Yeah, I know, but I didn't want to say that out loud."

"Don't worry about it, everyone thinks the same thing."

"Well, I just came to ask you if I could have my paperwork for tomorrow, please."

"Here ya go. Just make sure you pick it up on time. White Lightning is supervisor on that job, so check with him on when he wants to go to location. It's a blow and go."

"Okay, thanks Mondo. I'm going to sleep now."

"Alright. Did you use proper safety procedures in the shower?" he asked, spotting her still wet hair.

"Oh, not you too." Shelby swatted at Mondo with her paperwork.

"Just kidding, Shelby. Get some rest."

◊◊◊

The trip to Fresno was quiet. Shelby arrived on time, but there were several trucks waiting to load in front of her and she had to wait. She went inside the office. "Hi, my name is Shelby, and I'm here to load for ESCC."

The man shook Shelby's hand and took her paperwork. "Hi, Shelby. My name's Vann and it will be a little while before we can get to you."

"Okay. I'll just wait at my truck over there. She pointed to a vacant spot in the yard. Come get me when you're ready."

Shelby saw Phantom 309 and White Lightning in the parking lot, talking. "Hey, guys. What's up?" Shelby asked as she walked up to the two men.

"Hi, Shelby. How are you?"

"Good, thanks. So do you think we'll be here long?"

"No, they load pretty fast," said White Lightning. "We're just waiting for our paperwork."

"Oh, well Mondo told me to ask you when you want to go to location."

"I want to go as soon as we get back. No reason waiting since the box is already on location."

"Alright, that'll work."

"Yeah, after you get loaded just head to the location."

"Okay." Shelby went back to her truck and waited to load.

◊◊◊

Highway 6 was full of stoplights, and it took Shelby quite a while to get on Highway 59, which was busy with traffic too. She noticed several weigh stations when she was headed into Fresno for her load, but none of them were open when she passed them. Just as she got onto 59, however, Shelby had to pull into a weigh station. Although she hadn't ever had any problem with them, she hated having to pull in.

"Good afternoon, ma'am. Can I see your truck information please?"

Shelby handed the uniformed man the folder that she kept on her truck.

"Well, everything is in order, but you're a little over on your front drivers. It's only 200 pounds. I'm going to let you go this time, but please tell your loader to be more careful next time." The man handed the folder back to Shelby.

"Thank you."

"You're welcome. Have a safe trip."

Shelby pulled her truck back out on the highway and continued down the road toward the south yard.

◊◊◊

"Pull in over there and turn it around. What compartment are you in?" Shelby showed White Lightning the paperwork. "Okay, it says you'll be going into compartment number two, so turn around and back it in." Shelby did what White Lightning told her to do. Once she was in position, she hooked her hose up. As usual, when she was finished, she went to help the other drivers. After everyone was hooked up, White Lightning told everyone to go ahead and begin blowing off their sand.

Shelby powered up her PTO and exited her truck, waiting for the pressure to reach ten PSI before releasing the sand. Suddenly White Lightning came around the corner of her truck at a full run, "SHUT IT DOWN, SHELBY!"

Shelby ran to the front of her truck and shut it down immediately. "What's wrong Lightning? Did I do something wrong?"

"No, you didn't do anything wrong, but this paperwork isn't right for some reason and you're going into a compartment that already has yellow sand in it. I need to call the office and find out what the deal is. I'm glad I decided to check the compartments before we started to blow, or we would have a real mess. Just hang tight for a minute, and I'll let you know what they want us to do."

"Not again!" Shelby blinked backed the tears forming before they could slip down her cheeks. "It seems like every time I turn around I'm screwing up."

"What? No Shelby, this isn't on you, it's a typo or something. Give me a minute and I'll find out."

"Okay." Shelby stood next to her truck with her arms crossed in frustration.

White Lightning was on the phone with the office. "Bolt, check the computer and find out for sure what compartment Shelby was to blow off into. He waited for a reply. "Yeah, I know that, but that compartment is full of yellow sand." He waited again. "No, I checked her paperwork and it says compartment two," he replied. "No, she hasn't blown anything yet," he sighed. "Okay, so it says compartment one? You guys need to be more careful in that office. She almost blew off in the wrong compartment and that would have really been expensive."

"Alright, Shelby, we need to change you over to compartment one."

Shelby and White Lightning began moving her hose to the new compartment. "This is just wonderful. For the last two weeks all I have done is correct mistakes. I must be cursed or something. Between a wrong location, a wrong load, and now a wrong compartment, I'm three for three."

"That's really weird, but don't worry about it Shelby. Shit happens. Go ahead and kick it off. You're clear to blow off now."

"Thanks, White Lightning. I appreciate you catching the mistake."

"That's why they pay me the big bucks." Both drivers laughed as Shelby started up her PTO again and started blowing off her sand.

Meanwhile, Betty stomped out of the south yard office with Ted close in tow. "Damn it. I can't believe it, Ted! She got saved again by another one of those morons we work with. What in the hell do I have to do to get rid of that little bitch? I'm going to get her if it's the last thing I do."

"Betty, relax," said Ted. "Maybe you should just back off for a little while and see what happens."

"Back off and let her tell everyone what is going on between us? Just think about it Ted, all that child support you'll have to pay, and nowhere to live."

"Nowhere to live? I figured if anything happened I'd live at your place."

"No way!"

◊◊◊

Shelby was thrilled when she finally was loaded out of George West and heading for home. "I'm on my way home, sweetheart! I'll be there in about nine hours."

"Great. It's about damn time. I sure miss you."

"Me too. See you soon."

CHAPTER THIRTEEN

Sandy was busy answering the phone and doing paperwork when Shelby stuck her head through the door to her office. "Hey, girl. What's up?"

"Busy, as usual. I put your next load assignment in your box."

"Okay, I put in for a PM a couple days ago. Do you think Ed will be able to get to it pretty soon?"

Sandy put down the phone and gave Shelby a somber look. "You didn't hear?"

"Hear what?"

"Ed got in an accident a couple weeks ago."

"What happened?"

"He was on his motorcycle and got hit by a car."

"Oh my god, is he alright?"

"He's recovering. PM's are backed up until they get a new mechanic in here. Danny is working on them, but there's a lot to do. The new mechanic should be here soon."

Shelby learned she was going to pick up a load out of Tatum and deliver it back to West Texas. She looked at the wall map and saw that Tatum was in East Texas about eight hours away—an overnight run. She needed to go home for a few things and let Jack know she wouldn't be home for the night.

◊◊◊

Shelby had become so familiar with I-20. She felt she knew every bump, crack, and turn of the highway. The drive to the Bid D had minimal traffic, the CB chatter was clean, and the weather was cold, but sunny. Shelby drove in peace and quiet. By evening, she found a place to park and then called

Jack. "Hey, baby. I'm at Van. I'm going to take a shower and get something to eat. How's everything at home?"

"Just as you left it this morning. Will you be home tomorrow?" Jack insisted.

"Yeah, but I saw a bunch of work on the board, so I doubt I'll be home for long."

"Sounds about right," Jack complained.

"It sure is getting cold out here, and there are some ominous clouds rolling in."

"I told you this job isn't safe. You need to be home."

Shelby ignored his comment. "I'm going to go take a shower. I'll call you before I go to sleep. I love you, sweetie."

"Love you, too."

◊◊◊

"Look Ted, she's going inside for a shower. Now's my chance to get into her truck and take her log. If she doesn't have her paperwork she'll be driving illegal, and I can call the cops. She'll get a ticket for driving over hours and poof, fired. I don't know why I didn't think of this before. Using the DOT to get rid of my problem is genius."

"I don't know, Betty. What if someone sees you take her stuff, or what if she comes out and catches you?"

Betty jumped out of her truck and moved toward Shelby's truck with Ted in tow. "That's why I have you and that's why I have this…." Betty held up the key she'd stolen from Eddy's office drawer. "I'm going to clean her out."

She moved around behind the truck and slinked back to the front on the driver's side. The shadows gave Betty and Ted some cover, but they were still exposed in the dusk's lingering light. Betty unlocked Shelby's truck and got inside. She loaded Shelby's things onto her bedding, rolled it up, and pushed it through the driver's side door to Ted. "Take it to my truck and keep out of sight."

"Okay," Ted mumbled. He nearly fell to the ground from the weight of the cumbersome bundle. Betty got out of the truck and left the door unlocked.

Ted helped her push the bundle through her truck door when she met him back at her truck. Betty got in, turned, and glared at Ted, still standing by her open door. "Go to your truck, dummy. We've got to go on down to the rest area in case someone gets suspicious."

"But, Betty, I haven't eaten yet," Ted whined.

"Oh, shut up, Ted. You won't die if you don't have a double meat cheese-burger tonight. Get in your truck and let's go. I'll be able to see Shelby go by when she leaves here, and then I can call the DOT and let them know she's out of hours. It's perfect." Betty reached for her door and forced Ted to move back so she could close it. "See you at the rest area."

◊◊◊

With her shower bag, purse, and dirty clothes in hand, Shelby left the truck stop and walked back toward her truck. She felt good after her shower and dinner and was looking forward to a good night's rest. She put her key into the lock and turned it, but the door locked instead of unlocking. "Weird," Shelby said and turned it in the other direction. *I could have sworn I locked the door before heading to my shower.* Shelby turned it the other direction and unlocked it again. She climbed into her truck and fell with a thud into her driver's seat.

"Oh my god." Her heart sank as she saw that everything in her truck was missing, even her bedding. "Who in the world could have done this?" She felt sick to her stomach, and dropped the last of her possessions on a now empty bed. "Now what?"

She decided to go into the truck stop and ask the clerk if they had a se-curity guard around or if she needed to call the local police to make a report. As she walked back toward the truck stop, a couple of men came up behind her. "Ma'am?" they said, startling her.

She stopped and looked at them, cautiously.

"Sorry, ma'am, we didn't mean to scare you, but we saw a couple people taking things out of your truck. We didn't think too much about it until they took the stuff to another truck and then took off."

"You saw someone break into my truck and take my stuff and you didn't think it was odd?"

"No, ma'am. Well I mean…."

The other driver intervened. "Hi, I'm Wild Child and that's Outlaw and what he is trying to say is that the woman who got into your truck had a key. She handed the stuff to a man right in broad daylight, so we thought they were just cleaning out their truck. But then they took off in some other trucks, with emblems like yours. Then, when you came out, we knew something was amiss."

"First, I need to make a police report, I guess…. And since they took everything, including my bedding, I guess I better find me a store."

"We're sorry, ma'am. We would have stopped them if we'd known they were stealing from you."

"Oh, it's not your fault. Just some crazy people out looking for free stuff, I guess. I can't replace most of it; it's sad people have to steal. "Sorry, but I need to make a report and find some bedding so I can rest."

"Alright. Have a better night."

"You too." Shelby went into the truck stop and talked with the clerk.

"Man, I'd love to get my hands on the assholes who did that to that nice lady," said Wild Child, fuming.

Outlaw put his fist into his hand. "Me too. I knew something was funky when I saw them come up to that truck from the rear."

"Hey, let's get on the radio and find out if anyone wants to help this little lady out," Wild Child said. "We can take up a collection or something and take her over to the Wally Store."

"That's a great idea." The two men got on the CB and explained what had happened to Shelby in broad daylight and asked if anyone would like to help her.

Shelby returned to her truck with a local cop in tow about an hour later. "This is my truck. I know I locked it when I left, but it was unlocked when I returned. A couple of drivers came up to me a little while ago and told me that some woman had a key and she unlocked my truck. Then she took the stuff out of my truck and handed it to her partner. They said the two people were driving trucks like mine, but I'm not sure whether they meant sand hauler or company."

The cop was making notes as Shelby talked. "Does anyone else in your company have a key to this truck?"

"Well, no, just the office. They have a spare key, I assume."

"This is a Peterbilt?"

"Yes."

"Okay, did you get the names of the two witnesses?"

"No, not their real names. Just their handles. But, I'm sure they're around here somewhere."

"Their handles?"

"Yeah, their CB handles." Shelby looked up and noticed the two men coming toward her and the cop. "There…those two guys who are coming this way."

The two men answered the cop's questions. Then the cop got into Shelby's truck and looked around. "They didn't take the things on your bed?"

"I was in the shower at the time, and that's all I have left."

He looked at Shelby's truck information folder and then at her door. "Well, I'll make out a report. How much do you think you lost in value?"

"I don't know." Shelby shrugged. "Maybe two hundred dollars, I guess."

"Okay. We'll do what we can, Mrs. Mathews. We'll call you if we find any of your things."

Shelby shook the officer's hand and he left.

"Thanks, guys. I really appreciate you coming over and talking with the cop. I'm pretty sure I'll never see my stuff again."

Wild Child and Outlaw reached into their pockets and pulled out the money they'd collected from other drivers in the lot. "Here, we got on the CB and took up a collection for you. Wild Child and I'll take you over to the local Wally store."

Her fatigued mixed with their kindness caused her to burst into tears. "Wow, I can't believe you guys did this for me."

"We're all drivers out here and although there are some bad eggs, most of us are just hardworking family people just like you. We try to take care of our own, and when someone gets hurt we try to help."

Shelby gave both men a hug and went to the middle of the parking lot and waved at as many drivers as could see her. She knew she had reached some of the drivers who had helped out because the whole parking lot was filled with the sound of big rig horns letting her know she was welcome.

"Come on, the cab is here. Time to go shopping," Wild Child said.

◊◊◊

The next day, Shelby walked into the ESCC office and went directly to Sandy's office.

As soon as Sandy saw her she said, "Did you get your load off okay? I need you to get your paperwork finished and head to Arkansas tonight. I got loads out of the Fort going to North Dakota. Plus, the sooner you can get there the better, because the snow and ice are coming."

"First, yes, I got the load off fine today. Second, I need to go to my house and get some more clothes and things since most of mine were stolen yesterday. If it hadn't been for some really nice truckers, I would've been sleeping in the cold because I had very little money with me. Third, I have never driven a big truck in snow or ice. Do you think you're wise in sending me?"

Sandy stopped what she was doing and looked at Shelby. "What? You got robbed? How did that happen, and where?" Shelby gave Sandy the details of what had happened.

"Oh god, I'm sorry, Shelby. Why didn't you call us? We would have wired you money."

"Well, I was just going to buy a blanket and all these drivers gave me money for new bedding, so it all worked out. But I need to go home and get some more clothes before taking off for The Fort. I'm a little nervous about going into ice and snow."

"You'll be fine, Shelby. Besides, it will give you a chance to learn since there isn't a big hurry on these loads."

"Okay, if you think so."

◊◊◊

Jack wasn't happy when he found out his wife was going to be gone again for several days, especially in the snow and ice. Shelby assured him she would be fine and she would take lots of pictures.

Running her usual route to the Big D right down 20 was the quickest way to The Fort, but the weather was beginning to worry her. The temperature dropped and a fine mist was falling. She decided to check with some of the westbound drivers and find out what the conditions of the roads were like in the Big D area. "Do you know what the conditions of the roads are like in the Big D?"

"Well little lady, they were wet when I left the city, but by the time you hit town with the cold rolling in, you're looking at a real mess. Big D drivers aren't used to driving on ice and they tend to cause more accidents because of it. If you're headed that way, you need to watch the four wheelers and drive real careful over those bridges. It's going to be slick out there tonight."

"I appreciate that. I'm Shelby, what's your handle?"

"You got Nature Boy here."

"Hi, Nature Boy. You're looking good all the way back to Odessa—didn't see a thing. The roads were dry until I reached the 409."

"Alright, lady driver, I thank you for that info. You be safe."

"Same to you, Nature Boy." She would heed his advice.

Shelby made it safely to Highway 45 despite a few slick spots running down 30 through Dallas. Once she reached 45 things changed, though. It was getting colder, and it was now raining. The rain was turning into ice on the roads and the bridges were treacherous. Nature Boy knew exactly what he was talking about when it came to the four wheel drivers. They just didn't understand ice driving. Shelby had geared down and was rolling in traffic at about 35 mph, which was slow but safer. Several of the little cars had slowed down in front of her and she found it hard to stop without jackknifing. She didn't want to take a chance on hitting one of them.

Once she was out of the city traffic, things seemed to get worse. The roads were now thick with frozen ice and without as much traffic she felt her trailer fishtail more with every mile. She now understood what "white knuckling" meant. Shelby made it as far as Anna and decided she'd fought the weather long enough. She called the office; Sandy wasn't there so she left a voice message. "Hey, Sandy. I'm shutting down near Anna. The roads are really bad and I'd rather take it slow than wreck my truck."

◊◊◊

Shelby took her time getting to The Fort in the northwest corner of North Dakota. Because of the potential for black ice, she decided to go north out of Arkansas into Missouri and then catch 29 through the Dakotas. The weather actually held the further north she traveled. It was blistering cold, but other than some spots of snow, she had dry roads.

"How about you, northbound?"

Shelby responded, "Go ahead, southbound."

"Yeah, little lady driver, you got the Bull Rider here. Just wanted to let you know you got yourself some real tricky weather coming into this area tomorrow, so you might want to keep your eyes open."

"Yes, sir, you got Shelby here, and I've been keeping my ear to the weather station, hoping to be to my destination by midnight tonight."

"Good 'cause the storm that's a brewing is going to be a doozie. I'd hate to see a pretty little thing like yourself stuck in the snow."

"Thank you, driver. I'm working hard to get to Williston as quick as I can."

Highway 85 leading up into Williston was a beautiful ride but Shelby knew that it wasn't going to be beautiful when the snow and rain got there. She quickly made her way to the yard and blew her sand off into a silo. She wanted to get off the mountain and to a truck stop. *I don't want to spend the night in the middle of nowhere, and I need to take a break.*

She found a place in Bowman and was settling in for the night went she got a call from Sandy. "I need you to head back to The Fort for a load back to here."

"Okay. But I can't leave until in the morning. I'm out of hours. Is that going to be a problem?"

"Not at all. Get in your break and then head that way. I already know about the storm, so don't push it, just be careful."

"Okay, you got it."

The next morning, Shelby woke to a blanket of white powder and more coming from the sky. She didn't know exactly which direction to take, but she knew she needed to get south.

Traveling south seemed logical, but the further she traveled, the slicker the roads seemed to get. *I wonder if I made the right choice.* She reduced her truck speed because she wasn't loaded and the slick spots were causing her truck to fishtail. With the slow speed and the unknown territory, Shelby figured she was in for some education if she couldn't get through the slick stuff before dark. Driving on ice during the day was hard, but driving on it at night was a whole different ball game.

As darkness began to fall, Shelby realized the snow was coming down harder. She felt like she was in a fish bowl rolling down the highway. All she could see with her headlights on was the white snowflakes falling all around her truck with an occasional set of headlights from another oncoming vehicle. She wasn't that far from Missouri, but the roads were becoming snow packed and her nerves told her she wasn't handling things well.

Suddenly, a big rig flew by her as if there wasn't a blizzard. "Moron!" Several minutes later, she came to the spot where the same rig had slid off the road and jack knifed into the ditch. "Not such a hot shot driver now, are you?"

There was no way to move around the truck, but several four wheelers that had been out fighting the storm had stopped to check on the driver. Shelby decided that she was not going to stop since she knew she wouldn't be able to help anyway. She'd had enough of the storm. She looked for a decent place to park for the rest of the night, or for a few days, however long it took to wait it out.

CHAPTER FOURTEEN

Shelby was loaded again and heading toward West Texas. Her nervous feelings began to subside. In fact, she was rather proud of herself for making it through the snow and ice without wrecking her truck. The roads in Oklahoma were still ice- and snow-packed, but clear enough to travel at careful speeds. Interstate 40 was not bad as long as she stayed out of the passing lane. Four wheelers didn't seem to be having too much trouble with that lane, but when she tried a couple times, the rear of her truck seemed to want to come forward. Staying in the left lane was fine for her. Right now she just wanted to get back into Texas.

"Hey there, driver. How are you today?"

Shelby was surprised at the voice coming over the radio. Unsure if they were talking to her, she decided to just listen. The little girl's voice came over the radio again. "Do you have your radio on, ESCC driver?" Shelby knew then that the little girl was talking to her.

"Yes, little lady. I got my ears on."

"So what do you think about all this snow?"

"It's pretty, but dangerous."

"Yeah, I'm out here riding with my daddy right now, and he lets me talk on the radio."

"Well, you're doing fine there little one."

"I don't see too many lady drivers out here, especially in this kind of weather."

"Oh, you'd be surprised," Shelby said, smiling. This little girl—reminded her of one of her first graders. "There are a whole lot of women drivers out here now," she continued. "Some of them drive really well in weather worse than this all the time."

"Yeah, that's what daddy says. So what's your handle, lady driver?"

"I don't really have one yet. It's been kind of hard to decide. I want just the right one. My name is Shelby."

"I understand. I don't have one either. Some of my daddy's friends have given me a few, but I'm kind of like you—I want one that's just right."

"That's right, a handle that fits. So where are you guys headed today?"

"Oh, we're going over near Oklahoma City and then back home to The Fort."

"Well, little one, it has been awesome rolling with you, but I have to get off here at the 69, so you guys be careful going west."

"Alright, lady driver, I mean, Shelby. You be careful too. Oh, Daddy said to tell you that the roads toward McAlister are about the same as this one, so watch that left lane. The talk is that things are good and dry through to the Big D."

"Thank you, Sweet Pea. You take care now."

"THAT'S IT SHELBY, I LOVE IT. THAT'S MY HANDLE. SWEET PEA!"

"I thought you might like that one. Well, this is my turn. See ya on the flip side."

"Thanks, Shelby. See you again, I hope."

"Me too, Sweet Pea."

Shelby had a good week and thought that the curse she had been under was lifted. On top of that, she proved to herself she could handle the cold weather. She would be home just as soon as she got this load off.

◊◊◊

Shelby woke up the next morning thinking, *How wonderful it feels to sleep in my own bed, snuggled under the covers with my honey who was overly excited about my being home.* Unfortunately, her reverie was cut short by the sound of her cell phone. "Damn it! I need a break," Shelby muttered as she reached for her phone.

"Hey Shelby. This is Sandy. I got a load I need you to pick up out of Brandy today. Oh, I'm sorry. Did I wake you up?"

Shelby reached for a pen and paper. "No, I was just laying in bed thinking about getting up."

"Okay, well I need you to pick up out of North Voca, and deliver near Garden City. They want it there tonight, and it's real tricky on those Ranch roads late at night. Be sure and take your spotlight."

"I got it. I'm going to take a shower and do some stuff around here since I'm not delivering before tonight."

"Sounds good. Call me when you're done, and be careful."

"Alright."

Shelby fell back on the pillows and covered her head. "I love this job Jack, but I never get any time off. And when I do, it's usually on the road. I miss cleaning and cooking and taking care of you sometimes."

"I miss that too. Maybe you should just quit." Jack pulled Shelby on top of him and kissed her. "Want to take care of me, baby?"

"Gladly!"

◊◊◊

"I don't care what you say, Ted, I want her gone. I have backed off long enough and fortunately for her, we haven't been running in the same job circles lately. Tonight, however, I'm going to get her." Betty was pulling hoses off of Shelby's truck, making holes in them with a butcher knife she had brought from her house.

"But Betty, putting holes in her hoses isn't going to get her fired, it just might get her or someone else hurt."

"All the better."

"Don't be crazy. If they find out you did this, they might fire *you*."

She continued to punch the hoses and then put them back. "They can't fire me. I'm a lead driver and the best driver they got. Besides, quit being such a pussy!"

Ted walked toward his truck.

"Where are you going?"

"I'm out of here. We need to get going. She might pull in any time now, and I'm not getting caught. Come on, Betty, let's go."

"Fine. I have one more." She quickly jabbed several holes in the hose and then smiled proudly. "There." She replaced the final hose before heading to her truck.

"I need to stop by the office before we take off." Betty told Ted as they pulled up next to the scale house. "Be right back."

"Okay, but hurry up. We need to get on the road."

"I don't know what your problem is lately, but you better cool it and stop talking to me that way."

Ted didn't respond.

"Understand?"

He nodded reluctantly. "Yeah."

"I'll be back in a minute."

"Fine."

Betty went into the office and turned on the computer. "Now to make sure Shelby gets in trouble for sure. I'm going to change both her directions and compartment this time. You, little Miss Shelby, are going to have a hard time getting out of the mess I have waiting for you tonight." She pulled up Shelby's assignment sheet, changed the directions, and gave her a different compartment number.

"There. Get out of this one, little girl." She laughed to herself as she changed out the worksheets and left the office.

◊◊◊

Shelby spotted Betty and Ted leaving the parking lot just as she pulled in. Several other drivers who had been assigned the same job were behind her. Shelby went into the office and got her paperwork out of her box.

"Hey, Shelby. What's up?" Speedy asked as he reached for his paperwork.

"Not much."

"You heading for Brady?"

"Yeah. Hey, Sandy said that this location we're going to is a little complicated. Do you think I could tag along behind you guys so I don't get lost?"

"Sure, no problem, Bobcat and Fast Man should be here shortly. I think there are a few others going, but you can roll with us if you want."

"Yeah, I appreciate it. I'm going to pre-trip my truck and get ready."

"Alright, see you out there."

Shelby rolled with her coworkers toward Brady, but when they got to Sterling City Shelby needed to use the ladies room. "Guys, I'll meet you in Brady. I need to stop at the restroom."

"Okay. Hurry, by the time we make location tonight it's going to be really cold."

"Alright, be right behind you." Shelby pulled into the little store and went inside.

◊◊◊

"Let's get unloaded and then I want to go over to that location near the stop sign and watch what happens." Betty and Ted had reached the location before any of the other drivers. They hooked up and started to blow off their sand. Betty climbed into her truck and told Ted, "Let me know when each pod is done so I can stay warm. Watch my load, and let me know when I need to get out and make a change."

"Betty, you know it's against policy to leave the gauges unattended. You can't sit in your truck while you're unloading, in case you plug off. I can't watch your truck and mine too."

"Policy? You don't have a problem climbing in my truck and fucking me when that's against policy. It will be fine! Just let me know when the pods get low." Betty got into her truck; she wanted to hear anything that came over the radio from the other drivers just in case they should get to the ranch roads before they finished unloading.

Getting loaded and back to Garden City took the drivers a good four hours. Shelby was glad she was rolling into location with the other drivers because Sandy had been right about the dark and tricky layout of this ranch. "Hey, Speedy. My directions say we're supposed to be taking a left here."

Fast Man interrupted. "Mine says we're supposed to be going right."

"Yeah, that's what mine says too." Bobcat chimed in. "Shelby, are you sure you're looking at the right assignment sheet?"

"Yes, I'm getting so tired of this bullshit. Every time I turn around I'm getting wrong directions, wrong loads, and wrong compartments. What the hell is going on in that office?"

Bobcat spoke up. "Don't worry about it, Shelby. Just stay with us and we'll get you there."

"Sorry, guys. I'm just tired, and it's just frustrating when I try to do a good job and can't because of the information I'm given."

"I know, but it's all good tonight. You can take it up with Sandy tomorrow." Speedy led the group of drivers to the location, and Shelby showed everyone her paperwork. "See, I told you."

Speedy read the directions, and they were not even close to the ones the other drivers had. "This is crazy and look…" Speedy showed the other drivers the paperwork. "The compartments are different too." The air was blistering cold as Shelby was hooking her hoses up to the compartment that she had been assigned according to the paperwork she had received. "Wait, Shelby. Don't hook up yet. I don't think you're going in that compartment either."

"Damn it, when is this going to stop?"

◊◊◊

Betty and Ted had already unloaded and had moved over to the other location. Their lights and engines were turned off, and they waited in the dark to see what would happen with Shelby. "Damn, I didn't think about her following some other driver onto location. Oh well, she'll put that sand right on top of that CLT, and there will be hell to pay for that one."

"I'm moving closer, I want to see Shelby put that sand in the wrong box."

"I'm staying here," said Ted. "It's cold, and I still haven't thawed out from unloading."

"Get out of the truck Ted and go with me. I want to get a closer look. You wouldn't want anything to happen to your pussycat now would you?"

"Fine." Ted swung open his truck door and stormed out.

The two snuck up on the location and strained to listen. "See, she's hooking up to the wrong compartment," Betty said. "Wait. Speedy just stopped her. Damn it! They're looking at her paperwork. Shit, they know.

How the hell did they figure it out again? I WANT HER DEAD! I'm so tired of everyone helping her."

"Wait, I forgot about the punctured hoses."

◊◊◊

Sandy picked up her cell phone. "We need you to find out what compartment Shelby is supposed to go into," she heard Speedy say.

"What? I'm not at the office. Why isn't she using her assignment sheet?

"She got her assignment sheet, but it's wrong. The whole thing is wrong. The directions, the compartment, even the PO is wrong."

"Oh god, not again. Okay, give me a few minutes and I'll find out. But if I remember correctly she's going into compartment three."

"No, I'm in three."

Speedy knocked on Shelby's truck door. She'd climbed in it to keep warm while he was sorting things out. "She's checking on it."

"Does anyone else ever have this much trouble with their paperwork?"

"I've never had any trouble, but things happen in a busy office; things get mixed up."

"I'd believe that if I wasn't the only one. I thought Sandy liked me, now I think she's trying to get rid of me."

"It's just mistakes."

"Yeah, maybe."

Speedy's phone rang. "Okay," he said and motioned to Shelby for them to leave the truck. "You're going in compartment one, let's get you hooked up." The other drivers were already unloading and taking care of Speedy's load but came over to Shelby's truck to help hook up. Bobcat pulled Shelby's hose to the compartment and then stopped. "Wait look, Speedy this hose has been cut."

"Not again!" Shelby lamented.

"Shelby, get another hose."

She went and got another hose. "Damn," she said, "this one is punctured, too."

Speedy came to Shelby's deck, asking, "What's up, Shelby?"

"Look, all my hoses have holes in them."

"Shit, I'll get one of mine. Come on, it's cold as fuck out here."

◊◊◊

"I cannot believe this! What the hell I do I have to do to get rid of that slut?" Betty looked around at the huge rocks along the side of the hill. "I got it!"

"Oh, come on, Betty. It's freezing out here, and I want to get in my truck."

"Fine. I can do this myself. GO, DAMN IT! GET THE FUCK BACK IN YOUR STUPID TRUCK, YOU PUSSY!"

◊◊◊

It took the drivers about an hour to get everyone unloaded and packed up. Shelby didn't say much. She couldn't get over the feeling that everything happening was her fault. She felt guilty that the other drivers were dealing with stuff they wouldn't have had to contend with if she weren't there. Before getting back in her truck she said, "Thanks for all the help, guys. I really appreciate it."

They soon heard her screaming over the radio. "OH MY GOD, NO!"

Speedy, Fast Man, and Bobcat stopped their trucks and ran back to Shelby's truck. "What's wrong?" Speedy asked.

Shelby was sitting on the ground next to her rear tandem. "What the hell else can go wrong tonight? It just rolled down that hill, and I couldn't stop fast enough to keep from hitting it."

Fast Man and Speedy looked at the damage the boulder had done to Shelby's truck. Fast Man went to the other side of the truck and then came back around after his examination. "Looks like it just damaged the inside rear driver's side tire, but this fender is fucked from the blowout. We aren't too far from the yard. If you take it slow, I think you can baby it back there. Think you can do that, Shelby?"

"Yes. If you guys can just stay with me till we get the hell off this lease, I'll drive it back real slow."

Bobcat touched Shelby on the shoulder. "I'll stay with you just in case you have trouble with it on the interstate."

"You're going to be okay there, little ma'am." Speedy said. "Let's move this rock and get out of here."

The drivers complied.

◊◊◊

"You stupid little witch. That boulder may not have gotten rid of you for good, but this is only the beginning." Betty ran back to her truck. "Let's get out of here before they see us. I really fixed her this time. Eddy is going to be pissed about the damage to her truck. I can't wait to see her try and get her ass out of this jam with her hoses punctured and her truck damaged. This is too good. Come on Ted, move it. They'll be leaving as soon as they get that boulder out of the way."

"Okay, Betty, but if we move too fast they will see the dust and know someone else is out here."

"That doesn't matter as long as they don't see us. Now, get the fuck going."

CHAPTER FIFTEEN

It was dawn by the time Bobcat and Shelby pulled into the yard. Shelby parked her truck near the mechanic's shop. "Thanks, Bobcat. I sure appreciate you sticking around for me."

"No problem. Stan and Manly will repair the damage."

"I've already got the repair slip filled out. I just hate telling Eddy. I hope he won't be angry."

"No, he won't be. Stuff happens out here, believe me."

Shelby entered the office but didn't say anything to Sandy. She still had it in her mind that Sandy was, for whatever reason, messing up her paperwork on purpose. She went directly to Eddy's office. Eddy was talking with Stan when she knocked on the already opened door. "Sorry to interrupt boss, but when you and Stan have a minute, I need to talk to you."

"We're done. Come on in. What's up?"

"Well, to start with, every hose on my truck has been cut. Plus, a boulder rolled down the hill near the location we were on last night. I ran over it before I could stop and damaged a tire and fender."

Stan spoke up. "I'll go have a look," he said and left.

"Alright, we'll be right there." Eddy motioned for Shelby to take a seat. "I don't know what is going on, Eddy, but I seem to be the only one having problems with my paperwork. I'm getting wrong loads, wrong locations, bad directions, wrong boxes, and chief numbers. The other drivers don't seem to be having those problems, and I'm always finding holes in my hoses."

"Do you check your hoses before leaving the yard?"

"No, not always, but I haven't seen anyone else check their hoses each time they leave the yard either. I'll try and be more careful, but that still doesn't explain how they're getting damaged. Or my paperwork problem."

Eddy got up from his desk and put on his hard hat. "Let's go check out your truck, and I'll look into the paperwork issue later. Did you fill out a work report on the truck?"

"Yes, sir."

"Okay, let's go have a look and see if we can figure out why your hoses have holes."

"I'm really sorry I ran over that boulder last night, but it just came out of nowhere and I couldn't stop before hitting it."

"Don't worry about it. We'll fix it. Stuff happens out on these locations."

Just as Eddy and Shelby were walking out of the building, Betty and Ted walked into the office. Eddy greeted his two drivers. "Hello, Betty, hello Ted. Just getting in this morning?"

"No, boss, got in late. We slept in our trucks in the yard last night."

Shelby had not spoken to Sandy, and she wasn't in the mood for pleasantries with Ted or Betty either. She couldn't help thinking as she walked out the door, *I'll bet you slept in your trucks.*

Sandy was extremely busy in the office with phone calls and trucks coming in for loads. Tiff was in her office, but came into the dispatch office with some paperwork. Betty and Ted sat down at the break table. Betty motioned for Tiff to come to the table. "What's going on around here? Eddy seemed upset, and Shelby wasn't her usual bubbly self. What's up?"

Tiff shrugged her shoulders. "Not sure. All I know is Shelby ran over a boulder and had some bad hoses on her truck."

"Bet Eddy was upset about all that."

"No, not really." Tiff left the break room and went into her office.

Betty sat there, fuming.

"I got to go, Betty," Ted said. "Annabel has been calling all morning, and I need to go home and help her with the kids. See you later."

Betty was so pissed she just ignored Ted. She stood up and gathered her paperwork. "Sandy, here's my paperwork. Hey, do you think I could borrow my spare key to my truck for a minute? I left mine in my car."

Sandy moved the phone away from her mouth. "Yeah, sure. Give me a minute and I'll get it."

"That's alright, you're busy. I know where they are, I can get it." Sandy went back to her phone, waving at Betty that it was okay.

Betty went into Eddy's office and snuck behind his desk. She wasn't really looking for her key. She wanted to find something else. After rummaging through several drawers, she finally found what she was looking for. "There! This will work perfectly." She put the item in her coat, shut the drawer, and quietly slipped out of the room.

◊◊◊

Exhausted, Shelby opened the front door to her house and took off her trademark pink steel-toed boots.

Jack was in the kitchen, making breakfast, when he heard the door open. "Is that my little mother trucker?"

Shelby fell onto the couch and only moved when Jack pulled her up for a kiss. "I take it you didn't have a very good night."

"You could say that. Between the holes in my hoses again, the screwed up paperwork again, and the freezing cold…. Oh, not to mention the boulder that came out of nowhere…."

"A boulder? Come on, I just made eggs, toast, and some fresh coffee. Tell me about the boulder." Jack pulled Shelby up.

"Oh, Jack, I'm too tired to eat, but I could use a cup of coffee."

Shelby sat at the breakfast table and sipped at her coffee. "It was totally awful, baby. I ran over a boulder that came out of nowhere. I couldn't stop in time and blew out a tire and messed up my fender. I just don't know what to do about all the messed up paperwork. Seems like every time I turn around, something is wrong with it. I told Eddy about it, but who knows if he'll really check into it or not. I don't understand why Sandy is doing this to me. I thought she was going to be a good friend."

Jack brought plates of scrambled eggs and toast to the table. He placed one in front of Shelby and one for himself. "Well, I'm sure there is a reasonable explanation. Eddy will check into things. I'm trying hard to feel bad for you, and all your troubles, but I don't want you out there anyway. There's too many things that can go wrong, and who's there to help you out? Lots of other men."

Shelby pushed the plate away. "Thanks, Jack, for all your support. I'm going to bed. I'm tired."

Jack finished his breakfast and cleaned up the kitchen while he stewed about wanting Shelby home. His phone rang.

"Is this Jack Mathews?"

"Yes. Who is calling?"

"Well, I'd rather not say but I wanted to call as a concerned friend."

"Really?"

"Well, I just wanted you to know that your wife, Shelby, is not exactly being faithful."

Jack felt his insides grow cold. "What does that mean?"

"Well, she has been seen messing around on location with other men."

Jack forced himself to take a deep, calming breath. "Really? And just what locations has she been messing around on?" he asked, stiffly.

"Well, the specifics aren't really necessary. We wouldn't want to get those men in any trouble, now would we? I mean after all, it's Shelby who is leading those men in the wrong direction."

"Really, and you expect me to take your word for this load of crap without specific information or names? I don't know who this is, and before I believe anything you're saying, you better come up with more than what you got."

"Well, I just thought you might want to know that your wife is being a slut."

"Well, I think you better give me your name, lady, so I can check you out and be sure you're telling me the truth."

The phone went dead. "Moron," Jack said to no one.

Jack felt sick. *Is the caller telling the truth? Is Shelby playing around? Surely, Shelby wouldn't do that to me.*

◊◊◊

The office was dark, except for the glowing computer screens. Sandy kept the computers on all the time. Betty had become very familiar with the files that Sandy had stored on her computers, so finding her call list and daily drivers load availability lists was not difficult. Betty brought the files up on the computer screen and pulled the phone out of her pocket, which she had taken from Eddy's office earlier. Eddy's office was always locked, so taking the phone when she did was a smart move.

The phone list was her first chore. She removed Shelby's real number from the list and put the number of the phone she had taken from Eddy in its place. Then she checked the phone by calling it from the office to make sure that Shelby's phone calls would come to that phone. After dialing the number, she answered it to see what kind of answering message was on it. Luckily, it had one of those automated voices. Next, she deleted Shelby's home number and her husband's cell phone number so that the only number Sandy would have for Shelby would be the phone in Betty's hand.

"I'll finally be rid of Shelby Mathews forever," Betty whispered to herself as she worked on the second part of her plan. She accessed the driver availability list and moved Shelby's name to the bottom. She realized that she would have to move Shelby's name to the bottom every day if her plan was going to succeed. Occasionally, Shelby would receive a call for a job when she wasn't able to get into the office. The phone she had taken would solve that problem. Betty knew that Shelby came to the office early in the mornings sometimes just to see what was going on and would land a job or two that way. If her plan worked, Shelby would get fed up with not working and quit.

◊◊◊

Shelby had been busy all day cleaning her house. Although she thought it strange that she had not heard from Sandy for a couple of days, she was actually enjoying the time off.

Jack came into the living room, "Well, it's about time you got this house cleaned up." He laughed and put his arms around Shelby's waist. He kissed her neck as she dusted the television screen.

"Yeah, someone needs to keep up with the dirt, 'cause my little house bitch isn't doing a very good job." Shelby giggled as Jack turned her around and kissed her passionately.

"Well, this house bitch needs the house maid to take a break."

"Really, and what might you have in mind?"

Jack led Shelby toward the backyard. "Come on. I have a surprise for you. Close your eyes."

"I'll fall, Jack."

"You'll be alright. I'll guide you. Keep your eyes closed."

"Okay."

"Okay, open your eyes." Sitting in front of Shelby was the prettiest pink sport bike she'd ever seen.

"Oh my god, Jack. It's beautiful." Shelby walked to the bike and touched the new paint job and shiny chrome handlebars. "Whose bike is this?" She assumed it belonged to a client or friend of Jack's.

"Yours."

Shelby turned toward Jack and jumped into his arms. "MINE? Oh, Jack! When did you get this? Can we afford it?"

Jack kissed her, put her down, and pointed out the special details. "Well, I got it a couple months ago from a lady who wanted to trade up. I airbrushed it with all these custom designs, decked it out with some chrome, and tuned up the engine. Yes, we can afford it. I'm back on payroll at work, at least part-time. It's all yours, my sweet baby."

"Oh, Jack, it's beautiful! Can I take it for a ride?"

"Sure, but it's not tagged or insured yet, so just around the block, okay?"

With Jack's help, Shelby pushed the bike into the cold afternoon air.

"You better get a coat," Jack said.

"I think with the gloves and helmet I should be warm enough for just around the block." She kissed him before she put on her helmet and got on the bike. She took off down the driveway, loving every shift of every gear as she rolled into the street.

Shelby was freezing by the time she pulled into the driveway after several times around the block. She parked the bike back inside the shop and took off her helmet. "If it wasn't so cold, I'd have really taken her for a spin. Baby, thank you so much; I love it."

They were standing, holding hands, admiring the bike when Shelby said, "I better get back inside. You never know when they'll call, and I'll be on the road. I want to make sure the house is good and clean before I go out."

Jack locked up the shop and walked with Shelby back to the house.

"I think I'll go to the yard in the morning and see what's happening. I'm not sure why I haven't been called out lately. Maybe things are a little slow."

◊◊◊

Sandy was perplexed. She ran through her computer files and printed out some inconsistencies. "Eddy, I need to talk to you," she said as she walked into his office.

"Yeah, I need to talk with you about some things, too."

Sandy put the files she had just printed out in front of Eddy. "Look at these. I think there is something wrong with my computer. Everything is connected to Shelby's assignments and job availability. Either there is a glitch in the program, or someone is messing with my computer."

Eddy looked over the assignments and compared them with printouts and found that several things had been changed. "This doesn't make any sense. These changes would have had to be made manually, unless there is something in the software causing the mistakes."

"I know, and that isn't all. Shelby's name keeps falling to the bottom of the list without being assigned a job."

"How is that happening?"

"I don't know, but it's causing a lot of confusion—especially for Shelby."

"No wonder she's been so upset lately." Eddy looked at the files again and then went with Sandy to her office to look at the computers. "Does this happen to every job she goes on?"

"No, it only happens every once in a while, but it seems to be only in Shelby's files and I don't know why."

"I'm not sure why it's happening either, so let's try and put a security block on your computer for now and see what happens."

"A security block? Do you think someone is getting into my computer?"

"Not sure, but I think the only way these things are getting changed is manually, and if you're not doing it, someone else is. Also, if it's something in the software we'll at least be eliminating the possibility for manual changes. Who besides you could make those changes?"

Sandy frowned, a little offended. "I think the security block is a great idea, but do you really think I'd sabotage one of my own drivers?"

"Of course not, but something is going on and we need to take out the obvious in order to find the problem."

"Alright, I'll get right on setting up a block. What was it you needed to talk with me about anyway?"

"Oh, I forgot…, I'll think about it and talk to you later."

"That's not the only problem," Sandy said. "Whenever I try and call Shelby, all I get is her voicemail. I called yesterday and left her a message for a load, and she never showed up. I had to send someone else."

"Maybe her phone's out or something. Did you call her house?"

"Yes, or at least I would have, but we don't have a home number for her. We don't even have an emergency contact, actually. I'm not what happened but her whole personal file seems to be missing a lot of information."

"That seems odd. I specifically remember getting all that information from her when she started. When did you notice the information missing?"

"Well, I just noticed it today, so it's hard to tell how long the information has been gone. Until lately, she has always answered her cell phone, so I never needed another number to get in touch with her. I don't know, maybe I need to go over to her house and check on her. This just isn't normal."

"We'll go over there after lunch today. Do you have a load for her?"

"Yes, I left her a message, but I guess I better get someone else to haul it until we find out what has happened to her."

◊◊◊

Shelby reached for her cell phone for the tenth time since breakfast. It had been four days, and she had not heard anything from Sandy. She hadn't called the office since she had been able to catch up with responsibilities at home. She was, however, becoming concerned and decided she would go to the office. *I want to know what the hell Sandy's problem is with me.* She grabbed her purse and keys, jumped in her car, and drove to the office.

Shelby opened the door to the office, but before she could get it closed Sandy yelled, "Where the hell have you been? Don't you ever answer your phone?"

"Excuse me? My phone hasn't rung once. I've been at home, waiting to get some work!"

"How can I assign you work if you don't answer your fucking phone? I had a job for you two days ago and you never even bothered letting me know you wouldn't be taking it. I had to send another driver and he delivered late because you didn't bother to check your messages or answer your phone."

Shelby was livid. "I NEVER GOT ANY PHONE CALLS OR MESSAGES!" She threw her phone onto Sandy's desk. "Check it! This is obviously another one of your paperwork mishaps. I don't see any other drivers having any problems with their paperwork. Just what is your damn problem with me anyway? I thought you were cool at first, but now I'm beginning to wonder."

Eddy and Tiff heard the women yelling and ran over to intervene. Eddy took charge. "Enough, both of you! Shelby, go to my office, and Sandy you sit down and cool off."

Shelby plopped down angrily in the dusty chair in Eddy's office.

Eddy came in and shut the door. "Now calm down. What is going on?"

"Honestly, I have no idea. Sandy says she's been calling me with jobs, but you can check my phone, Eddy, I haven't received any calls or messages from her."

"Okay, give me a minute to check things out. Sit here and calm down."

"Alright." Shelby crossed her arms.

Eddy left his office and went back to Sandy's. Sandy was sitting in her chair looking at Shelby's phone. "There's nothing on here but calls from her family. Nothing from me, but she could have deleted the messages."

Eddy took the phone. "Now, why would she do that, Sandy? Think about it? She *wants* to work, remember? Why would she delete anything from you?"

"I don't know, but I know I called her and got her voice message."

Eddy looked at the phone and then picked up Sandy's office phone. "Give me the number that you've been calling." Sandy pulled up the drivers list and gave Eddy the number. Eddy dialed the number and waited with the phone in his hand. The phone never rang. "It's not her number. Tiff, go ask

Shelby for her cell phone number." Tiff went into Eddy's office and came back shortly with Shelby's number written on a piece of paper.

"Here, Eddy."

Eddy took the paper and dialed the number. The phone in his hand rang. "This is her number. The number on your computer has been changed."

Sandy looked at the two numbers. "Oh my god, Eddy. I have never changed any of her numbers, and I sure haven't been doing anything to her paperwork, I swear."

"I know, but someone has been messing with her assignments and with her personal information. I need you to come into my office so we can get this straightened out. Then we need to get Shelby's personal information back into the computer under the security block."

Eddy entered his office with Sandy and Tiff on either side of him. There was obvious tension between the two women. "Shelby, we need to apologize to you for all the mishaps that have occurred over the last few months. These things have been done on Sandy's computer without our knowledge. Sandy has not been doing these things. In fact, until a few days ago, we didn't have security on our computers, so anyone could have messed with the paperwork. We now have security on the computers and we need to get your personal information again because someone has obviously deleted yours."

Sandy spoke next. "I'm sorry, Shelby. I really don't know how all this happened, but I assure you it was not me. I like you, you're a good driver, and until all this stuff started happening, one of my best. Please forgive me for being such a bitch to you."

"It's alright. I didn't want to think it was you, but I just didn't know what to think. Do you have any idea who might have done it?"

"No, but when we find out, they'll be fired immediately," Eddy said. He turned to Sandy, "I'm sorry too, Sandy. I should have known you wouldn't sabotage your own driver."

"I'd be cutting my own throat. Without my drivers, I don't have a job."

Shelby and Sandy hugged each other and went back to Sandy's office. Sandy sat at her desk and pulled up Shelby's personal information file. "I have to get all this information again. I also gave your load away for today, but I'll put you at the top of the list for the next load. If you don't have any plans this evening, maybe we need to get together for some beers."

"Sounds like a great idea." As Shelby shared her information, she was relieved that it wasn't Sandy who'd been sabotaging her. Shelby noticed Betty's name on the work board across the room. *Could be Betty behind all the trouble?* she wondered.

◊◊◊

Jack had come home early from his job, but Shelby wasn't home. *She didn't call to tell me she's going on a job. Maybe she's at the store*, he thought. He opened the door and a white envelope with his name on the front fell to the ground. Jack went inside the house and opened the envelope.

Mr. Mathews,

I had to write to you and let you know that I saw your wife with another man the other night. They were at a local bar drinking, dancing, and kissing each other. I hate to tell you such bad news, but if it had been my wife, I'd want someone to tell me. She has also been seen on several locations getting very friendly with other men. I truly am sorry to have to tell you these hurtful things but thought you should know.

Sincerely,
A Friend

Jack looked the letter over again and then put it back in the envelope. He wasn't sure what he wanted to do about it yet. He couldn't believe it—*Shelby isn't like that, but I did receive that phone call a few weeks ago…. And then she went out with Sandy last night for a few beers. I love her and want to trust her. I'll keep this letter for now and see if anything else surfaces before I confront her.*

CHAPTER SIXTEEN

Betty and Ted were spooning in Betty's truck sleeper. "How is she getting away with everything?" she lamented. "If one of us had done half of the things she's done in the last few months, we would have been fired. I have tried everything I can to get rid of her, but I guess I can't expect too much. Sandy's an idiot who can't see a bad driver when she's in front of her."

"Shelby isn't that bad of a driver. I've been on several jobs with her and she does okay."

Betty jumped up, gathered her clothes, and began to dress. "You fucking moron."

"What did I do?"

"It's not what you did Ted, it's what you said." She poked him in the chest with her finger. "She's a terrible driver and would never have lasted this long if she hadn't manipulated the boss. She has to go, Ted—one way or another."

She sat in the driver's seat and lit a cigarette. Ted began to put on his clothes. "I thought you gave those up?"

"I did, but I still have one occasionally, especially when I'm stressed."

"What do you have to be stressed about?"

"I can't stand her. She has to go, Ted. I can't work here any longer with her taking our loads, moving in on our turf and, above all, knowing that she knows about us. Every day I wonder when she's going to drop the bombshell and tell everyone. She hasn't even been in the trucking business for a year yet, and it seems like every trucker in the country is willing to help her out. What's up with all that? It took me years to establish myself in this business, and she's does it in just a few months. Maybe I should dye my hair blonde, get a boob job, and wear pink boots."

Ted moved close to kiss Betty. "I like your boobs the way they are, and I don't think you'd look good as a blonde."

She turned her head. "Shut up, Ted. I've decided it's her or me. Little Shelby has to go, and if you're not going to help me, you'll have to get your play time at home from that fat wife of yours."

Ted liked having sex with Betty because it was dangerous, not because he couldn't get it at home. He wasn't sure why Betty thought he wasn't getting it from Annabel. Still, he didn't want Annabel to know about him and Betty. He really wasn't quite sure what getting rid of Shelby meant, *But it can't be that bad,* he reasoned. "Okay," he exhaled. "How do we get rid of Shelby?"

Betty threw her cigarette out the window and turned around in the driver's seat so her back was against the door. She placed her feet up into the seat and wrapped her arms around her knees. "We have to get rid of her permanently. No Shelby, no problem."

"You mean kill her?"

"Well…not up close and personal. We'll have to make it look like an accident. Don't use the word kill. We aren't going to kill her—just help the little angel get her wings a little sooner. After all, little Shelby wouldn't want to grow old and get all wrinkled, would she?"

"I guess that would be better, but how are we going to help her get her wings?"

Betty grabbed another cigarette and put her legs over the steering wheel. "Well, Sandy took my access away from the computer. I can't get us put on any jobs automatically with her, so we'll have to just set things up when we can. I do need to get a hold of another one of her truck keys. I lost the one I took a while back when we took her shit. I think they still have those locked up in Eddy's office."

"Do you want me to get it the next time I'm in there?"

"Do you think you can get it without anyone catching on to what you're doing? You need to be discrete."

"Course I can. All I have to do is pretend I'm getting one for my truck because I left mine at home, which I do all the time. Why do you need her key anyway?"

"It makes things easier when you need to make little adjustments to equipment, if you know what I mean," Betty explained as she sat up straight and threw her cigarette stub out the window. "You get that key and I'll try and probe Sandy for information on our next big run and see if Shelby will be on it too. I have an idea for getting rid of her if we get sent out of state this weekend. If not, I need you to get that key as soon as possible, because I have another idea that might work if we don't happen to get sent on the same job. Hell, it might even work out even better if we don't get sent with her. If things happen like I hope they will, Shelby won't come back in one piece. The only thing I hate is that I won't be there to see it."

"Sure, I'll get it tomorrow but…" Before Ted could finish, his cell phone rang. "Yeah honey, I'm coming. The job just took longer than expected. Yeah, we're still taking the kids out. Okay, I'm on my way, just have to clean out my truck and turn in paperwork. Yeah, okay. Me too, see you soon." Ted hung up and went to open the door. "I have to go, Betty. I promised to take Annabel and the kids to Mickey Ds."

Betty rolled her eyes and crossed her arms. "Like that fat cow needs more fried foods and those kids need more junk. Whenever I need you here, you up and leave me to go home to her." Betty pouted, pretending to care if he left.

"Look, Betty, I want to stay, but I promised her. I'll get the key tomorrow and email you later." Ted reached to kiss Betty, but she pushed him away.

Ted left.

Once again Betty put her legs over the steering wheel and stared out the front windshield. *Once Shelby is eliminated, I'll have my life back. Maybe I can get Sandy fired…and Eddy transferred. After all, they were nothing but problems for me, too. I can run this place better than any of those idiots. Then… maybe I can get Ted's wife out of the picture and have the boy toy all to myself.* Her last thought snapped her back to reality. *What am I thinking? Ted, every day…all day long? Oh hell no! I like the sex, but being around him all the time?…No way.*

Betty was proud of herself. *I'll do what I have to so I can get what I deserve—the top.*

◊◊◊

Shelby arrived early the next morning to get ready for her Arizona trip. She was surprised to see Betty and Ted in the break room with the other drivers. The two never associated with the other drivers unless they had to, but today they were actually conversing over the Arizona job. Shelby got her paperwork from her box and found a place at the table. "Hey, guys. How is everyone today?" Several drivers responded to Shelby, but most were busy discussing the up-coming long haul. Ted ended his conversation with Betty, got up, and went into Eddy's office.

It wasn't long before Sandy came into the lounge and handed out assignment sheets. "Okay, I have ten of you leaving for Arizona. You'll pick up the sand Saturday and bring it back here by Sunday for delivery on Monday. I want senior drivers helping younger drivers find the yard and getting loaded. This is a big job, and we want to keep this customer, so don't screw this up. Most everyone will stay at the truck stop at mile marker one. No need to rush this run. You'll have plenty of time. Just be back by Monday for delivery."

Everyone in the room understood the instructions and how important it was to get loaded and back on time. Shelby liked running the long hauls, especially when she got to run with the senior drivers. However, she hoped she wouldn't get stuck in the pack with Ted and Betty.

Sandy looked at two of the senior drivers. "Shotgun Rider and Speedy, you run with Shelby and make sure she finds the place."

"Sure, no problem," said Shotgun Rider. Shelby liked Shotgun Rider. He was always nice and never left her behind when she ran with him. Some of the other drivers would get annoyed at her when she lagged behind, especially when she was in her old truck. She was able to keep up in the new one.

Everyone got up, gathered their things, and moved toward the door, still talking about the job. Shelby conversed with White Eyes and Phantom 309 as they walked to their trucks. "I'm excited about getting to go west this time. I brought my camera, so maybe I can get a few pictures while we're out there."

"Yeah, there are some pretty mountains on the other end of New Mexico," White Eyes said. They chit-chatted for a while about the scenic west, neither of them noticing Betty watching them from the corner of the room with a glint in her eye.

◊◊◊

The trip to Arizona was an incredible ride for Shelby. She had already been into New Mexico as far west as the oil patches near Artesia. Now she was going to get to see the mountains near the big city. Shelby liked New Mexico. The culture was rich in the Native American life and rituals. Shelby held her camera to the window as they rolled through the mountains and took several pictures. She wanted to stop and take some good shots but didn't want to upset her coworkers. "Oh wow, look at the beautiful scenery out here! It's gorgeous."

Luscious came over the radio. "Shelby, you haven't been in these mountains before?"

"No, this is my first time, but I'm definitely going to get Jack to bring me here for a vacation."

"Hey, Speedy. How far are we from the truck stop?" Shotgun Rider asked.

"I guess about three hours. Why?"

"Well, you've been running us hard and heavy now for several hours. I think we should break for lunch. I'm hungry."

"If you'd said something earlier, we'd have stopped. I think we can stop at the Casino up here. They have pretty good food on their buffet."

"That sounds like a good idea," Shelby chimed in. "I need to use the little girls' room. And maybe get some better pictures there, too."

Betty came over the radio. "Speedy, Ted and I are going on to the truck stop at the one marker. We'll see you guys there later."

"Okay."

Shelby was glad that Betty and Ted weren't going to stop with them, but she wondered why Betty never wanted to hang with the other drivers.

"Alright, guys, I see a bunch of parking in the back. Be careful coming through that curve there, it's tight."

◊◊◊

Ted called Betty on her cell phone. "Hey, why aren't we stopping to eat? I'm hungry."

"We have to get to the truck stop before everyone else, Ted. I have a plan to get rid of Shelby tonight. Didn't you get my email?"

"I didn't have time to read anything this morning. I'll read it when I get to the truck stop, but I'm hungry."

"Suck it up, Ted. You can eat at the truck stop at the one mile marker. Now I have a couple calls to make. Just drive."

"Fine."

Betty placed a call to a local rental car agency. "Yes, I need to rent a car for the evening." She listened to the agent. "Yes, I have a Visa card." Betty read off the sixteen digits, the expiration date, and her zip code. "I'll have a taxi bring me to pick up the car in a few hours. Thanks."

Betty got on the radio with Ted. "Alright, I have everything set up for tonight."

"What is set up?"

"Never mind, Ted. I'll tell you later. Just drive."

"Okay, but I'm really hungry."

"We'll be there in a little while, Ted. JUST DRIVE."

◊◊◊

The team arrived at the Casino and found plenty of parking places. Shelby went in and found the ladies' room. Before she could get back to her truck, however, Jack called her cell phone. "How are things going, sweet baby?"

"Things are okay. No problems yet. We have to be in the sand yard at 7:00 a.m. so I'm going to take a short nap, shower, eat some dinner, and watch a movie until I fall asleep. There's talk about coming back for another load after we deliver this one to Farmington. So I might not be back for a few days, baby."

"Okay, how many drivers are with you?"

She was curious, he'd never asked that question before. "I don't know, several, I guess. Why?"

"Oh, just making sure you got some help if you need it. I want you to be safe."

"I always try to be. I'll call you before I go to bed."

"Alright, talk to you later."

Shelby couldn't help but feel that something was up with Jack.

◊◊◊

"Get up, lazy bones! We're all going into the restaurant for dinner." Shelby woke up with a start to darkness in her truck. She used her hands to push her hair back and then moved her curtain to see who was pounding on her door. Fastman and Phantom 309 where standing by her truck. She smiled and opened the window a little. "Hey, guys. Give me a few minutes to pull myself together and I'll be right there."

"Alright, we'll save you a place. You're buying, right?"

"Uh, NO!"

They all laughed. "See you in a minute." Shelby brushed her hair and touched up her makeup. She put on her coat, slipped a wool cap over her head, and put up her collar before stepping out into the freezing temperatures.

She locked her truck before heading toward the restaurant. In the parking lot, Shelby noticed several men standing in front of their trucks, talking with a man who had his hood open. Shelby waved to them.

Suddenly, from out of nowhere, a small grey four-door car came around the trucks, headed straight for Shelby. With her head and ears covered, she didn't hear or see the vehicle. The men who hung out around the trucks raced toward Shelby. "LOOK OUT!" they called, "LOOK OUT!" It took Shelby several seconds to understand what they were saying, but before she could, one of the men grabbed Shelby and pulled her out of the way of the racing car. She slipped and fell on her rear end.

The car screeched its wheels around through the parking lot. Another two men ran over to Shelby and the others. "You guys okay?"

"Yeah, GO! GO GET THAT CRAZY BITCH DRIVING THAT CAR! SHE MIGHT KILL SOMEONE THE WAY SHE'S DRIVING!"

"Are you okay, miss?"

Shelby was still in shock, "Yeah, I'm fine."

"I'm Little Mule," he said, sticking out his hand. Shelby shook it. "Wish I could say we met under better circumstances."

She nodded. "Shelby. Nice to meet you."

"Stay here." Little Mule ran to his truck. The other drivers who had witnessed the incident headed toward the parking lot exit and tried to head off the car. Little Mule got on his radio. "Any of you drivers on that back row got your ears on? There's a car driving out of control in the parking lot, and if you can, I want it stopped. It almost ran over a lady driver in the front row."

Little Mule didn't wait to find out if any of the other drivers heard his call. He headed back toward Shelby who was still sitting on the ground near a light pole. The parking lot, however, was evidence enough that several drivers heard his call. Trucks that had been sitting still were moving forward and backwards in an attempt to block the now frantic driver. The drivers who were on foot had made their way to the exit, but didn't know if they would be able to stop the crazy driver.

"Move up, Dream Weaver, and try and block her."

Dream Weaver moved his truck forward in front of the car, but the car was too quick and made it around the truck before he could block her. "Shit, she went around me. Bad Company your truck's close to the exit. Angle it out and see if you can block her. What the hell is up with this crazy person?"

"Got it, Dream Weaver. Baby Boy, you move your truck backwards and see if we can block the whole exit."

Bad Company moved forward while Baby Boy moved back. It seemed to the drivers that maybe they had the car blocked. "Shit, she went in between us. She's headed toward the guys standing in the exit and it doesn't look like she's going to stop, either. I hope they get out of the way—she's not slowing down."

Little Mule had made his way back to Shelby, along with a couple of other drivers who had noticed what was happening. Little Mule helped Shelby to her feet. "You're sure you're alright?"

"Yeah, I'm fine. What was that all about?"

"Oh, probably just a drunk." The group of drivers standing with Shelby watched as the truckers in the parking lot did their best to stop the driver.

As the car approached the exit, Shelby moved her gloved hand toward her mouth. "Oh god, that crazy driver isn't going to stop. I hope those guys move, or someone's going to get hurt! Move guys! Just let her go," Shelby called.

"I think they're smart enough to know they can't stop that car with their bodies." Little Mule tried to reassure Shelby as they watched the spectacle unfold near the exit.

"Hey, Dream Weaver. This is Detroit. I'm coming into the truck stop off the service road. Tell the guys to let the car through, and I'll try and put her in the ditch out here."

"Alright, Detroit, I'll try and get their attention."

The car was weaving in and out of trucks after making a U-turn at the entrance. The driver apparently didn't want to hit the men standing in the exit and sped through the parking lot looking for another exit.

"Damn it, get the fuck out of my way you idiots!" Betty was getting nervous as she frantically looked for another way out of the parking lot. "Fine, stand there, you shit heads, and I'll run you down. You already ruined my plan by saving that little bitch, so running you down will only make up for it."

Meanwhile, Dream Weaver made his way to the men standing in the exit. "Okay Detroit, she's all yours. The guys are going to let her through."

"Gotcha, Dream Weaver, let her through."

Betty headed the car one more time straight for the exit and was happy when the men in the exit moved aside to let her out. She hoped it was dark enough that none of them would notice her, but at this point she didn't care. This attempt at getting rid of Shelby was too up close and personal. She realized, as she sped out of the parking lot that she would have to make the next attempt less personal.

Outside the parking lot, Betty felt she had a clear shot to her friend's house, but was taken by surprise when Detroit had his truck headed straight for her. She was either going to have to take him head on or head for the ditch. Betty chose the ditch, but with her driving skills, she easily maneuvered the little vehicle in and out of the ditch without too much difficulty. "Asshole, you must think you're something, too. Well, you have no idea who you're dealing with."

Betty sped away down the freeway just as the police were running lights and sirens up the freeway on the opposite side toward the truck stop. Betty dropped her speed and blended into the night traffic. She was glad she had removed the rental company's license plate and had replaced it with one she had lifted from a salvage yard the day before leaving for Arizona. She would get the car washed and replace the plate before returning it to the rental agency.

As the cops questioned Shelby about what had happened, the truckers where putting their trucks back into their parking spots. "I'm being really honest here, sir. I did not see the driver. In fact, if it wasn't for Little Mule, I'd have been road kill. The driver was driving very erratically all over the parking lot. Maybe he or she was drunk or something."

The officer took Shelby and Little Mule's names and got a partial description of the driver and car. No one was able to get a complete plate, but the cops took the partial of what appeared to be an out of state plate.

The drivers who'd tried to help stop the car in the parking lot gathered around Little Mule and Shelby. "Well, we tried Little Mule, but she got away."

Shelby spoke up. "Are you sure it was a female driving?"

"Yeah, pretty sure. She had dark hair and evil looking eyes. She didn't look drunk, she looked like she was out for blood or something."

"Really…"

"Well, she's gone now," Little Mule interrupted. "And, I'm hungry. Anyone want to join me for dinner?"

Shelby looked at her watch. "Oh, damn. I was supposed to have joined my friends for dinner an hour ago. They must think I'm really rude."

"Well hell, we were all going to the restaurant anyway; we'll go with you and explain things. How angry will they be when they find out you almost got ran over by a crazy lady?"

"You have a point."

"Well, look who finally woke up?" joked White Eyes when he saw Shelby enter with the other drivers. "And she brought her body guards with her."

"Sorry guys, but you'll never believe what happened in the parking lot." Shelby pointed to her new friends. "These are the guys who saved my life tonight." Shelby and her new friends joined her coworkers at the table.

"Saved your life? Alright, what did you get yourself into this time, Shelby?"

All the drivers laughed and talked in detail about what had happened in the parking lot. They talked about their jobs and the loads they were carrying. Shelby enjoyed the company.

It was getting late when the drivers decided they needed to get some rest for work tomorrow. Shelby walked out with the crowd, but Little Mule seemed to be hanging close by her side. In fact, he seemed to have stayed close the entire evening. Shelby decided she needed to break the attachment and head to her truck before he got the wrong idea. She did find him very attractive, and considered that maybe it was her attachment she needed to break. "Well, thanks, Little Mule," she said, turning to face him. "I truly appreciate you saving my life tonight."

"No problem, Ms. Shelby, glad I was there. Would you like for me to walk you to your truck?"

Shelby wanted to say yes, but she knew she had to decline. "No, I believe I'll be safe with all these drivers out here. But thank you anyway."

"Alright, you be careful and maybe we'll see each other out on the road sometime." Little Mule walked towards his truck and Shelby walked towards hers.

"Maybe so, Little Mule, maybe so."

CHAPTER SEVENTEEN

"Hey, home girls. How's it going?" The two girls Shelby had befriended at the fuel stop near the yard turned to greet her as she walked past.

"Hi, Shelby. How's it going?"

"Going good, Josie and Fressy. Are you girls behaving yourselves?"

"Nope, wouldn't be any fun if we did."

"Good answer. How's the coffee?"

"Decaf just like you like, fresh and hot."

"That's my girls."

"So, where you headed, Shelby?"

"Headed to Mississippi." Shelby took her receipt for her fuel and used her reward card for her coffee.

"Wow, that's a long haul. Are you running by yourself or with other drivers?

"Oh, there are eight of us going, but most of us are running alone until we get to the location. We do that a lot. It makes it easier when you can travel at your own speed and not have to hurry or wait for anyone. I can sleep, eat, and pee when I want without worrying about inconveniencing someone else. We just have to be on location at the same time."

"Be careful, Shelby. Don't let the snakes and gators get ya."

"See you girls in about a week."

Shelby ran into Rude Dog Rider, Southwest Grizzly, and Cowboy in the parking lot. "Hey, guys. Headed to Mississippi?"

"Yeah, we'll be right behind ya, little Shelby," Cowboy said sweetly.

"See you in Mississippi, guys. Be careful."

"You be careful, Ms. Shelby. We've heard about the things that happen to you."

Southwest Grizzly and Rude Dog Rider laughed. "Yeah, you're the one that needs to be careful."

"Okay, I'll be careful, but hopefully nothing will occur on this trip."

Shelby knew she'd be able to make it into Louisiana before she'd have to shut down for the night. She was excited about this trip. She was going to get to see a new state: Mississippi. Except for the little mishaps that had happened to her over the last few months, Shelby was enjoying the traveling required on her job.

◊◊◊

Shelby figured she would arrive at the truck stop within an hour of when everyone had agreed to meet before leaving the yard. She wasn't in a hurry, but the roads weren't marked, so she was taken by surprise when the driver she just passed came over the CB with a warning, "Be careful running too fast down here in these parts, little lady. Them there police like to generate that revenue for their little towns."

"But I'm only rolling 65."

"Yeah, and down here that's speeding. The people down here like it slow and easy. You'll find 55 and below is more the speed for the drivers in these parts."

"Wow, 55, how does anyone get anywhere down here running that slow on a freeway?"

"I know what you're saying, but if you're going to run that fast be careful. They'll write you in a heartbeat."

"I appreciate that, driver. They don't mark their roads very well either, do they?"

"Nope."

Just as Shelby brought her speed down to 55, a local cop came around the corner in the on-coming traffic. "Look, there's one of Mississippi's finest."

"Thank you driver for letting me know. I could have gotten myself a big ticket if you hadn't said something. What do they call you?"

"They call me JJ."

"I just go by Shelby."

"Nice to meet you, Shelby. You take it nice and slow down here and you'll be alright."

"I will. Thanks again, JJ, for saving my bacon from those locals."

"No problem. Be safe, Shelby."

"You too, JJ."

◊◊◊

"Okay Ted, take the next exit and make a right down that narrow street."

"Betty, are you sure we should be taking our trucks down that road?"

"Yes, Ted, I've been down it many times. There is a parking lot at the end of the block we can park in and then walk to Samoan's."

"Why are we going to this woman's house again?"

"Oh, god, Ted. I told you I need to buy something from her."

"What could you possibly need from a witch doctor?"

"She's not a witch doctor, she practices voodoo."

"Same difference."

"No, you idiot, they're not the same. Now just pull into that parking lot and shut the hell up."

They parked their trucks and walked two blocks to Samoan's house. Betty knocked on the rickety screen door several times before a long, grey-haired woman appeared. She wore a long cape-like dress of vibrant colors. "Betty, how are you, dear?" The woman took the hook off the secured door and let her two visitors into her dark, cluttered home.

"I've been fine, Samoan. How have you been?"

The woman pointed to a couple of chairs next to a table in what appeared to be a dining room. "Come sit and have a cup of tea with me Betty and…"

"This is my friend Ted, and yes, we would love some tea."

"Very close friend, I see. But be careful, Betty. He does not belong to you."

Betty wasn't surprised at anything Samoan said to her. She knew her ability, but Ted was taken by surprise. Ted whispered in Betty's ear. "How does she know that?"

Betty whispered back, "Shut up, Ted. I'll explain later. Just sit and be quiet."

Samoan went into a kitchen behind a swinging wood door. She came back with a tray of cups and a pot, placing it on the table. She placed a cup of tea in front of each of her guests and then sat in a chair at the head of the table. After sipping at her tea, she looked up and said, "So, you want something slithering from me, do you, Betty?"

"Yes, Samoan, three if you have them."

"The reason for them is not wise, Betty."

"It's something I have to do, Samoan, and although I know you're not in agreement with my desire to eliminate the obstacle I have in my life right now, I need you to just let me do what I must do."

"Oh, I'm not in any position to stop you from doing as you wish, but you're right. I do not agree."

Ted sat quietly and didn't hear Betty ask for anything from the woman. He figured she must have called her ahead of time.

"You're not a very strong man, are you, Ted?"

"Oh, I can lift quite a bit of weight if I have a mind to."

"Not much of a mind I see, either." The woman took her focus off Ted and put it back on Betty. "So, you wish to buy three?"

"Yes, three poisonous, the more poisonous the better."

"Betty, this is a dangerous road you travel, but I'll supply you with what you wish."

"I appreciate it."

"Finish your tea. I'll take you to the backyard and you can pick the ones you want. Sip slowly, it's good for your soul."

Betty ignored the instruction and drank her tea in a hurry. She was here for one thing and she wanted to get on with it. The woman sipped slowly and then eventually moved toward the wooden swing door of her kitchen. "Come, Betty, I'll show you my pets. They're costly, so I hope you're prepared."

"I have a pocketful, Samoan. You could give me a discount."

"No discount for these, Betty. They're hard to replace."

"Alright. I don't care what they cost."

Ted was a little frightened by the dark swamp-like atmosphere of the backyard. Weeping willow trees surrounded the house and the yard was filled with cages containing different types of snakes and reptiles.

"Betty this place is creepy. Can we get out of here?" Ted whispered as they followed Samoan to a group of cages under a carport.

"Oh, shut up, Ted."

"I see your friend is a little unnerved being in my garden."

"He's a pansy. Don't pay him any mind."

Samoan showed Betty several different types of snakes and suggested her favorites. "I think these three would do what you want them to do."

"Tell me how much you want, cage them up, and I'll be on my way."

"They're three of my favorites, I can't take less than $200 a piece."

"TWO HUNDRED DOLLARS A PIECE? You're out of your mind, Samoan."

"No, Betty, my mind is sound. Perhaps you're the one who is not one with your mind."

Betty pulled the cash out of her pocket and handed Samoan $600. "These snakes had better do what I want or I'm coming back for my money, my friend."

"They will do all they need to do, but you're welcome to bring them back if you like." Samoan handled each snake as if they were her children and gently placed each one into their own cage. "Oh, my sweet baby, I shall miss you most." She kissed the snake and allowed it to wrap itself around her arm. "Take care of my pets, Betty."

Betty grabbed one of the cages, and Ted took the other two. "For the kind of money I just gave you for these slimy things, I'll grill them on a barbecue if I want."

The old woman led the two out of her home and to the front porch. "Remember, Betty, vengeance will only bring about more vengeance. Be careful my friend, I read your future to be full of much confinement, and your friend Ted doesn't have a long life span."

"Thanks, Samoan." Betty waved goodbye over her head as she and Ted walked toward their trucks. Betty and Ted heard the woman's last words to them but Betty didn't seem to care.

Ted was shaken, however. "What did she mean I don't have a long life span?"

Betty was trying to keep the cage from touching her leg. "Don't get yourself all worked up over that old woman and her bullshit. She's full of more crap then you are, Ted. Now, help me put these damn things in my storage compartment and let's get the hell out of here. We need to get to the truck stop before the others wonder where we've been."

◊◊◊

The truck stop was small, and the place was packed with customers. Shelby found a table where a lady named Rose brought her a menu. "What can I get for you to drink, sweetie?"

"I'll have water with lemon if you don't mind."

"I'll be right back. The special today is ham and beans with greens on the side."

"Thanks, I'll look at the menu for a little while."

The menu had a few things that she liked, but was mostly full of good old Southern cooking.

Rose came back to her table with her water, a basket of bread, and silverware. "What can I get for you, honey?"

"I'll take a chef salad with ranch dressing, please."

"No problem. Be right back."

Shelby sipped at her water while she watched the people in the café. Everyone seemed to know each other and it was nice watching the neighborly behavior that was so hard to find these days.

Rose brought Shelby her salad. "Okay, if you need anything just yell. We're kind of busy tonight, so you really might have to yell."

"Thanks, Rose. Is it always this busy in here?"

"Yeah, most of the time. When you're the only café in town people tend to flock to the gossip spot."

Shelby finished her meal and was about ready to leave when Betty and Ted came through the door. Shelby decided to drink the last of her water and say goodbye to Rose, that way she wouldn't have to cross paths with the two. There were a couple open tables at the back of the restaurant, but Shelby figured Betty was too lazy to walk that far since they sat at a dirty one near the front door.

Unfortunately for Rose, the table they had chosen was one of hers. Betty pointed to spots on the table as Rose did her best to clear and clean the table for the less-than-patient guest. "What can I get for you today?"

"A clean table to sit at would have been nice when we came in, but I'll take tea and so will he, sugared if you have it."

"We have sugar on the table, ma'am."

"Of course. We should have gone down the street, Ted. These little rinky-dinky places never have anything you want."

Ted nodded his head in agreement while looking at the menu Rose had just placed in front of him. Betty sat sideways in her chair crossing her legs outward in the walkway, making people have to go around the table in order to get by while she looked at her menu. "Told you they never have any real food in places like this. Guess I'll have to settle for a hamburger."

"I think I'm going to try the special."

"Oh god, you ain't getting into my truck tonight after eating beans."

Rose brought the couple their tea and took their order. "We're in a bit of a hurry, so if you could tell that cook of yours to make it snappy."

Rose pointed around the room. "As you can see, ma'am, we are pretty busy, but I'll see if he can put a rush on it."

"Well, he better hurry if you want me to eat here again. You know what they say, the customer always gets what the customer wants."

Rose took the menus and Shelby could tell Rose didn't like Betty at all. "Yes ma'am."

Shelby decided to sit for a while and see how much more of an ass Betty was going to make out of herself. It didn't take long for that to happen when Rose brought Betty and Ted their food. Ted looked at his with anticipation as he took his fork and began to eat.

Betty, however, looked hers over and sure enough found a flaw. "I asked for mustard, there is no mustard on this burger."

"The mustard is on the table ma'am, right there."

"But I wanted it put on the burger for me."

Shelby could tell Rose was losing patience with Betty. Rose picked up the mustard bottle off the table, picked up Betty's plate, and took it back to the kitchen. It took Rose about two seconds to put the mustard on Betty's hamburger before she returned and placed the plate in front of Betty.

With Rose still standing there, Betty looked over her burger again. "Thank you. See, Ted, never just accept something without checking it out first. Most of these places hire people without any education and they just don't know much of anything."

Rose's face flushed with anger, but she let the comment slide and left the table. As Betty was placing her mouth around the rather large burger, Shelby got up from her table and walked to where the two were sitting. "You know, Betty, you're a smart gal and a good trucker. If you'd just be nice to people, and not make such an ass out of yourself, life would be a lot more pleasant not only for you but for the rest of us."

Shelby was surprised when the other customers applauded her remarks. She hadn't realized she was talking that loud, but the other guests appreciated her putting Betty in her place. Betty almost choked on her food and Shelby made a quick exit before Betty could respond.

Betty fumed. "Bitch," she muttered under her breath. She threw her half-eaten burger on the plate and slid her chair back. "Hurry up, Ted. I want to get out of this rat hole."

Before leaving, Shelby stopped at the register, paid her bill, and gave Rose a large tip. Rose tried to protest her generosity. Shelby said, "I know that woman will probably not tip you. I'm really sorry she was so horrible to you."

"Thank you. I'm working my way through college and hope before too long I won't have to deal with people like her anymore. I really wanted to dump that plate of food on her head."

Shelby laughed "I don't blame you. You showed great restraint."

◊◊◊

Betty complained all the way back to her truck. "I can't believe she talked to me like that in front of all those people. Where the hell does she get off?" She opened her storage compartment to check on the snakes. "So, my little killers, you need to do a good job for me tomorrow and get rid of that witch, okay?"

The snakes slithered about in the confinement of their cages, causing Ted to groan with worry.

"They better do what I want, or there will be hell to pay." Betty slammed the compartment shut and climbed into her truck. Ted followed, but Betty turned to him and said, "I'm not in the mood, Ted. Sleep in your own truck tonight." She turned, stepped into her truck, and closed and locked the door.

CHAPTER EIGHTEEN

The group of sand haulers rolled in single-file to the location. Slick Stick and Phantom 309 were the first to arrive and went to check things out. Shelby tagged along. She felt better about getting into position when she knew the situation.

Betty and Ted stayed with their trucks. Once she was sure everyone was out of sight, she told Ted to get the snake cages. "Don't you think we should wait until later to put them in her sleeper?"

"I'm doing it now." Betty climbed into Shelby's sleeper and pulled the curtains closer together. Then she and Ted released the three snakes.

◊◊◊

It took a couple of hours to get the first four trucks unloaded on location and get the last four backed into position and hooked up for unloading. As Shelby returned to her truck, she paused. She did not remember pulling her curtain closed all the way. She rolled her truck down the road and turned behind the other drivers onto the split highway that led home. There was a rattling noise coming from her sleeper but it didn't sound mechanical. The sound continued to bother her, so she reached back with her left hand to pull the sleeper curtain back. "OH SHIT!" Shelby screamed over the CB. "GUYS, THERE ARE SNAKES IN MY TRUCK!"

Shelby's scream alerted the snakes and they began to look for somewhere to hide from the noise and the light that spilled into their resting spot. Shelby closed the curtain as quickly as she could, causing her truck to swerve. "HELP ME, GUYS, I'M SERIOUS! THERE ARE REAL FUCKING SNAKES IN MY SLEEPER, AND THEY'RE MOVING. DAMN IT, THERE IS ONE COMING TOWARD ME!"

Slick Stick said over the radio, "Shelby, what the hell is going on?"

"Princess, did you say snakes?" Cowboy asked.

Shelby was busy trying to find a place to pull over while keeping an eye on the snake that was now slithering under the curtain and coming toward her feet to respond. "OH MY GOD!" Shelby screamed and slammed on her brakes, bringing her truck to a stop between the side of the road and the middle of the lane she was traveling in. She managed to pull her air brakes and put on her emergency flashers. Then she jumped out of her truck, and caught one of the snakes in her door as she slammed it shut. She ran across the two lanes to the middle median, almost getting hit by a car that honked and flipped her off. Once she reached what she thought was a safe spot in the grass, she leaned over and threw up what was left of her breakfast.

Her abandoned truck brought traffic to a crawl. Several truck drivers were on the CB trying to find out what was causing the hold up. Slick Stick tried to get Shelby on the radio but she was stranded on the median.

"Phantom 309 can you see if Shelby is behind you."

"She isn't and her truck is in the roadway. I'm going back to see."

"Oh shit, what is it with that girl? She is always getting herself into something. I'll be right behind you. I missed that turn around and I got to go to the next one."

There was chatter on the radio:

"Hey, does anyone know what is going on in the westbound lane?"

"Not sure yet, driver. Only thing I heard was a woman scream that she had a snake or something in her truck."

"Damn."

"I'm just about to the truck causing the slow down. I'll let ya know."

"The halted truck has half a snake hanging out the driver's side door. I'm guessing the lady on the median is the driver. There are a couple other trucks already stopped. What do you know…the disco lights just showed up. I'm going to stop and see what's up."

The driver got out of his truck and joined Shelby and several others on the median. The patrol car pulled up, a policeman got out and walked up to the assembly of people. "What's going on?" he asked the first person he approached.

"This poor lady trucker was attacked by snakes that somehow got into her sleeper."

"Has anyone checked out the truck?"

"No, see that snake hanging partway out of her door? How do you feel about snakes?"

"Snakes, plural? You're sure there are more?"

"She said she saw at least three."

"Let me go speak with her."

The cop talked with Shelby and then went to her truck to check it out. The snake was caught but not dead and was frantically trying to get loose. Shelby watched from a distance and when the snake wriggled and writhed against her door, she vomited again.

"Are you going to be alright, ma'am?" A woman came over and put her hand on Shelby's.

"Yeah, I just can't stand snakes."

"I understand; I don't like them either."

The cop didn't know if the snake was poisonous and got on his radio to contact Animal Control, as well as request back up from traffic control. He went back to the median. "Okay, I've got Animal Control on the way. If you're not with this woman I need you all to get in your vehicles and clear out of here."

Most of the people complied. The only drivers who stayed were Shelby's coworkers. Cowboy talked with Shelby while Slick Stick and Phantom 309 talked with the cop.

"Well, Princess, looks like you caught yourself a few friends," Cowboy said.

"I guess, but I have no idea how they got into my truck or how long they've been there. God, I think I'm going to lose it again just thinking about those things."

"Don't worry, Shelby, they probably got in when we were on location."

"I hope so. I hate to think I've been sleeping in that truck with those creatures."

Once Animal Control wrangled the snakes and traffic was flowing again, the cop, Slick Stick, and Phantom 309 walked to Shelby's truck. She stayed where she was, not convinced her truck was free from the reptiles.

"I think these babies are pets. They're not even afraid of me," the wrangler told the cop.

"Pets?"

"Yeah, I'm pretty sure they're harmless."

"Thanks, I need to talk to the driver over there."

"You mean that attractive blonde?"

The cop approached Shelby. "Ma'am, are those snakes yours?"

"Mine? No disrespect officer, but are you out of your mind? Snakes make me sick." Shelby pointed toward areas where she'd relieved her nausea.

"Well, those snakes might be pet snakes. Do you know anyone who might have put them in your truck as a joke or anything?"

"Pets? Who in their right mind has snakes for pets? I can't think of anyone who'd play this kind of joke on me." Shelby looked around at her co-workers; they shrugged.

Rude Dog Rider and Southwest Grizzly pulled in behind the other trucks along the roadway. Betty and Ted weren't far behind, but when they came through the one lane of traffic around Shelby's truck, they simply looked and kept on going. Shelby caught Betty's stare as she passed.

Could it have been Betty? Shelby wondered. *Where would Betty get snakes and how could she get snakes into my truck without someone seeing? Sure, Betty's an evil witch, but is she clever enough to pull of such a trick...and was it just a trick?*

◊◊◊

Betty turned livid when she saw Shelby standing on the median...alive!

She grabbed her cell phone and called Ted. "Did you see that? That bitch is still alive. What do I have to do to get rid of her? Did you see that man near the Animal Control truck? He was playing with those snakes like they were tame as puppies. We have a stop to make on the way home. I'm getting my six hundred dollars back from Samoan."

"She said you had to bring the snakes back, remember?"

"Fuck that! She gave me pet snakes. Who in their right mind has snakes for pets?"

"Be careful, Betty. That woman has powers. She might hex you or something."

"Bullshit. She's a con artist. Trust me—I know a con when I see one."

◊◊◊

The team of sand haulers were several hours behind by the time the cops let everyone go. As they crossed the border into Texas, Shelby felt the weight of her exhaustion settle in.

She had called Jack to let him know what had happened, which caused his worry to intensify. "I'll be running with coworkers all the way home. They'll watch out for me," she assured him.

Before going to bed, Shelby had taken everything apart and checked through everything to make sure there were no more snakes, but she still couldn't shake the creepy feeling that someone was out to get her.

She had a sleepless night in her truck.

CHAPTER NINETEEN

Shelby, Tiff, and Sandy walked into the bar together. Sandy excused herself for a few minutes and walked back outside for a phone call. Shelby hadn't been in a dance/pool hall in years. Shelby was reminded of the places she and Jack used to go to twenty years earlier. Sandy came back in and the three walked to the bar and ordered beer.

"So, how come Jack didn't come with you, Shelby?" Tiff asked.

"Oh, he didn't want to," Shelby, shrugged. "I guess he thought I needed a girls' night out after all that's been happening lately."

"Well, that was sweet of him, but I'd still like to meet him sometime."

"Maybe next time."

Sandy's boyfriend, Walter, came in and joined them around their table. Then Sandy and he took to the dance floor.

Shelby tapped her feet to the music as she watched them dance and a little part of her wished Jack had decided to come with her after all.

"Wow! That was fun!" Sandy said, a little out of breath, as she and Walter returned to the table. "Shelby, you want to dance with Walter?"

"No, thanks," Shelby sighed. "I have two left feet. Jack is the only one who has ever been able to dance me around a dance floor and still have his feet left after a dance."

After a couple of hours, Shelby announced, "Well, I need to get going guys. I promised Jack I wouldn't be out too late."

"Alright. Are you sure you're okay to drive?" asked Sandy asked.

"Yeah, I've only had a couple of beers," Shelby, said. "I've been drinking Sprite most of the night. I'm fine."

"Good—I wouldn't want my favorite driver to get arrested." Sandy smiled.

"No need to worry. Oh, do I have anything for tomorrow?"

"Yeah, I forgot to mention it. I'm sending you and some others to Louisiana for a job on Monday."

"Yuck, I have to go back to snake country?"

Sandy frowned. "Well, I can send someone else, but I thought you might want the money…"

"I'll take it. I could use the money. I just hope I don't catch any more snakes."

◊◊◊

Shelby started for Louisiana early the next morning. She decided to do this trip alone. It was just a delivery and she'd just be taking the sand already loaded to a port near the Gulf. She looked forward to a peaceful drive.

As soon as she returned after the snake incident, she made Jack and Steven help her search for any possible holes that may have allowed those snakes access to her sleeper. They searched every inch and with no access holes, they came up with only two possibilities: either Shelby had left her truck door open, or someone had deliberately put the snakes in her truck. With no way to know for sure, she concluded, *I probably left my door open at some point*, she told herself, trying to shrug it off. It was preferable to thinking about the alternative.

The road Shelby would be traveling was a man-made road built out into the ocean. She would also be going across several wood bridges that had been damaged some years ago by storms, but by all accounts had been repaired and were safe. Shelby liked water, but she wasn't sure about driving a big truck out into the middle of the ocean. She also knew that the load she'd be delivering was going to be transferred onto a barge. *This will be just one more adventure*, she thought.

◊◊◊

"Hey, Roy. This is Betty."

"Hi, Betty. What do you want?"

"Is that anyway to talk to an old friend?"

Roy laughed. "Old friend? Are you serious?" He said sarcastically. "The only reason you're calling me is to hassle me about the money I owe you, or you want something. How the hell did you find out I was out of lock up already? I just got out a week ago."

"Oh, I have my ways…but you're right, I'm calling about the money you owe me. And I do want something."

"Well, I don't have any money, and I don't have anything you could possibly want."

"Oh, I think you do, and I have a plan to square things between us."

"I can hardly wait to hear this," he sighed.

"I have a job for you, and all you have to do is push a little problem I have off into the water. You know, like maybe off one of those really rickety wood bridges you guys have down there in the bayou?"

"Really? And does this little problem have a name? Or maybe it's a make and model."

"Both, smart ass. She's a little blonde named Shelby and she drives a truck like mine. All you have to do is help her find her way to the bottom of the Gulf, and we are square forever."

"I just got out of jail, Betty. Now you want me to run someone off the road and risk going back?"

"Or…you can bring me the money you owe me tomorrow. One or the other, Roy. Otherwise I'll call Zack and let him know you're out and he'll collect what you owe him as well as mine."

"Still the same hardcore bitch."

Betty laughed. "Thank you for the compliment. So, do we have a deal?"

"Yes, we have a deal," Roy said, resigned to his predicament. "I'm going to need a few more details. Just remember, if I get caught, I'm not going down alone. I'm going to squeal like a stuck pig."

"So don't get caught. It wouldn't be healthy for you if you do."

Betty proceeded to give Roy the information on Shelby's load. They discussed everything that Betty wanted done and how she wanted it done. "I can't give you the exact time she'll arrive because they're just supposed to unload on that barge by Monday. You may have to wait until she arrives, and then follow her out until you come upon a good opportunity along those marsh roads to take her down."

"I'll call you when I'm done."

"I look forward to your call. Get it right, Roy."

◊◊◊

Shelby stopped for dinner in Lafayette. The town was congested with evening traffic and not being familiar with the city, she was forced to keep moving without stopping. The main highway she was on ran through the middle of the downtown area. Several big rigs were following the same route. "Break one nine for some local information," she spoke into her mic.

"Go ahead, break."

"I was wondering if you could tell me if a truck stop is in the area."

"There's a store in New Iberia that has truck parking, fuel, and food. Not sure if they have a driver lounge or showers though."

"I'm just looking for something to eat. Thanks."

After stopping for dinner, Shelby wasn't tired, and she still had plenty of hours, so she decided she'd continue toward the port. It was her first time at the Gulf. There was no Wi-Fi and she couldn't use her GPS, so she depended on her map.

A few hours later, Shelby found herself on the road that was supposed to take her to the port. It was dark, curvy, and nothing like what her map showed. She found a soft shoulder and pulled over. She put her flashers on as a precaution. She studied the map, but she couldn't make heads or tails of where she was on the road.

Perhaps I should stay right here until it gets light outside, she thought. She worked on her log and then turned off her light. She crawled back into her sleeper and put her head on her pillow. She was about to fall asleep when a man's voice came over her CB, which she had left turned up. "Hey, ESCC driver. Are you alright?"

Shelby jumped up and keyed up her mic. "Yeah, I'm alright, just a little lost. I was just going to wait until daybreak to find the port I'm headed to, but if you could tell me how to get there I'd really appreciate it."

"What port are you looking for, lady driver?"

"The ESCC's yard is supposed to be around here somewhere."

"Just up in front of you are a couple of tanker trucks stopped at a stop sign. That's me and my partner, Hotwire. Fall in behind us and we'll take you right to your yard. We're headed that way right now."

"Thanks! Will do."

When Shelby arrived at the stop sign, the drivers led her through the dark, narrow, curvy roads. Shelby tried to watch for landmarks so that she could find her way back, but it was difficult to see anything in the dark. "I guess coming down here at night was not the best idea I've ever had, especially not knowing exactly where I'm going."

"Yeah, and if you make a wrong turn you could end up in the Gulf. You're actually in the man-made gulf area. These roads are built into the water. One wrong turn and you're swimming."

Within a few minutes, Shelby was where she needed to be. "Here you go, little lady. Just follow this road to the right and you'll drive into ESCC's yard."

"I sure thank you guys for the help. Following you down here leaves no doubt that I'd have gotten really lost if I'd have tried it on my own."

"You're welcome, lady driver. If you need help out when you get unloaded, just get on the radio. We're always running these roads at night."

"I'll keep that in mind. It's hard to tell when they'll unload me, though."

"Take care, lady driver."

"You too, guys."

Shelby pulled into the small, crowded ESCC yard. The shipping office was on the top floor of a three-story building. There was no elevator, so she climbed the stairs.

"I'm Shelby Mathews, from the ESCC west yard; I have a load for you."

"Yeah, we weren't expecting you 'til tomorrow, but since you're here you can go on over to the barge and unload."

"I don't mean to be rude, but I've never been here before. I have no idea where the barge is or even how to unload into one. I can do whatever you want, I just need some direction."

"Sorry, I just assumed you knew. Well, best thing for you to do then is just park your truck and wait for Gus and Sam to get here."

"Okay. Is there any place specific that you would like me to park? The parking lot is pretty small, and I feel like I'm in the way."

"Oh, you're fine where you are. Just take a nap until the guys get here, and I'll have them wake you up when they arrive."

Several hours after resting in her sleeper, Shelby was awakened by a knock on her door. "Hey, driver. Time to get your ass up."

Shelby straightened her hair and went to her window. "Oh, sorry, ma'am, about the language! I didn't realize..."

Shelby smiled. "Don't worry about it, driver. I've heard worse. Can you give me a minute to get myself together and maybe use the restroom first?"

"Sure, I'll show you where it's at."

Shelby grabbed a couple things and followed the man up the steps. "Man, you guys must really get your exercise climbing these steps every day."

"Yeah, but they build everything up high since we are out in the water. It saves a lot of property from being washed away during hurricanes."

Shelby freshened up and followed Gus back to their trucks. The drivers led her out of the yard and further down the road she had come in on last night. Shelby was amazed at what she saw through her windshield. Everywhere she looked she saw water. *I'm in the Gulf for sure; it's beautiful, but also kind of terrifying.*

It took only a few minutes to get to the barge, and with the help of Gus and Sam, Shelby was unloaded and on her way back home in short order. "Thanks, guys, for the help and the map for getting out of here."

"Not a problem, Shelby. Be careful going home."

Shelby followed the map as best she could, but somehow managed to get onto a wooden bridge that didn't appear to be on her map. "Damn, now what do I do?" she muttered. "Guess I'll just keep going and hope I don't fall into the Gulf." Shelby kept looking for a different road to take, but there wasn't even a place to turn around. "Great," she said. "I'm lost."

Shelby was so focused on her predicament she didn't notice the truck behind her, which had been behind her since her first turn the ESCC yard road. She kept looking for a place to either turn around or a road that might lead her in a different direction. Seeing neither alternative made her nervous. The wooden road seemed stable, but it was built on water. *How safe can it be moving farther into the water, especially in a big truck?* She wondered.

She finally spotted a sign ahead for a town called Grand Isle. Relieved, she grabbed her map and realized her mistake, but she needed to find a place to turn around. The truck was still following her, but it was far enough back that she was not aware of it. Suddenly, she found a small abandoned parking lot in front of a place that was either closed or no longer open for business. She turned on her blinker and after traffic was clear made a U-turn in the parking lot and headed back toward Port Fourchan.

Shelby was finally headed north on Highway 1. "I'm headed home," she sighed. Suddenly, she noticed the light blue long nosed Pete coming racing up behind her. Figuring the truck was going to go around her, she slowed her speed and moved slightly to the right to give the driver visual of oncoming traffic.

The truck, however, stayed right on the bumper of her trailer even when there was no traffic. Shelby got on the CB to find out why the driver was waiting to go by. "Hey, driver. You have a clear shot around me if you want it."

The driver did not respond. Instead, he bumped Shelby's truck. Shelby thought the impact was an accident. "You just hit my truck!" she said into her mic, trying not to sound pissed. "We better stop and check to see if you did any damage."

Still no answer; he simply bumped Shelby's truck again.

"Hey, mister. I'm not sure what your problem is, but I'm calling the cops if you don't knock it off."

Then the driver put the nose of his Pete right into Shelby's bumper and started pushing her.

"YOU WEIRDO, KNOCK IT OFF!" Shelby screamed over the radio. She had to work hard to keep her truck straight and not let the driver push her trailer sideways. She reached for her mic and keyed it up. A couple of trucks were up in front of her and several were in the lane heading in the opposite lane. "HELP! IF ANYONE CAN HEAR ME, I NEED HELP! THERE'S A

CRAZY DRIVER TRYING TO PUSH ME OFF THE ROAD INTO THE WATER!"

"Where are you, little lady?" asked a concerned voice over the radio.

"I'm northbound on Highway 1, just outside of Port Fourchan. Can you help me, please?"

"We see you, lady driver. I'm Chevy Man, and Lonely Driver and Slammin are right in front of me. We're directly in front of you. That truck still pushing you?"

"Yes." Another driver in the opposite lane was leading several other trucks down the road. "Yeah, Chevy Man, this is Swinging Coyote, Tennessee Canine, Slim Pickens, and Tumbleweed. We just passed them heading south, and he is pushing her hard. The boys and I'll get turned around and fall in behind them."

"Alright, Swinging Coyote, I'll keep her straight and steady. I guess the best way to get him off her is to take him out in the marsh mud."

"Yeah, I know that area. We just found a turnaround spot, so we'll be there in a few minutes."

Chevy Man got on the CB with Shelby. "Okay, little lady. What's your name?"

"Shelby!"

"Okay, Shelby. I take it the driver hasn't responded to talk?"

"No," Shelby answered breathlessly, trying not to sound too panicked. "He just started pushing me even when I tried to let him go past me!"

"Alright, I want you to maintain your speed at 65 as best you can and stay as straight as possible. My buddies and I will maintain at 65 until the other guys get behind you with their trucks. When we get near the marsh mud, I'll let you know and we'll have you pull hard to the left. You may put your truck in the mud, but the guys behind you are going to try and push that crazy driver to the right and into the mud. Just keep it steady and straight 'til we get things set up."

"Okay, Chevy Man. I'll do my best."

"Chevy Man, we are right behind the flatbed that is pushing Shelby," said another voice.

"I'm right on his bumper. Tennessee Canine and Slim Pickens are ready to pull out next to him, so just let us know when to make our move."

"Okay, we got a couple more miles, Shelby. And then I'm going to brake hard, you're going to brake to the left and take the mud on the side of the road. Keep it as straight as you can so you don't roll that pretty red truck. Swinging Coyote and his boys are going to push that son-of-a-bitch off into the mud to the right."

"Alright," said Shelby. "I'm scared, but I think I can do this."

"I know you can do this. Just watch for my brake lights and put your truck in that mud, READY…? NOW!"

Shelby braked to the left and her truck headed into the mud as predicted. She kept it straight and when she finally came to a stop, the front of her truck was deep in mud. She quickly got out to see what was going on up on the highway. Tennessee Canine and Slim Pickens had moved their trucks up in the left lane to block the flatbed from pushing Shelby as she braked to the left. Chevy Man and Swinging Coyote had him blocked in on the front and rear. Lonely Driver and Slammin were up front as lookouts for oncoming traffic.

Shelby couldn't see much more than Chevy Man and the other trucks trying to stop the flatbed. Suddenly, there was a puff of smoke coming from the stacks on the flatbed and brake lights from the trucks in the left lane and Swinging Coyote's trucks. Shelby figured they must have put the driver in the mud. She watched as Slim Pickens and Tennessee Canine moved over into the right lane. She had to step back as several four wheelers sped past her on the road. *It's a good thing the drivers ditched the flatbed before those vehicles got too close. That could have been disastrous,* she thought.

Swinging Coyote and the other drivers were stopped behind Chevy Man on the far side of the right lane. Shelby saw truck flashers glaring but couldn't see the light blue truck anywhere, *probably deep in mud,* she figured. Before long she saw Chevy Man turn his own flatbed around on the road. All the drivers who had helped sat on the truck bed and were headed toward her.

Within a few minutes, they were standing next to Shelby. "Hi, I'm Shelby. I sure appreciate you guys helping me out. That driver was trying to kill me, I think, but I don't even know why."

Chevy Man shook Shelby's hand. "I'm Chevy Man. It's hard to tell, but he did seem to have a problem with you. We had to let him out of our little trap because of an oncoming vehicle that came around that curve a few miles up."

"Oh, so he got away?"

"Yeah, we didn't want to cause an accident with the oncoming cars, so we let him go around."

She nodded. "That would have been disastrous."

"I think the two guys that were up in front of us are going to watch and see where the flatbed lands, if he lands."

"Okay. Now it's my turn to get out of the mud. I guess I'll call dispatch and have a wrecker sent to pull me out."

"No need for that. We have enough horsepower right here to pull you out ourselves. Are you loaded?"

"No."

"Good, that should make it easier."

Swinging Coyote was looking at the front of Shelby's truck.

"How deep is she in the marsh, Coyote?" Chevy man asked.

"Not too bad. I think your truck will do fine. Does she have any chain?"

Shelby went to the deck on her truck behind the cab and climbed on through the mud. She pulled out a long, steel chain and with the help of Tennessee Canine they put it behind the trailer where it wasn't muddy. "Will this work?"

"Yeah, great."

Chevy Man gathered everyone around. "We're going to need to stop traffic, so get on the horn and see if you can get some trucks up the highway and down the highway to block things off for us till we get her out. Shelby, I want you to get into your truck and when I'm in position, we'll first tighten the chain and then you'll put her in reverse. We won't move until I say, though. That way we can keep the chain tight and let my truck pull."

Shelby nodded. "Got it."

Chevy Man pointed up and down the highway. "The rest of you need to keep an eye out for any problems and traffic that might get through the blockades."

Slim Pickens went to Chevy Man's truck and got on the CB looking for Slammin and Lonely Driver, but they were out of range. He was able to get Left Lane and One Track to block traffic from the south with Pigtail and Droopy blocking traffic from the north. "Thanks drivers, we sure appreciate the help. We should have her out of the mud in just a few minutes. We'll let you know shortly."

Left Lane confirmed, "We got you covered, starting now. But there are some hot four wheelers not liking truckers right now."

Pigtail confirmed the same. "Yeah, we got you on the north end Slim Pickens, but they ain't too happy here either."

"Guess they'll just have to get over themselves for a little while, right? We'll let you know when she's out."

◊◊◊

Betty answered her cell phone. "Hello?"

"We are even bitch, and don't ever call me again."

"Don't talk to me like that, Roy! We're only even if you got rid of my problem. Did you?"

"No. We're even because if I ever hear from you again I'll be going back to prison for murder."

"DID YOU FUCKING GET RID OF THE BITCH?"

"NO, but I almost got caught by about a dozen truckers who were helping out your little problem. To be honest, I think you're the problem, not her."

"Go to Hell, Roy. You still owe me."

"Bullshit. You stay away from me or I'll take care of *my* problem, got it?"

Betty threw her cell phone against the wall. "DAMMIT! WHY IS IT SO HARD TO GET RID OF THAT BITCH?" She found her phone and called Ted. "Roy failed, and the bitch is still alive. I'm going to lose my mind if I can't figure out a way to get rid of her."

Ted had never heard Betty sound so desperate. He hated hearing her so upset. "We'll figure it out, baby. Maybe we should shoot her or…."

"Oh, sure, we'll shoot her and got to jail. I was hoping you'd help me think of something, but obviously I'll just have to keep trying by myself."

◊◊◊

In Larose, Shelby met up with the truckers who had helped her out on the highway. Over coffee and a sandwich, she shared her experiences with them. "I think I'm cursed or something. Or maybe I'm just not meant to be a driver. You would not believe all the things that have happened to me since I've been out here."

"Trust me, darling, you have no idea about what happens to drivers out here on the road," Slammin said. "Between wrecks and assholes who think they own the roads, we're all cursed. Wait till you've been on these roads for twenty years."

The other drivers assured Shelby she wasn't cursed. "You're a good driver; hang in there. You'll get used to the crazies and will learn how to deal with the assholes," Lonely Driver said as he took Shelby's ticket from the waitress. "I got this one, little lady."

"Oh no, I need to be paying for you guys."

"No, we drivers stick together. And besides, I'm sure you don't make that much hauling sand." That comment got a laugh from everyone around the table.

"It's been really great meeting you guys. Thanks so much for helping me today." Out in the parking lot, Shelby said goodbye to the drivers again as they all geared out and headed back on the road to their own destinations.

CHAPTER TWENTY

Jack had been working afternoons, but was to be cleared to work full-time soon. *I hope Shelby will consider going back to teaching. I know it's unlikely, she obviously enjoys her new career*, he thought.

Steven hurried out the door. "Hey, Dad. I've got to get to work."

Jack let his son pass. "Have a good night."

"Alright, you too. Oh, Dad, there's a letter on the entertainment center for you. It was in the door when I got in from class."

"Thanks, be careful, son."

Jack took off his shoes, threw his jacket on the couch, and went to the entertainment center. The white envelope only had his name. He opened it with trepidation. As before, it was about Shelby's infidelity.

"This is garbage," he muttered as he read. He was tempted to throw the letter in the trash and not give it another thought. But he kept reading and wondered if there might be some validity to the accusations. Jack took the letter and put it with the other one he'd received. He thought about it as he fixed dinner, but decided to wait before confronting her.

◊◊◊

"Jack, baby, I'm home!"

Jack met Shelby in the hallway.

"I missed you, sweetheart," she said as she put her arms around his neck. "Did you miss me?"

"No, I didn't even think about you the whole time you were gone," he lied. "Silly girl, of course I missed you." Jack pinned her up against the wall and kissed her with a passion Shelby hadn't experienced in a long time.

"Well, you really have missed me."

They enjoyed a scrumptious dinner, and after doing the dishes together, spent the rest of the evening, watching a movie, making love, and snacking on PB&J sandwiches and oranges. As she lay next to Jack, Shelby wondered if her job and absence were causing a rift in their marriage. She hoped not.

Shelby got up and went to take a shower, knowing that by dawn someone would be calling her about a job. A lot of the time she simply went to the yard to check on work, but this morning she just wanted to stay in bed and be with Jack. She still hadn't told Jack what had happened in Louisiana. In fact, she hadn't told Jack much about any of the recent incidents. She wanted to avoid him pressuring her to quit.

As she stepped out of the shower, Shelby was greeted with a warm-from-the-dryer towel and a fresh cup of coffee sweetened just as she liked it. "Your coffee, my love."

"Jack, you spoil me."

"Yes, but after last night, I think you spoil me." He flashed her a seductive smile.

"Oh, I think we manage to spoil each other quite nicely in that area." As Shelby kissed Jack, her towel fell to the floor. Jack placed the coffee on the counter near the sink and took his naked wife into his arms. "Want to spoil me again?"

Shelby kissed him passionately but then broke away. "I want to, baby, but...."

"I know…you've got to get to the yard. I'll make you some breakfast—that is if you have time."

"I'd love some."

◊◊◊

"Hey, Shelby. How was your night off?" Sandy asked when Shelby entered the office. Shelby went to her box, reached in, and pulled out two assignment sheets. The first sheet was for a local job delivery for that day and the other one was for Bakersfield, California, delivering in three days. "Bakersfield California! I didn't know we went that far? Hell, I didn't know California even allowed oil wells in their state."

"I know it sounds crazy, but California has oil."

"I didn't say they didn't have oil, I said I found it hard to believe they allowed oil to be drilled in their state."

"It's all about the money, honey."

◊◊◊

Jack sat in his pickup a few blocks from the yard, feeling uncomfortable about spying on his wife. *What am I going to say if she see me?* He wondered. But he stayed until Shelby pulled out of the yard; then he followed her to the head of the lease road. *She's going to recognize the pickup if I go any further*, he concluded. Jack turned around and headed back to the house, feeling foolish about doubting her. *How can I believe that after all we've been through together over the years that she'd want to cheat on me now? Shelby loves me; she's not doing anything that would harm our marriage or hurt me.*

◊◊◊

"When does this local load need to be delivered?" Shelby asked.

"By one p.m. for Halls and Bert."

"I like hauling for them. I hope Carlos, Clayton, or Jess are there. They're real nice guys. Marshall is a really good supervisor, too."

"Well that's a change. I've heard a lot of the drivers complain about hauling for Halls and Bert."

"That's odd. I've never had any problems with them. Could it be that other drivers just don't like their rules?"

"Probably."

Shelby got the load off for Halls and Bert quickly. She returned to the yard and loaded for her trip to California. Although she was excited about going to California, several drivers told her California was not a trucker friendly state and that it was really hard on truckers when it came to weight and speed limit. "They don't even allow trucks to idle there," she was told. She hoped it would work out so she could spend the night in Arizona.

◊◊◊

"Hey, Mark. This Betty. How ya doing, baby?"

"Good, Betty. How have you been? Haven't heard from you in a long time."

"Well, I'm doing alright. Thought I'd give you a call and let ya know I'm coming to Cali. I thought maybe we could hook up while I'm in town."

"That sounds great. When will you be here?"

"We're leaving in just a few hours. I should be in Bakersfield in a couple days."

"Dammit, sounds like old times."

"I've been thinking about all the fun we had when we long-hauled together. Are you still trucking?"

"Yeah, but just local stuff. Pays pretty well, and I'm home more."

"You still married, or can I come over to your place now?"

"Got divorced a year ago. After having you, sleeping with her wasn't fun anymore."

"Well, let's get together and have some fun."

"Can't wait. Get your sweet little ass to Cali, baby."

"I'll be there soon."

Betty smiled. "Mark was always a good fuck," she murmured. "Maybe he'll be good at taking out Shelby, too." Betty was always able to get Mark to do anything she wanted, especially after giving him a night of good sex. She planned to get a half day's jump on the other drivers by leaving that evening. *I'll hook up with Mark and let him know my plan.* She intended to make it look like a mugging in a dark area of Buck's truck stop in Bakersfield.

Betty did not tell Ted about her plan. She wanted to make sure the two men did not know about each other so she could get what she wanted out of each of them.

◊◊◊

"Hey, Mark. Been a long time, big boy." Betty wrapped her arms around Mark's neck and kissed him deeply.

"That's my Betty, getting right to the point."

"What other way is there but straight to what you want?"

"Come on, baby. Let's go to my apartment and you can show me how much you missed me."

"Better yet, you can show me how much you want me." They disappeared into Mark's pickup.

After foreplay in his truck, the two moved into Mark's apartment. Betty playfully rolled next to Mark on the bed while he panted from the lust-filled two hours of sex the two old friends had enjoyed. "Want some more?" she asked.

"In a little bit," he gasped. "For now, let's just lie here and enjoy the moment. I haven't had a good lay in a long time, and I want to savor it." Betty snuggled her naked body close to him, waiting for the perfect moment to manipulate him into her little scheme.

"So, how has work been for you?" Mark asked. "Ever think about giving up driving and maybe settling down with someone?"

Betty fought the urge to roll her eyes at Mark. *Is he going to ask me to stay with him?* The thought almost made her want to vomit. *Give up driving? Share a home and a bed with one man for the rest of my life? Is he insane?* She swallowed her bile and thoughts and decided to use the moment as an opportunity to get what she wanted.

"Work's alright. There's this one bitch though who has really been giving me trouble. I'm trying to be strong." She pouted. "As for settling down, I don't know. I guess it would have to be the right man. You know, someone who knows how to take charge, protect and take care of me. This job's starting to wear on me, but I really need to get a few things paid off before I decide to make a change. I'm just afraid this new bitch we got working for us is going to mess things up for me."

"Who's the bitch and why is she messing with you? You know I don't like anyone messing with my girl."

"Well," Betty sighed. "She's been doing really mean things to me and I don't know why. I know it's her, but I can't prove it. Like the other day she got Sandy, the dispatcher, to change a load on me so she could get a better one. That really hurts the pocketbook, and I can't get away from Texas if I can't pay off my bills."

"Your dispatcher gave her a better load than you? Are they friends?"

"Real good friends. They go out together…I'm thinking they might even be lovers or something. That's not the worst of it. She's also been doing shit to my truck. I know she put holes in my hoses the other day, and I almost got hurt on location. Then there was the day she put snakes in my truck and stole all my clothes. It's really been bad since she started working for us, but no one will listen to me when I complain. She has them all fooled into thinking she's this great driver, and to tell ya the truth, she can't drive anywhere near as good as I drive."

"That's awful, baby. Wish there was something I could do to help. Why don't you just quit and come live here with me? I make plenty of money. I can get you a job with the company I'm working for. I'll even help you with your bills."

"Oh, Mark, you're sweet, but I really need to work this out myself…. I may have an idea to get rid of her while she's here in California. I know it sounds bad, but she deserves it."

Mark turned to face Betty. "Tell me, baby, maybe I can help."

"No, I don't want to get you involved."

"Just tell me and let me decide."

Betty rolled over and put her tits against his chest and rubbed his back. "I don't know."

Mark drew her closer and ran his fingers through her hair. "Tell me."

"Well, what if she was attacked by a mugger in Buck's parking lot? Nothing too serious, maybe…stabbed…enough to put her out of commission for a while. I think I could do it, but even if it's dark, she would probably recognize me…then I'd really be in trouble…probably end up in prison. I don't know…I know it sounds horrible, I really just want her dead. That would solve all of my problems. Do you think I'm a bad person for thinking that?"

"No, baby, of course not. She's the one harassing you. She needs to learn a lesson. Mugging her is not a bad idea. Do you really want her dead? I mean, I think I could hurt her, but I'm not sure about killing someone."

"But if she's not dead, she'll just come back to work, and somehow I'll get blamed…probably fired, so I won't get my stuff paid off and be able to move here with you."

Betty kissed Mark and he pulled her even closer.

"Let me think about it for a little while," he said.

"Don't think too long. I only have tonight. We unload in the morning and head back to Texas. So if you can't do it…I may have to get someone else…but who? Nothing is going to change for me as long as she's around." Betty got up and started to get dressed.

"Where are you going?" Mark asked.

"I'm hungry. You got anything to eat?" Betty put on her bra and panties and walked to the kitchen.

Who else could she get? Mark wondered as he watched her leave the bedroom.

"Oh my god, Mark. All you have in her is beer and some leftover take-out." She closed the refrigerator and walked around the kitchen. She saw a butcher's block with knives next to the sink. She walked over and pulled out the largest one.

"Yeah, I know. I've been meaning to go to the store but I just don't eat much at home," he said, looking down and buttoning his shirt. Her back was to him. He grabbed Betty from the back around the waist. "If you lived here, we could enjoy lots of meals at home together. Hell, I might even buy you a nice little house with a full-size kitchen for you to cook in." He spun her around and she almost cut his cheek with the knife she held.

"Oops, sorry, she said, lowering her hand. "Oh, baby, that sounds romantic. You and me in a little house together. By the way, do you think I can borrow this?"

Mark took the knife out of Betty's hand. "No!"

"But…"

"If you're really serious about coming to live with me, I'll take care of your little problem for you tonight."

"Oh, Mark you're wonderful. I can't wait; we'll be together forever."

Mark gave her a passionate kiss, and then led her back into the bedroom for another round of hot sex.

◊◊◊

Ted had spent over an hour wandering around the truck stop and parking lot, trying to find Betty. She wasn't even answering her cell phone. Several of the ESCC trucks had made it to the truck stop and were backing into position when Shelby arrived and pulled into the fuel isle. Ted walked over to her truck as she was getting out. Normally he wouldn't talk to her, but he felt desperate. "Hey, Shelby. Have you seen Betty?"

Shelby walked toward the truck shop entrance. "No, Ted, not for several days. I didn't even see you guys at the briefing the other day before we all left for this job."

Ted followed Shelby and held the door for her as she walked through. "No, Betty wanted to get here early for some reason, so we left the night before, but I can't find her. I'm becoming concerned. It's getting late and she usually never leaves without saying something."

"Maybe she's in the shower. Did you check the log?"

"Did that, and checked the restaurant and bar. She isn't in her truck either."

Shelby frowned, not sure what to think. "Check with the security guard or the front desk if you really think something has happened to her."

"Oh, I'm sure she just walked to the store or something. I'll let it go for a little while longer and then I'll ask the desk clerk to check it out."

"Alright, well, let me know if you find her."

Shelby handed the clerk her credit card for fuel and walked back to her truck with Ted right behind her. "So did you have a good trip out here?" he asked.

"Yeah, I met a couple new drivers along the way," she said cautiously, wondering why Betty's boy toy was being so friendly. "One was from L.A. His name was Fiancé. I don't know if that is his real handle or not, but he was telling me all about his love life. Then there was this "Gloom and Doom dude," he talked to me about the end of America and how God is getting ready to judge us and stuff."

"Yeah, I used to meet a lot of drivers when I long hauled," said Ted. "But since I've been hauling sand with Betty, she pretty much runs the show and doesn't like to be too sociable."

"Why do you run with her so much? You could run with some of us once in a while. Are you afraid of hurting Betty's feelings? I guess it's just better to stay on her good side."

"Yeah, I guess." He started walking back toward his truck.

"Well, let me know if you need help finding Betty."

"Okay, thanks."

Just as he approached his truck, Betty came walking through the parking lot from the direction of the street. Ted met her half way. "Where did ya go? I was worried."

"Oh god, Ted. Can't I even go to the store without you on my heels?"

"Well, I figured that's probably where you went, but you usually tell me when you're going somewhere."

"What, so you can go along?"

"No so I won't worry."

"Oh hell, Ted. Grow up and stop treating me like your wife. If I want to go to the fucking store without telling you, I'll go. Besides, sometimes I need time away from you. You tend to get on my nerves."

Ted noticed the only thing Betty had with her was her purse. "So what did you buy?"

"Nothing."

"Oh."

"I just walked through the store, okay?"

"Okay."

Betty climbed into her truck with Ted right behind her. "Get out, Ted. I want to get a shower and take a nap. I'll talk to you later tonight."

"Okay. Do you want me to wake you up for a late dinner?"

"Yeah, that'd be great—around eight o'clock, and then we'll go to the bar."

"Alright." Ted moved in for a kiss but Betty just pushed him away. He left her truck and walked back to his own.

Betty wanted a shower. As she walked through the parking lot, Shelby drove past. Shelby waved at Betty and then turned her truck around and parked next to Ted's rig. Betty ignored Shelby's wave. Shelby got on the CB and said to Ted, "I see the lost is found."

"Yeah, she just went to the store."

"Well, at least she's safe."

"Yeah."

◇◇◇

"Hey, Shelby! It's about time you got here," said Bobcat as he spotted Shelby. "We've been here for three days and thought maybe you got lost."

"Very funny. We were only a few miles apart, but I got stopped at the weigh station. How'd you guys get past the lady in the office? I thought for a while there she was going to strip search me and my truck."

"I'd love to have been there for that pretty sight."

"Alright, Luscious, are you flirting with me again?"

"Well, I was trying, but I'll settle for having dinner with you."

"Sounds like a plan, but I really need to take a shower first."

"Need help?"

"Luscious!"

"Just kidding. A bunch of us are going for a drink in the bar before dinner so you can meet us there."

"It's just around the corner and behind the truck stop, right?"

"Yep, we'll see you over there in a little while."

Shelby gathered her things and walked to the truck stop for a shower. Betty was getting to her truck about the time she walked past so she stopped to speak to her. "So, did you have fun shopping this afternoon?"

"What?"

"Ted mentioned you went shopping this afternoon and I was just curious if the shopping was good around here. I was thinking about checking it out for myself before heading back tomorrow."

"Oh yeah. It was fine." Betty didn't wait for any further conversation; she moved into her truck and shut the door.

She's just one rude bitch, Shelby thought as she continued to the showers.

"Ted, get over here, NOW!" Betty yelled into the CB.

Ted obeyed and without responding went to her truck.

"What were you doing telling my business to Little Miss Princess?"

"What?"

"You told the bitch I was shopping? What else did you tell her about me?"

"I just asked her if she had seen you. I couldn't find you and was worried."

"If I'd wanted you to know, I would've told you."

"You left without a word, and I had no idea where you were."

"You're not my mother. I'll let you know what you need to know, got it?"

"Got it."

"Good. Now, let me tell you what I have planned for her tonight."

CHAPTER TWENTY-ONE

The restaurant was crowded with truck drivers and Shelby felt a little self-conscious being one of three women in the place—the other two being waitresses. "So what would you like to drink, gentleman and lady?" a young redheaded waitress asked.

Luscious and several of the others lifted their beer mugs. "We'll all have another round. How about you Shelby? Want a beer?"

"Yes, please. Whatever you have on tap that's lite."

"Oh my god, a light weight," Speedy teased.

"I'm not a light weight…just watchin' my figure."

"No need for that, Ms. Shelby. We manage to watch that for you."

The table burst out laughing and Shelby blushed.

"Look, she glows bright red."

"Be careful, she's going to blow!"

"You boys are full of crap today, ain't ya," Shelby kidded. Although she was embarrassed, she couldn't help enjoying the men's flirtatious behavior just a bit.

"Come on, Shelby, just one more and then you can go to your truck and go to sleep," the others encouraged her after dinner.

"Alright, guys, but I need my beauty rest."

"Any more of that and you really won't look like a trucker."

"Very funny, Luscious, I do too look like a trucker."

"Not any trucker I've ever met."

"Yeah, and you don't smell like a trucker either."

"Oh, Doc Snow, you say the nicest things."

The bar was smoke-filled, loud and bustling with even more drivers than before dinner. Shelby and Jack had gone to bars earlier in their marriage, but after having children and maintaining steady careers, bars had become a thing of the past. She didn't mind having a couple of beers with the guys, but this bar just wasn't her thing. "Well, I'm tired guys. I'm going to my truck to go to sleep. Ya'll have a good time and remember we have loads to deliver tomorrow."

"Don't leave, Ms. Shelby! Stay and have one more with us."

"Yeah, stay, Ms. Shelby."

"No, I want to go to bed, guys."

"Oh alright, do you want one of us to walk you out? It's dark in that parking lot."

"Nah, I'll be alright, it's not that far. Besides, as much as ya'll have had tonight, I don't believe you'd be much help even if I needed it."

"Oh, that's cold."

"Yeah, that's just not right."

"She speaks truth, though."

The table busted out in laughter again as Shelby got up and walked out of the bar. "Be good, guys. Don't make me have to get out of bed and bail you out of jail."

"Damn, and I wanted to spend the night in lockup."

"Behave."

"Yes, Ms. Shelby."

Shelby walked out of the bar and headed into the darkness. She felt a little unsettled walking alone and didn't realize until that moment how dark the place was. *Maybe I should have taken one of the guys up on their offer to walk me to my truck. Too late now.* She took a deep breath and quickened her pace, thinking if she walked faster she wouldn't feel quite so alone.

As Shelby rounded the corner someone grabbed her from behind. She tried to scream, but a hand was over her mouth. Glistening in the dim light of the moon—a knife! It was in the hand of whoever had a hold on her. She gathered her thoughts as the assailant pulled her away from the corner of the building and closer to the wall. Shelby had taken some self-defense training years ago, but at the moment all she could think about was getting away from this person any way she could. She struggled against the strength of the perpetrator, trying hard to avoid the sharp blade of the knife.

"I'm going to kill you, bitch, for messing with my girlfriend."

What is this guy talking about? I'm not messing with anyone's girlfriend. He's got the wrong person. Shelby tried struggling with the man until she felt a piercing pain in her left thigh. She stopped struggling as the blood ran down her leg. The man then took the knife and plunged it into her arm. Although the stab hurt her like hell, she could tell that it only grazed her skin through her jacket. The knife was still in her arm and the perpetrator's hand was wrapped around the handle. Shelby screamed and then bit down as hard as she could on the man's wrist.

"Bitch," he barked as he pulled his punctured hand away from her!"

Shelby let out the loudest scream she could muster, causing the man to realize his mistake. He plunged the knife back into her arm and then took his fists and beat her face bloody. "I'll teach you to bite me and take money from my woman."

"I didn't take anything from anyone, you son-of-a bitch!"

The man kept pummeling her until she couldn't fight back. She collapsed flat on the ground near the wall. Suddenly, a group of men came out of the bar and headed in the direction of the blood-curdling scream.

"Shit." The man took off through the parking lot.

"Get some help, guys, she's in bad shape."

Shelby tried to wake up when she heard the far away voices. She saw outlined figures through her blood-crusted eyes. She felt weak and disoriented, the beating was over and she hoped the pain she felt would cease. As she moved in and out of consciousness she heard voices and felt her body being moved. She tried hard to focus on what was happening, but she just wanted to sleep. Finally, she closed her eyes, and gave herself over to sleep.

◊◊◊

"Get that bastard! I saw him run just around that truck over there." Super Saddle and Turtle searched from truck to truck looking under every box, flatbed, and bulk trailer parked in the lot.

"It's no use. He either left the lot, or is hiding in one of these trucks. He's not going to show his face after doing what he did to that girl."

Bert and Shadow joined the other two drivers in the middle of the lot after checking the other side of the parking lot. "Can't find the son-of-a-bitch anywhere."

"Man, did you see what he did to that little girl?"

"Yeah. What kind of man does that?"

"I don't know, but I wish we could find him and give him what he has coming."

"Come on, let's go see what the medics are doing for her. That asshole is probably long gone by now."

Mazulla Man had stayed with Shelby until the ambulance arrived. He tried to keep her warm by taking his coat off and putting it over her body. Before long several drivers had come out of the bar.

"Oh no, it's Shelby. Bobcat, go get the others and call Sandy," Luscious said, bending down next to Shelby and helping Mazulla Man hold the open wounds. "What the hell happened?"

"Not sure. We came out of the bar and found her on the ground. Some guy was running into the parking lot. Several of my friends went after him but they haven't come back. Not sure if that's a good thing or a bad thing."

"Man, Shelby, can you hear me?"

"You know this girl?"

"Yeah, she's a coworker."

"I knew I should have walked her back to her truck. Damn."

Sirens rang out as flashing lights from several cop cars, an ambulance, and a fire truck arrived at the truck stop. The medics and police quickly took charge of the scene, moving all unnecessary spectators back so they could take care of Shelby. "Patient is approximately 45-year-old, female, and un-conscious, with knife lacerations to the left thigh and left upper arm. Doesn't look like the knife has punctured any vital arteries. The knife is still lodged in her arm and the bleeding is heavy with the wounds deep. She has extensive bruising and lacerations to her head as well. Her pulse is erratic and patient is unresponsive." The medic radioed in the information to the local emergency room as he prepped Shelby for transportation.

The police focused on finding out as much as they could from the people who had gathered around the crime scene.

◇◇◇

Betty moved her curtain back slightly and watched through a small corner of her driver's side window. "Yes, I think Mark did it. I think he got rid of that horrible, nasty woman for me."

"Mark, who's Mark?"

"He's my friend and he offered to help me out tonight, unlike you, Ted."

"You didn't say the guy was a friend of yours. You just said someone was going to get Shelby for you tonight."

"Does it really matter, Ted? The job got done, and I'm so happy!"

Betty watched as the ambulance and fire truck left the scene. The police were still taking statements and patrolling the parking lot looking for the suspect.

"Let me in, Betty." A small knock caused Betty to let go of the corner of the curtain and open her driver's side door.

"What the hell are you doing here, Mark?"

Mark was breathing heavy as he climbed into the driver's seat. Betty motioned for Ted to get into the sleeper while she moved into the passenger seat. "You're covered in blood and it's getting all over my seat."

"Sorry, I got surprised by some guys coming out of the bar, and I had to get the hell out of there before they saw me. I think they even followed me into the parking lot, but I know they didn't see me. Coming to your truck was the safest thing for me to do until the cops leave and things quiet down."

"Well, to be honest, that was probably the stupidest thing. Especially if they check trucks. They'll think I had something to do with it."

"You did, baby."

Mark turned and looked at Ted in the sleeper. "Who are you?"

Betty interrupted before Ted could answer. "He's just a coworkers who came to check on me with all the commotion. So did you finish the job?"

"Yeah, I think so. If not, she is hurt really bad and won't be going back to work any time soon. Should we be talking about this in front of him?" Mark whispered and pointed toward Ted.

"It's alright, he hates her as much as I do."

"Oh, that bitch causing you trouble, too? Man, she was a scrapper. She must really be hell for you if she makes work as difficult for you as she fights."

"Yeah, she's a real wild one. Right, Ted?"

◊◊◊

Shelby couldn't feel much as she opened her eyes to a white room and the smell she hated that permeated in all hospitals. Very little of what had happened was vivid to her, but the pain was undeniable.

"I think she's coming around! Get the nurse." Shelby recognized Luscious' voice. "Hey, girl. How ya doing?"

Shelby's mouth and face hurt. She found it difficult to say much of anything. "Okay, I guess."

"Good. Don't talk right now. Save your strength. That bastard really messed you up."

"Call Jack."

"Already done girl, he and Eddy are on the company jet right now headed this way. They should be here in a minute."

"What about my load?"

"Don't worry, baby girl. The team is taking care of everything. It will get delivered. You just relax and get better."

The nurse came in to the room, followed by Speedy. He and Luscious backed away from Shelby's bed and let the nurse check Shelby's vital signs.

"You're one lucky little lady, Shelby. Those knife wounds just missed vital arteries, and your friends were smart enough to help stop the bleeding the best they could. Now, let's see how you're doing. I think you have a special guy coming from Texas to see ya. He sounded really anxious on the phone. Let's see if we can't get you cleaned up a bit before he gets here. Gentlemen, give us a few minutes, please."

Shelby moaned as the nurse lifted her off her pillow and put another one behind her head. Shelby managed a small voice. "Thanks, guys."

"No problem, Shelby," said Luscious as he and Speedy left the room. "We'll be right outside."

In the hallway, Luscious and Speedy found chairs to sit in while they waited. "Man, I want to find the mother fucker that did this to her."

"Me too. I can't understand why anyone would want to hurt Shelby."

Jack and Eddy walked down the hall. "Hey, guys. This is Jack—Shelby's husband. Jack, this is Luscious and Speedy, two of my drivers."

Jack shook hands with the drivers. "Have you heard anything?"

"She just woke up. The nurse is with her right now."

Jack hurried into Shelby's room.

The nurse had just given Shelby a sponge bath, getting rid of all the dry blood and dirt that had not gotten removed in the ER. The nurse lowered Shelby gently onto her pillows after washing her back. Shelby was exhausted from the bath and closed her eyes just as Jack came close to the bed. "How is she?"

"Banged up pretty good, but she's strong. She'll be alright. You must be her husband?"

"Yes, I'm Jack."

"Well, Jack, you have one little fighter on your hands. If it had been anyone else, she might not have been as lucky."

"That's my little Shelby."

Shelby opened her eyes and gave Jack a small smile. "Hi, babe."

"Hey, slugger. I understand the other guy looks a whole lot worse, but I find that hard to believe cause you look like hell." Jack laughed a bit and kissed Shelby on the forehead, holding the hand of the arm that had no bandages.

"Asshole."

"Yep, she's better." The nurse and Jack laughed while Shelby closed her eyes.

"Well, I tell you what—any woman who can handle a big rig and still wear pink steel toed boots around rough ass truckers is okay in my book."

"She does love those boots. They're okay aren't they, or do I need to buy her a new pair?"

"Oh no, the boots are fine. In fact, she's the talk of the hospital right now. Come on, let's let little Miss Celebrity rest, and I'll fill you in on what's happening with her. You can come back in after we have a little chat."

◊◊◊

Betty was furious when she heard from Doc Snow that Shelby was going to be alright. She kicked the tires on her truck as she reached for her phone to call Mark. "Well, it doesn't look like I'm moving to California. The bitch isn't dead and sounds like she's going to be just fine."

"Wow! I thought I really did her in, baby, but she'll be out of commission for a while. You can pay off those bills and still come here with me."

"Fat chance, asshole. There is no way in hell I'd be with you. You make me want to vomit." Betty shut her phone and yelled at Ted who was pre-tripping their trucks, "Come on! Now that little Miss Barbie is hurt and everyone has come to her rescue, we have to not only deliver our loads, but her load too."

"Who said?"

"Eddy. He called from the company plane this morning and he's here. Damn it. That woman has got to be a cat with nine lives or something."

CHAPTER TWENTY-TWO

It took Shelby about a month to recover from her injuries after flying home from California with Jack and Eddy. She had spent the largest part of the time off around the house and in therapy for her leg and arm. Other than visiting the office to chat with Sandy occasionally, Shelby had not seen or driven her big truck in four weeks. But once she'd regained strength in her arm and leg, she was ready to go back to work. Eddy informed Sandy that Shelby was to only be on local hauls for a while. Shelby and Jack both liked that idea.

It was a little strange for Shelby at first when she sat behind the wheel of her big truck. *I hope I still remember how to drive,* she thought.

Everyone in the company had welcomed her back…everyone except Betty and Ted. They had been sent to Wyoming to run loads for the northwest yard and they wouldn't be back until the end of the month. Shelby hadn't been to that yard yet, but there were some loads for that area on the board for the end of the year, along with a huge run into the Utah Mountains near Vernal. She hoped she would be in good shape when those runs came to fruition.

◊◊◊

"Look, Ted," Betty said one night as they lay in her sleeper. "I have had it with Sandy trying to keep me and you from Texas. We've been in this hellhole for six weeks now, and I'm determined to return home tomorrow with or without her permission."

"Sandy said she wanted us to stay here for another week."

"Like hell. I'm going home tomorrow."

"Alright, I'll tell Sunshine we won't be hauling with her to North Dakota in the morning."

"Wait, North Dakota? That's a good paying run. I'll do that run and then head south from there."

"Okay, we leave at five."

"Damn, do they ever sleep around here?"

◊◊◊

The local runs bored Shelby. *At least it's a paycheck,* she thought. *After all, isn't that why I took the job in the first place?*

She took a call from Sandy. "Hey, Sandy. What's going on?"

"Hi, Shelby. I was wondering how you're feeling?"

"Great, why?"

"Well, Eddy has cleared you for long hauls, so if you're feeling up to it, I have a haul for you down near the south yard. Then you'll check in with Casper and haul a few loads with the guys down there. I have a few other drivers going, so you won't be alone."

"Sure!" Shelby grinned. "I feel great, and to be honest, I'm ready for a long ride. Don't you worry about me. That was just a freak occurrence in California."

"I don't know, it seems to me trouble should be your middle name."

"Funny. Yes, I want the run."

"Great. I'll put you down for it. You'll need to deliver Wednesday morning. I'll put the paperwork in your box."

"Great, I'm going home. See ya later."

"Later, chickadee."

◊◊◊

Betty and Ted pulled into the yard and parked their trucks on the line. It was late and all the lights were out in the office. "I'm going into the office to get my paperwork for the job Sandy said she had lined up for us on Wednesday. I'll get yours too while you post trip the trucks."

"Okay."

Betty went into the office and got the paperwork out of her's and Ted's boxes. She looked over the job assignment sheet and the list of drivers who would be going. "Shit, I thought that bitch was stuck on local runs," Betty hissed as she threw the paperwork on the table and sat down. *There has to be some way I can get rid of Shelby without getting my hands dirty. But I can't depend on other people. Maybe I'll have an opportunity on this trip.*

Ted came into the office. "Why are the job assignments scattered here?"

"I put them here, you idiot."

"Why?"

"Because I felt like it. Guess who's going south with us?"

"Who?"

"Shelby. She's off local runs. I can't believe she's still alive."

◊◊◊

The trip to south Texas was wonderful, and Shelby enjoyed the long roll. She had delivered the load she carried to Eagle Pass and then went on to the yard in south Texas. It was late when she rolled into the yard, so she parked her truck next to the silos in the yard and went to sleep. She hadn't slept in her truck in a long time but it was comfortable, and she fell asleep right away, looking forward to the next day's assignments with her friends.

◊◊◊

As Shelby slept, Betty schemed with Ted. "It won't be long now. Casper just gave me the perfect opportunity to finally get Shelby Mathews out of my life. We need to get down to the border before the others, so I can make contact with a connection I have down there. This is going to work…I need for it to work… It's getting harder to be assigned jobs with her."

"When do we need to leave?"

"I want to leave in an hour so we can be down there before it gets dark. It's going to be hard enough finding the man I need to talk to, let alone doing it in the middle of the night."

"Okay. Just give me a call when you're ready to leave."

"You better be ready."

◊◊◊

Shelby was talking and joking with the guys at the table outside the driver's office when Ted walked by. "You and Betty going to the border with us tomorrow Ted?" Woodchuck asked.

"No. Betty wants to get down there before dark tonight."

"Be careful. Do you guys know where the caliche pit is down there?"

"Yeah, Betty has been there several times."

"We'll see y'all down there tomorrow."

"Whatever," Ted said and sulked off.

"What the hell is up with that guy? Betty can't be that great in bed. He does whatever she says, no matter what."

"I know; he's got issues."

◊◊◊

The sky was beginning to darken as Betty and Ted reached the Mexican border near Rio Grande City. They found a truck stop on the west end of the city and walked to the entrance gate into Mexico a few blocks away. "Now, let me do all the talking," Betty hissed. "I don't want to get us killed by these people, and you're mouth might just make that happen."

"My mouth? I can't even speak Spanish so how would I…"

"Shut up, Ted. Just shut up, okay?"

"Okay."

Betty walked to the border patrol station and showed the guard her passport with Ted right behind her. "The reason for your visit?"

"I have a friend I've come to see."

"Very good. Have a nice visit."

Betty and Ted walked headed straight toward a hotel notorious for some really dangerous people. The lobby had a musty smell and was lit by a small lamp positioned in the middle of the registration desk. The only other light was daylight that came from the cracks in the walls. The two walked toward the front desk almost stumbling over chairs and tables that blocked their path.

Ted didn't like the vibe he got from several of the men that were sitting in chairs, smoking cigars and drinking from liquor bottles spaced through-out the room. "Betty, we need to get out of here."

"Shut up, Ted. I need to talk to the girl at the desk." Betty approached the scantily dressed woman. Speaking in Spanish, Betty asked if the woman spoke English.

"Sí…"

"Gracias. I'm looking for Rico." The room got deathly quiet when Betty said the man's name.

"Rico not here."

"Do you know where I can find him? It's important."

"Rico may be here later. Why?"

"I need to give him money for a job."

"Are you from the Federales?"

"No, I'm just an American."

The girl put down the towel she had been using to dust off the front desk and went to a door to the rear of the room. "RICO!"

"What?" An older Mexican man appeared through the smoky haze. He looked at the young woman, angrily. After a brief secret conversation, the man puffed on his cigar and walked toward Ted. "You owe me money?"

Betty quickly put herself in front of Ted. "You speak English?" she asked.

"Yes." The man pushed Betty out of the way and spoke to Ted again. "You owe me money?"

Betty again tried to intervene, but the man wanted his answers from Ted. "Sir, I'm here to speak to you, not him."

"So what is he doing here?"

"I just wanted him to come along."

The man diverted his attention away from Ted and thrust his face directly in front of Betty's, blowing cigar smoke at her. "So what, *you* owe me money?"

The man's intimidation tactics were working. But Betty forced herself to suck up her fears. "Sir, I don't owe you money. I want to pay you money for a job I need done."

"What makes you think I'm looking for a job?"

"A while back a friend of mine—Carlos Riviera—pointed this place out to me when we came here to party. He said that some friends of his hung out here and if I ever needed any help I could just come in here and ask for Rico."

"Carlos Riviera isn't with us any longer. He managed to get himself killed while doing time in the States for delivering some product for us."

"I didn't know that."

"We still respect our brother Carlos, so if you're a friend of his, I'll honor his word. What is it you need?"

"I'm interested in buying a shooter."

Everyone in the room burst out laughing. "A shooter, why would you need a shooter?" Rico asked.

"I'm having a problem with a woman, and I want her dead."

Rico raised an eyebrow, "Why?"

"The reason isn't important. I have money and I'll pay to have her killed, but it has to be tomorrow."

Rico considered her proposition. After a while he spoke. "I have a shooter, but because you want it done in such a hurry, it will cost a lot."

"How much?"

"I want five thousand American dollars."

"Five thousand! I only have three thousand with me. What if you don't get the job done?"

"That is the risk you take for such short notice. In fact, I'll send out three of my best shooters just to make sure. It must be done in Mexico, though."

"It can't be in Mexico. They're only going as far as the caliche pit in Rio Grande City. They'll only be there tomorrow."

The man looked at his friends in the room and then sat in a chair next to one of the empty tables. "I don't know what to tell you, *señorita*. That is my price and those are my terms."

"I can't pay what I don't have, and I can't get her into Mexico." Betty and Ted turned to leave. "Is there anyone else I can talk to who might be able to help me out for the price I have and in the States?"

"I'm not sure anyone would do what you want for that price, and definitely not in the States."

Betty and Ted left the hotel and walked back down the alleyway toward the border. "Damn it to hell," Betty muttered. "I thought for sure that would work."

"Well, I'm glad we are out of there. Those guys might have killed us."

"Oh, quit being such a pussy, Ted. What would they gain by killing us?"

"Three thousand dollars."

"Shut up, Ted."

Just as they reached the gate that led back into the States, a young boy approached. "Señorita, my papa wanted me to bring you back to the hotel."

"Crap! You little shit—do you think you could scare me just a little more?"

"I sorry, but my papa wants you to come back, please."

"Fine, but I don't have all night to get this set up."

Betty and Ted walked back to the hotel with the boy. When they arrived, the little boy disappeared, leaving Ted and Betty to enter the hotel alone again. "I don't want to go back in there this time, Betty. I'll just stay out here."

"Like hell you will. You'll come in there with me if I have to drag you by your balls."

They entered the hotel again. This time there was a lady at the front desk who brought them a beer and had them sit down at a table. "Please sit down here. Rico will talk with you in a minute."

Betty and Ted sipped on their beers while they waited for Rico to return.

"This is spooky," Ted whispered. "What if they've decided we know too much or something and they're planning to kill us?"

"Well, I guess we'd be dead then, wouldn't we, dumb ass? You watch too much TV. Besides, if they wanted us dead they would have killed us in the streets and not in here where we would have made a mess for them to have to clean up."

Rico entered the room. "Good, I'm glad you returned. I discussed your offer with my compadres and I have reconsidered. I'll only send two shooters and no money back if we miss. My guys won't miss if she's a clear shot."

"Great, they'll roll into the caliche pit around ten in the morning, and besides me, she will be the only female in there. Do you know where the pit is?"

"Yes."

Betty stood and took off her boot. She retrieved money from the bottom of it and then put it back on. She did the same thing with the other boot until she had a stack of bills next to her feet on the floor. She picked up the money from the floor and did the best she could to straighten out the bills that had become crumpled in her boots. "This is all I have, three thousand."

The man took the money and shook Betty's hand. Two men with guns came out of the back. "These are my best shooters. They will do a good job."

Betty shook the men's hands. "I hope so."

"We'll take care of her."

"Thanks."

Rico moved Betty close to him and whisper into her ear. "Be assured señorita, if any of my men get hurt or caught, I'll come looking for you. Make sure nothing goes wrong tomorrow if you want to keep your life."

Betty knew the man was serious and backed away from him quickly. "I understand." Betty moved toward the hotel door with Ted right at her side.

In the dark alley, Ted looked at Betty who was still slightly white in the face. "What was that all about?"

"Shut up, Ted. Just walk."

◊◊◊

"Alright, is everybody ready to roll?" Buck asked over the CB.

Shelby, Doc Snow, Phantom 309, and Bobcat from the west yard were rolling with Buck. Leba, Scratchy, Elwood Blues, and Mario from the south yard had already left. "We'll be meeting the Mexico drivers at the caliche pit and we'll blow our sand into their trucks so they can take it across the border."

"Sounds like an easy job, today."

"Yep, should be fast, too."

"I like that—easy and fast."

"Bet you do, Scratchy," joked Shelby.

"Oh, she got ya on that one, Scratchy."

"Yeah, bet she's just my type, too."

"No way, Scratchy. I like things slow and easy, just ask my old man."

Everyone laughed.

It took the drivers several hours to reached their destination, but they had left early enough so that when they reached the pit it was still dark outside. "It's creepy out here. Explain to me again why we needed to be here so early?" Shelby asked.

"Sometimes when we get here early the drivers from Mexico will be here, and we'll get to unload sooner. Looks like just our drivers are here though." Buck observed.

"This place looks like a garbage dump." Shelby commented.

"I guess it could be, but I think it's just become a convenient place for people to rid themselves of their old junk," Scratchy explained.

Buck came over the CB. "Okay, we'll park these trucks along the east side and then just wait 'til the Mexican drivers get here."

"Is there a place to use the restroom?" asked Shelby, suddenly needing to pee.

"Yep, look out your door, Shelby you got all kinds of bushes and trees."

"Yuck, guess I'll hold it."

"We won't watch."

"Shut up, Scratchy."

Shelby sat in her driver's seat and noticed several of the drivers she was running with were gathered outside their trucks, talking. She decided to join the group. She grabbed the coffee she had picked up at the store earlier and got out of her truck.

"Look who decided to join the living?"

"Did you bring me some of that coffee?"

"She don't share," said Scratchy.

"Scratchy, you've been pushing it all the way down here. Maybe I need to draw a yellow line and whip your ass."

Suddenly, shots rang out throughout the pit, causing an explosion of quick movement from the drivers who stood talking. The first shots flew past Shelby on both sides of her body. "WHAT THE HELL?" she screamed.

Buck grabbed Shelby and pushed her to the ground. "Crawl under the truck and keep your head down." The next shots flew in Shelby's direction again, but because Shelby was under the sand hauler, the shots were useless. Shots began flying all though the pit in all directions, taking any target they could find.

Scratchy hit the ground after trying to hide behind the rear of a sand hauler. "Damn it, what the hell do these bozos want?"

Elwood Blues fell down next to Scratchy, holding his arm. "I don't know Scratchy, but they hit me in the arm."

Scratchy moved over next to Elwood Blues. "Let me see, man."

Just as Shelby was wondering if the shooting would ever stop, things suddenly went quiet. She lifted her head up out of the dirt and saw several drivers quickly getting to their feet. They were running in the direction of where the shots had come from on the hill.

Buck had worked his way through the gunfire by using the sand haulers as shields in order to get close to the suspects. Once he got close to them, the shooting stopped and he was on the ground holding his leg. "I'm hit, damn it I'm hit. They're running east. Get 'em."

Woodchuck, Equalizer, Mario, Phantom 309, Bobcat, and Doc Snow were already on their feet, moving cautiously toward the hill that had been the cover for the shooters.

Woodchuck yelled at Mario and Bobcat who were climbing the hill toward Buck. "Be careful. Get him down from there and get back to the trucks for cover! It's hard to tell when they might come back and start shooting again."

"I'm fine!" Buck yelled back. "See if you can see where they're headed. If they continue to head further east they're not locals, they're from Mexico."

Phantom 309 and Doc Snow kept climbing until they reached the area the shooters had occupied. They looked through the tall brush and down toward the valleys, trying to locate the direction of the gunmen. "They're heading east, Woodchuck."

"Okay, come on back down. They're long gone by now."

Shelby decided she was probably safe now, but still used the sand haulers for protection as she ran to check on Elwood Blues. She didn't get to check on Buck until the other drivers brought him down from the hill. When she reached Elwood Blues she checked his arm wound. Scratchy tried to help him but didn't really know what to do, so Shelby took over. Shelby looked at Scratchy. "What the hell just happened?"

"I have no idea, but those bullets came directly toward you when they started, Shelby. And, they didn't start until you came out of your truck. Who have you pissed off?"

Shelby ripped at Elwood Blues' shirtsleeve exposing more of the injury. She motioned for Scratchy to take off his shirt. "I have no idea, but it seems someone wants to get rid of me pretty damn bad. Give me your shirt." Scratchy opened up his shirt and took it off so that Shelby could use it to help stop the bleeding coming from Elwood Blues' arm. "Can you go to my truck and get a couple bottles of water out of my refrigerator, please?"

Scratchy got up and moved cautiously toward Shelby's truck. He opened the driver's side door, exposing the multiple bullet holes in the door panel. Scratchy didn't take time to check out any of the other damage but he could tell that Shelby's truck had purposefully been targeted. He retrieved the water and took it back to Shelby.

Shelby wet the shirt strips she had made and placed them around Elwood Blues' arm. "Scratchy, stay here with Elwood Blues while I go check on Buck."

Scratchy moved in closer to Elwood, but then pointed toward the entrance to the pit. "Help's coming, Shelby. Maybe you better just stay here until the guys bring Buck off the hill."

"Yeah, you're probably right. I just hope he's alright."

"He's barking orders at people, Shelby. He's alright."

"I guess so, I just feel so bad about what happened."

"Why, did you ask those shooters to cross the border and shoot at us?"

"No, but you said it looked like they were targeting me. You can't believe the things that have happened to me lately. It's like someone is after me."

"Don't be silly, Shelby. Who would be after you?"

"I know it sounds stupid, but it sure feels like it between this, the stabbing incident, and the guy that tried to push my truck into the Gulf."

"Nonsense. Now, concentrate on your patient here."

"You should have been a nurse instead of a trucker. You're pretty good at fixing people up," Elwood Blues said as he looked over her bandage job.

"It comes from having three boys."

It wasn't long before the pit was filled with lights and sirens from the local police and ambulance services. Ted and Betty had been watching the whole thing, but didn't leave their trucks until the shooting stopped. Betty looked around, then stomped her feet like a child throwing a temper tantrum in the dirt when she saw Shelby putting bandages on Elwood Blues.

"This is bullshit! All that money, and they missed," Betty whispered to Ted as they moved toward some of the drivers who were talking to the police. "That son of a bitch said he gave me his best shooters. The bastard lied to me and took my money. Shelby is costing me a lot of money and favors. I guess I'm just going to have to do this myself. I wanted to keep my hands clean, but the bitch has got to go!"

The drivers who had made it to the top of the hill to pursue the shooters were headed back down the hill. The medics were helping the drivers who had been helping bring Buck down the hill. The whole place was buzzing with questions about why this had happened and who did it. Mario and Bobcat let the police know that the shooters were heading for the border and had probably crossed over by now. "They're enjoying a beer by now, I imagine."

"I can't figure out why anyone would shoot at a bunch of sand haulers. We have nothing except maybe a little cash that wouldn't be worth stealing."

The cop taking the statements interrupted. "We have a lot of drug-related wars going on along the borders these days, so it's probably just a mistaken location for a shootout."

"Great. We were just mistaken targets," Mario said with frustration.

CHAPTER TWENTY-THREE

Shelby spent several more days in south Texas delivering loads and checking on her friends who were transported to the hospital with injuries. The police attempted to locate the perpetrators, but were unable to even locate witnesses who could identify the suspects who ran back over the border after the shootout. As she rolled down Interstate Ten toward home, she mulled over in her mind all the things that had happened over the last few months and wondered, *Do I really want to be in such a dangerous line of work? I didn't make much money teaching, but at least I was home safe every night. Is this worth it?*

◊◊◊

Jack answered the phone and spoke sharply when the caller refused to reply. "Hello, is anyone there?"

"Mr. Mathews?"

"Yes."

"I know you obviously haven't believed anything I have told you so far, because your wife is still fooling around on you. And, you're letting her."

"Look, I don't know who you are mister, but I've checked on my wife and she is always where she has been assigned. Why are you trying to cause trouble for us? Why don't you mind your own business?"

"Okay, but she's been seeing someone from out of town, so unless you've been checking on her while she's gone, you probably wouldn't know she's being unfaithful."

"If you know so much about what she's doing—why don't you give me times and dates and names so I can check it out for myself?"

"Oh, I wouldn't want to get the other people involved in any trouble. You might go crazy, or something, and hurt them."

"I think you're full of bullshit, and you need to stop calling my house before I call the police and complain about you harassing my family."

"Suit yourself, Mr. Mathews. Just hope she doesn't bring something home to you."

"Shut the fuck up and get off my phone."

Jack slammed the phone down just as Shelby walked through the door. "Hey, baby. I'm home." Shelby kicked off her boots at the front door and could tell from Jack's expression that something was wrong. "Who was on the phone, sweetheart?"

"Oh, just some bullshit."

She pressed him for more information as she moved in for a kiss and put her arms around his neck. "Bullshit, sounds kind of smelly to me. Would you like to elaborate a little further with your wife over a cup of coffee?"

Jack was not in the mood at the moment for getting cozy. He took Shelby's arms down from around his neck and gave her a quick peck on the lips before walking toward the kitchen.

"Wow, that was some greeting from a man who hasn't seen his wife in a few days. What the hell is going on, Jack? What kind of bullshit has got my husband so upset that he can't even kiss me when I walk in the door?"

Jack handed Shelby her cup of coffee, walked to the breakfast table, and sat down. Shelby took her cup and sat down next to him waiting for a response.

Jack sipped at his coffee for a few moments. "Shelby, I need to tell you about something that has been going on, but I just don't know how to talk to you about it. I don't think it's true, but I have all these questions."

"Just tell me, baby. What's going on? I love you, and we can work through anything."

Jack began telling Shelby about all of the letters and phone calls he'd been receiving.

Shelby was stunned as she listened to Jack explain what had been going on. "Why didn't you tell me about the letters and calls when they first began?

"I wanted to… I just didn't know how to bring it up…."

"Let me see. I think it would have been really easy, something like… *Hey, Shelby. I got this letter today that says you're fucking around.* Or maybe:

Shelby, I received a phone call today that let me know you were screwing someone while you were on a trip somewhere. Sounds pretty simple to me unless you just didn't want me to know someone was talking shit about me to you. Better yet, maybe you believed that crap and wanted to check up on me and see if it was true. Well, tell me, Jack. Did you find me doing anything wrong? Was I cheating, Jack?"

"No."

Jack knew the minute the word came out of his mouth that he had said the wrong thing.

"WHAT? You checked up on me? How could you do that without asking me first? I can't believe this; you really think I'd throw everything we have together, everything we have built together, away on some other ass-hole? Well, you're an asshole for thinking I would cheat."

Shelby got up from the table and slammed her coffee cup down. She left the kitchen and went to the bedroom to take a shower and cool off while Jack stewed over the one-sided argument he had just had with his wife. *How did this whole thing get turned around on me? How did I become the bad guy in the situation? I'm not going to take this from Shelby. I haven't done anything wrong. The phone calls and letters were about her, not me. Maybe she does have something to hide. Shelby is not going to make this my fault.*

He stomped into the bedroom just as Shelby had disrobed and was getting into the shower. "How dare you call me an asshole for not discussing it with you before now. Did you ever stop to think that maybe I didn't believe it and didn't want you to feel embarrassed or hurt about someone saying something bad about you?"

Shelby was in the shower, washing her hair, listening to Jack. "I wouldn't have been hurt or embarrassed over something so ludicrous. If you trusted me then why did you check up on me? You don't trust me, Jack, and that's what hurts me, not those stupid phone calls or letters. I have been very faithful to you, Jack, and you're a jerk for thinking I haven't been."

"It wasn't that I didn't trust you, Shelby. I just wanted to make sure."

"So you spied on me when you could have just asked me directly."

"You're saying if the tables were turned you would have asked me about this stuff instead of checking on me first."

"That's what I'm saying, Jack. I'd have trusted. Unless, of course, you lied to me about where you were going or what you were doing—then I'd have a reason not to believe you."

"So, if you didn't check on me, how would you know I was lying?"

"Believe me, Jack. I know you, and I know when you're lying."

Shelby finished her shower and wrapped herself in a towel.

Jack continued to stand in the doorway while Shelby dressed. "Why are you putting on jeans? It's almost time to go to bed."

She walked pasted him, grabbed her coat and purse and headed toward the door. "I'm going to go out and cool off."

"You're going to what? I don't think so. You're going to stay right here and finish this conversation."

Shelby opened the front door and walked to her car. "I'm going to go out, because if I don't, I'm going to get even angrier at you, and you really don't want that, now do you?"

"No, but where are you going?"

"I'm not sure, but don't wait up."

"Shelby, this is ridiculous!"

"Not as ridiculous as thinking I'm sleeping around." Shelby shut the door to her car and pulled out of the driveway.

"Shelby stop!" Jack called as she pulled away. "Let's talk some more."

But she didn't hear him. She was already gone.

As he stood there in the driveway, Jack felt like even more of an idiot. He decided to get in his truck and see if he could find her and talk things out. He drove down the street in the direction that Shelby went but had no idea where she might go. *She doesn't like bars that much, unless she's with a group. It's too late for her to go to a friend's house, and most of the department stores are closed. She wouldn't involve Jack Jr. in something like this.* Jack thought for a moment and then it came to him: *Work.*

Jack decided he would give his wife a little time to cool off before he went to her truck. He went by the local store and bought a little bouquet of flowers.

Shelby loved flowers and he always got some for her whenever he made an ass out of himself. He stopped by the local ice cream store and got some of her favorite ice cream just in case the flowers weren't enough this time.

Jack pulled into the ESCC yard and just as he suspected, Shelby's car was parked out in the yard near her truck. She had parked it back far enough that it wasn't visible from the street, but it was there. He pulled his truck in with the headlights off and parked as close to hers as he could, hoping that she wasn't able to hear his truck over the noise of her big rig. He took the ice cream, spoons, and flowers out of his pickup, then gently knocked on Shelby's truck door. Shelby looked out her driver's door window. She pulled back the curtain and got back in her sleeper. "Go away, Jack."

"Come on, Shelby. I brought flowers and ice cream…," Jack pleaded.

Shelby knew Jack was trying. She got out of her sleeper and opened her driver door. "Rocky Road?"

"Yep, your favorite."

Jack climbed into the truck and presented Shelby with the flowers and ice cream. "Am I forgiven?"

"Only if you brought spoons."

Jack pulled the spoons out of his pocket and showed them to Shelby. "Spoons."

Shelby took the flowers and smelled them while Jack found a seat on the bed next to her and opened the ice cream. "Forgiven."

"I'm sorry, baby. I should have told you about everything instead of playing spy."

"It's alright, but do you really think I'd do that to us? Who else knows what it takes to get me to not be mad anymore?" Shelby put her head on Jack's shoulder and licked the spoon off that had just been full of ice cream. "Nobody."

Jack and Shelby each took turns at the pint of ice cream. Shelby laid the flowers in the driver's seat and took off her shirt with the spoon from the ice cream still in her mouth. After removing her shirt she took the spoon out of her mouth then touched Jack's nose with it while placing her body between his legs while he sat on the bed. "Would you like to spend the night with me in my sleeper, you bad boy?"

Jack placed the ice cream container and spoon on the shelf next to the sleeper bed. Taking off his coat, he pulled Shelby in close to him and kissed her breasts that were slightly exposed at the top of her bra. "I don't know… Do you want me to spend the night with you?"

Shelby rubbed Jack's hair with her hand and then pulled his head in closer as he kissed her chest. "Yes, I do."

Jack kissed his way up Shelby's neck, making his way to her lips. The passion in the kiss gave no room for question as to how Shelby and Jack would be spending the next few hours in Shelby's truck.

◊◊◊

"Look, Ted. I don't care what you think, but that bitch has got to go. And since nobody else has been able to do it, it looks like it's going to have to be us this time."

Ted turned over and put his hand on his forehead. "I don't know Betty, I'm not sure I can really hurt someone directly like that. You know, kill them."

"Oh shit, Ted. Quit being such a pussy. We just have to figure out a good time and place and just let it happen. Don't worry, I won't ask you to do it up close and personal. I'll figure out how to do it from a distance so we won't get dirty."

"Good."

"I know there are some big jobs coming up soon, and the next big one we get put on with her she's going down."

Betty got off the sleeper bed and grabbed her clothing. She picked up Ted's clothes from the floor and threw them at him. "Get dressed. It's getting light outside and we need to go before the office groupies get here."

Ted sat up on the bed and dressed while Betty put on her shoes in the driver's seat. "Office groupies?"

"Oh, shut the hell up, Ted. Sometimes you drive me insane. When I think about just how stupid you are, I wonder why I'm even with you."

Ted ignored Betty' insults he didn't care what came out of her mouth as long as she kept using her mouth in other ways he liked.

◊◊◊

The brim of light that showed itself briefly under the curtain that Shelby had placed around the windows in her truck woke her from the sound sleep that she was enjoying in her husband's arms. *I probably overreacted to the whole thing. I won't admit it, but it makes me feel better knowing that he loves me enough to come looking for me. And certainly knows how to apologize.* "Hey, baby. We better get up and go home for showers. People will be coming into the yard soon and wonder what's going on."

Jack snuggled next to his naked wife. "Let them wonder."

Shelby held Jack for a few moments. "Jack, baby, we really need to go home."

Jack moaned while letting go of his wife.

Shelby got up and began to dress while Jack slowly sat up on the bed and reached for his clothes. "Okay, but I'm not finished sleeping with you yet."

"Got ya, but we need to finish that sleep time in our bed at home."

Jack bounced his hand on the bed as he dressed. "This bed isn't that bad. A little small, but really not that bad."

Shelby was brushing her hair when she slid the curtain away from the passenger side window slightly, trying to see if anyone had arrived at the front office yet. She began to giggle as she dropped the curtain and continued brushing her hair. "Guess we weren't the only ones taking advantage of a free night of rest and pleasure in a company truck."

Jack zipped his pants and pulled back the curtain to see what his wife was so amused about. "What are you talking about?"

"Betty and Ted apparently spent the night in the yard last night together, too."

Jack watched as Ted, then Betty, climbed out of Betty's truck. "Are they the ones you accidentally caught in the warehouse?"

"Yep. Now that's a couple having an affair. We better let them leave before we do, so they won't say anything."

"I don't mind waiting," he said with a kiss.

"It's a real soap around here sometimes," she laughed and kissed him back.

"Jack, I've been thinking. Maybe we should reconsider me driving trucks. I love what I'm doing, but it just seems like every time I turn around something bad is happening. I'm not a quitter, but maybe we should at least think about me going back to teaching now that you're going to be cleared to work full-time."

Jack listened, but there was not conviction in Shelby's voice. "You can't really be serious about giving up driving? You're happy, Shelby… really happy, driving this big old truck. I'm not sure going back to teaching will make you this happy. Maybe you should just give it a little more time and see if things are still going badly before you decide. You know, with all that's happened, surely things have got to get better."

"You could be right. Maybe it's time for things to improve. I'll give it a little more time, but I may consider going back to teaching. If for nothing else, so I won't feel like someone is trying to kill me."

◊◊◊

Shelby spent the next few weeks driving her truck in the mountains of Wyoming and Colorado. She was running loads of sand from Rock Springs to several different locations in the Rocky Mountains. Sandy seemed to have a hunch even without being told that Shelby was beginning to question her choice in careers. Not wanting to lose one of her best drivers, Sandy sent Shelby alone to Rock Springs.

The weather was still cold in several places, and Shelby was greeted with ice and snow on the roads. But she was having a great time, even with the treacherous weather conditions. Her trips to the hills in North Dakota introduced her to several drivers from the northern yard. Paul was a nice man who ran with her several times, along with his sister, Sunshine, and nephew Darren. She also met two drivers named Wizard and Hand Full. The drivers had helped her find her way to a small town in North Dakota.

◊◊◊

Betty was smoking a cigarette in her driver's seat while Ted lay naked on her sleeper bed. "I heard in the office yesterday that we have a big job in Utah,

221

just before Christmas. Sandy told Speedy that every available driver's going and even some from T.R.I. I think that will be the perfect opportunity for me to get at Shelby, especially if I can work it out somehow to get her and us separated from the rest of the drivers. What better way to make sure she gets dead then to show her the edge of a mountain from the front window of an eighteen wheeler?"

"But, I thought she was working out of the northwest yard for a while."

"Yeah, she is, but from what I heard yesterday, they have her rerouted home now. So, she should be back in plenty of time to take one of those loads with us."

Ted rolled over on his side. "So what's the plan? We just going to push her off the mountain or something?"

"Yep, that's the plan. I just have to work out a few of the details and figure out how to keep her from getting any help from other drivers."

"How are you going to manage that? She knows you don't like her. Why would she go anywhere with you?"

"I don't know yet, Ted, but I'll email you and let you know what I've come up with. Now, get your dumb ass dressed and out of my truck before everyone starts showing up this morning."

"Okay. Jeez, you don't always have to be such a bitch about things."

CHAPTER TWENTY-FOUR

At seven thirty, Jack had made a sandwich and was heading back to his shop to work on a motorcycle he had agreed to fix for a friend when the doorbell rang. He put his sandwich down and went to the front door to see who it was. A short little red-haired round lady with one child on her hip and one holding her hand stood at his door. "Can I help you?" Jack asked as he noticed the rather run-down minivan in his driveway, containing several more children.

The young mother spoke softly and apologetically. "I'm really sorry to bother you, Mr. Mathews. You're Shelby Mathew's husband, correct?"

Jack's heart sank and his mind began to race with all kinds of thoughts about a possible truck accident, or worse, since Shelby had just left earlier that morning for her run to Utah. "Yes, I'm Jack Mathews, Shelby's husband. What can I do for you?"

"I'm really sorry to come to your home, but your phone is unlisted and the office at ESCC wouldn't give me your number, and well, I have something really important to show you." The young woman let go of the child who was holding on to her hand and tried to pull a stack of untidy papers from a diaper bag she had on her shoulder. The baby on her hip slipped downward as the young woman dropped several of the papers on the porch while reaching for the other child who was now attempting to wander off.

Jack, seeing the difficulty the mother was having, gently took hold of the wandering child's hand and sat him in a chair near the door on the porch. He then quickly gathered the now scattering papers. The young woman balanced the baby back on her hip and handed the remaining stack of wrinkled and muddled papers out for Jack to examine. "Thank you, oh, I'm Annabel." She informed Jack as she let go of the papers that remained in her hand. She moved near the child that was now rocking nicely in the chair Jack had put him in.

Jack couldn't make heads or tails of the mess of documents, but they looked like copies of emails from one person to another. While Jack looked over the emails, the young woman elaborated further on the reason for her being there. "Mr. Mathews, those emails are to my husband from a woman that your wife and my husband work with at ESCC If you read those emails, you'll see where my husband—soon to be ex-husband—and that woman, Betty, he has been seeing are planning on hurting or killing your wife when they get into the mountains in Utah.

"I've suspected for some time now that Ted had been seeing Betty, but until I found those emails on his computer today, I didn't have any proof. When I began to read them though, I knew I had to warn Shelby that Betty and Ted were going to try and hurt her. I guess she caught them some time or another having their little affair and well, Betty being Betty won't stop until she gets what she wants. I've known Betty for years and I know exactly what she is capable of. Just look, what she's done to my marriage."

The woman rambled on while Jack patiently listened and read the material. "I went to school with her before she went on the road with her dad, and she was always causing trouble. I can't believe she would really go this far though. She's crazy."

Jack interrupted the woman. "Thank you for this information, but do you really think this woman, Betty, and your husband are going to go through with what they're planning in these emails?"

Annabel looked squarely at Jack and responded with confidence. "Absolutely. She's nuts, and she has Ted under her spell. She'll get Ted to do anything. I think she might be an evil witch or something."

Jack was concerned about Shelby's safety. "Did you show these to Sandy or Eddy at the office?"

"No, I thought coming to you would be better. I didn't want Ted to get fired or in trouble. Then he won't be able to pay child support on all my kids."

Jack realized the woman had other motives for this visit besides Shelby's safety. He wasn't belittling the pain she must have been experiencing from the knowledge of her husband's infidelity. However, it was obvious she was not focused on the more dangerous situation at hand.

Jack reached for the door handle, needing to go into the house with the papers for a closer examination. All he wanted to do was warn Shelby she was in danger. "Thanks, Annabel. I need to go inside now and call Shelby. I appreciate you bringing this to my attention." He went inside, leaving her to the task of getting her children to her van by herself.

As Jack entered the house he heard Annabel mumble something while walking down the driveway. It sounded like, "If Shelby sees Ted, tell him he's in trouble when he gets home." He ignored whatever it was he thought he heard and headed straight for the phone.

Shelby answered on the second ring. "Hello?"

Jack took a deep breath. "Shelby, where are you?"

"I'm almost to Farmington, New Mexico, sweetheart. Why?"

"Shelby, I'm not sure what is going on, but Annabel, Ted's wife, came by the house just a minute ago. She gave me some emails she recovered from Ted's computer today. What I've been reading seems to indicate Betty and Ted are going to hurt you when you get into the mountains. I know it sounds bizarre, but I tend believe her. You need to stay away from them and come home as soon as you can. In the meantime, I'll call the police."

Shelby couldn't believe what she was hearing especially since today had been such a great day. Betty had actually been civil towards her all day. "No Jack, I don't want you to call the police, and I'm not coming home right now, either. Everything is fine here. You're overreacting. I'll keep my eyes open and be careful around them, I promise. I don't trust her or like her, but I don't think she'd really try to kill me with all the other drivers around. Everything seems alright up here, in fact, we are all about ready to shut down in Farmington for the night."

Jack wanted to believe Shelby and trust her judgment, but he had a bad feeling. He thought about all the things that had happened to her over the last few months. Now he knew those incidents were not just accidents or coincidental. The emails proved that something else was going on. "Shelby, I understand what you're saying, but I'm worried. Annabel believes that Betty is very capable of doing something bad to you. What about all these emails I'm looking at?"

"I don't know. Maybe Annabel made them up to get you to help her get back at Ted, now that she has proof about his affair with Betty. Jack I'm fine. I'm with ten other drivers besides Betty and Ted. How do you suppose they plan to get rid of me with all those people around? Please, Jack, don't worry."

"Fine, but you call me when you shut down, when you get up tomorrow and when you get to the mountains. I'm not going to stop worrying about you. Remember, if you don't call me I'm going to call the police. Promise me, Shelby. I love you and I don't want anything to happen to you."

"I love you too, baby. I'll call, I promise. Stop worrying. Bye, sweetie."

Jack reread the papers Annabel had left with him. When Steven came in from work, he found Jack milling through the papers at the dining room table. "What are you doing, Dad?"

"Oh, this woman came by tonight with all these emails. She says that her husband had been communicating with another woman from your mother's workplace, and they're having some kind of affair."

"Mom's having an affair?"

"No, don't be ridiculous. This woman's husband is having an affair with another woman that your mother works with. These emails indicate they might be planning to hurt your mom."

"Why does someone who's having an affair want to hurt Mom?"

"I guess your mom knew about them. Now it appears that all those things that have happened to your mom these last few months were not exactly accidents," Jack explained. "I tried to warn your mom when I called her a little while ago, but she says she's fine. I made her promise to call when she shuts down tonight, but I just can't shake this terrible feeling."

Steven's eyes widened as he read through the emails. "These people are crazy. Did you see this? There's proof here that they were behind several of the things that happened to Mom. Look."

"I know. I've read them all…multiple times."

Steven continued anyway. "They're talking about when Mom got shot at on location, remember? Man, Dad, if they had balls enough to have mom and those other drivers shot like fish in a barrel, you know pushing her off a mountain wouldn't be that hard for them. I think you need to call the police."

"I know, but your mother will never forgive me if I call the cops on these people and nothing happens."

"Yeah, but you'll never live with it if you don't. Look at this. It proves that Betty and Ted were behind the stabbing. These two should be in prison."

"You're right. I have to call the state police in New Mexico and Utah, even if your mother gets upset with me."

As Jack and Steven were talking, Mark arrived with some of his motorcycle buddies. Mark had come home on leave for the holidays and was hanging out with his old friends. "That's a first… Steven is right about something?"

Steven scowled and Mark's friends laughed. "What's all this?" Mark asked, pointing to the printouts.

"Someone has been trying to hurt your mother. Steven will fill you guys in, I've got to make some calls."

"What's wrong?" Mark asked when Jack rejoined them.

"Well, they want me to fax copies of the emails to them and give them the route your mother is traveling. They say they can't really do much except keep an eye on them until something happens. The emails only suggest that they might do something, not that they will, and they won't stop them on a hunch. We'll just have to wait and see if anything happens. Damn it."

"To hell with the police, I'm going to Utah and get me a piece of these two psychos. You guys can stay here and wait to see if something happens to Mom, but I've got proof enough here for me. They've already done plenty. They won't be doing anything else to her if I can help it."

Mark put on his helmet and pointed at his friends. "You guys want to come watch me kick some ass?"

"Hell, yeah," they shouted in unison.

"Wait," Jack said. "We'll all go, but we need a plan. They have ten or twelve hours of driving time on us and although we do have their shut down time on our side, getting there will be difficult."

"Steven, go call Jack Jr. and get him over here. Mark, get the map from the office and I'll find your mother's little black book; it's got all the names of the drivers who she's met since going on the road. We'll probably need help from some of them if we plan on getting to your mother in time."

◊◊◊

"Hey, Shelby," Betty announced on the radio, "Ted and I are going to stop at this little café we know of in Bloomfield. They have great food and a nice parking lot we can stay in for the night if you want to stay there with us. I think the other drivers are going on into Farmington, but they have to split up because there isn't any real big truck stop there. You can go on with them if you want, but parking is a little more difficult there."

I'm not sure I want to be separated from the other drivers, especially after Jack's call. "How far away is Farmington?"

"Oh, about eight or so miles."

"The parking isn't good?"

"No, they just have some parking areas you can use to shut down in for the night."

Farmington's close, I'll be okay. Betty is making an effort to be nice. "Yeah, I guess I'll stay with you guys. I'm hungry anyway."

"Great! It's on the left side of the road at the bottom of the hill, just as you get into town. It's called King something."

"Okay, I'll be right behind you."

A couple other drivers overheard the conversation. "Sounds good to us too, we'll join ya'll."

Betty wasn't thrilled that others were going to join them, but she'd already decided how she was going to separate Shelby from the group. "Great," she said, stiffly. "One big party."

◊◊◊

One by one, the drivers pulled into the café and parked their trucks. Shelby gathered her phone and money and comb from her purse and headed into the café right behind Ted and Betty. Speedy and Shot Gum Rider were already seated at a large round table looking at menus. "Buying dinner, Shelby?" Speedy asked as she sat down next to him.

"Yeah right, steaks all around." The table was full of laughter as the waitress took drink orders.

"Where are your restrooms?" Shelby asked.

"I'll show you," Betty said before the waitress could respond.

"Okay." They got up from the table, and the others stared in silence as the two women headed to the rest room.

"Wow, that's a first," Shotgun Rider said. "Betty is actually being civil to another female?"

"I just wonder what she's up to." Speedy said.

"Got that right. Betty isn't nice to anyone for any reason."

Shelby laid her keys and phone on the counter and washed her hands. Then she began combing her hair. She pulled the strands from the comb with a paper towel and turned to throw them in the trashcan. Betty was washing her hands, watching Shelby in the mirror. When Shelby's back was to her, she reached up and stuck Shelby's phone into her pocket.

Shelby turned back to collect her things. "That's weird, I could have sworn I laid my phone up here." Shelby patted the counter and then went back into the stall to see if she had left her phone there. "Hey, you didn't happen to notice if I brought my phone in here, did you?"

Betty was wiping her hands with paper towels now. "No, maybe you left it on the table."

"Maybe…" Shelby was trying hard to remember and hurried out the door to check the table.

Betty lagged back so that she could turn off Shelby's phone in case someone tried to call her. Betty disabled the phone and put it back in her pocket.

Shelby looked over the table and at the spot she had been sitting in to see if the phone was at her seat. The phone wasn't there and she was becoming concerned, especially since she promised Jack she would call him when they shut down for the night. "Anyone seen my cell phone?"

The other drivers moved their menus and checked the table. "No, I think you had it when you went to the bathroom," Ted said.

"Yeah, that's what I thought, but it wasn't anywhere in there."

"Maybe you left it in your truck," Betty said as she sat down at the table.

"Maybe. I'm going to go check. I promised Jack I'd call when we shut down."

"Oh, have dinner and then go check. He can wait for you to eat, can't he?" Speedy suggested.

"I guess, but I did promise and if I don't call soon he'll have a cow." *I don't want him to get crazy and call the police*, she thought.

"Wow, quite the demanding hubby, isn't he? What's he going to do, call the cops if you don't call him?" Betty mocked.

"No, but he worries about me, especially with all the bad luck I've had on the road. I'm going to go out to my truck and look right quick."

Speedy reached into his shirt pocket and pulled out his phone. "Here, use mine. You can look for yours later."

"Thanks." Shelby took Speedy's phone and dialed Jack. She ordered a chef salad from the waitress while she waited for him to answer.

"Hello?" Jack answered.

"Hey. We made it to Bloomfield, New Mexico, and I'm having dinner with a bunch of the drivers."

"Whose number are you calling from?"

"Oh, Speedy let me use his phone. I left mine in the truck."

"I thought you were shutting down in Farmington?"

"Yeah, well Betty said that this place was better and that the food was really good, so a few of us stopped here."

"So you're still with Betty and Ted?"

"Yes, Jack, among others."

"I take it you aren't able to talk because of the company you're around?"

"That's true, but everything is fine. I promise."

"Alright, Shelby, but something isn't right, and I'm concerned. You call me when you get back to your truck. We have to talk about this, you're not thinking clearly, this woman is dangerous."

Shelby got up from the table and walked to the back of the room. "Jack, I'm fine! Don't you dare do anything to embarrass me in front of the people I work with. I mean it."

Jack and the boys had already decided what they were going to do…with or without Shelby's permission. "I know what you're saying, baby, but I have proof she's going to try and hurt you, and I think you need to at least be cautious of her."

"I will, Jack, just calm down and trust me."

"It's not you I don't trust."

"Jack! I love you, just knock it off, please."

"Love you too, babe. I gotta go. The boys are here and they want to go riding."

"Good, go riding, but don't be out too long in this cold weather. I don't want you to get sick. Remember you're going back to work full-time soon."

"Okay, I won't."

"Tell the boys I love them…and I love you, too. Don't worry, baby. I'm fine. I promise, okay?"

"Okay, I love you, too."

Shelby hung up the phone and headed back to the table. *Jack doesn't give up that easy. I wonder what he's up to. I'll deal with him after dinner on my own phone in the privacy of my truck.* She handed the phone back to Speedy. "Thanks, Speedy."

Betty was eating a salad and looked up. "Trouble at home with the hubby?"

"Not really. He's just a worry wart."

Ted interrupted. "I wondered how your husband did with you out on the road like this."

"He doesn't really mind, but he has been a lot more protective since the incident in California."

Shotgun Rider spoke up. "Yeah, I heard about that. If that had happened to my wife, she wouldn't be driving anymore."

Shelby picked at her salad. "Would you think the same thing if I were a guy?"

"Probably not. But you gals have to be a lot more careful out here than us guys. We can protect ourselves a little better than you can. No offense, but that's just the facts. Some of these places we go to aren't really safe and unless you're an expert in some type of defense or martial arts. You need to be real careful."

"So you're saying women shouldn't be out here?" Betty sniped.

Shotgun Rider held up his hands defensively. "No, I didn't say that. I just think women have to be more careful than men, and they have to know how to defend themselves because there isn't always going to be someone around to help them in case they get into trouble. Like with what happened to Shelby in California. If she would have known some defensive moves or been with a group in a better lit area that never would have happened."

Shelby already felt guilty about not taking more precautions that night and didn't really want to rehash past mistakes. She kept quiet and ate her salad.

◊◊◊

Jack put the map in the middle of the table. Jack Jr. had joined his father, brothers, and bikers. They planned a route based on the route Shelby was taking with the sand haulers. He discussed with them places they would meet if they encountered trouble and possible fuel stops. "Now, if they take their full ten-hour break, we should just be a couple hours behind them if we can get some help making time through New Mexico and Texas.

"Mark—you, Jack Jr., and your friends can ride lookout. You might have to be decoys from time-to-time. Steven and I can get through in the pickup in case any law enforcement rolls up on you. I'm hoping we can pick up some of your mom's trucker friends along the way. Your mom talks about how they've helped her out while she's been on the road. Maybe they'll help distract the police, should we encounter any. That way we can move faster.

"If any of you get stopped I'll gladly pay the tickets. Our objective is saving Shelby, but please don't do anything that could get you hurt. Don't do anything stupid, Mark."

"Gotcha, Dad."

"Good."

Mark reached for his helmet and he and his friends headed through the front door, chanting, "We feel the need…THE NEED FOR SPEED!"

I hope I'm doing the right thing, Jack thought.

Jack Jr. joined Mark and his six friends in the front yard as they put on their helmets and mounted their bikes. Jack and Steven got into the pickup with the map, black book, and cell phones. They all headed to the local convenience store for fuel before heading through Texas and into New Mexico.

◊◊◊

After dinner, Shelby returned to her truck and searched every possible spot she could think of for her cell phone. It was nowhere to be found. She decided she should check the restroom again, but found the café was closed for the night and knew she'd have to wait until morning. *Jack's not going to be happy if I don't call. Maybe Betty will let me use her phone.* Once she got to Betty's truck, she had second thoughts about waking Betty up and walked back to her truck. *I wish pay phones were still around.* Shelby crawled back into her truck. *I'll just call Jack in the morning. I just hope he doesn't do anything stupid because I haven't called.*

Betty was nervous about getting caught with Shelby's cell phone. She peeked out of her truck window to make sure no one was around. She got out of her truck and walked behind Shelby's truck. She threw it under one of Shelby's truck tires and hoped Shelby would run over it when they left in the morning.

◊◊◊

Shelby had insisted that Jack put a CB radio in his pickup a few months ago, and he was glad he'd complied. Although he couldn't use it to communicate with the bikers, and would use lights and hand signals with them, he'd be able to communicate with truck drivers and other CB operators in the event he needed some help. He decided to test it out once they were on the highway. "Hey, my name is Jack. I'm not really familiar with how to talk on this radio, but my wife, Shelby, is a truck driver and she's in trouble. I need some help

233

getting to her in a hurry before something terrible happens to her. Does anyone out there hear me?"

"Yeah, we got a copy on you, Jack. This here is the Lone Star Base Station and we'd be happy to help you out. What's your twenty and where you headed?"

"Twenty, what's that? I'm headed into the Utah Mountains."

The voice from the base station came back. "Sorry, forgot you don't speak CB yet. Twenty means, where are you? Why you going into the mountains this time of year?"

"We're headed north on 385. Shelby is a hauler headed up there with a load of sand. A couple of her coworkers are going to try and hurt her in the mountains, and we need to stop them."

"Shelby? Cute little blonde? Yeah, everyone around here knows that sweet little lady. You're her old man?"

"Yes."

"Well, we'd be happy to help you out, anything for little Shelby. Just give me your route, and I'll get on the radio to other base station. Those stations will get in touch with drivers along that route so they can help clear a path for you."

Jack wasn't too shocked to find out that folks knew his wife. Shelby was very outgoing. *Maybe being trusting has contributed to her present situation, but I love that my wife is friendly.* "Thanks, I really appreciate the help, Lone Star Base," Jack said and then relayed the route to the base station.

"Got it, Jack. It will take me a few minutes to make contact with the other stations, so you just hang tight. We'll have you spotted and protected in just a little bit."

While the base station was setting up the line of protection for Jack and the boys, several other drivers came over the radio and talked with Jack about the situation. Many of them were local drivers who knew Shelby and wanted to help. "How about you, Jack?"

"This is Jack."

"Jack, my name is Shifty Gears," the driver responded, "and I'm rolling northbound on 385 with General Lee, Roadrunner, M&M, Texas Viking, One-handed Man, and Dirty Whore."

"Glad to meet ya."

"We all work for a competitor of the company that your wife works for and we'd be happy to take the front door for ya. We can take you guys as far as 380 in North Texas."

"I appreciate that, Shifty Gears."

"Not a problem. Shelby's a sweetheart. It just doesn't make sense that someone would want to hurt her. Who is it?"

"A couple of people she works with, we think."

"She couldn't hurt a fly. Why would anyone want to hurt her?"

"We don't understand it ourselves. We just want to get to her and fast. She doesn't believe that they're going to try anything. I tried to tell her, but she's in her own little world sometimes."

"I hear that," Shifty Gears said. "Most women only hear what they want to hear."

"I'd be happy for you guys to take the lead. I got a couple of my boys and their friends on bikes up there. I hope we don't have to, but they will act as decoys if I need them to. I don't have very good communication with them, so having you guys take the lead would give me ears and eyes up front.

"Gotcha, Jack. If you can let the bikers know we are taking the lead."

"Sure, no problem."

Jack flashed his lights at the boys and Mark backed off enough to get beside his dad. Jack rolled down his window and yelled at Mark that the trucks behind them would be taking the lead.

Mark waved. "Gotcha, Dad."

"Okay, Shifty Gears, the boys will back down and let you guys take the lead. I sure appreciate the help." He was becoming concerned with the speed that they had taken on but knew Shelby needed them, so he just kept moving.

"No problem, Jack. Anything for Shelby." Within minutes five grey and silver sand haulers rolled by Jack's pickup.

Shifty Gears spoke up on the radio. "Okay, Jack. We got the front door and we'll let you know if we see any full grown, baby, or mama bears running loose out here."

"Thanks, Shifty Gears. Not sure what a full grown is, but I'm assuming you're talking about cops."

"Yep, cops. Oh, just so you know, I left a couple of the boys at your back door so they can watch your flank. Sometimes those DOT boys can be kind of sneaky. Wouldn't want them to get you from behind."

Before Jack could reply, the Lone Star Base Station came back on the radio. "Hey, Jack. You got a copy?"

"This is Jack."

"Okay, I contacted base stations in New Mexico, Arizona, and Utah, and they have your route. These are the towns that will pick you up by radio." Lone Star listed off the towns.

"Thanks, Lone Star. I'll be sure and let Shelby know she has good friends out here." Jack sat back in his seat and checked his phone for the hundredth time. He still hadn't heard from Shelby and when he called, all he got was her voicemail. *Shelby promised she'd call, and she is always kept her promises. I hope it's just service problems.*

CHAPTER TWENTY-FIVE

J ack and the boys made their fuel stop and introduced themselves to some of the sand haulers who they'd talking with on the CB. "Hey, I really appreciate all the help, guys," said Jack. "If you ever need anything let me know."

"We're only going to be able to be with you for another few miles because we're close to our drop off point. We'll take you as far as our turn off on Highway 380. Be sure and tell that nice lady hello from us."

As soon as Jack reached the 380 turn off, another driver was on the radio with him.

"Overheard your conversation, Jack. I'm Triple L, and I'm on my way into New Mexico. I can take the front door if you like, and I have a number of friends on the roads in that area right now if you would like their help."

"Triple L, that would be great. My boys and I really need to get to Farmington as quickly as possible."

"Let's go, then. I'll get in touch with my friends and let you know where they will be to help."

"I made a few phone calls to some motorcycle friends of mine too," Jack said. "They're going to meet up with us at Wagon Wheel. I think going through the city and safety corridors up there will be one of our biggest obstacles, especially at these speeds."

"Okay, I'll get my buddies on the horn and have them ready and waiting. With their help we should be able to get you through that area in record time."

Shelby was right; these truckers are friendly and helpful. What is it about this breed of working men and women that make them so generous?

Triple L interrupted Jack's thoughts, "I know a shortcut around alien town, so just stay on my bumper and we'll be on 285 in no time."

"Got it; I'm right on your bumper. I got a phone call; be right back."

Jack hoped that it was Shelby, but the voice on the other end was a friend from an old motorcycle club he and Shelby had ridden with years ago. "Hey, buddy. What's up?" Jack asked, trying not to sound too disappointed.

"We're making our way around alien town right now. "We should be there in a couple hours."

"We have had lots of help from base stations and truck drivers and they're all going to help, so the trip through the city should go quick. Oh damn, Buddy, got to go. Looks like we got a cop checking us out. Bye."

"Jack, might be a good time to use those boys of yours to give this local blue something to do." Triple L said as he watched the cop make a U-turn and fall in behind the speeding convoy.

"Yeah, I noticed him pass. I'll give the boys the go ahead." Jack rolled down his window and motioned to the bike riders to go around. Jack Jr. and Mark knew exactly what their father wanted and gladly gave him what he expected. Mark motioned to the other riders to follow him and his brother. Within minutes, the chase with the cop was on.

Mark and Jack Jr. went around their father and the truck driver along with the other bikes. When all the riders were in the oncoming lane in full view of the cop, the bikers kicked their bikes into high gear and put them in the air. "Yee haw!" Mark yelled as he and Jack Jr. passed their father on one wheel. Jack wasn't thrilled with the dangerous tricks that his boys performed, but he knew they were very skilled and able to control their bikes.

It wasn't long before the cop fell in behind the bikers with lights flashing. Jack had already discussed with the boys where they would meet up in each town if this sort of thing occurred. "Triple L, as you can tell, the boys are splitting away from us and will meet up at the rest area on 285. I hope they all make it. They've all been riding together for a long time, so I'm sure they'll be okay."

"They'll be okay," Triple L assured him. "Follow me, and let's get to that rest area."

◊◊◊

Jack Jr. split off quickly with several of the other riders, hoping to cause the cop confusion. Mark, however, loved the thrill he was feeling as he rode through the cold air away from the cop. He was a great Marine, but when he was riding his bike, he was free. Within minutes of the other boys splitting off in different directions, the cop had to decide who he would stay with… he chose Mark. Lights flashing, the cop skillfully stayed right on Mark's tail as Mark took him on a chase of turns and curves through the town. It was late, so traffic was minimal and Mark avoided most of the main streets, not wanting to be slowed down by stoplights.

While Mark was keeping the cop busy, the other riders managed to make their way to 285 from different directions and streets. The thrill for Mark was soon replaced with nervousness when he realized that he might not be able to shake the cop. Mark's nerves eased when he reached a split in the highway. He maneuvered his bike toward one direction of the split and then quickly took the other direction. The cop, not having the maneuverability of a motorcycle, was left making the split away from Mark's chosen direction.

Once he was out of the cop's sight, Mark gunned his bike and sped toward the rest area. Jack Sr., Steven, and Jack Jr. were all standing next to the pickup when Mark pulled up taking off his helmet. "Damn it, Dad. Didn't know if I was going to get away from that rookie cop or not. He was really good, but I'm better."

Jack handed his boy a bottle of water, messing up his hair a bit. "Glad you could make it, Marine."

Mark laughed as he drank the water, and talked a little about his adventure with the other riders. Jack motioned shortly for everyone to mount up. "Let's go." He got into his pickup with Steven, knowing they'd better get moving in case that cop decided to adventure out further in their direction looking for Mark.

Mark, Jack Jr., and the others put on their helmets. Triple L got back into his truck when Jack radioed, "Everyone's ready, Triple L. Let's get to Wagon Wheel."

Triple L moved out onto the highway. "Okay let's go."

It took the group another hour to get to the meeting place on I-40. While they had no further trouble with cops, everyone expected there to be a vast presence of law enforcement in and around the city. Jack was shocked when he, the boys, and Triple L pulled into the parking lot of the rest area. There was little to no parking available due to the trucks and motorcycles that had showed up to help out their friends.

Jack shook hands and hugged several riders that were obviously close friends. "Damn, it sure is good to see ya, Bones. Slater, how are ya?"

Triple L introduced Jack to several of his trucker friends, some knew Shelby. "Jack, this is Bootlegger, Bull Dog, and Sweet Daddy."

Jack shook the driver's hands. "Glad to meet ya."

Jack's sons and friends gathered around with the hog riders and truckers listening to Jack explain what he needed from them. "Shelby, last I knew, was in a little town outside of Farmington called Bloomfield with several other sand haulers. Some are from her company and some are from another company, but they're supposed to be rolling together. However, I haven't heard from Shelby in hours and that is not normal for her. She called when they stopped for dinner and said they were bedding down for the night and that she would call me when she got back to her truck. But, she didn't, and I haven't been able to raise her on the phone since. Something is wrong, and I suspect that the people who are bent on hurting her have obviously broken off her communication somehow."

A tall man with a scruffy beard broke into the conversation. "What about contacting some of the other drivers, or even the police?"

"The police would only take it under advisement, and Shelby was hell bent on me not doing anything to embarrass her. I contacted a couple of the drivers that she rolls with. She doesn't know it, but they're supposed to keep an eye on her. However, the woman who is behind this whole thing is really creative, and I think she has plans to separate Shelby from the rest of the pack. Even with those drivers keeping an eye on Shelby they might miss something, and I'm not taking that chance."

A shorter blond man spoke up this time. "What's your plan, Jack?"

Jack took a deep breath and then began to explain. "I want to get to her as quickly as possible. I'm hoping we can get to them before they leave

Farmington. If we miss them, and I still can't get Shelby on the phone, then I'll know we have a real battle on our hands trying to catch them before they make the mountain bypass. If we need to follow the sand haulers all the way into the mountain bypass, things are going to get really dangerous, especially if we get into any snow or ice."

"What can we do, Jack?"

"Getting us through the safety corridors and helping us avoid being stopped is really what I need from everyone right now. Once we find out how far this thing is going to go will determine what we'll need later in the mountains. I'll have to decide then how far I let that go. Shelby's life and all of your lives are the most important things."

In a few minutes, everyone was back in their trucks or on their motorcycles heading down the corridor. As expected, it was well-patrolled, so it didn't take long at the speeds they were rolling before a patrol unit interrupted the convoy. "Jack, we got company. A black and white unit is coming up on our back door." One of the truckers explained. "We got, it Jack. Just keep a-hauling."

Jack watched as two trucks moved in side by side and slowed down enough that the cop and the traffic behind the rigs were blocked and unable to go around. Triple L, Dirty White Boy, Bootlegger, Bull Dog, and several other drivers had scattered themselves in front of Jack and the bikers. "Guess he radioed in for some back up, boys, 'cause we got one coming at us from a side road, on the westbound side, and three with lights in the eastbound lane."

Another driver further in front of the convoy informed them. "You got a few waiting on ya down here too, drivers."

Triple L informed Jack as to how they would isolate their friend. "We got ya, Jack. Just stay behind us, and we'll do the rest. When I tell you, I want you and your boys to move in behind me and then Wild Child and Sweet Daddy will protect you from the rear and side. Once we hit the street that allows the cop access to you from the right side, we'll move Bull Dog and Bootlegger over to protect you from the right side. These boys are not going to be too happy with us at the bottom of the hill, but they won't try and stop all of us, so just keep rolling."

"Jack, this is One Track. My buddy Loco and I will block the two DOT running the east side for you. Not sure how long they will let us detain them, but we'll try and keep them busy."

"Jack, this is Gypsy and Shadow. We'll help out on the eastbound side, too."

"Thanks, guys. I sure appreciate all the help."

"No problem, man. We need to give the bears some hell every once in a while since they give us hell all the time, right?"

"Right."

Although Jack didn't have radio contact with any of the bikers, he watched as several used their bikes to go in and out of traffic, causing the cops to not only realize that they now had to deal with runaway truck drivers but motorcycle riders as well. "I bet they're wondering what the hell is going on about now."

As the convoy arrived at the bottom of the hill, they were greeted with several police units with their lights on. None of the units were blocking the roadway since that would have been disastrous, but they were waiting to fall in line behind the other units and move in on either side of the convoy.

Triple L saw a way of blocking the left side units but knew he wouldn't be able to block the right side without some more trucks. "Hey, Jack. When I tell you, we're going to move the convoy to the right lines. If any drivers in front of us can hear me when we make this curve, I hope I can count on a couple of you blocking those left lanes with Wild Child."

"Got ya already, driver."

It worked like it had been planned out for days. As the convoy moved into the right lanes, the trucks from in front of Triple L slowed up just enough to block the police units from moving into the left lanes. "Damn, you guys are good," Jack said. He couldn't help but grin.

"That's right, we are PROFESSIONAL DRIVERS!" The chatter over the radio let Jack know that these drivers were not only hard working men, but loyal to their fellow drivers as well.

The police settled for a couple of truck drivers that willingly gave up the chase since they weren't even in it to start with but figured they could help by moving over and getting stopped by the now frustrated police units. The eastbound boys were having fun with their units as well, and the bikers that were weaving in and out of traffic led several units off the corridor for smaller street battles. It was amazing how quickly the group made it to I-25, but Jack knew that until they reached the hills closer to Farmington, they would still need to hold their cover if they didn't want to get stopped.

◇◇◇

The morning light hadn't even begun to peek through the cracks under Shelby's curtain when she was startled by a knock at her driver's side door. "Shelby! Time to get up. Ted and I are leaving in about an hour."

Shelby threw her curtain back and saw that Betty was the one delivering the bad news of the morning.

"Okay," she muttered, her voice still hoarse from sleep. "I'll be ready in a few minutes." Then she fell back on her sleeper bed, wishing it wasn't morning yet. "God, I just want to sleep," she mumbled, looking at the clock. *No wonder I'm tired—I didn't even get eight hours of sleep. Why is Betty getting me up several hours earlier than she should? Her ten-hour break isn't up for at least a few more hours. If Betty and Ted aren't taking their full ten hours, maybe I shouldn't run with them.*

Another knock. "Come on, lazy bones. It's time to roll."

Shelby pulled herself out of her sleeper and took down her curtain. She grabbed her shower bag and went into the little café to freshen up. She looked around more but her phone was still nowhere to be found.

After cleaning up, Shelby went into the café and asked the manager if anyone had turned in a cell phone. The manager just shook his head. "Not this morning."

"Okay, thanks," Shelby said, sighing. "Do ya'll have a pay phone I can use?"

"No, but I think there's one down the street a few blocks."

"Okay, thanks."

Shelby walked out to the parking lot and saw Ted and Betty talking near her truck. "Hey, Betty. Do you have a cell phone I can borrow? I promised Jack I'd call him back last night, but I still can't find my cell phone."

"Yeah, I got one, but you won't get any service on my phone. It's a cheap son-of-a-bitch. Wait till we get near Green River, you'll get better reception there."

"Okay, how far away is that?"

"I don't know. About five hours or so."

"Alright, well if we see a pay phone I've got to call Jack or he's going to go nuts."

"Alright," said Betty.

◊◊◊

Jack and the boys were feeling tired as they drew closer to the Farmington, New Mexico area. It wasn't light outside yet as they rolled into Bloomfield. Jack had already stopped a while back and put two of the rider's bikes in the back of his pickup, allowing the riders to sleep in the back seat.

"Hey, Dad. Wake up. We're in Bloomfield and Triple L is trying to talk to you on the CB."

"Okay," Jack said, yawning. "Yeah, Triple L. I'm here. What's up?"

"I just went by the café you said your wife was shut down at, and I didn't see any ESCC trucks in the parking lot. I checked with a driver that's ahead of us and he saw a few of those trucks earlier this morning heading toward Moab. Looks like we probably missed them by a couple of hours."

"Okay, Triple L. We better stop for a little while and get the boys up and out of your truck so you can shut down."

"No way, buddy. I got my partner in here and there is no way I'm shutting down 'til we find your little lady."

"Well, okay, but don't you think we better get the boys up?"

"No, let them sleep. We'll get them up in a little while for food and fuel."

"Okay, I was hoping we would catch Shelby here, but I guess they left early. That means we are in for hell if we have to try and catch up with them in the mountain bypass. Hey, have you heard anything on the weather in that area?"

"Not yet, but give me a few minutes. I'll check with dispatch and see what they can find out for me."

"Aren't you going to get in trouble with your company for going out of your way like this?"

"This is my truck. I lease it to this company for now. I can go where I want and take the jobs I want."

"Oh, I see."

Jack looked to the east as they passed the café that Shelby had stopped at for the night. Jack hoped that by some chance Triple L had missed seeing her truck there, but as they passed, Jack only saw two trucks in the parking lot and neither of them were Shelby's truck. As they drove on through the towns, Jack got a glimpse of several ESCC trucks parked in some parking lots but none had Shelby's number on them. He tried several times to reach her by phone but only got her voicemail.

Suddenly, his phone rang and he jumped at the sound. "Hello, Shelby? Is that you, baby?"

A strange male voice answered. "No, I'm sorry, sir. My name's Jason and I found this phone in the parking lot of King Café in Bloomfield. I assume it belongs to someone you know by the name of Shelby?"

"Yes, it's my wife's phone. Apparently she dropped it in that parking lot. Do you think you could give it to someone in the café there, and I'll pick it up, or send for it on another day?"

"Yeah, sure." They exchanged contact information and Jack thanked him for calling. As he hung up, Jack tapped his hands on his wheel, more worried than ever. *That's why she didn't call. But why doesn't she borrow a phone? Something's not right.*

The weather was holding for now, but there was a storm from the north moving into the area within forty-eight hours, and Jack hoped to have Shelby out of harm's way by then. Since they hadn't been able to stop Shelby in Farmington, Jack knew that he and the boys were going to have to stop whatever Betty had planned for Shelby in the mountains. Several truckers and biker friends were going to meet up with the convoy in Salt Lake and travel with them through the mountains to Vernal.

Jack decided to phone the drivers that he had contacted before leaving the house to see if they knew where Shelby might be. Triple L had said that several ESCC trucks had been seen near Moab, so it might be possible they would catch them in Salt Lake if those trucks had Shelby with them.

◊◊◊

Shelby got out of her truck at Green River and started to fuel up. She was becoming nervous about what Jack might do since she had not contacted him since dinner last night. She decided that once she finished fueling up, she'd find a phone and call him.

"Hey, Shelby. Are you about ready to roll?" Betty had come from the trailer end of the truck, causing Shelby to jump.

"Kind of jumpy aren't ya? Didn't mean to scare ya."

"No, I'm just a little nervous about all this snow. Do you think the roads will be alright where we are headed?"

"Don't know, but I did hear while I was in the truck stop that there is a storm coming in from the north. Not sure when that is supposed to hit, but hell, driving in snow isn't that hard. It's the ice you need to worry about, especially in those mountains."

"Really? Well, that doesn't make me feel any better."

"No worries, Shelby. Just don't get close to the edges."

Betty walked around the front of the truck while Shelby replaced the nozzles to the fuel pump and went inside to pay. As she signed for her fuel, she asked the clerk where she could find a pay phone. The clerk pointed toward a row of pay phones along a wall. Shelby reached into her pocket and pulled out a ten dollar bill and asked the clerk for change. Then she hurried to the phones.

"Go inside and keep an eye on her, Ted," Betty instructed. "If she uses the pay phone be sure and listen. I want to know who she's talking to and what she's saying. We're really close to finishing her off, and I don't want any kinks in the plan this time."

"Fine Betty, but do you think I can finish fueling our trucks first? I need to use the restroom, too."

"Fine, but watch her. I'd do it, but it might be suspicious." Betty walked to her truck and got inside.

Meanwhile, Shelby listened as the ringing on Jack's phone stopped and went directly to his voicemail. Shelby was a little annoyed, so she tried the house phone, hoping Jack had just turned his cell phone off for some reason. This time Shelby got the home phone answering machine. She decided to leave a message in case Jack was in his shop or something. "Jack, it's Shelby. We are in Green River, and I can't find my phone. I'm fine; so don't worry. I'll call again when we get to Salt Lake. I love ya, babe."

Shelby took her change and headed back to the parking lot. She saw Betty sitting in her truck, smoking a cigarette. Ted was just coming out of the store behind her, so she felt better knowing she hadn't held things up too much. She looked over at Ted as he was rushing to his truck. "Ready to roll?"

"Yep."

Ted walked to Betty's truck and got up on the steps on the driver's side. "She called her husband," he reported. "But I don't think she talked with him personally. It sounded like she just left him a message. Other than that and using the restroom, she didn't do anything."

"Great. Everything is going according to plan. Leaving early put several drivers behind us and if I know Phantom 309, he had the other drivers up and running before us anyway. That's perfect. We have a few behind us and a few in front of us, but none except her with us." Betty laughed. "Let's get this ball rolling. I want to get to Salt Lake and into the mountains."

◊◊◊

Jack and Triple L opened up the trailer doors, waking up the sleepy bikers. "Damn," one of them muttered, shielding his eyes from the light. "Isn't this a hell of a load to be hauling through the mountains?"

Jack pointed out the riders who were slowly pulling themselves up off the floor of the trailer. The bikes had been strapped to the floor and walls of the trailer with bungee cords so they wouldn't move around. Several of the riders were moving toward their bikes to unhook them. "Time to get up and ride, boys. We only have a few minutes for food and fuel, so let's go."

Jack and Triple L met with several drivers and riders to devise a plan for the mountain bypass if they weren't able to catch Shelby in Salt Lake. "Okay, this is what I suggest we do if we can't catch Shelby in Salt Lake," Jack began. "We won't be able to set the plan in stone until we see what the road conditions are like, and the traffic flow will definitely be a factor. With all the help, and the help that I'm working on with the drivers that are in front of Shelby from her company, I think we'll be able to defuse the attack without any problems."

Jack pulled out a map of the area. He currently had four flatbed drivers and several box trailer drivers either running with them or waiting to follow them into the mountain bypass when they arrived. He also hoped to have several sand haulers that were currently ahead of Shelby willing to help on the reverse end of the attack. "I've been trying to get in touch with some of her co-workers, but phone service has been limited. I've left messages, so I suspect when they get into better reception, we'll hear from them. Triple L and Sweet Daddy have feelers out, and we've been told that three ESCC trucks were spotted at a truck stop in Green River thirty minutes ago. So, we are gaining on them, but it still looks like we are going to have to take Betty and Ted on in the mountains."

Jack's plan seemed simple enough if everything went right, but Triple L and several of the other drivers knew from experience that driving on flat and straight four-lane highways was never an exact science. They also knew that driving on curved mountainous two-lane highways with possible weather impaired conditions was not going to be a picnic either. Jack needed to be more prepared for what would probably happen, and not what he hoped wouldn't. "Hey, Jack. Can I talk to you in private for a minute?" Triple L asked.

"Sure." Jack and Triple L walked away from the group.

"Look, Jack, I know that you're concerned with the safety and welfare of Shelby and the rest of us, but you really need to know that once we get into those mountains, things aren't going to go exactly the way you want them to. It is going to get rough up there, and not everyone is going to make it out alive. I understand how you're feeling right now, but those roads aren't exactly the easiest to handle, especially in bad weather."

Jack was shocked by the driver's candor. "I know what you're saying Triple L, but I really just want all of us to do everything we can to bring everyone out of there alive."

"We'll try, but those people we're chasing obviously have no concern for anyone's life, and those mountains aren't very forgiving. You need to realize there are probably going to be casualties and prepare yourself and the others for that possibility ahead of time. Let's not head into this thing with blinders on for the sake of everyone."

"Okay," he said, nodding. "I'll prepare everyone," Jack conceded.

Triple L gathered everyone for a group meeting. Jack stood in front of the drivers and bikers and took a deep breath. "What we are planning to do is dangerous," he told them, looking around and making eye contact with each one individually. I really appreciate everyone's willingness to help; however, nothing is ever perfect. When you try to plan a rescue, things go wrong. It's possible someone might get hurt, so if you want to stay behind I totally understand and appreciate everything you've done this far."

Not one driver or biker backed out of the group.

◊◊◊

Betty was nervous as she, Shelby, and Ted pulled into the truck stop in Salt Lake. Several State Troopers were in the parking lot inspecting trucks at random. Betty got on the CB with her usual whiny voice. "Hey, maybe we better go to another truck stop. Looks like the DOT are having a heyday with this one."

"Okay," Ted responded obediently.

Shelby, however, was annoyed and didn't care about the DOT. She had fixed her log earlier so that it was legal despite leaving early out of Farmington. She wanted to get something to eat, freshen up a little, and above all, use the phone to call Jack, despite Betty's objections.

"I'm stopping here, Betty. You and Ted can do what you want, but I need to talk to my husband, so you guys go on, and I'll catch up with ya'll later."

Betty didn't want to let Shelby out of her sight, so she decided fending off a few DOT men was worth keeping an eye on Barbie. "Alright, we'll stop here. But I think it's a bad idea with all the cops around."

"We haven't done anything wrong except leave a couple hours earlier than we were supposed to out of Farmington. If you worked your log right you should be right on time by now anyway, so what are you afraid of?"

"Nothing. Fine, I'm stopping."

Shelby pulled into the fuel island and after fueling, moved her truck into a parking spot. *I'm going to eat and call Jack before going into the mountains whether Betty waits for me or not.* She entered the store of the truck stop alone.

Betty and Ted fueled up and went inside the truck stop for a short time before returning to their trucks.

"Okay, while that little bitch is in the truck stop you need to work on her air brakes so that once we get into the mountains and she starts using them she loses air pressure. Do you think you can manage that while I go inside and keep her busy?"

"I thought we were going to just give her a helping hand off one of those mountain cliffs?" he asked, confused.

"We are, dumb ass. But if she has brakes, she might be able to stop long enough to get out of the truck before we get her over the edge."

"Oh yeah, I see."

"You just do what I tell you and let me do the thinking."

Betty went into the truck stop and noticed that Shelby was trying to use a pay phone. She walked over to Shelby just in time to see Shelby slam the receiver of the pay phone down into its holder. "Damn it, I hate these things. I wish I had my cell phone."

Betty reached into her pocket and handed Shelby her personal cell phone. "Here, use my cell phone."

Shelby took the phone and dialed Jack's cell phone. "Thanks, Betty."

Shelby walked away and Betty walked toward a table and sat down. *Even if she gets Jack, we're too far away for him to do anything.*

"Jack, its Shelby. I'm in Salt Lake, baby. I've tried to get in touch with you but apparently reception out here is really bad. I'm using Betty's phone. I still can't find mine, so when you get this message just call Betty and let her know you got the message. We're almost ready to go into the mountain bypass. Call, please, and let me know that everything is alright with you and the boys. I love you."

Shelby hung up the phone and walked over to where Betty was sitting. She handed Betty her cell phone. "Thanks again."

"No problem. Did you get a hold of the hubby?"

"No. Reception out here is horrible, but I did leave him a message and he might be calling you back to let me know that he got my message. I hope you don't mind."

"No, not at all."

"I'm hungry. Want to grab a bite before we leave?" Shelby asked.

"Yep, was just about ready to head that way.

"Hey, where's Ted?"

"Oh, he had some things he needed to check out on his truck. I told him I'd bring him a hamburger, so don't let me forget."

"Alright. Hey, how much further is it to Vernal?"

"Not much further, but if the roads are bad in the bypass it could take a little longer."

"Oh. How bad does it get up further?"

"Sometimes it gets pretty nasty. Just stay with us, and we'll get you through it."

"Okay."

◊◊◊

Jack reached for his phone when it rang but there wasn't enough of a signal where they were at as they neared the highway leading to Salt Lake to be able to talk with the caller. The phone number was not one he recognized, but he figured, or at least hoped, it was Shelby trying to contact him. His frustration and fears were building the closer they got to the mountain bypass. Mostly because he still hadn't been able to get in touch with Shelby and partly because he was afraid they wouldn't get to her in time.

CHAPTER TWENTY-SIX

Jack figured they would be in Salt Lake in about an hour, but Triple L's friends that were waiting on them in Salt Lake just informed him that three ESCC trucks were parked at the truck stop. Those trucks had been there for at least an hour and had not shown any signs of moving yet. "They're still there, Jack. Maybe we'll get lucky and intercept them at the truck stop."

"That would be great, Triple L. Except, how am I going to explain all the overreaction to Shelby if Betty doesn't do anything to her?"

"Don't worry about that, Jack. Shelby will understand. Besides, Salt Lake is the last big place to stop before the bypass. If Betty and Ted are going to disable Shelby's truck, they will do it there. All you have to do is show her the impairment and she will know you did it to save her."

"You're right. I hope we can catch them before they leave."

"Me too."

Jack's phone rang again and this time he had plenty of service. "Hello?"

"Jack, this is Slick Stick. I got your message, but Shelby isn't with us anymore. She stayed in Bloomfield with some of the other drivers, and we got separated from her. Sorry about not being able to stay with her, but you said not to be obvious. I was afraid if we insisted on her staying with us she might get suspicious that we were keeping an eye on her."

"That's alright, Slick Stick. I appreciate you trying anyway. We know pretty much where she's at anyway. We have been tracking her through some trucker friends of a man that is traveling with us. She's somewhere in Salt Lake and we hope we can intercept her there."

"I see. Hope you can. Betty is a real witch."

"Thanks."

"Hey, where are you guys anyway?"

"We're almost into the bypass. Why?"

"Well, if we miss Shelby in Salt Lake and we have to get to her in the bypass, I sure could use your help in blocking off traffic from the east end of the bypass. Maybe even some help in keeping control of that end in case we have to move the interception down further into the bypass."

"Yeah, sure, Jack. We would be happy to help out. Just give me a call if you miss Shelby in Salt Lake, and I'll get the guys to set something up for you."

"Great, Slick Stick. Thanks."

◊◊◊

Shelby finished her sandwich and went to the pay phones to call Jack again when Ted walked into the restaurant. "Hey, you guys. Ready to take off?"

Shelby looked at the phones. "I want to try and call Jack one more time before we leave."

"You couldn't even get him on my cell phone, Shelby. What makes you think you'll get him on one of those crappy things? You can call him when we get to Strawberry at the bottom of the bypass. I used my phone there a whole lot the last time I was up here, so I know they have good service. Besides, we really need to get going if we're going to make it through there before dark."

"Alright, but do you promise I can use your phone as soon as we get to Strawberry? I know Jack is probably losing his mind about now, especially because…" Shelby stopped talking, remembering she didn't want Betty to know what Jack had said about her.

"Especially because what?"

"Oh, nothing. Jack's just a worrywart. Let's get going."

The three drivers walked to their trucks, but Shelby felt like she was being watched the whole time as they proceeded across the parking lot. Shelby leaned over and told Betty what she was feeling. "Don't you feel like someone is watching us?"

Betty laughed. "You're a female driver. Most male drivers watch the females in these places, looking for a piece of ass."

This feels different, she thought. She went to her truck feeling uneasy while Betty and Ted walked to their trucks.

Betty waited until they were on the other side of their trailers before checking with Ted about the brakes. "Did you do what I told you to do?"

"Yep, they should hold until she starts using them in the mountains."

"Great. Let's get going and show little Shelby a close up view of the side of one of those mountains."

◊◊◊

"Jack?"

"Yeah, Triple L? What's up?"

"I just got word from my buddy Snowmobile Flyer in Salt Lake that the trio is leaving the parking lot now."

"Damn it!" Jack said. "We're still thirty minutes from Salt Lake. Well, let's meet up with your friends. I guess we'll have to try and stop them in the pass."

"Yep, looks that way. Sorry, man."

◊◊◊

Shelby couldn't believe the amazing beauty of the Uinta Mountains. Everywhere she looked she saw mountains with snow-covered peaks. The further into the mountains they traveled, the more she was able to see the snow up close. "Oh wow, this is so beautiful. I just hope we don't run into any of the pretty white stuff on these roads."

"Hate to say it, but we'll definitely run into some the higher we go," Betty said, trying not to sound too pleased.

"That doesn't sound fun."

"Just stay on the packed stuff and away from the dirty snow."

Ted overheard what Betty was telling Shelby and realized that she was telling her to do the exact opposite of what she needed to do to handle the snow. As usual, he kept his mouth shut. *Maybe if Betty's plan is successful, I'll finally get a little action tonight. It's been a long time.*

◊◊◊

Jack and his convoy of trucks and bikes fueled at the same truck stop that Shelby had been at not thirty minutes earlier. "Jack, these are the guys that will be helping us the most when we get into the pass." Triple L said of the truckers who had been waiting to accompany them into the mountains.

"Glad to meet, ya'll. I really appreciate all the help."

"No problem, Jack. All of us have met Shelby at one time or another and we are glad to be helping you save her stubborn ass."

"Oh, I see Triple L has already filled you in on my wife's attitude."

"We already knew she's stubborn. Just didn't know she was *that* stubborn."

"She definitely is. Anyway, Triple L mentioned you might have a short-cut that could bring us right in behind her. Is that true?"

"Yep, and as soon as you guys get ready we'll head that way."

"Well, I think everyone is fueled and ready to roll. Did Triple L fill you in on what we think would be the best way to intercept their attack?"

"Yes, and once we get in behind them, we should be able to get into position for the counterattack."

"Let's go."

Jack knew it was time to contact Shelby's coworkers who were in front and behind her for their help. "Hey, Slick Stick. This is Jack again. We missed Shelby in Salt Lake and we are going to need you guys to help control traffic."

"We're ready, Jack. Just let us know what you want done."

"Okay, I need for at least three trucks to come toward us on the high-way to try and force the front truck to stop. I need to block off traffic so that no one can get onto the highway until we have the situation defused."

"Alright, Jack. I personally, along with Luscious and Little Boy Blue, will move toward you on the highway. I'll have Bobcat, Speedy, Scooter, Phantom 309, Whiskers, Speedy, and Long Legs block traffic near Strawberry."

"Sounds good, Slick Stick," said Jack, trying hard to keep track of all the different truckers' handles. "I sure appreciate all your help. Do you have any contact with the two drivers behind us?"

"Yeah, what do you need with them?"

"Contact them and have them watch for Sweet Daddy, Bad Boy, Bootlegger, and Kat Doctor near Fruit Way. There will also be a local there named Winston who will be organizing the blocking of the west-bound traffic."

"Okay, no problem. I'll get in touch with Hemi and Elwood Blues and let them know what to do. We're on it, Jack. Just be careful. I ran into a few slick spots in the high areas of those mountains earlier."

"Got ya, Slick Stick. We'll watch out. Thanks again."

◊◊◊

Snowmobile Flyer led the group through the shortcut that he knew to the bypass, and within about an hour the convoy was within hearing distance of Shelby. "I can hear her, Snowmobile Flyer, but I can't see her yet."

"Yeah, I know. I hear her too, and it sounds like they're attempting to get her into position for their attack."

"Patience, Jack," interjected Triple L. "We are probably only a couple miles away. We'll get there in time. Trust Shelby's instincts and abilities to handle her truck. We'll get to her, I promise. Just hang in there."

"Okay but it sounds like she's in trouble already."

"I know, calm down. We'll be there soon."

◊◊◊

"There is something wrong with my truck, Betty. I can't stop like normal."

"Oh, I'm sure it is just out of adjustment, Shelby. Don't worry."

"It's kind of hard not to worry, Betty! The thing doesn't have any brakes."

"Okay, I'll tell ya what. I'll get behind you and Ted can stay in front of you and we'll hold you like a sandwich in case you have trouble."

"Alright, but do you think that will work?"

"Yeah, of course. I'll fall behind you and Ted will stay in front. That way if you get to rolling too fast he can stop you with his truck, and I can guide you into his if things get fishy."

Shelby paused before answering, remembering Jack's theory about Betty. *Is this all part of some big strategy to hurt me? But what choice do I have? My brakes aren't working, and some help is better than nothing.* "Alright," she said at last. "If you think so."

Shelby didn't have to do much to let Betty get behind her since she had already let off of her accelerator and Betty was able to easily move in behind her. Ted had stayed in front of her and now Shelby was unsuspectingly trapped between the two people who wanted to see her dead. "Okay, I think we got you, Shelby. You should be easy to control now."

Shelby knew she was in trouble. "I don't like this, Betty. I'm going to try and pull over and let you get in front of me again. This seems too dangerous."

Betty came back on the radio and talked directly to Ted. "Ted, go to our channel."

"Okay."

"Betty, what the hell is going on? What channel?"

She got no response back from Betty, but what she did get was a bump from Betty's truck in the rear of her now run away truck and trailer. "Betty, what the hell are you doing?" Shelby worked the steering wheel and kept her truck straight before grabbing the mic again. Betty still did not respond. Shelby did her best to run through the channels on the CB while still holding onto the wheel of her truck to see if she could find the channel that Ted and Betty had changed to, but it was impossible.

Shelby went back to channel nineteen and decided that maybe she would be able to find someone on that channel who would be able to help. "HELP! IS ANYONE OUT THERE? HELP ME, PLEASE."

Meanwhile, Betty and Ted spoke directly on their private channel. "Okay, Ted. We have her exactly where I want her, and I'm giving her some good shoves with my truck. Once we get to the high point of this mountain, I want you to slow up and bring her truck in close to mine so I can give her a good push off the edge."

"Okay, but there is a lot of traffic coming. Don't you think we should be careful about trying to do this in front of witnesses? Look behind you."

"Shut up, Ted, and do what I tell you."

"Fine."

"Can anyone hear me?" Shelby pleaded.

"We hear you, Shelby!" said a familiar voice. "We are coming."

"JACK!"

"Yes, baby. It's me and the boys. So just hang tight for a few minutes until we get to you. Where are you? Can you give me a mile marker or some kind of landmark so we know about how far ahead you are? Also, let me know what Betty and Ted are doing so we know how to handle them when we reach you."

Shelby was shocked but relieved to hear her husband's voice. "Alright," she said, her voice shaky. "I'm not sure of the marker, but we just passed a log cabin-type building on our right that has a side road leading to it. We're heading into some really horrible looking climbs and slopes. Betty and Ted have gone to another channel."

Jack was so glad he could finally hear Shelby's voice again. "Okay, baby. Just stay calm. What are Betty and Ted doing?"

"Betty is bumping the back of my trailer with her truck, trying to make me go faster down these slopes and Ted is in front of me keeping me boxed in. I don't have any braking power, Jack. They did something to my truck. They're controlling everything I do right now. I'm trying to keep it as straight as I can though."

"Great, sweetheart. Just keep it between the black flags and we'll be there soon. I love you."

"I love you too, Jack, and I'm sorry I didn't listen to you." Tears began welling in Shelby's eyes.

"It's alright baby," he said. "Stay strong. I want you to go to our wedding day channel so that I can tell you what we are planning to do without giving it away to Betty and Ted in case they're monitoring nineteen."

"Alright, but how are you going to do this alone, Jack?"

"Shelby, turn to our channel and I'll explain everything. Since you lost your phone, I can't call you. So just go to that channel for now."

"OK," Shelby said, moving to channel thirty and waiting for Jack to talk to her.

"Did you make it, sweetheart?"

"Yeah, I'm here. Jack, this is scary. She keeps running into my trailer and the roads are getting slicker the higher we climb. I'm afraid she's going to fishtail me and put me over the edge."

"Shelby, remember what the guys in the Colorado Mountains taught you on those slick roads? Stay out of the packed snow areas and run your tires in the dirty snow."

"Okay, but Betty told me just the opposite a little while ago."

"Why do you suppose she did that, Shelby? I'm not the one running up your ass, am I? So listen to me baby, please."

"Right. Sorry. I still don't know how you plan to help me out here by yourself, Jack—two big rigs against one little pickup."

"Shelby, I brought lots of help with me. Besides, the boys are on their bikes too. I have twenty truckers and several of our motorcycle friends out here trying to save your stubborn ass, so be calm and let us get you out of this mess."

"Oh god, Jack! I can't believe you drove all this way with the boys to save me. What truckers do you know?"

"Well, I know a bunch now, and several are friends of yours. We don't have time for small talk right now, Shelby. You're fixing to get into some really rough inclines and declines. Plus, we are still at least three quarters of a mile from you. I want to confirm that Ted is in front of you and Betty is behind you?"

"Yes."

"How far ahead of you is Ted?"

"About two truck lengths, until he slows up to box me in for Betty."

"Okay, and how about Betty?"

"About one truck length, until she moves up to bump me."

"Okay, baby. Do the best you can to keep that truck straight, and don't worry about what we are going to do until I tell you. I want you to go back to channel nineteen and monitor it. When I tell you to do something, I want you to do it and do exactly what I tell you without question."

"Okay, Jack."

"Now go back to nineteen. Keep it straight and between the black flags. We should be at your back door in just a few minutes."

"Alright."

Jack got on the radio and let everyone that was monitoring know that he had Shelby on board with the plan. Jack called Slick Stick and got him to contact Elwood Blues so that the truckers they had with them could block off the east and west entrances to the bypass. Snowmobile Flyer and Triple L let GTO and Ramjet go around them. They would be the separation between Ted and Shelby. They would also attempt to box him in at the front with the help of Slick Stick, Luscious, and Little Boy Blue coming from the east. For the first time in several hours, Jack felt confident. *We have a plan, and damn it, that plan is going to work!*

◊◊◊

"Betty, there are two trucks coming around you," Ted said on their private channel. "It looks like they're going to pass me."

"Let them pass, dumb ass."

"Okay…" Ted said, slowing down a little to let the trucks pass. But for some reason, they didn't. Ted spoke into the mic again. "Um, Betty, these guys aren't going around me."

"Well slow up, idiot," Betty told him. "Maybe they got governors on those trucks and can't get around."

"No Betty, they want in back of me for some reason."

"FUCK! MUST I DO EVERYTHING? Slow up and get into Shelby's front dumper. Make the bastards go around you."

Ted tried to do what Betty wanted, but the truck behind him didn't seem willing to let him. He nosed his truck over, forcing Ted to move up in speed to avoid being hit from the rear. "SHIT, Betty! These guys aren't letting me back," Ted said, his forehead beginning to sweat. "I think they're here to help Shelby out. Sorry, Betty, but these guys mean business. I'm out of here." Ted moved up and allowed the truck to slide in behind him.

"YOU COWARD!" Betty screamed. "SON OF A BITCH! GET YOUR ASS BACK HERE, AND HELP ME FINISH THIS BITCH OFF!"

"Sorry, Betty, you're on your own. There are two more trucks coming around you. These fuckers are flat on my ass. You can take care of Shelby alone. I got troubles of my own with these two bad boys."

Betty looked in her mirror and saw the other two trucks Ted was talking about coming around her on the left side. She knew without even thinking twice that somehow Shelby had managed to find herself some help. *So what? The little bitch is going down this time no matter how many trucks show up to try and save her.* "Come on, mother fuckers! You out here to help out little miss Barbie? Come to momma. I'll show you the edge of these mountains too."

◊◊◊

Meanwhile, Road Trash and Richie Rich had moved in quickly behind the first two trucks. Their trucks were going to be used to hopefully slow down Shelby's truck once they had her isolated from Ted and Betty. If they couldn't manage to slow her down, Jack, Steven and Jack Jr. would come up beside Shelby. Which side would depend on their access to her at the time. With help from Jack's biker friends, they would attempt to extract her from the runaway truck.

Road Trash moved in next to Betty, making his way toward Shelby's truck. But just as he got even with Betty, she jerked over, ramming his truck. "Take that, you prick."

"Bitch!" Road Trash called out as he moved over quickly into the oncoming traffic lanes to avoid the clip.

Richie Rich was behind Road Trash and saw his jerk over into the other lane but didn't know why. "What happened?" he asked over the CB.

"That bitch just tried to clip me, but she has no idea who she's messing with." Road Trash took his flatbed trailer and fished it over into the tank on Betty's truck, almost causing her to leave the road. "There, bitch. Now, you know who's the best driver on these roads."

Betty caught her truck just at the edge of the cliff and brought it back into position before the two drivers could get around her. Then she got right back on Shelby's bumper. This time she pushed Shelby with all the power she could get out of her truck. "Fine!" she called out of the window. "You want to save your little friend? How about you find her at the bottom of the mountains and take her home in a body bag?"

Road Trash realized that he was going to need some assistance if he and Richie Rich were going to get around Betty. "Jack, send a couple of your bravest biker dudes up here so we can force this bitch to back down."

"Okay, I have to get them up here. Give me a second."

"Hurry. I'm not sure Shelby will have a second if this witch keeps pushing her like this."

Jack rolled down his window and motioned for Bones and Slater to move up next to him. Bones moved up next to Jack. "Road Trash needs you to help make Betty back down off Shelby."

Nodding his head, Bones motioned for Slater to follow. Without a plan or any idea of how they would accomplish such a feat, Bones and Slater rode their motorcycles around Richie Rich and got in beside Road Trash. Road Trash yelled at them over the noise of the truck and pointed in the direction he wanted them to try and open between Shelby and Betty. He also pointed at the hill in front of them, hoping on the climb that they might be able to make space for one of the trucks to maneuver in between the two female drivers. "Get in between us on the next hill climb if you can!" he shouted.

"Got it, boss!"

Betty saw the bikes come around from the side of the trucks now cruising on her left side. "I don't think so," she muttered. She wasn't sure what they were doing, but when she saw the hill coming up, she pushed on her accelerator even more, causing Shelby to become completely unnerved.

"JACK! SHE'S PUSHING ME EVEN HARDER, AND I'M HAVING TROUBLE AT THIS SPEED."

"I know, baby. Just stay calm. See the riders behind you? They're going to try and give one of the trucks enough room to get in between you and Betty on that hill coming up."

"Okay."

"Just keep her straight."

"Alright."

Betty saw the hill coming up and did her best to keep in close to the rear of Shelby's trailer, but the incline was steep and she was having a hard time pushing Shelby's truck with her own load on board. "Damn it, come on, baby. Don't let me down now. SHIT! YOU PIECE OF CRAP TRUCK!"

About halfway up the hill Betty lost her momentum and wasn't able to stay close enough to Shelby. She was forced to back away slightly from Shelby, leaving enough room for the bikers to ease their way between the two female truckers. The bikes quickly made room for Road Trash to get his truck in, causing separation between Shelby and Betty. Richie Rich then moved on around both Road Trash and Shelby, putting his truck in front of Shelby.

"We got in, Jack!" called Road Trash called. "I'm going to stay behind Shelby, and Richie Rich is in her front door."

"Great job, guys. Thanks. We're still a little ways behind ya'll, but you should be able to see us in your mirrors."

"Yeah, we got ya. Betty isn't going to give up easily so you better send those other two trucks in here soon so I can get around Shelby and try and get her slowed down if we can."

"Alright."

Snowmobile Flyer spoke up. "Jack, I think it will work better if you get in behind Shelby and in front of Road Trash. Let Sweet Daddy and Kat Doctor swing in beside Betty so you can be a barrier for them. Betty might try to slide in behind Shelby again if they can't move into position quick enough."

"Yeah, I agree. Okay. Road Trash, me, and the rest of my biker buddies are going to come around Betty first."

"Sounds good, Jack. I'll hold her back. Boy is she a fighter, bumping the rear of my truck like this. I can't wait till we get her stopped. I'm going to personally show her the rear end of my truck and use her ass to pull out the dents. She wants to act like a man, she can be treated like one."

"I hear that. We're on Betty's back door, so go ahead and back her down if you can."

"Gotcha. Come on around."

Jack moved out with several bikers, Sweet Daddy, and Kat Doctor in tow. Sweet Daddy and Kat Doctor pulled in behind Jack with ease until they got up next to Betty. Betty saw Jack and the bikers going around her, but she wasn't aware that it was Shelby's husband so she let them go past. When the truckers came around however, she wasn't going to let anyone help Shelby. She jerked her truck over into the left lane and blocked Sweet Daddy and Kat Doctor from coming around her on the left side.

Sweet Daddy instantly moved toward the right side, causing Betty to rethink her action. She knew her new position left the right lane open and she could easily be blocked out. She moved back into her old position before Sweet Daddy could close it up. "Damn, this mean bitch has a death wish."

Road Trash keyed up his mic. "You got that right, Sweet Daddy. She's one reckless, mean ass bitch. Be careful, she isn't going to give this thing up easy, but thanks for getting her off my tail for a little while. Come on around me and I'll keep her back for you and Kat Doctor."

"Gotcha."

"Jack and the bikes are already in position in front of me, but I really need to get up there with Richie Rich if we're going to stop Shelby."

"We're coming."

"10-4."

The last part of the plan was for Triple L and Snowmobile Flyer. They were going to try and stop Betty with their flatbeds. Jack's boys would be back up if Betty continued to be a bitch and wouldn't stop. The boys would get on the flatbeds with their bikes and then use the flatbeds and tractors to get onto Betty's trailer. They were then going to get into her truck and make her stop, or stop the truck themselves.

Snowmobile Flyer and Triple L, followed by the boys on rockets, moved in behind Betty. Things were happening fast, but they wouldn't do anything until GTO and Ramjet had Ted isolated. Then Richie Rich and Road Trash needed to be in position to help Jack get Shelby stopped before Sweet Daddy, Kat Doctor, Snowmobile Flyer, and Triple L could completely put Betty in their pocket.

Suddenly, GTO keyed his mic. "Hey, Snowmobile Flyer. There's a side access road coming up in what looks like about two miles ahead of us. It's in the valley of the last group of mountains we'll be taking on before the final decline into the populated area. It should be okay for the riders if you need them, but we'll be making a steep incline once we pass that access road, so you might decide now if you're going to use them."

"Damn, that means we really have to hope Betty doesn't give us any trouble or make the mark exact for the bikers to intercept."

"Yeah, you got that right, man."

"Well, let's do this thing. Jack. We're going to go ahead and push forward so we can use the boys if we need too."

"Sounds good, Snowmobile Flyer. We have everyone in position to try and stop Shelby's truck, so Sweet Daddy and Kat Doctor it's up to you to make Betty back down. GTO, go ahead and get Ted stopped if you can. Everyone be careful and see ya at the bottom of the hill."

"Gotcha, Jack."

"Right behind ya, man."

"Lead the way, brother."

Ted looked in his rear view mirror and saw GTO and Ramjet right on his back door. Then, just as he was rounding a corner toward the final incline, he saw the mass of trucks waiting for him at the bottom of the hill—not to mention the three sand haulers headed straight at him up the decline he would soon be taking. "SHIT! WHAT THE HELL HAVE YOU GOTTEN ME INTO, BETTY? I GOT TRUCKS COMING AT ME, BEHIND ME, AND WAITING ON ME AT THE BOTTOM OF THIS MOUNTAIN. I SHOULD HAVE NEVER GOTTEN INVOLVED WITH YOU!"

Betty didn't come back over the radio because she wasn't in range.

GTO and Ramjet moved side by side and ran their trucks within inches of Ted's trailer. GTO moved in for a bump to let Ted know they were there. "Alright, you son-of-a-bitch. Make this hard or make this easy, but one way or another you're getting shut down."

Ted realized he was not in a good position with all the trucks coming at him. GTO backed off slightly just long enough to see Ted attempting to pull his fast-moving truck off the road and into what appeared to be a pullover spot. Ted didn't realize that the spot wasn't deep enough for his big rig. He was going way too fast to get stopped in the small space. "OH NO!"

GTO and Ramjet couldn't believe what they saw next. Ted's truck flew over the side of the mountain like a toy truck falling off a table. There wasn't a sound until the truck hit the bottom of the cliff and burst into flames from the impact. The truck crinkled up like a soda can crushed in a man's hand. The explosion threw flames and smoke to the top of the ridge.

"Shit, Jack! Ted just put his rig over the side of this mountain."

"No way! Are you guys alright?"

"Yeah, we're heading toward the other trucks so we can get them out of your way. I doubt he made it. The smoke and fire down there looks pretty bad."

"Damn, I was hoping no one would get hurt."

Betty had changed channels and was now monitoring nineteen. "Serves him right for abandoning me," she spat. "But there is going to be one more death, and that's your little Shelby, Jack."

"Why don't you give it up, Betty?"

"Like hell I will!"

"Fine, whatever you want. Alright, guys, let's get on with the rest of the plan."

Sweet Daddy and Kat Doctor moved side by side in front of Betty and down shifted their trucks, causing Betty to have to back down. "What, you think that's going to stop me?" Betty, using the decline of the mountain, moved around the trucks but was blocked off when they separated and blocked her move.

"Jack, she's trying to get around us! You better get Shelby stopped."

"Gotcha."

Road Trash and Richie Rich put their trucks side-by-side and backed down until Shelby was able to put her truck in their back doors. Road Trash keyed his mic. "Okay, Shelby. What I want you to do is gear down and use your engine brake to slow yourself down with our trucks."

"Okay."

Shelby did exactly that, but the decline coming up was not going to allow for them to have enough room to stop her. Richie Rich keyed up. "This isn't going to work, Road Trash. We don't have enough straight away for the stop."

"I know. Jack, it's not going to happen. She's loaded too heavy, and the decline isn't going to do anything but push us all over the edge."

"Alright then, we'll just have to get her out of there and let the truck go."

Jack motioned for the bikers to move into position. Steven crawled through the window and into the back of the truck with the bikers between the truck and the pickup. Jack's friend, Racket, was on the far side of Shelby's truck near the edge and jumped off his motorcycle grabbing the handle of Shelby's passenger side mirror. Shelby saw the man struggle to get a footing on her truck and didn't breathe until she could see that he was able to hold on and have his feet on the steps. Racket managed to open her passenger side door and get into the truck. "Hey, Shelby. I understand you're having a bit of trouble today."

Shelby laughed a bit, even though she was scared shitless. "Yeah, Racket, just a little."

"Well, let's get you out of here."

"Okay."

Racket got on the CB to let Jack know he was ready. "Okay, Jack. I'm going to help her out and then steer this bad baby off to the left. You guys better be ready when I jump out of here."

"We're ready."

"Alright, here we come." Racket pointed to Shelby's door. "Open it up and get ready to jump into the pickup bed with Steven."

"Okay, but what about you?"

"I'm going to steer this thing until you get clear and then I'm going to get a lift from Pauli."

"Oh my god. You're going to do that motorcycle thing you guys do at the rallies aren't you?"

"Yep, that's the plan. But we are moving a hell of a lot faster right now, so I hope I make it."

"Oh, Racket. Please be careful."

"I will, but you got to get out of here so I can. Now go!"

Shelby looked at the ground and then looked at her youngest son who was holding out his arms to catch his mother. "Come on, Mom. You can do this."

Jack had rolled down the windows in the truck so he could talk to Shelby, too. "Come on, baby! Not much different than being caught by some guys after being thrown in the air during a football game."

Shelby knew exactly what Jack was talking about. He was referring to her years as a cheerleader. "Alright," she said, gathering her courage. "Here I come!"

Shelby took a deep breath and flung herself toward her son in the back of the pickup. Shelby and Steven landed in the bottom of the pickup bed in a pile of legs and arms. Jack looked through the back window and saw that they were both okay before getting on the CB again. "Alright, Racket, we got her! Now I'm going to head down the mountain so I won't be in the way while you get out of there. Be careful, my friend, and thanks."

"Not a problem, Jack. Anything for my friends."

Jack sped away from the runaway truck and moved down the road in front of the two trucks that were holding Shelby's truck with their rear trailers. Racket got on the radio. "Alright, Road Trash. I'm fixing to swing this thing wide to the left and exit it fast, so when I say clear, you guys move your trucks to the right so they won't get caught in the swing. Then please haul ass so when Pauli catches me we can fly right by you."

"We gotcha, Racket. Just give us the word."

Racket opened Shelby's driver door as wide as it would go and, still holding onto the wheel, stepped out onto the metal step. Pauli was waiting right near the door for his old friend to exit the truck and hitch a ride on his back seat. They had performed a similar trick many times in front of crowds at rallies, but it was never at these speeds and never from a big truck. "Alright, CLEAR!"

At the sound of the word "clear," Richie Rich and Road Trash accelerated their trucks and moved off to the right. Racket turned the wheel of Shelby's truck as best he could toward the left and let go of the wheel, causing the truck to veer to the left alone. Racket steadied himself slightly as Pauli moved in close to the runaway truck. With one precise jump he landed butt first into Pauli's rider seat. The impact and speed caused Pauli to have to fight with the bike's balance, but within a few seconds of skillful guidance, Pauli brought the bike into complete submission. He throttled the bike with complete ease and rolled it in between the two trucks that had moved to the right and left of him. "Yes! That's one for the memory books!" Racket said as he slapped his old friend on the back.

"Damn right, you son-of-a-bitch. We are the best, aren't we?"

Racket waved at Road Trash as they passed, letting them know they had made it and were heading off the mountain. Richie Rich keyed the mic, "Alright, Jack. Bikers are safe and now it's up to the rest of the gang to stop

Betty before they get down that mountain and into the crowd of trucks and people waiting at the bottom in that little town."

"There are a bunch down here. Thanks guys for all the help."

Shelby and Steven moved to the front part of Jack's pickup and huddled together. Shelby watched as she saw her beautiful red Pete tumble over the edge of the mountain and crumple at the bottom into a bloom of fire and smoke. She heard a loud explosion as she held her face down into Steven's jacket for the short but very cold ride to the bottom. "Oh god, I loved that truck."

"It's okay, Mom. You'll get another one."

Shelby and Jack had finally reached the bottom of the hill and were not surprised to see not only the trucks they had been using to block things off, but several groups of local spectators. Not to mention the DOT officers that were attempting to clear out the less-than-cooperative truckers so that they could get to whatever was happening on the mountain. Jack parked his truck, and got out quickly to check on his wife and son who had huddled together to keep warm against the cold winter air.

"You guys okay?"

"Yes Jack. We're fine," Shelby said as Jack helped her out of the pick-up and held her in his arms. Steven hopped out of the truck his mom reached for his hand. "Thanks, sweetheart. That was so brave of you."

"Kind of cool to be a hero."

The trio looked toward the mountains, realizing that this thing wasn't over yet. Betty was still up there and she wasn't going to go down easy. Jack just hoped that she would come to her senses before anyone else got hurt. The boys were still up there and it was beginning to get dark. Jack and Shelby watched as they caught a glimpse of the group of trucks and motorcycles moving up and down through the last of the mountains.

Sweet Daddy and Kat Doctor had managed to keep Betty from getting around them, but she was ramming their trailers at every turn. "If I'm going down, you bastards are going down with me!" she growled into the mic.

Snowmobile Flyer and Triple L had managed to get their trucks on either side of Betty and make her move to more of the center of the road. However, not only was Betty ramming the trucks in front of her, she was also jerking her truck from one side to the other, causing the side trucks to move away from time to time to avoid possible collisions. "Betty, give it up babe. You can't get out of this box."

"Want to bet, you son-of-a-bitch?" Betty jerked her truck to the right and tried to ram into Snowmobile's truck.

"Okay, guys. This isn't working. I say we go with plan B."

"Yeah, I think you're right. That road is just ahead."

Betty keyed her mic. "That's right, bitches. It isn't working so take that road and get the hell out of my way."

Snowmobile Flyer rolled down his window and gave Jack Jr. the hand signal they had worked up earlier, letting him know that it was time to send in the rockets. "Go boys, bring her down."

Jack Jr. signaled Mark that it was going to be up to them to stop Betty. Pointing toward the access road up ahead, Mark and Bentley moved around the parade of trucks with great speed. They took off and got ahead of the trucks by almost a half-mile before exiting the road. They turned their bikes around facing straight back to the road they just left. Jack Jr. stayed behind the convoy, knowing that his part in the take down was going to ask him to give up his rocket since he would be leaving it in a few moments. Snowmobile Flyer and Triple L had already backed away from Betty and were now single file behind her waiting for their new loads to park themselves onto their flatbeds.

Betty watched as the trucks backed off as the bikes took the exits, but she was still trapped by Sweet Daddy and Kat Doctor. "Why don't you shit-heads join the rest of those pussies and get the hell out of my way?"

No one responded to Betty. They simply waited as the boys lit up their tires and sped as fast as they could toward the now approaching convoy of trucks looking for their marked flatbeds.

Within a few seconds, Mark and Bentley had jumped their rockets into the air and placed their bikes onto the flatbed trailers of Snowmobile Flyer and Triple L's trucks. The boys were now sliding on their sides down the wooden trailers toward the pipe bumper that was waiting for them at the front of each trailer, hoping that the impact they were about to experience wasn't going to hurt too much.

It took only a few more seconds for the boys to hit the bumpers and then extract themselves from their damaged bikes. Getting to their feet, they signaled to the drivers of the flatbeds that they were good and ready for the next part of the plan. The flatbed drivers moved their trucks again on either side of Betty. Snowmobile Flyer only went as far as her trailer for Mark, who jumped off the flatbed and grabbed onto the ladder.

Jack Jr. then took his cue and moved in next to Betty's truck with his bike after Snowmobile Flyer moved up further to complete the pocket around Betty again. He grabbed onto the ladder behind his brother and kicked his bike out of the way. "What?" she screamed. "I thought you sons of a bitches had enough, but no. I guess you're back for more. FINE!" Betty moved her truck with jerking motions toward Snowmobile's truck, almost causing Jack Jr. to lose his footing and fall off the tank.

"Damn it, this bitch is crazy."

Bentley, with Triple L's assistance, was able to mount Betty's truck at the front. He jumped from the flatbed and onto Betty's passenger side steps, almost missing his mark with a slip of his foot on the now icy metal. Grabbing the mirror, he steadied himself and then reached for the outside truck handle for balance. "I don't like this," he muttered. "I don't like this at all."

Betty didn't see Mark climb the ladder, but she was now well aware of Jack Jr. who was presently climbing the ladder behind his brother. "Oh, I see you. Think you're going to try and make me stop? Well, I have news for you. I'm not stopping and I see all those people down there. I'm going to head straight into you assholes because I know Shelby's there, and if I'm going down so is she and her prick of a husband. Come on boys, give it your best shot, but I'm not stopping 'til I get Shelby."

Betty moved her truck back and forth into the trucks on either side again and again, then rammed the trucks in front of her several times, letting everyone around know she was pissed off. Bentley was holding on for dear life, but did manage to check to see if the passenger side door was locked. Unfortunately, it was secured. He would have to hold on until Jack Jr. and Mark could implant themselves into Betty's truck from the driver's side.

Mark was a trained Marine, so most of what he was doing wasn't that difficult. But the movements Betty was making with her truck were causing him some distress, especially when he slipped and hit his knee on the back deck of Betty's tractor. "Damn it! I'm going to kill that bitch!" Mark yelled as he held his knee for a moment before standing to help his brother down onto the deck. "Okay, I'm going to go first and try to climb into the tractor through the emergency door. You follow in right behind me unless you want to come in through the driver's door. Bentley is still outside the passenger's door, so I assume it is locked."

"Doesn't matter, let's just stop this bitch before she hurts someone."

Mark moved toward the emergency door but backed away slightly to avoid Betty from seeing in the mirror what he was up to. "I need you to hold my arm while I open the emergency door and climb inside. Since you're taller you can climb in behind me or use the emergency door to swing out and jump onto the driver's side steps. I'll let you in when I can from the inside."

"I think I want to come in from the driver's side door. I'm not sure I'll have enough room to get my legs into that door from here."

"Okay."

Mark reached around the corner of the tractor from the deck and opened the emergency door while Jack Jr. held onto his little brother's arm. The wind from the speed of the trucks rolling down the road made it hard to keep the door open and difficult for the two boys to communicate. "Got it, but there's something across the entrance on the inside."

"Yeah, that's a leather piece that just snaps in for looks over the door. Just push on it and it will give way."

"Alright, big brother. I'm going for it. I need you to do what you can to keep me from falling off this big bastard."

"Got it."

Betty had seen her emergency door fly open and although she had been doing her best to try and knock the boys off of her truck, she had not. Snowmobile Flyer and Triple L had been holding her in the pocket they had created with Sweet Daddy and Kat Doctor pretty well. Betty was becoming more angry and frustrated with each closing mile as she rounded the curve toward the final incline and descent. "You fuckers aren't getting into my truck!"

Swerving her truck toward Snowmobile Flyer's, Betty watched through her mirror as the emergency door flew open and a leg appeared through the door. Mark fell through the leather cover and onto the sleeper bed. He quickly composed himself and looked at his surroundings before getting to his feet. It took him only a second to position himself behind Betty. "Howdy, ma'am. We can do this one of two ways. You can stop this truck yourself by backing her down right now, or I'm going to stop it for you."

Betty took her left hand and swung it at Mark, not even coming close to hitting him. "Get the fuck out of my truck, or I'm taking you and your little friends with me right over the edge of that cliff coming up."

Mark saw that this woman was not going to give it up easy. He reached over and unlocked the passenger side door while Betty tried with all of her power to keep him from letting Bentley into the truck. Bentley slowly maneuvered himself around the steps through the force of the wind to where he could open the door and slip into the passenger seat. Breathless and cold he sat relieved in the seat for a moment. "Thanks, buddy." He looked at Mark who was busy clearing things out of his path and fighting off punches from Betty so he could make his next move.

"No problem."

Betty was furiously cussing and throwing punches at both boys while holding one hand on the wheel. "You bastards are dead." With one big jerk Betty moved her truck over into Triple L's truck and would not let up. She pushed with her truck, making Triple L have to push back in order to avoid going over the edge of the mountain. Mark lost his footing some when she made the jerking move but got back up quickly and looked out the front windshield. Seeing that she was forcing not only Triple L in the direction of the cliff but taking her truck there too, he knew he had to do something quick.

Mark looked at Jack Jr., who was still outside the truck and had managed to get onto the driver's steps and then looked at his friend Bentley. He whispered his plan to Bentley while blocking hits from Betty. "When I signal you, grab the wheel and keep it straight. Get Jack Jr. in here, and I'll do my best to keep this bitch hemmed up in the sleeper."

"Got it."

Mark blocked Betty's hand with his arms and grabbed the woman in a less than gentle way with his muscular arms. "LET GO OF ME, YOU BASTARD!" Betty was a fighter, but she wasn't strong enough against Mark's strength. It took a few fierce pulls to force Betty away from the driver's seat and into the sleeper, but he managed to pin her face down on the sleeper bed and put her hands under his body that was now sitting on top of her. "FUCK YOU! FUCK YOU! LET ME UP, RIGHT NOW! THIS IS MY TRUCK!" Betty screamed and tried everything to get out of the pinned position Mark had confined her to.

"Calm down, you're not going anywhere except to the waiting arms of those officers down at the bottom of the mountain." Betty wrenched and wiggled even more at Mark's words, but everything she tried was completely unsuccessful.

Bentley had done his best with the help of Triple L to move Betty's truck back onto the highway and away from the cliff. He had opened the door for Jack Jr. who quickly found his way into the swerving big rig from the cold and wind. He plopped into the driver's seat and grabbed the wheel from Bentley, who was more than happy to let go of it. Bentley sat in the passenger seat and reached for the CB mic. "Okay guys. We got the truck under control now."

"Good job." Snowmobile Flyer praised the young men.

Snowmobile Flyer and Triple L backed down and got in single file behind Betty's truck. Sweet Daddy and Kat Doctor took the front door and all five trucks geared down for the final descent toward the crowd of people and cops waiting at the bottom of the mountain. "How about you, Sweet Daddy?"

"Yeah, go ahead."

"We are some mighty good driving sons-of-bitches, ain't we?"

"Got that right, Snowmobile Flyer, you got that right."

"Hey, Jack Jr. You handle that rig pretty good. Want a job?"

Jack keyed the mic. "No thanks. I think I'll go back to the oil field—it's a hell of a lot safer than this."

The drivers all laughed as they drove down the mountain.

CHAPTER TWENTY-SEVEN

The big rigs that were at the bottom of the mountain were now moving out of the way after hearing over the radio that the final five trucks were headed safely toward them. The police were doing everything they could over the cheers and claps from the large gathering of people, four wheelers, trucks, motorcycles, and even children that had gathered to watch the spectacle.

Jack held Shelby as they watched the trucks move down the mountain and into the street below. Shelby held her breath as the trucks came to a stop in single file in the middle of the street. She hoped her boys and all their friends were okay. The first to exit Betty's truck was Jack Jr., who motioned for a cop to speak with him. Jack Jr. talked with the cop for a few minutes and then entered Betty's truck, taking out his cuffs from his back pocket. Other police moved in to get information and explanations of the events in the mountains from the drivers as they exited their trucks.

Bentley was next to exit Betty's truck, followed by Mark. Then, with Mark's help, a kicking and screaming Betty was forcibly removed from the big rig. "LET ME GO, YOU FUCKERS! LET ME GO! I HAVEN'T DONE ANYTHING WRONG. THESE ASSHOLES TRIED TO STEAL MY TRUCK AND RAPE ME. LET ME OUT OF THESE CUFFS NOW."

The cop motioned for assistance from some other uniforms so that he could get Betty to his unit.

Betty lifted her head up and saw Shelby standing next to Jack a little distance away. "THIS IS ENTIRELY YOUR FAULT, YOU STUPID LITTLE BITCH! IF YOU HADN'T COME TO WORK AT ESCC NONE OF THIS WOULD HAVE HAPPENED. WATCH YOUR BACK BARBIE, 'CAUSE I'M COMING FOR YOU. I WON'T STOP 'TIL YOU'RE DEAD, I PROMISE. NOBODY STEPS ON MY TURF AND MESSES WITH MY TRUCKS WITHOUT PAYING FOR IT!"

Shelby grabbed Jack's hand, grateful for his foresight. Then she broke away from Jack and ran to her two boys who were now standing around wondering what the hell just happened. She grabbed each of them into a group hug. "God, I'm so glad you guys are all right." She hugged each of them around the neck and gave Bentley a huge hug as well. "Thank god. I'm so proud of you."

Jack Jr. looked at his dad who was standing next to the circle with Steven. "You owe me a new bike, Dad." The family laughed and hugged each other, realizing that things could have turned out very differently.

"We'll go pick it out when we get home." Jack pulled at Shelby's hand. "I sure have missed being in the field at work. That office is so stuffy. I'm thinking we need to team drive."

Shelby was a little shocked. "You want to drive a truck with me?"

"Sure, why not?" Jack shrugged.

"I don't know, I guess it's something to think about." Shelby walked away from Jack. "I have to talk with the police and call the office."

Jack blew her a kiss. "Okay, babe. I'm going to hang out over here with my biker buddies." Shelby waved, acknowledging what he had said.

Shelby figured that Eddy and Sandy probably already knew what had happened, since two of their loads to Vernal, were now scattered at the bottom of a mountain bypass in Utah. But she wanted to get away from Jack's crazy idea about driving together, before he convinced her it wasn't crazy.

She walked toward the group of company drivers parked near a small truck stop. Before she could reach the group, several of the trucks that had been blocking four wheelers and other traffic on the west end of the bypass started rolling into town. Hemi, Elwood Blues, Winston, Bootlegger and Bad Boy all drove the now crowded truck-lined Main Street. Shelby waved as they passed and pointed toward a small parking area that was still left in the only truck stop in the little town. She went to greet them.

Bobcat, Scooter from TRI, Phantom 309, Whiskers, Fast Man, Speedy, Long Legs, Slick Stick, Little Blue Boy, and Luscious were all standing around the parking lot.

"Hey, guys," Shelby said as she approached them with Jack's phone in her ear, waiting to hear Sandy on the other end and hoping she wasn't about to get fired. "Sandy?"

"Well, it's about time girl! Are you alright?" Sandy asked.

"Yeah, I take it you already know what's up."

"I've been informed by just about every driver up there."

"Hey, I lost my load."

"I know. I already have two more drivers on their way to bring in the two lost loads. Slick Stick is going to deliver his load and come back for Betty's if the cops let him have the truck, so don't worry about anything right now. Go ahead and take some time off. Be back to work after Christmas, alright?"

"Okay, thanks. Is Eddy mad?"

"As hell, but not with you, so don't worry about it."

"Alright, see you in a few days." Shelby hung up the phone and talked with her friends from ESCC and TRI.

Many of the truck drivers that had been involved stayed on in the little town overnight, but some had loads to deliver and homes to get to.

"Thanks, guys. You're true friends," Shelby said.

"That's what we do, Shelby. We stick together."

GTO came up behind Shelby and tapped her on the shoulder. "Lady Driver, I was wondering if you had decided on a handle yet? I mean, since you're a real driver now, don't you think maybe you should have one?"

Shelby laughed. "I don't know, maybe I should really piss Betty off. How about Barbie?"

GTO and most of the others hanging around loudly agreed with whoops and whistles. "BARBIE. We got us a real Barbie doll rolling with us, boys."

ACKNOWLEDGMENTS

I would like to thank Danielle H. Acee, Mindy Reed, Douglas Brown, and all those involved in editing and perfecting the text. Their guidance made the book release possible.

I also can't forget all of the individuals who supported me with their encouragement—my daughter-in-law, Cydney and my friends, Tina, Tamra, and Tammy. To so many others (truckers, friends, family members) who helped me in this endeavor, sometimes without even knowing it, thank you.

I will always remember all those who helped make this dream a reality.

With all my heart forever.
    —Robyn Mitchell
    robynmitchellauthor.com

About the Author